the kookaburra creek café

Sandie Docker grew up in Coffs Harbour. She first fell in love with reading as a teenager when her father encouraged her to take up his passion for books. Sandie decided to put pen to paper (yes, she writes everything the old-fashioned way before hitting a keyboard) while living in London. Now back in Sydney with her husband and daughter, she writes every day. *The Kookaburra Creek Café* is her first book.

www.sandiedocker.com

 @SandieDockerwriter

sandie docker

the kookaburra creek café

MICHAEL JOSEPH
an imprint of
PENGUIN BOOKS

MICHAEL JOSEPH

UK | USA | Canada | Ireland | Australia
India | New Zealand | South Africa | China

Penguin Books is part of the Penguin Random House group of companies
whose addresses can be found at global.penguinrandomhouse.com.

Penguin
Random House
Australia

First published by Penguin Random House Australia Pty Ltd 2018

10 9 8 7 6 5 4 3 2 1

Text copyright © Sandie Docker 2018

The moral right of the author has been asserted.

Cover design by Laura Thomas © Penguin Random House Australia Pty Ltd
Cover illustrations: (watercolour floral pattern) Skorik Ekaterina/Shutterstock.com;
(kookaburra) Anastasia Lembrik/Shutterstock.com; (teapots) Elzza/Shutterstock.com;
(summer flowers in glass bottle) Le Panda/Shutterstock.com; (spring flowers)
Depiano/Shutterstock.com
Typeset by Midland Typesetters, Australia

Printed and bound in Australia by Griffin Press, an accredited ISO AS/NZS 14001
Environmental Management Systems printer.

A catalogue record for this
book is available from the
NATIONAL
LIBRARY National Library of Australia
OF AUSTRALIA

ISBN: 978 0 14378 919 2

penguin.com.au

MIX
Paper from
responsible sources
FSC® C009448

For Dad, for always believing I could

Prologue

Kookaburra Creek, 2010

She ran as fast as she could.

'Where are you?' she screamed, her voice cracking.

Her throat hurt. Every gasp for air was difficult. She couldn't see very far through the thick black smoke, but she was sure she was close now. She had to be.

Angry orange flames danced across the tops of the gum trees behind her, chasing her down. But she wouldn't stop. She wouldn't leave him out here alone.

Be brave.

She coughed. No air.

'Are you here?' she rasped.

Trees cracked beside her. Branches exploded, sending hot black shards into the air. She ducked. She weaved.

Be brave.

There in the clearing she could see a quiet shadow.

'There you are. Silly boy, running off. It's okay. I'm here now. But we have to go.' She could see fear in his eyes. 'Are you hurt? Can you walk?'

He whimpered. She fell to her knees and ran her hands through his thick coat.

Tears started to fall down her face, before evaporating into the hot, dry air. 'It's okay. I'm here.' She coughed again. Each breath was harder than the last.

'We'll be okay,' she said, as she lay down in the dirt beside her best friend. He nuzzled into her arm. 'We can rest a little bit, then we have to go.'

She closed her eyes, coughing, wheezing. A minute was all she dared rest.

One

Kookaburra Creek, 2018

Alice Pond opened the door to the Kookaburra Creek Café and the brass bell hanging from the entrance frame didn't clang.

Most people entering the café wouldn't have noticed the absence of the bell's ring, but for the last fourteen years every morning of Alice's life had been exactly the same. Nearly every morning. And that meant Alice certainly did notice.

The oven timer's discordant buzz, in contrasting harmony with the door chimes, should have assaulted her ears as she opened the door. But there was only silence.

The smell of freshly cooked bread left to bake overnight should have greeted her. But there was no delicious doughy aroma wafting through the room.

Something was wrong.

Alice looked above her head to see the bracket holding the bell to the door frame was slightly bent. Her eyes darted around the room. Everything else seemed to be in place. The green ging-ham curtains were drawn shut, the piles of serviettes were on the counter where she'd left them the night before, the chairs were still atop the tables.

Then her gaze fell on the counter. The register was open.

Alice's stomach tightened as she moved slowly through the dining room.

Carefully she inched open the white shutters that divided the dining room and kitchen. The oven was off. She frowned. The pantry door was slightly ajar and she picked up the rolling pin as she tiptoed past the bench. Not that it would do her any good against a band of thieves, or even one thief if they were serious. But false confidence was better than none.

She stepped towards the pantry door. The sound of something hitting the floor, a lid perhaps, made Alice jump. The buggers better not be into her flour. Surely no one would think to look in there for her stashed savings. Well, whoever they were, they picked the wrong café to break into.

She pushed the slatted door open. A crumpled mess of grey spun round to face her.

'Ha-ya!' Alice screamed out, adopting her fiercest ninja pose, rolling pin poised for attack.

'What the —?' The grey mess jumped back and grabbed the closest object to its flailing hands – a tin of beetroot.

The hand holding the beetroot tin was very small and there was a slight curve beneath the grey hoodie. Alice's thief was a girl. A young girl with pieces of half-cooked bread crumbs caught in the folds of her tattered jumper. At least that explained what had happened to her baking.

'The door was open. I didn't break in,' the girl said at once, stepping back and forth looking for a way past her captor.

'What are you doing here?' Alice asked, trying to control her breathing. It was just a child. 'If you put back whatever you've taken, I won't call the police.'

'Don't you dare call the cops.' The girl pushed her greasy black hair behind her ears and raised her eyes to Alice in defiance.

From Alice's trembling hand the rolling pin crashed to the floor, a resounding thud echoing through the silent café, and she gasped.

Those two piercing blue eyes.

The girl shoved past her and sprinted through the café.

'Sorry.' Alice ran after her. 'Wait. I just . . .'

But the girl rushed past, out the café and into the trees across the large grass clearing that stretched in front of the café before Alice got to the bottom of the steps.

Alice sat on the deck that wrapped around the café and tried to calm her racing thoughts. It wasn't the first time she'd seen his eyes gazing back at her from a stranger's face. It wasn't the second or third. There was a time when she saw those eyes in every male she met. In the stare of the postie who'd delivered her bills; the mischievous gazes of the boys in the pub who were probably too young to drink; every second customer that came into the café when she first arrived in Kookaburra Creek. No, it wasn't the first time she'd seen Dean McRae's eyes in another. But only once before had she seen his eyes in a young girl, and that was so long ago, in a life no longer hers.

It was several minutes before Alice felt calm enough to rise on shaky legs and head back inside. Fractured images from her past fought for attention, but she blocked them out. She had a café to open. She couldn't dwell on wasted memories.

She stood in her kitchen, her heart beating fast, not sure where to start. It was too late to make more bread. Betty would be upset, no doubt. So would Claudine. They loved her homemade loaves. But they'd forgive her, just like they had that time a town-wide blackout had turned the oven off in the small hours of the morning. She'd make up some excuse or other. Joey would be able to bring over a few loaves from the bakery if she texted him now, and he'd be popping by for his coffee in about twenty minutes anyway.

Coffee! She hadn't put her coffee on. Nothing could be achieved before that ritual was taken care of. The drip of the Colombian blend falling into her favourite yellow mug was just the tonic she needed. She switched on the coffee machine to heat up and freshly ground the beans. She'd make enough for two.

She took down the wooden chairs, each a different colour – blue, pink, red, orange, purple, green – from the round white tables they perched on overnight. She rearranged them in new combinations, as she did each morning. Except Joey's chair. He liked the aqua and he liked it beside the east-facing window. He was her best customer, after all, even if his motives weren't altogether benign, so she kept his favourite spot for him, just the way he liked it.

As her coffee cooled she wiped down the tables and set them with the salt and pepper shakers collected from around the world: Babushka dolls, English phone booths, an Eiffel Tower set. Every time someone from town travelled overseas, they brought shakers back from their trip as a gift for Alice. Joey had started the tradition with the Leaning Tower of Pisa set and Betty had continued it with the two camels from Dubai. One day, on the table in the middle of the café, Alice would place a set she brought back herself.

She hoped the young thief was all right, that she hadn't been too frightened. Alice knew a little something about being discovered where you shouldn't be. She could never forget those early days when scared, alone and afraid, she'd stumbled upon the neglected café in the tiny town of Kookaburra Creek nestled in the hills in the middle of nowhere and somewhere.

As always, the routine of setting up the café soothed Alice completely, and she slowly sipped her coffee in front of good old Sylvia while waiting for inspiration to strike.

Sylvia always provided an answer, of course. Her warm expression and kind eyes looked down on Alice from her framed place on the wall above the oven, her grey hair collected in a white cotton bonnet. At least they were the colours Alice imagined behind the sepia tones of the picture. Sylvia wasn't her real name, though there was no reason it couldn't have been. Alice had simply called her that all those years ago when she first stepped into the kitchen and looked up in wide-eyed terror, wondering how on earth she'd ended up in this town.

Sylvia had told her that day, by way of the recipe that fell to the bench when Alice reached up to touch the picture hanging on the wall, to bake chocolate fudge cupcakes. So she had. It was the first cake of any description she'd ever made and the world stilled. It was as if everything around her had quieted. It was the first time in Alice's life she'd been able to switch off the constant thoughts in her head. The first time she'd been able to forget the scars and bruises collected in her life and enter The Silence. And so it had been that way ever since.

Alice looked into Sylvia's eyes and waited, asking her silently what to bake today. The answer came at once: strawberry and white chocolate.

Alice lowered her cup, her heart pounding, and stared hard at Sylvia. 'What?'

Sylvia gazed straight back, her eyes giving nothing away.

With shaking hands Alice pulled out the red and white polka-dotted patty cases from the pantry and lined the cupcake tin. She hesitantly reached for her bowls, beaters and measuring cups. Sylvia had never been wrong before. But strawberry and white chocolate?

Alice closed her eyes and, when she opened them again, the morning chorus of magpies and lyrebird no longer floated through the open window, the constant, gentle buzz of the old fridge could not be heard: The Silence.

Her hands steadied as she hulled the strawberries, chopped them into small pieces and folded them into the batter. She pushed a square of white chocolate into the centre of each waiting cupcake and her breathing quickened. Strawberries and white chocolate was not a combination she'd ever used before. Or ever wanted to use. Strawberries, yes. White chocolate, yes. But never together. Memories of that night so long ago teased the edges of Alice's mind. How could Sylvia have known?

Alice slid the tray on to the oven shelf and shut the glass door. She cranked up the music on the radio and moved her hips in time with the beat as she cleaned down the bench and started washing up.

The three-tiered cupcake stand on the counter was Alice's very favourite thing in the room. After the photo of Sylvia, her favourite thing in the whole café. In itself it was nothing special – plain white ceramic that you could probably pick up in any homeware store in any town. But it was the same stand she'd displayed her first batch of cakes on and each batch since, and she always felt such pride every time she loaded the tiers with creations she'd made on her own from scratch.

This particular morning was different, though. Her hands were unsteady as she arranged the strawberry and white chocolate cakes. She shook her head. *Stop being so silly.* It was a coincidence, that's all. How could Sylvia possibly have known the significance of strawberry and white chocolate and that night so very long ago? She was an inanimate object, for goodness' sake. And how could she possibly have known the girl with Dean McRae's eyes would be in Alice's pantry that same morning? She couldn't have. That's right.

'They look good.' A deep voice startled Alice from her thoughts of the past and she dropped the last cupcake, frosting down, on her bright blue bench. 'Sorry, Alice. I'll take that one with my coffee.'

'Good morning, Joey. The usual?' she asked, handing him the double espresso she'd started making before he'd even turned up.

Monday was Joey's only day off from his bakery, and at 9 a.m. Mrs Harris, the reverend's wife, started her shift in Moretti's Bread House. Every Monday Joey then made the walk to the Kookaburra Creek Café and 9.06 on the dot he arrived for his double espresso and cupcake after a long morning baking.

'I got your text. Here are those loaves you wanted.' He put one white, one wholemeal and one tomato and olive loaf on the bench. 'What happened this time?' He asked fondly. 'Or do you finally concede your bread will never be as good as mine?'

'Haha. I just, um . . . I forgot to set the timer. Silly me.' Alice couldn't tell him the truth. He'd only worry if he found out the café had been broken into.

Joey shook his head. 'How long have we known each other, Alice? I can always tell when you're lying. Something's got you rattled.'

He reached across the bench and took her hand, his gentle touch warm, yet hesitant. Still. After all these years.

She started to tug her hand away and he immediately released it, frowning.

'I'd better head.' He nodded and Alice watched him leave. His old dog, Shadow, waited patiently at the bottom of the deck, big eyes staring up, ever hopeful Alice would let him back into the place he once knew as home. But she couldn't.

Despite the morning's disarray, the day passed without much note. As Alice closed the blinds of the café that evening, her thoughts turned to the girl with Dean McRae's eyes, then to the strawberry and white chocolate cupcakes. Surely it was just a coincidence.

Alice was too on edge to head up the external staircase to her apartment and call it a night. Instead, she made her way along the ambling creek that ran past two sides of the café, wrapping its way from the back around to the side before meandering off to the right to cut the town in half about half a kilometre downstream. The single bridge there, joining the east and west banks, was one of Alice's favourite parts of town.

The grass by the creek edge was long this time of year and Alice slipped off her shoes to feel the soft blades between her toes. The fields of Massey's farm to her left had been turned. Planting would begin soon. To the north she could see the lights of town blinking on as the sun began to set. She would only walk as far as the bridge, as far as Dandelion Dell this evening. With little chance of running into anyone, she could stop in her special place. She could sit on the bench hugged by dandelions and run her hands along the wood, like she often did when her thoughts were a mess, and draw on the sense of calm that always washed over her there.

She followed the creek as it curved to the right, stopping just before Dandelion Dell. Curled up on the white bench was the girl in grey.

'You didn't get very far,' Alice said gently, stepping forward.

The girl sat up, and Alice's breath caught as the familiar blue eyes pierced right through her.

Two

Lawson's Ridge, 2003

Alice Pond sat in the school playground whispering with Louise. She pushed her long brown plait behind her ear. This wasn't a particularly unusual event in itself, the whispering or the plait fiddling. Best friends since kindergarten, the two girls had spent at least part of every lunchtime over the past twelve years absorbed in urgent, hushed discussions. When they were in Year One it was who had the prettiest pencil case. In Year Three it was whose lunch was more interesting, and now as teenagers it was how Wendy Dobson's new hairdo definitely made her look like a boy and what was she thinking, or whether Bobby Jones really was the cutest guy in school, or the ridiculousness of Mr Young's latest gimmick to try to get them interested in the topography of some far-off country like Uruguay.

They sat on the hot metal bench, pressed together with foreheads almost touching, lips moving quickly, simultaneously, which wasn't strange at all. What was strange was the fact they had some-thing altogether new to discuss. Some*one* altogether new.

'Where's he from?' Louise whispered in Alice's ear.

'I heard Sydney.' Alice tried not to look over towards the new boy.

Dean McRae's arrival at Lawson High School had caused quite a stir. To look at he was like any other teenage boy – limbs that seemed too long for his scrawny body, shirt untucked, hair in need of a good brush. The only real difference between him and the other boys in school was, simply, that he was new.

'Well, I heard he got kicked out of his old school.'

'Someone,' Alice turned her head ever so slightly to sneak a peek, 'said his mum bought the old Richards place.'

'Well, my mum said he was only going to be here a month.'

And Louise's mum would probably know. She knew everything about everyone in town. Not that that was hard.

Nothing ever changed at Lawson High, population 125. The principal had been a teacher there when Alice's mum was a student. Alice sat in a chair for English that had her dad's name carved into the back of it. When Louise's mum got behind on the washing Louise would wear her mum's old uniform and, aside from the missing piping on the shirt pocket, no one could tell the difference. The last time anything exciting happened was five years ago, when Alice and Louise had started high school and Brian, Louise's twin brother, blew up the science lab and chemistry had to be done in the hall. The same hall that Louise's grandfather had built. Not a lot happened at Lawson High. Not until Dean McRae showed up. Population 126.

'He's kinda cute,' Louise said.

'You reckon?' He certainly didn't compare to any of the guys from Silverchair, whose faces were plastered all over her maths exercise book.

Louise shrugged her tiny shoulders. Alice was always jealous of Louise's small frame. Not that she was big herself, but compared to her best friend she always felt like a giant. Compared to her best friend, well, Alice wasn't anything special at all. Her curly brown hair, which she tried to tame into plaits, was no match for Louise's thick golden strands that cascaded down her back. Alice's boring brown eyes never sparkled like Louise's blue. And Alice always felt awkward manoeuvring her less than elegant frame anywhere near Louise's graceful body. If only Louise was taller, she could have been a model. Still. It meant no one ever paid Alice much attention, and she liked it like that.

The bell rang loudly and the girls headed off to maths.

Taking their seats together up the back of the room, Alice grabbed out of her bag the answers to the homework she knew her friend wouldn't have finished. Louise didn't ask for them like she usually did, though, and Alice followed her gaze. Dean had entered the room and was looking for a spare chair. He held his hessian backpack in one hand and smiled at Wendy Dobson, who no one ever sat next to, or smiled at really. The girl with the boy haircut slid to the left to make room and Dean sat next to her.

Louise turned her head back to Alice, her eyes wide with disbelief.

Alice knew how much the new boy sitting next to Wendy Dobson would have irked her friend. She handed Louise the homework she'd done for her. Ever since Year Six, when Mr Nash threatened to repeat Louise and keep her from going to high school, Alice had helped her friend with her schoolwork. She turned and looked out the window, only half listening to Ms Robertson go over the previous day's trigonometry that most of the class had struggled with. She'd finished the homework in one night and read two chapters ahead. Maths was her favourite subject, after all.

Not because she found it easy, which she did, but because it gave her the chance to look across the school playground and into Faraway Forest. With equations she could solve in her sleep scrawled across the board in dusty chalk, Alice could stare outside and imagine herself walking past the trees through her very own Narnia-esque portal leading not to a land of magical creatures trapped in permanent winter, but to the skyscrapers and heaving crowds of Sydney 700 kilometres away.

Anytime anything happened on the news it happened in Sydney. Anytime Alice read about a successful entrepreneur, they'd found their fortune in Sydney. Anyone who was anyone came from Sydney. The view from the maths room was a chance for Alice to travel through Faraway Forest all the way to magical Sydney, so very, very far from Lawson's Ridge, and imagine the day she'd get there herself.

'So, Alice?' Ms Robertson stood in front of Alice's desk.

She quickly looked up to the board and scanned the problem Ms Robertson was seeking the answer to.

'So x is greater than fifteen,' Alice replied.

'Thank you, Miss Pond.' Ms Robertson casually opened Alice's notebook and tapped the blank page. 'So . . .' she continued as she walked back to the front of the class.

Alice scribbled down the equation and the solution and let her pencil drift to the side of the page where she drew flowers and butterflies floating over the top of a somewhat crooked Opera House.

'You coming?' Louise asked, nudging her. Alice hadn't even heard the bell.

'Hold your horses.' Alice packed up her books.

'Did you see the way Wendy was batting her eyelids at that McRae boy all lesson?' Louise leaned across the table.

'Hadn't noticed.'

But clearly Louise had. She always noticed the boys. Ever since they were little. And they always noticed her back. Alice remembered Louise's first crush, aged five, when she followed Andy Johnson all round kindergarten, sitting next to him every recess, every lunch, sharing her food with him. When Andy Johnson's family left town, Louise cried for a whole twenty seconds before deciding Billy Trainor was more to her liking. Aged eight, it was Mark Kelly. Aged nine Greg Fletcher. And then she discovered that letting the boys chase her was a lot more fun and, by the time they were sixteen, Alice spent a lot of time watching Louise be pursued by various boys till they won the chase and she'd get bored and move on. Dean McRae was the first new prospect to pass through Lawson's Ridge in a long time and Louise was certainly going to notice.

Taking her usual route home from school, Alice approached Faraway Forest. No one else called it that, of course. No one else called it anything, really. 'The scrub by the school' was probably the most common way to refer to the few clumps of trees, the scattering of messy bushes, the overgrown grasses covering the forlorn stretch of land on the other side of the schoolyard. If anyone bothered to refer to it all. Alice had taken to calling it Faraway Forest when she was ten and had discovered the red ironbark in the very centre of the green and brown tangle. That was when her mum got sick. With slender, pointed green leaves dripping from pale branches that reached out from a sturdy black trunk, her ironbark produced flowers that, to a young girl, looked like red fairy tutus. Alice would climb up a few branches and make a perch. From there she'd drop her fairies, twirling and dancing through the scrub beneath, down into tiny pixie villages. The trails in the grasses turned into highways along which magical elves could travel, the rocks into secret caves tiny trolls patrolled. Even before she'd learned the tree was impervious to the hottest of fires, she'd always felt safe there. And as time wore on Alice needed to feel safe. For eight years she'd sought shelter sitting in her old friend, the tree.

'Hello, mate.' She put her scuffed black school shoes on the rock that allowed her to reach the fallen branch caught between the unusual twin trunks of her tree and from there she hoisted herself further up. She settled on the ironbark's lowest limb, strong and thick, and leaned against the ridged trunk. It wasn't time to go home just yet.

'Hey up there.'

Alice looked down to see the new boy standing in front of her tree, legs astride, fists on hips.

'Hey.'

'Is that a private branch, or can anyone join?'

Before Alice had a chance to tell him it was, in fact, a very private branch, he'd scaled the trunk and was sitting beside her.

'Hi.' He smiled at her as she inched away a little, her eyes cast down. 'You go to my school, right? Or, I go to yours is more like it.'

Alice pointed to the school crest on her white blouse and rolled her eyes.

'I'm Dean. Dean McRae.' He held out his hand.

Alice looked up to answer and her breath caught in her throat. Gazing back at her were eyes so blue, so bright, she almost slid off the branch.

'Whoa, steady there,' Dean said, catching her. 'Don't climb trees much, hey?'

'Actually,' Alice coughed, 'all the time. Just not used to sharing my branch with anyone.'

'Your branch?'

Alice shrugged.

'So, have you got a name? You know, so if anyone asks if they can come up here I can say, no, this branch belongs to . . .'

'Alice.'

'This branch belongs to Alice. Nice to meet you, Alice.'

Alice tried to think of a way to get rid of the trespasser. 'I heard you were booted out of your old school.'

Dean laughed. 'Really? What else are they saying about me?'

'Lots of things.'

'Well, I guarantee you the reality isn't anywhere near as interesting as the gossip.'

Alice frowned. He certainly didn't speak like a streetwise thug, one of the many rumours already swirling. He also didn't seem like the delinquent son of a rich politician sent far away so as not to hurt daddy's campaign.

'So, what is the truth, then?'

'Just a boring old divorce.' He looked down, avoiding eye contact for the first time since plonking himself on her branch. 'Mum and Dad's. Not mine.' He looked up and grinned, a dimple in his left cheek appearing.

Alice giggled. Alice rarely giggled and she wasn't sure she was okay with him being the reason she did.

'What's this town like?' Dean looked at her and she had to turn away.

'It's as boring as it seems. Nothing compared to Sydney. Must be a real shock coming out here.'

'It's not that bad.'

'Give it time.'

'What's not to love? Quiet streets, friendly locals.' He winked at Alice.

'There's no theatre, no shopping, no nightclubs, no decent sporting events, no beaches.'

'Okay, I'll give you no beaches,' Dean nodded, 'but Sydney isn't all it's cracked up to be.'

'I doubt that.'

'Well, I've never been to a nightclub or the theatre. And shopping isn't exactly my thing.'

Alice giggled again.

'And there are some pretty dodgy parts of Sydney, you know.' Dean lowered his voice.

She nodded. Of course she'd heard about places like Kings Cross. Who hadn't? But surely even seedy underbelly action was more exciting than no action at all.

'Speaking of which, Alice of the Branch.' He bumped her shoulder with his. 'Is it safe to be wandering around here on your own?'

'Ah, yeah. Seriously, nothing ever happens in Lawson's Ridge. Good or bad. Absolutely nothing.' She shook her head. 'But I probably should be heading home.'

When Dean didn't move she cleared her throat.

'Right, yes,' he said, and climbed to the ground.

As Alice reached the bottom she lost her footing and stumbled. Dean grabbed her hands.

'You okay?' he asked.

Alice nodded, unsure of why she was suddenly unable to speak. She turned and ran towards home.

When Alice got to her front lawn, she picked up the newspaper that had been delivered, set Gus, the gnome, back to standing and brushed the dirt off his orange checked trousers. Harry Brown always liked to target poor Gus on his paper run and his accuracy had improved dramatically in the last six months. She raked the gum leaves that noisy cockatoos had broken off from the large eucalypt that stood guard outside her house. The house with the neatest front yard in the street. The house with seven gnomes neatly on display that showed no signs of the truth inside.

'Today is going to be a good day,' her dad had said that morning. 'I can feel it, Tadpole.' He'd rubbed her shoulders.

'Me too,' she'd said. Every morning he said it. Every morning she believed him.

Turning the key slowly, Alice opened her front door with a gentle push. She closed it softly behind her and went into the living room where her dad would be, just like he was every afternoon. Littered on the floor beside the brown sofa were empty beer cans. Alice didn't bother to count them. She used to. She'd make a game of it – predict each afternoon how many there'd be and congratulate herself when she got it right. For a short time she even kept a chart inside her closet to track how close she got. But there hadn't been any point lately. Thirteen. It had been thirteen every afternoon for the last few months. And the monotony had only reinforced how pathetic her situation was, so she'd stopped.

Alice grabbed a garbage bag out of the kitchen drawer and put the cans inside. She slipped her dad's shoes from his feet and pulled the blanket over him. He was snoring softly and she kissed his lined forehead, brushing his greying fringe aside. One day he'd come back to her.

She made herself a cheese sandwich, one slice no butter, and cleared a space at the dining table to do her homework. When her English essay was finished, Alice changed into her pyjamas, checked on her dad, who was still safely snoring, and crawled into bed. She pulled the photo of her mum out of her bedside drawer and held it in front of her.

'School was good today. Ms Robertson has given me even more homework to do, which is good. You wouldn't believe Wendy's new haircut. She looks so much like her dad now it's a bit scary.' Alice laughed. 'We started a new unit in economics today. I'm not sure I'm ever going to need to know what the gross national product of Brazil is, but I guess it makes a nice change from the fiscal policy of the Australian government. In *The Courier* this morning there was an article about the new road out of town. Can you believe the idiots at council still can't come to an agreement? How long's that now? Four years? I guess that's about all the news.' She ran her thumb down the side of the photo. 'Oh, except that the footy club needs new goal posts and Louise's dad has a fancy new truck. Tells anyone who'll listen all about it. Spends all his time in it apparently, and Mrs Jenkins calls it his mistress. Reckons when she's on the late shift at the hospital, he goes out and spends time with it. Oh and there's a new boy at school. Nothing special.' Alice swallowed hard. 'Well, that's it. Goodnight, Mum.'

She kissed the photo and turned out the light, but sleep wouldn't come. One image kept appearing every time she closed her eyes. She tried to block it, to think of something else, but those two piercing blue eyes and that left dimple just wouldn't go away.

Three

Kookaburra Creek, 2018

'Well?' The girl in grey stood up and took a step towards Alice. 'What are you staring at?'

Alice blinked. 'I . . . um . . . nothing. Sorry. What are you doing here?'

'I was just trying to get some rest.'

'Out here?'

'Where else?' The girl started to scratch her arm.

Alice recognised the mix of fear and anger in the girl. She recognised herself.

'What's your name?'

'B . . . Becca.' The girl smoothed her heavy black fringe over her downcast eyes, pushing it slightly to the left.

'Well, Becca. Are you hungry?' Alice asked.

Becca shrugged.

'We can head back to the café and I can make you something to eat?' Alice stepped forward and Becca inched back.

'Okay,' Alice said, frantically thinking of what to do next. 'Or maybe I could bring you something.'

Becca shrugged again.

'If you wait here, I'll bring you some dinner.'

When Alice returned to Dandelion Dell, Becca was nowhere to be seen. Alice lowered herself onto the bench and placed the bowl of pasta beside her. She should have known the girl would run. She should have stayed and talked to her more.

The second she saw her lying on the bench, on this bench of all places, Alice knew deep down there was more to this than coincidence. There had to be. But she'd let Becca slip through her fingers.

'What have I done?' She sighed.

Above her a possum jumped from one tree to another. Alice stood and looked around, but the dark of night had set in. She left the bowl of pasta on the bench, in case Becca returned, plucked a dandelion and left it next to the bowl.

Walking back along the creek towards the café, Alice couldn't help but feel regret.

In the morning Alice fixed the doorbell then stood in the kitchen and looked up to Sylvia.

Apple and custard.

'Well, that's new.'

Alice gathered the ingredients, moving around the kitchen with automated ease. As she measured out flour and sugar, all the previous day's worry left her body and she started humming.

From the height of her outstretched arm she dropped the diced apple into the bowl. She mixed the batter with easy rhythm and closed her eyes as she used the ice-cream scoop to spoon it into the patty cases.

'Morning, petal,' Hattie called as she entered the kitchen, breaking Alice's trance.

'Hattie.' Alice greeted her with a hug. 'Welcome back. How are you?'

'As well as anyone my age can be expected to be.' She flicked her black chiffon scarf over her shoulder, and the matching black hairpiece clipped in place created a bold stripe in her grey hair.

'Tea?' Alice asked.

'Thank you. Why don't you make yourself one too, and join me out on the deck?'

Hattie's polite suggestions were never really suggestions, so Alice dutifully got two cups ready.

'Sit, sit.' Hattie waved a bejewelled hand Alice's way as she carried out the camomile blend. 'It's always so lovely being home.'

'How was Sydney?'

'Fine, thank you.' Hattie pulled her scarf tighter. 'Just fine.' The old woman took a long, slow sip of tea.

'And how was the show?'

Every year Hattie went to Sydney to see whatever show was playing at the State Theatre, her old stomping ground.

'Sublime. I have some great ideas for this year's dramatic society performance.'

'I bet you do.' Alice said. She studied her friend. The usual sparkle in Hattie's eyes when she spoke of the theatre wasn't there. She'd been in the city longer than usual this time too.

'Did something happen this trip?'

'Of course not.' Hattie waved her hand in dismissal, but Alice didn't believe her. She knew her friend well and something was definitely bothering Hattie. But she'd learned long ago not to push Harriett Brookes.

'And how were things while I was gone?' Hattie asked.

'Um, great.'

'Except?'

'Except nothing.'

Hattie gave her a look and Alice knew she wasn't buying it.

'I got broken into.'

'What?'

'It wasn't that bad. A young girl. She just took some food.'

'Where is she now?' Hattie asked.

Alice shrugged.

'You let her go?'

'Sort of. I found her again. Well, came across her. I offered her dinner, but she took off.'

'My dear girl. Have you learned nothing from me?'

The café doorbell rang. First customer of the day.

'Saved by the proverbial.' Hattie waved her finger as Alice got up.

'Morning, Betty, Claudine.' Alice greeted the two ladies as they made their way to their usual table.

Betty pulled out her chair with a loud scrape and sat her slight frame on the yellow wooden seat. Her grey hair had been freshly trimmed close to her scalp, as usual. Her half-moon glasses hung round her neck on a red chain that she adjusted as she waited for the third in their party to join them.

'Morning, Clive.' Alice nodded to the old man, always a few steps behind, as he took his seat with them.

'Menus, please, Alice.' Betty's crisp voice cut across the chatter that always came with this group.

'Is that really necessary, Betty?' Hattie stepped up to the table with three menus in her hand. 'Clive will have the bacon and eggs, Claudine will have the muesli, and you, of course, will have the raisin toast, butter on the side.'

'Whether or not we order the same items is irrelevant, Hattie. There are certain protocols of civility one must maintain.'

'How silly of me to forget.' Hattie handed them their menus with exaggerated flair.

'Welcome back, *ma chère*.' Claudine took Hattie's hand. 'Never the same without you.'

'How was the big smoke?' Clive mumbled, running his fingers through his big white beard. He removed his tweed flat cap and revealed a mess of tangled white hair that fell chaotically around his round face.

'It was fine.'

'Are you all right, Harriett?' Betty narrowed her eyes.

'Of course.' Hattie waved a bejewelled hand in dismissal.

'Wretched place, that city.' Clive grumbled.

'I agree,' said Betty. 'Paris. Now that's a city.'

'Well, some of us don't have the funds to go gallivanting around the world whenever the whim strikes us.' Hattie shot her old friend a look. Though perhaps friend was a loose use of the term. Alice never could quite figure the two of them out.

'I did suggest you come with me last year.'

'Oh, that would have been a treat,' Hattie snapped. She turned on her heel and strode into the kitchen.

Hattie never snapped at Betty. Clive, yes. All the time. But never Betty.

'Poor poppet is probably tired, *oui*, Alice?' Claudine tucked her perfectly turned-under auburn bob behind her ears, her green eyes warm and smiling.

'I think so.' Alice looked at Claudine.

The briefest hint of a frown crossed Betty's face before her usual rigid expression returned. 'I think we're ready for our order, Alice.'

The kookaburras laughed as the afternoon sun lowered in the sky. All the customers had left and Alice and Hattie began cleaning up. Alice had watched Hattie closely all day and, while there were no further signs of anything worrying her old friend, Alice wasn't convinced she was just tired.

The café bell rang and Alice turned around. Becca stood in the entrance, holding Alice's white pasta bowl in her hands.

'Thought you might want this back.' She held out the bowl.

'Thank you.' Alice's heart was racing, but she knew she'd have to stay calm. A wrong word and the girl would run.

'Would you like to stay for supper?' Alice asked.

Becca shrugged and glanced at Hattie.

'Oh. This is Hattie. My business partner. I'm Alice by the way.'

'I should go,' Becca said quickly.

'No. No, please.'

Becca stepped back, then forward. Then back again.

'Do you have anywhere to go?' Hattie's voice was soft and sweet.

Becca shrugged.

'Well . . .' Alice looked to Hattie. The old woman nodded. It was all the encouragement Alice needed. 'Well, we've had a busy day and we could use a spare pair of hands cleaning up. Hattie's not as young as she used to be.' Alice grinned. Becca stared, blank-faced.

Alice thought quickly. 'There's dinner in it for you, as payment.'

Becca scratched her forearm and shrugged.

Without a word, Alice handed her a mop and Becca started swooshing it across the floor.

The three women sat on the deck of the café and ate the stir-fry Alice had whipped up. Alice had no idea what to say and Hattie was surprisingly quiet.

'I need to go.' Becca stood up before she'd even swallowed her last mouthful.

'You can stay here,' Alice blurted out, faster than she'd intended. Becca stepped back.

'If you wish,' Hattie added.

'No. Thanks. I got somewhere.'

'Well, maybe you can come back tomorrow. Lend me a hand. I can pay you. Might help with a bus fare or something.'

'I can't cook.'

'There's more to a café than cooking.' Hattie smiled encouragingly and Becca's expression softened.

'Think about it,' said Alice, trying not to sound desperate.

Becca nodded, then stepped off the deck and into the night.

Hattie put her arm round Alice's shoulders.

'Do you think she'll come back?' Alice asked.

'Don't know. She's scared. I do know that.' Hattie sighed. Hattie never sighed.

'Are you okay? Really?'

Hattie wrapped the black scarf around her neck with a flourish. 'Of course. An old war horse like me is always okay.'

Alice looked closely at her and noticed, for the first time, the downward creases in the old woman's forehead. Sensing Alice's scrutiny, Hattie drew on her acting prowess and her face became a picture of serenity. 'Well, I must get an early night. I've got that wretched drama workshop at the high school tomorrow. Perhaps I'll sabotage this year's community theatre so they'll stop asking me to try to teach those ungrateful teenagers. No appreciation for the artistry and beauty of the theatre, that lot.'

Alice laughed. Hattie would never sabotage the Kookaburra Creek Amateur Dramatic Society's productions – they were her pride and joy.

'Goodnight, petal.'

Alice watched her steady herself at the top of the steps. As Hattie descended the three wooden treads at the end of the deck that surrounded the café, her shoulders dropped. Was the one person in the world Alice knew she could count on keeping something from her?

Secrets were poison. Alice knew that better than most. What could be happening in Hattie's life that she couldn't share with her?

Four

Kookaburra Creek, 2018

Hattie sank into her dressing-table chair. The small lights surrounding the mirror no longer turned on, but she still imagined their luminous glow lighting up her face. She unclipped the black hairpiece and brushed her grey strands. Fifty strokes each side, fifty at the back. From the rack of tiny hairpieces she chose tomorrow's colour, red, and lay it across the dresser.

She took the letter out of the envelope and looked at it again. The vile words remained the same, no matter how many times she read them. The lawyers at Smythe and Smythe, acting on behalf of the estate of Buckley Hargraves, regretfully informing her that the title deed to number one Mini Creek Lane was still, in fact, in the Hargraves' name and, as no legal change in ownership was ever recorded, the property belonged to the Hargraves' estate.

It was real. The letter actually did say that the Hargraves family were claiming ownership of the café.

How could he do this to her? After all this time, even in death, Buckley Hargraves had a hold over her.

November, 1966

The lights in the theatre went dark. The silence was broken by deafening applause, shouts of bravo, and even the odd wolf-whistle.

Harriett was shaking as the cast lined up behind the curtain to take their bow. Buckley Hargraves took her hand and she had to remind herself that this was real. She really was standing there next to England's leading man of theatre and he really had requested her to play opposite him. The curtain raised and the cheers went up again. The entire audience were on their feet, everyone smiling and clapping.

Everyone except the lone figure standing stage left in the shadows, her arms folded tightly across her chest.

Harriett focused on the adoration surging towards her from the people that mattered, and she and Buckley stepped forward for one last bow before the curtain fell.

'I told you,' he said, embracing her and twirling her around. 'There's nothing as invigorating as a live audience.'

Harriett giggled. 'It really was fun.'

'You'll never return to film after this.' Buckley touched her nose with his finger and she felt her cheeks warm.

'Well done. Bravo. Brava.' The director swanned across the stage. 'We're the talk of the town. A coup, Buckley. You have orchestrated a theatrical coup.' He slapped Buckley across the back and then manoeuvred his star offstage.

The shadowy figure waiting in the wings stepped out from behind the curtain and hugged Buckley, holding on long enough to be sure Harriett had seen them.

'You were brilliant, darling. Brilliant.' Delilah planted a kiss on his cheek and shot Harriett a look.

Harriett could see the tension in Buckley's shoulders as he pushed Delilah back gently.

The look in Delilah's eyes was unmistakable as she glared at Harriett, but Harriett simply smiled in return. Who had Buckley insisted be his leading lady? Who had brought the audience to tears in act two? Who had received the most beautiful bunch of roses with a card signed 'your biggest fan, B'? Who had stolen a kiss under the moonlight on the last night of rehearsals? Not bloomin' diva Delilah, that was for sure.

Harriett didn't blame her, though. For wanting Buckley. Everyone wanted Buckley. And a starlet like Delilah, just starting out, was going to want him even more.

'Oh, Hattie.' Genevieve ran into her arms. 'You were fabulous. Just fabulous. You should hear what they're saying out there. And it's not just the crowd. The critics, too!'

'Let's celebrate.' Harriett linked her arm with Genevieve's.

Delilah appeared, cornering them in the hall. 'Before you go, Harriett,' she hissed, pulling Harriett away from Genevieve. 'Run along, pipsqueak. We have grown-up things to discuss.'

'It's okay,' Harriett said to Genevieve. Whatever Delilah had to say probably wasn't suitable for her baby sister. 'I'll catch up with you shortly.'

Genevieve walked down the corridor looking back over her shoulder until she turned the corner.

Delilah lowered her voice so no one could overhear. 'You may have bamboozled Buckley with your whorish ways, but I've news for you. You're not all that special.' She poked Harriett in the shoulder. 'You should go back to celluloid where you belong. If Buckley hadn't insisted —'

'But he did. And now you're stuck with me.' In her twenty-four years Harriett had never backed down from a bully and she wasn't about to start now.

'If you know what's good for you,' Delilah leaned in and Harriett could feel her cold breath on her neck, 'you'll step aside. The role should be mine. It will be mine.'

'Or what, Delilah? You need to learn you don't always get what you want.'

'That's where you're wrong, Harriett. Very wrong.' She grabbed Harriett's arm and squeezed it tightly. 'I always get what I want.'

Harriett reefed her arm free. 'Not this time.' She spun on her heel and strode down the hall to find Genevieve.

After the party Buckley walked Harriett and Genevieve the short stroll to their apartment. Under the lamppost outside her building, Harriett looked up into Buckley's blue eyes. She knew Genevieve was watching from the window, but it didn't stop her wanting to kiss the man in front of her.

'Don't worry about Delilah.' Buckley's fingers played with the back of Harriett's neck, sending shivers down her spine. 'She's just a little wannabe who thinks she's better than she is.'

'What makes you think I'm worried about Diva Delilah?'

'I saw you in the hall. I saw the look on her face,' said Buckley grinning.

'Well, she seems to think you two are destined to walk down the aisle together.'

'I make my own destiny.' He reached his arm behind Harriett's back and pulled her in tight.

The warmth of Buckley's body was so close to her, all she could think of, all she could feel, was him.

She knew it was wrong, bringing him inside the apartment with

Genevieve in the next room, but her heart disobeyed her head with such determination that she had no choice.

She'd been alone for so long that for someone else to love her was a drug she couldn't resist. And she knew he loved her. Without a doubt.

February, 1967

'It's beautiful.' Harriett looked down at her finger. The gold engagement ring, set with a large emerald-cut diamond, was the most beautiful thing she'd ever seen. She had no idea love could be so encompassing. Any second without Buckley was torture.

'So it's a yes?' He kissed her hand.

'Yes,' she squealed.

Genevieve burst into the room and threw herself at the two of them, tears streaming down her face. 'Congratulations!'

'I thought you'd gone to bed, squirt,' said Buckley, roughing up her fringe.

'And miss this? Not a chance.'

Harriett and Buckley laughed.

'I have another surprise.' Buckley got up from bended knee.

'I'm not sure I can take it.'

'Can you take this?' He handed her a set of keys.

She turned them over in her hands.

'They belong to this.' He gave her a photo of a cute little two-storey house surrounded by gum trees, a creek running alongside it.

'What is this?'

'A pre-wedding gift. I thought we could make it a summer house. Go there on holidays.'

'A summer house? For us?'

'For you. I bought it for you.'

They hugged and Buckley spun Harriett around.

'This is just the beginning. I'm going to give you the world.'

Genevieve clapped her hands. 'We're going to be a family. A real, proper family.' She twirled around the room.

Harriett filled with happiness. She turned her gaze to Buckley. A thin beaded line of sweat had appeared on his forehead.

Later that night they lounged on the couch, Harriett's legs draped across Buckley's. Genevieve was finally asleep and Buckley lit up a spliff.

'She isn't really going to live with us when we're married, is she Harry?'

'She hasn't got anywhere else to go.' Harriett frowned. 'But it won't be for long. A couple of years and then she can find her own place.'

Buckley frowned.

She took a drag of his joint and straddled his lap. 'It won't cramp our style,' she said, and unbuttoned his shirt, running her fingers through the thick brown hairs on his chest.

'Promise?'

'I promise.' She lowered herself and kissed his belly button.

2018

Hattie pushed her old memories aside. From the secret compartment at the back of her jewellery box, she pulled out the old ring. She hadn't taken it out in decades, though she never stopped thinking about it. She put it on and felt the weight of its history heavy on her hand. She turned and reached out for the trunk at the end of her bed, but stopped herself. She couldn't bear to look inside. Every mention of his name, every pixelated photo for the last fifty years, cut out of newspapers and magazines, was stashed within the shoebox inside. Hattie looked back into the mirror.

Staring back at her in shadowed reflection was a twenty-something starlet, bright-eyed, the world at her feet. Where had she gone? Tears streamed down her face, make-up pooling in the deep crevasses of her wrinkles. She tore the ring off. Damn Buckley Hargraves. How did she end up here, like this? So old, so desperate, about to ruin another life with her secrets and lies.

She would have to find the right time to tell Alice. Oh, poor Alice. There was no right time to destroy someone's life. There was no perfect moment to tell her she didn't actually own the Kookaburra Creek Café and the legal owners wanted it back.

Five

Kookaburra Creek, 2018

Sun streamed through the café windows as Alice pulled down her painted chairs and the brass bell clanged.

'Becca. I'm glad you came.'

Becca shrugged. 'I need bus money.'

Alice handed her a blue apron. She pulled out the smallest knife in the drawer, and showed Becca how to chop the carrots and cucumbers for the salad. Then she showed her how to grate the capsicum and zucchini ready to be mixed into the chicken mince for the patties that would be turned into burgers. Alice changed her burgers every day: beef, chicken, fish, vegetarian. And she always changed the flavours and spices, too. Today's flavour would be Moroccan.

Becca was a quick study and by opening time all the morning's prep was done.

'Wash up,' Alice said, handing Becca a cloth, 'and then come out front.'

Becca looked down her front and then back to Alice.

'There's another apron in the pantry.' Alice pointed to the yellow gingham hanging on a hook just inside the door.

Joey entered the café. 'Morning, Alice.'

'Morning. What are you doing here?'

'Just thought I'd pop by. Hoping to catch Miss Hattie.'

'She's not in today.'

'Oh. She's not sick, is she?'

'She's fine, just tired. Anything I can help you with?'

'Ah, no. It's fine.'

Becca came into the dining room carrying glasses.

'This is Becca. She's helping me out today,' Alice said.

Joey fixed his gaze on Becca, who took a step back, her eyes darting to the exit.

'Well,' Joey said. 'Nice to meet you, Becca. Don't let her work you too hard.' He turned to Alice. 'I'll take a coffee to go.'

'Is that your boyfriend?' Becca asked, scowling as she watched Joey leave.

Alice sighed. 'Ah, no. He's . . .'

What were they exactly? She didn't know. What they once were, what they were now – she didn't quite have the words.

'He's a friend.'

'He doesn't like me.'

Alice had seen the look that had crossed Joey's face ever so briefly when he met Becca. It wasn't dislike, though. It was shock.

'It's a small town. Newcomers are always noticed.' She thought back to the stares and raised eyebrows that had greeted her when she first came to Kookaburra Creek. 'They warm up, though.' At least, they had with her.

'Won't matter,' Becca muttered. 'What next?'

Alice showed her how to fold the serviettes and left her to it, watching carefully for any hints, any mannerisms that might be familiar.

At the end of the day Alice gave Becca 100 dollars – well over what she'd earned – and walked her to the bus stop just up the road from the café.

'The next one should be along in about fifteen minutes,' Alice said. She tried to sound chirpy, but somehow couldn't muster any real enthusiasm. She wasn't feeling good about this one bit. 'It'll take you to Glensdale, and they have buses to just about anywhere you might want to go.'

Becca looked up at her, her lips pressed tightly together, desperation in her eyes, and Alice felt her breath catch in her throat again.

'Unless . . .' Alice said, her voice wavering. 'Unless you'd maybe like some more work?'

Becca shrugged but Alice thought she saw relief behind those familiar blue eyes.

'You can stay here.'

'With you?'

'I have a spare room.'

Becca shook her head. 'No. The deck. Can I sleep on the deck?'

'It might get cold.'

'I don't mind.'

'Okay.' If that's what it took to keep her here.

'Just till I've got enough to get to Brisbane.'

Alice didn't point out that would only be about another day's work. 'You can stay as long as you want.'

They walked back to the café.

'There's a shower round the side. Feel free to use it.'

Alice headed upstairs to her little flat above the café and into her bedroom. From the back of the wardrobe she grabbed the jeans and T-shirt that hadn't fit her since she arrived in Kookaburra Creek. She'd always meant to give them to charity. She didn't know why she'd kept them all these years. A reminder of a life so very distant, perhaps. Well, they had a purpose now.

She gathered up a towel and some soap and left them outside the tiny washroom behind the café, along with her old clothes. The washroom was rarely used these days, only when the summer heat got to Alice and she'd duck out to splash herself clean between the morning and lunch rush. It certainly wasn't a luxurious place to bathe, probably the original outhouse of the property, but the water ran strong and hot.

It didn't take long for Becca to pick up the basics of how the café worked. In two weeks she'd mastered setting the tables and all the day-to-day cleaning. And she'd become quite good with a paring knife, though it made Alice a little nervous at times. Particurly during the torrential rain three nights ago, which had forced Becca inside. A troubled teenager, good with a knife, sleeping in the next room, wasn't exactly a pleasant thought. Yet most of the time, when Alice stopped thinking and just listened to her heart, she was comforted by Becca's presence. Even so, it was strange sharing her life with someone after living alone so long – having to wait to use the bathroom now that Becca was staying in the apartment, remembering to put extra water in the kettle, stopping herself from sobbing out loud when a random grief-filled memory took her by surprise.

Mostly, though, Alice was getting used to it. And she was definitely enjoying having someone help her in the café. Especially in the mornings.

Alice could see Becca was getting better with the customers, too. Except for Joey. She was still very wary of him.

'Can you grab the salad out of the fridge?' Alice called in to the kitchen.

'Tell me again why he has to come,' Becca yelled back.

'Because he's my friend and it's tradition,' Alice said when Becca came in to the dining room, carrying the large glass bowl stuffed full of lettuce, cucumber and capsicum. 'We've been doing this for so long now, I can't even remember how we got started.'

'He still doesn't like me,' Becca mumbled.

'He just doesn't know you.'

'You don't know me.' Becca shrugged.

'But I'm a much nicer person than grumpy old Joseph.' Alice thought she saw a hint of a smile cross Becca's face. 'You just have to give people a chance.'

'No one ever gave me a bloody chance.' Becca threw the serving tongs onto the bench. Alice stepped up to Becca. The girl shifted slightly away. 'Why are you bothering?' she asked, not looking up at Alice.

'Fair question. I guess . . . well . . . look. I don't know what's brought you here, Becca.' She shrugged. 'But I don't think it was an accident you ended up in my pantry.'

'Oh God, you're not one of those psychic kooks, are you?' Becca said.

'No.' Alice laughed gently. 'Not even close. But I reckon there might be something to fate and that maybe things happen for a reason.'

'I'm not worth trying to save,' Becca said. She looked at Alice with a defiant expression.

'I wasn't going to try,' Alice replied. She opened the fridge. 'I'm no saviour, but you've proved yourself useful and I'm kind of getting used to you. So I hope you'll stick around a little longer.' She took the salad from Becca. 'I know Joey can seem a little . . . rough around the edges, but he's the best of men. Really.'

The doorbell rang.

'I'm here. Are you ready?' Hattie burst through the café door.

'Always.' Alice grinned.

'Evening.' Joey came in behind Hattie, a little nervous if Alice wasn't mistaken.

'Becca,' Hattie called. 'Come out and join us, why don't you?'

Even Becca had learned that Hattie rarely 'asked', and she walked into the dining room, head slightly bowed.

'Sit next to me. I want to hear all about how you've been getting on here in the café. I hope your boss is treating you well.'

Becca sat dutifully, but remained silent.

'So,' Hattie said, trying to ease the tension. 'I ran into Reverend Harris today. It would appear Fiona is back in town.'

Alice's chest tightened at the mention of the oldest Harris child's name and she glanced at Joey, who didn't seem to react at all.

Despite her efforts to sound jovial over dinner, Hattie's thoughts were clearly elsewhere, and not in a happy place. She tried to tell stories, but they kept coming off flat. And that wasn't like Hattie at all. She was usually able to hold an audience's attention with consummate ease. 'And you wouldn't believe what Claudine said at bridge last night . . .' Alice could see through the facade, but said nothing.

As soon as Joey spooned the last pieces of sticky date pudding into his mouth, Alice jumped up to start clearing the table.

'I got this,' he said. He stood, collected everyone's plates and headed in to the kitchen.

'Becca, be a dear and help out.' Hattie pulled Alice back to her seat. 'Now, tell me,' Hattie continued, once Joey and Becca were out of the room. 'What's going on?'

'She's working out wonderfully. Doesn't give me a lot, you know, about her past. Well, about anything at all, really. But she is a huge help . . .'

'I wasn't talking about Becca. I can see for myself how that's going. I'm talking about Joey. He seems upset.'

Alice shook her head. 'I think he's struggling with Becca being here. It's probably nothing.'

'Petal, it's never nothing between you two. Neither of you ever seems certain of whatever the something is that passes between the two of you like this, but it sure as eggs is never nothing.'

'Sometimes I wonder, well, you know. If only . . .'

'Codswallop.'

'Codswallop?'

'You heard me. When you get to my age you realise how much life you waste on "if only". How much time you squander wishing things were different instead of making them so. And with Fiona Harris back in town, you can't afford to be wasting any —'

A crashing sound shot through the air and Alice jumped up and ran into the kitchen.

'What the . . .' she looked at the plates smashed into tiny pieces across the floor. Becca's eyes were glued to the floor, her hands open beside her, slightly raised.

'My fault,' Joey said. 'Tried to carry too much.'

Alice had known him too long not to know he was lying.

'Joey?' Alice glared at him.

'Sorry,' he said, bending down to pick up the pieces. 'It was an accident.'

'I thought it was Greeks, not Italians, who smashed plates,' Hattie said as she entered the kitchen.

Alice shot her a look.

'Would you walk me home, Joey?' She linked her arm in his.

As they left the kitchen Hattie turned back to Alice and mouthed, 'Never nothing.'

Alice turned around to see Becca walking out the back door. She counted to three and followed her out to the jetty.

'Jetty' was probably too grand a word to describe the old planks of wood that stretched over the water's edge running behind the Kookaburra Creek Café, but Alice liked to imagine small handmade rafts or tiny rowboats tied up to it on a lazy Sunday afternoon, a man and his son waiting patiently, fishing lines bobbing in the water. Alice made her way down to the jetty where Becca now sat, jeans rolled up, legs dangling in the gently lapping water below.

Alice sat beside her. 'Sorry if he scared you,' she said.

'Scared me?'

'Yes. You looked pretty frightened when I walked in. He really is the gentlest soul.'

'It wasn't him,' Becca whispered.

'Sorry?'

'It was me. I dropped the plates.'

'I don't understand.'

'I dropped them. By accident. But I panicked. They cost money and I thought you'd be angry.' Her eyes brimmed with tears. 'I begged him not to tell you it was me.'

'Becca, sweetheart.' Alice sighed. 'Why on earth would I be angry at you for breaking a few plates?'

She shrugged.

Alice went to put her arm around the girl, but Becca wriggled away.

'Have I ever given you any reason to think I would react angrily to something like that?' Alice asked.

'No.' Becca shook her head. 'But that's what they do. Make you think you can trust them, then bam.'

Alice hesitated. She didn't want to push too soon. 'Well, I'm not "they", and I'll never yell at you.'

They sat in silence and took in their surroundings. A tawny frogmouth began his evening serenade as the moon rose into the sky. Alice loved clear nights when the stars blinking above her went on forever. She searched for the Southern Cross, divided the pointers and traced the imaginary lines through the constellation.

'What are you doing?' Becca looked at her with a frown.

'Something my dad taught me.' Alice showed her, just the way Bruce had shown her when she ten, how to find true south.

'Why did Joey cover for me?' Becca asked, her finger dancing amongst the stars above her head.

'He covered for you because you asked him to,' Alice said.

I don't trust him.

The way he looks at me sometimes is unnerving. He didn't dob me in tonight, but that's what they do. Lure you in. Make you trust them. And then you're trapped. And trapped is bad.

Sometimes at night I slip back out to the deck and sleep there. Unlike a room with four walls and only one way in or out, easily blocked, the deck has options. Escape options.

There's no lock on the door of the room and when I do sleep there I push the desk across it just in case. I've got a bag of clothes, hand-me-downs the church ladies gave Alice, and a crate of tinned food I've been collecting buried in the bush out the back. At night I sneak out one tin at a time, slowly so she doesn't notice. I'm building up my getaway supplies. Just in case.

It is nice to be clean, though. It'd been six months since I'd had a shower. Six months of moving from one park to another, hitching rides from one deadbeat town to the next. Always running. Always moving. Six months since I'd had any real food. Hunger is a total bitch, a gnawing pain that never goes away. I don't miss that. But I can't get too comfortable. This won't last. Nothing good ever does.

Alice will show her true colours at some point. They always do. It's good to rest, though. To not run. Just for a little while.

Six

Lawson's Ridge, 2003

Alice walked her usual route to the general store and pinned her name tag to her striped uniform. Mrs Reynolds would be in around ten to do her weekly shop. Alice would try to tempt her into buying a fruit cake Louise's grandmother had made and delivered that morning, but it wouldn't be on Mrs Reynolds' list, so she'd say no. One day Alice would crack her, though. It was her mission. One of many missions she set to help while away the endless hours. Alice's boss, Mr Williams, would turn up around 10.30, his curls unbrushed, after having breakfast with his not-so-secret friend Donna Dobson, who was still married to Mr Dobson, the only one in town who didn't know of his wife's indiscretions. Sally and Sue, the aptly named Spinster Sisters, would wander in around one o'clock and buy an apple each. And at two, just as Alice was clocking off, the Trainor boys would speed past in their beat-up ute and toot their horn, creating a mini dust storm behind them. Just another Sunday at Lawson's Ridge General Store.

Alice unpacked the newspapers, delivered overnight from Sydney (everything happened in Sydney), and placed them in the rack by the front door. The alarm on the digital clock near the register chimed with three short trills and Alice raced back behind the counter just before the glass door opened.

'Morning, Bertie,' she said, looking intently down at the cracks in the counter surface.

'Morning, Alligator.' Bertie stood before her in his brown dressing gown, grey hair unkempt, grey stubble in need of a shave.

Reaching behind her for Bertie's cigarettes, Alice kept her eyes down. Without looking up she took his money and gave him his change. He didn't move.

Alice knew he wouldn't leave the shop till she looked up, so she raised her head. Bertie opened his dressing gown and put the cigarettes in the inside pocket.

'Blue today, Bertie.' Alice sighed.

'Bertie good boy.' He nodded, ever so proud as always of his boxers. Alice could only imagine how many times his mother must have told him as a child that every good boy changed their underwear regularly. She wished he wouldn't show her, though. Just once couldn't he put a singlet on under his dressing gown? Trousers, even? Not that it was his fault. There wasn't any help for people like Bertie this far from civilisation.

Just before closing she packed away the remaining two cakes Louise's grandmother had made. Six sales today. Grandma Jenkins would be pleased. She grabbed the envelope Mr Williams had given her before he'd left at twelve and she locked the front door, pushing the keys back through the mail chute.

As she turned to walk home she hit something solid and dropped to the ground.

'Sorry!' Dean McRae stood over her.

She shook her head. 'So you should be. Ouch.'

Dean bent down to help her up, but she refused his outstretched hand.

'Pond, huh?'

Alice followed his gaze to the name tag she'd forgotten to take off. She fumbled to remove it.

'I like it. Alice Pond.'

'It doesn't really matter if you like it or not. It's my name.'

'True. You're a strange one, Pond.' Dean followed her as she headed down the path.

'I have to go.'

'Okay. Where are we heading?'

'We?' Alice stopped walking and looked him in the eye. 'Of all the things people have said about you since you got here, crazy stalker hasn't yet come up.'

'Sorry.' He took a step back, his expression giving away how hurt he was by her barb.

'I normally walk home through Faraway Forest,' Alice said with a sigh.

'What-away what?'

'Never mind. It's this way if you want to come.'

Dean fell into step beside her and they walked through the brown, dusty streets. There was a time, Alice remembered, when she was really little, when the shop windows were full of colour, showing off their wares with pride. Cute little tea cups and pots arranged in sets in the gift store, and ceramic angels hanging from fishing wire; the haberdashery store her mum used to frequent, with stripes and dots and florals and checks stacked on top of one another next to the mannequin draped in some fancy silk or satin, always holding a basket stuffed full of wool skeins. Now most of the shops were empty, their windows boarded up and abandoned. The pub still thrived, though. So did the TAB. No matter what happened to the town, old men always had money for booze and bets. Middle-aged men, too. Alice knew that all too well.

It wasn't long before they arrived at Alice's ironbark.

'Did you just speak to the tree?' Dean asked as he climbed up behind Alice and sat next to her on the branch.

'We go way back.' Alice shot him a look. Why had she gone and greeted her tree in front of him?

'That's cool,' he replied. 'But if it ever starts talking back, we have a problem.'

Alice found herself smiling and tried hard not to laugh. She could feel Dean's eyes on her and she had to admit she didn't entirely hate his company. There was something gentle about him. All the boys she knew were loud and rough and only interested in farming or footy and teasing her about her father. Dean hadn't mentioned crops or scrums once. And if he did know about her dad, which wasn't inconceivable in a town where everyone knew everyone's business, he wasn't letting on.

'How long are you and your mum planning on staying in this paradise?' Alice broke the quiet.

He shrugged. 'Mum's actually thinking of starting a business, so who knows?'

'At least it's not long till you can take off and go wherever you want.'

'Maybe.'

'Maybe? You won't see me for dust come December.'

Dean smiled. 'And what will you do when you escape?'

Alice stared out across her forest. 'Go to Sydney. Go to uni. Never come back.'

'What about your family?'

'It's just Dad. When I've got enough money saved, I'll get him out, too.' Alice had heard there were places that could help her dad. Places in Sydney. Places that cost money. She had a plan and she knew deep down inside she could make it happen.

'Well, sounds like you've got it all figured out.'

Alice held his gaze, her heart beating fast.

'I really have to go,' she blurted out, and got up. She climbed over Dean and scampered down the tree so fast she stumbled when she hit the dirt. But she didn't stop, even when she heard him drop down and start following her.

'Seriously, Pond,' Dean said, gasping for air as he caught up with her. 'Wait up. I didn't mean to upset you.'

Alice slowed to a walk. 'You didn't.'

'I'm really sorry.' He smiled and, despite her best efforts to look angry, the corner of Alice's mouth turned ever so slightly up. 'Where ya headed?' he asked.

'I'm going . . . I was just . . .'Alice shrugged. When he looked into her eyes like that, all she wanted to do was stay. 'I was just walking. Nowhere in particular.'

'The boys have been talking about some dam everyone goes to,' Dean said.

'Pip's dam? It's ten minutes' drive that way.' Alice pointed west.

'What do ya say, Pond? Fancy a drive? My ute's over near the shop.'

'I s'pose.' It was just a drive. And it wasn't like he was interested in her. No one ever was.

*

Dean sped along the gravel road and Alice watched the speedo hit 130, then 140.

'You might want to slow down a bit.'

'Not scared are you, Pond?' He pressed down on the accelerator.

'No.' She swallowed hard. 'It's just the cops are usually out on this stretch.'

He slowed down and Alice felt the tightness in her chest release.

Pip's dam wasn't exactly what anyone would consider beautiful. In the middle of a field of yellow grass a thin strip of green ran around the perimeter of the deep water hole. It wasn't a huge dam but, in an otherwise brown and dusty existence, it did provide welcome relief on scorching summer days. When temperatures climbed above forty, as they inevitably did, the dam heaved with splashing teenagers, the old grey gum providing an outstretched branch just the right height, just the right extension, to hang a thick swinging rope off from which kids would fling themselves into the cool embrace of the dam below.

Pip never seemed to mind too much. It was his secondary dam, after all. As long as they stayed away from his sheep. Especially Bobbles, his prize ram. Every now and then, though, some idiot boy would try it on and bring Bobbles to the edge of the dam and the poor thing would start bleating, frightened out of its wits by the noise, and Pip would ban them all for the rest of summer. And they would all return two weeks later and Pip would watch them from the top of the hill, until he was certain they would behave. Until next time.

Come summer, Pip's dam would be crowded with sweaty teenagers trying to one-up each other with somersaults off the rope. But not today. On a mild August afternoon, it would be just them.

'The fellas haven't shut up about this place since I got here,' Dean said as they got out of his car.

'Only believe half of what you hear.'

'Not even half.' Dean nodded.

Alice led him to the big, old gum and sat herself against its thick trunk. Stretching out his long legs, Dean lay on his side beside her, propped up on one elbow, his head tilted slightly. Alice wished he wouldn't smile that way, the dimple in his left cheek deepening.

'So I hear you're a bit of a genius.'

Alice grunted. 'If only.'

'Really? What would you do if you were?' Dean asked, pulling himself up higher.

Alice sighed. If only she were smarter, she'd have found a way out of her situation already, found a way to help her dad. 'Achieve world peace, end famines.' She shrugged. 'The usual.'

Dean sat up and hugged his legs. 'I don't know, being that smart might have its drawbacks.'

'Like what?'

'Well,' he said, standing up and grabbing Alice's hands, pulling her up too. 'For one thing, if you were a genius, you'd be way too smart to go in on a day like today.'

'Go in where?'

Dean slipped off his shoes, took off his T-shirt and dared Alice with a wink.

'You're not serious!'

'See.' He smiled. 'Too smart.' He tapped her on the head. 'Not smart enough.' He hit himself on the chest and broke into a run. He leaped up and grabbed the rope, swung three times over the dam and let go with a Tarzan bellow as he flew across the top of the water.

'You're mad!' Alice screamed at him, following him to the edge of the water.

'It's beautiful,' he called back, splashing her while trying unsuccessfully to hide the fact he was shivering. 'But you're probably too smart and sensible to do something this crazy . . . and fun.'

'I know how to have fun.' Alice stood with her hands on her hips.

'Really?' He splashed her again.

Alice really wished he wouldn't smile like that.

She undid her trainers and took off her jeans. In her T-shirt and undies she grabbed on to the rope and pushed off from the bank of the dam.

'Holy crap,' she cried after she broke through the surface. 'It's freezing.' She swam as quickly as she could to the edge and climbed out. 'You really are mad.'

Dean climbed out behind her. 'Maybe. But you had fun, right?'

'I'm not sure that'd be the word I'd use.'

Dean bumped Alice to the side with his hip. 'Then why are you grinning like a Cheshire cat?'

Under the old grey gum in the setting afternoon sun, Alice and Dean sat. Alice in Dean's dry T-shirt that she'd put on behind the tree, her soaking top laid out on the parched grass to dry. Dean, his bare torso covered in goosebumps belying the fact he swore he wasn't cold.

'What sort of business is your mum thinking about opening?' Alice asked.

'A quilt store,' he said, rolling his eyes. 'Or something like that. I think Dad's a bit jealous she's going to be just fine without him.'

'They're in touch?'

'No. But I am. I think he was hoping that when we got out here she'd realise she needed him and go back to him.'

Alice nodded. 'Do you miss him?' She knew what it was like to be one parent down.

'Yeah. I guess. I'll visit him in the holidays.'

'Have you figured out what you're going to do next year?'

'All about school with you, isn't it?' Dean shook his head. 'Don't you think about anything else?'

'Only how not to catch pneumonia after jumping into a freezing dam.'

He laughed. 'And what about you? What are you going to study when you get to Sydney?' he asked.

'Law.'

'Why?'

'Why not?'

'Dunno. You just don't seem the lawyery type.'

'Oh? And what is the lawyery type?'

Dean shrugged. 'Argumentative, know-all, stuck up . . . oh, hang on . . .'

Alice threw a twig at his head and Dean laughed.

'I just don't think lawyer when I think of you.'

'Well, maybe you should stop thinking of me,' Alice said.

Dean lifted his hand and brushed a stray brown strand off Alice's face. 'Can't help it.'

Alice stood up quickly and backed away. 'Well.' She paused. 'I haven't got the stomach to become a doctor or the talent to be a movie star, so lawyer it is.' She'd done her research, looked into jobs that paid the most. She knew she had a head for facts, for remembering things. And lawyers, lawyers in Sydney, made a lot of money. And that was money that could save her dad.

'But,' Dean stood and stepped closer, 'what about your passion? Doing something you love, something that gets you, you know, excited?'

'I've never thought about . . .' Alice could see the flecks of gold in Dean's blue eyes. 'I need to . . . There's Louise.'

'What?'

'And Brian.' Alice stepped to the side and waved as the twins got out of Brian's ute. 'Hey, Lou,' she called, stepping further away from Dean.

'You guys didn't seriously go for a swim, did you?' Louise asked as she walked over to them.

'Hey, mate.' Brian greeted Dean.

'Hey.'

They slapped each other on the back.

'I can't believe you went in.' Louise cried. 'You guys are nuts.'

'Wanna give me a lift home?' Alice asked.

'What's the rush? We just got here.' Louise ran back to the ute and grabbed the old blanket from the tray and turned the radio up. 'May as well enjoy the sunshine.' She laid out the blanket and sat down. The two boys joined her.

As she pushed her blonde hair behind her ears, Louise turned her attention to Dean.

'How on earth did you get Miss Stick-in-the-mud here to jump in the dam? You must have some pretty powerful tools of persuasion. I love Pip's dam. Come here all the time. We should come together some time. Have you been to Cutter's Pass yet? Of course you have. Silly question. But have you been to the lookout? It's not all that great, I suppose, but it's about the best thing we've got going around here . . .'

Alice sat silently behind Brian and let her best friend do all the talking. That's how it always went: Louise front and centre, Alice in the shadows. And that was just fine by Alice. Every now and then she would turn her gaze from Louise to Dean and then look away again when his eyes met hers.

*

Brian dropped Alice home after Louise convinced Dean he absolutely couldn't wait one more day before he saw the lookout. Alice made some sorry excuse about having an assignment due and asked Brian to drive her back. She was glad to be away from them. Away from Dean. He was dangerous. And there was no room in her plan for danger. No matter how cute his smile was. She was pretty sure Kylie Trainor was regretting falling for a cute smile that passed through town last cattle auction season right about now, ready to give birth at the age of fifteen. And for Wendy Dobson's big sister, the smartest girl to ever attend Lawson High, falling for a cute smile from Cutter's Pass had landed her with five kids and a caravan on her parents' quarter acre and said cute smile shot through, unseen for the last six years. Cute smiles equalled danger and danger was best avoided. Alice was determined not to get trapped in Lawson's Ridge.

Alice's dad was in his customary position stretched out on the sofa when she got inside. She pulled a blanket over him and threw out the empty cans. On the bench was a TAB slip. She scrunched it up and threw it out, too. No need to check it. If he'd won, he'd still be at the pub. She put a pot of water on to boil for pasta. Sundays were the only days she allowed herself to use the oven, to save electricity. She made enough pasta for the both of them and put her dad's serve in the fridge so he could have it for breakfast.

She pulled her pay packet out of her pocket and divided up the notes, laying out her contribution to rent money, groceries, electricity. She put a small amount into her secret hiding place in a shoebox at the back of her cupboard. It would stay there until it was needed for school or, she counted the days on her calendar, for pads. She only bought what was necessary and she never gave her dad any of it. He had the dole to pay for his essentials – his beer and his betting. Alice only spent what she had to. Ever so slowly, her escape fund was growing and she knew, deep down inside, her plan would succeed.

Seven

Kookaburra Creek, 2018

Alice pushed the door to the bakery open. In all the years she'd known Joey, he'd never locked it after hours if he was inside. Even this early in the morning.

'Morning, Alice.' Joey stepped out into the shop from his kitchen. The heat inside was a welcome blast after the cool morning air. 'What brings you by so early?'

'I, well, I think maybe we should have a chat.'

'At five in the morning? Must be serious. Why don't you help me knead while we have this chat?' He gestured to the kitchen behind him.

Alice followed him and got to work mixing the wholemeal dough for his famous rolls. He'd taught her how years ago, and he'd taught her well.

'Becca told me what happened with the plates.'

He shrugged. 'Girl's got some issues.'

'I know. But I sense something in her.'

'Something of yourself?'

Alice blushed at how close to the truth he was. 'Maybe.'

Joey stepped round the bench and took Alice's floured hands. 'Or someone else?'

'You too?' Alice cast her gaze down. It was foolish to think he wouldn't be reminded of Tammy too.

'Hard not to.' Joey returned to his dough and started roping it into plaits. 'Becca's what, only a year or two older than she would've . . .' his words faltered. 'And those eyes . . . it's uncanny, the resemblance.'

'I'm sorry.' Alice took a deep breath, the fragile scar reopened. 'You understand why I couldn't turn her away, right?'

Joey stayed silent.

'She appreciates you covering for her. Though it might be a while before she trusts any of us.'

Joey shook his head. 'Like I said, girl's got issues. I can deal with it, though. Can you?'

Alice had no words.

'Miss Hattie was a bit funny when I walked her home last night.' Joey said. Alice was grateful for the change in subject. 'Anything going on?'

'I wish I knew. Something's not right, I know that much.' She divided her dough balls.

'Are you game enough to pry?'

'No way. I like my head right where it is, thank you.'

Joey handed her the canister of raisins and she started on the fruit loaf. He put the rolls and plaited loaves into the oven and when he came back to the bench Alice handed him the rolling pin that sat on the shelf below so he could start on the croissants.

Every time they baked together she wished they could freeze time and stay there. No past. No future. Just the two of them, flour, ovens, no words needed. Then things might be okay between them again. But life didn't work like that. They had a past, a painful one, and a fractured future, always in shadow.

As the clock struck eight, Alice washed the flour from her hands. 'I'd better get back to the café.'

'Thanks for the hand.' Joey passed her a tea towel. Their hands touched and Alice felt, just for a moment, a jolt of the magnetic force between them that was always just under the surface.

'Of course.' Alice stepped back.

'Right.' Joey brushed the flour off his apron. 'You have a good day.'

The week passed quietly and it was obvious Becca was becoming quite the kitchen hand. She'd already learned to throw together a good salad, didn't need any help with the sandwiches, and had managed to cook over a dozen burgers without burning a single one. Alice was impressed. When she'd first tried, it had taken her quite a few goes to get the pan just right (hot enough, but not too hot) and the timing perfect. Back then she'd never made burgers before. She'd never made anything, really. She'd learned the knack of grilling a good patty the hard, charcoaled way. Becca seemed to be a natural cook.

And that meant Alice had more time for baking. Earlier that morning Sylvia had told her to bake mini mixed-berry delights. Alice had left Becca to set up the dining room after she'd finished the morning's prep and Alice had baked three dozen of the cute little things. As she'd poured berry coulis into the cream cheese frosting, spinning the electric mixing bowl, Alice had begun dancing around the room. She'd filled the piping bag and with each swirl atop each cupcake, the flourish of her wrist became more elaborate.

'What are you doing?' Becca had asked, catching her in the act.

Alice had blushed. 'Cooking is supposed to be fun.'

'Oh . . . kay . . .' Becca had backed out of the kitchen and got on with her next task.

Alice knew she had to be more careful around Becca. The last thing she wanted was to scare her off.

Later that evening, they sat in the soft glow of the living room lamp. Alice snuggled in to her old sofa and looked at Becca sitting on the floor. 'You did great today,' she said.

Becca turned her head quickly, stood up and moved to the kitchen, but Alice caught a glimpse of the smile spreading across her face.

'Did your mum teach you how to cook?' Alice called out.

Becca didn't answer. Soon the loud bubble and steam of the ancient kettle prevented further discussion.

Alice pulled the blanket over her legs and let Becca make the tea. The nights still carried the leftover chill of winter, and she loved nothing better than to relax at the end of the day with a hot cuppa.

'I still don't get that you don't have a TV.' Becca returned, handing Alice a camomile brew, and sat on the rug in the middle of Alice's living room with her mug of Milo.

'I've never had one.' Alice shrugged.

'Never ever?' Becca pulled the woollen bed socks Alice had given her over her ankles.

'Nope.' Alice shook her head.

'Did you grow up on a hippy commune or something?'

Alice laughed. She was getting used to Becca's direct questioning. 'No. We just didn't have a lot of money when I was growing up and I've never really felt I was missing much, so I just haven't bothered.'

'What about the news?'

'That's what newspapers are for. Or Betty and her grapevine.'

'You've never seen *Home and Away*?' Becca continued. She looked at Alice in disbelief as she shook her head. She cast her eyes down and played with a loose thread on the rug beneath her. 'I miss TV.' She sighed. 'Silly, huh? Of all the things to miss.'

A wave of nostalgia hit Alice. 'I find we miss the strangest, smallest things when we're away from home. I miss my garden gnomes.'

Becca snorted milk out her nose. 'Gnomes?'

'Yes, gnomes.' Alice frowned.

'Sorry,' Becca said quickly. 'It's just . . . gnomes?'

'It's fine. As I said, smallest, strangest things.'

The two drank from their cups in silence.

Becca grabbed the Uno cards sitting on the coffee table and began to shuffle. 'I reckon I've got the strategy now,' she said as she dealt.

'Ah, but I play mean.' Alice's mouth turned up slightly. It seemed Becca wasn't just a quick learner with cooking.

'Yeah, sweet old lady mean. I'm street mean.'

'Who are you calling old?'

Alice played her first card, a pick-up four.

The next morning, Becca helped Alice load the two containers of cupcakes they'd carried into town into the back of Joey's van. 'Tell me why we're doing this again?'

'Because it's nice to do things for others.'

Becca grunted.

'Ready to go, girls?' Joey pushed his tray of rolls and pastries into the van. Becca groaned as she slumped into the back seat next to Shadow. The dog licked Becca's hand until she relented and patted him. Alice took her usual place next to Joey up front and kept her eyes forward.

Kookaburra Cottage was situated halfway along the winding road to Glensdale, an old sandstone house that housed the area's aged and frail. Alice had first gone there when Hattie took her to meet Genevieve. She wasn't quite sure what you were supposed to bring the first time you met the terminally infirm sister of the woman who'd changed your life, so she'd brought a box of cupcakes with her as a present.

Genevieve had been unable to eat them, but the other residents had snapped them up and told her, in no uncertain terms, she must return with more.

Then, when Joey had invited her to go with him on his monthly goodwill visit, she knew she had to go back to Kookaburra Cottage. Every month for the last fourteen years the two of them had sat with the residents. Every month except that one summer eight years ago.

The little yellow cottage was ten minutes out of town. It was bordered by hydrangea bushes, and baskets dripping with peonies and violets hung from the verandah roof. A five-metre-deep surround of perfectly cut grass led to gumtrees and bush that somehow seemed out of place around the cottage, despite it being the natural landscape for hundreds of kilometres in every direction.

Joey pulled up in the gravel car park and started to unload the van. Shadow ran round to the courtyard on the other side of the cottage, where there was always a resident or two waiting for him with treats.

'Do I have to come in?' Becca began to fidget. She'd got used to the customers in the café, but still wasn't good around new people.

'We could do with a hand. At least while we set up,' Alice said.

'Okay.' Becca reluctantly picked up a container of vanilla cupcakes and followed them inside.

Once they had unloaded, Alice went to sit with old Mrs Blackwood by the window overlooking the back garden. She'd sneaked in Mrs Blackwood's favourite, chocolate cupcake laced with Frangelico, and Mrs Blackwood thanked her with stories from her childhood. The carers didn't condone 'alcoholic' cupcakes, but Mrs Blackwood certainly did. In the far corner Alice could see Hattie sitting with her sister, which wouldn't have been strange if it were any other day. But it was Sunday. And Hattie never visited on Sundays.

Genevieve stared straight ahead, no recognition, no light in her eyes. To be absent in your own life . . . Alice could think of few things worse. Hattie's lips, close to Genevieve's ears, were moving quickly and she was concentrating so intensely on whatever it was she was telling her she hadn't even noticed Alice and Joey arrive. The scarf wrapped loosely around Genevieve's head slipped as Hattie talked. Alice sighed. The passing years had done little to fade the scars that disfigured the sweet old lady's face. Hattie quickly rearranged the green chiffon so only the right side, the unmarked side, of Genevieve's face could be seen.

Many times Alice had listened to the stories of the inseparable sisters who'd arrived in Kookaburra Creek suddenly one day and turned a rundown house into a café. She'd never got to know Genevieve, not properly, not before the dementia had taken hold. But she'd seen glimpses of the girl that might have been, back in her first days here. In those rare lucid moments Genevieve always talked about Hattie.

Joey looked over from his chess game with Mr Curran and winked at Alice, who had kept the secret cupcake hidden in her bag so none of the carers saw. She smiled back and looked around for Becca. The girl was sitting on the other side of the room, wide-eyed, having been cornered by old Miss Hayes who was happily regaling her with tales of nursing in World War Two, no doubt. Once ninety-four-year-old Miss Hayes had an audience, she didn't let them go. Becca would be stuck there till they left.

The late afternoon sun cast dappled light through the leaves of the tall gum trees outside Kookaburra Cottage as Alice and Joey packed the empty containers into Joey's van.

'That wasn't so bad, was it?' Alice asked Becca.

Becca shrugged and jumped into the back seat. Alice fought back her frustration. It was going to take longer than she thought to break down her defences. She'd hoped the visit to Kookaburra Cottage, a change in scenery, might do the girl some good. Apparently not.

'Ready to go?' Joey approached her.

'Who won this time?'

'Curran, of course.'

Alice grinned. Joey always let the old man win. She turned to get in the van and saw Hattie at the other end of the car park slink into her late-fifties Jag. 'Just a second, Joey.' She strode towards her old friend.

'Hattie. Is everything okay? Wind down the window.' She tapped on the glass.

'Good God, child. Are you trying to give me a heart attack?'

Alice could see the stain of tears on Hattie's cheeks. 'Is Genevieve all right?'

'Of course. Why wouldn't she be?' Hattie flicked her orange scarf over her left shoulder.

'You don't normally come on a Sunday.'

'So now I'm not allowed to visit my own sister whenever I like?'

'No. It's just that, well, the conversation you were having, it looked serious.'

'And you're an expert in conversations you didn't even hear?'

'No. I just . . .'

'Don't go looking for drama that isn't there, Alice.' Hattie drove off, leaving Alice standing in the gravel unsure of what just happened.

Becca remained silent as Joey drove them back to the café and Alice wasn't in the mood to prise a conversation out of her. Her own encounter with Hattie had unsettled her and she was happy to let the girl be. As evening fell, it was Becca who broke the silence.

'I'm off to bed,' she said as Alice put the dishes away.

'Becca?'

'Yes.'

'Is there anything . . . is everything okay?'

'Sure.' She shrugged.

'You can tell me, you know, tell me the truth.' Alice put down her tea towel.

'I know. Good night.'

Alice sighed as Becca left the room.

Whatever she'd been thinking when she invited Becca to stay, she hadn't thought it would be this hard. All she wanted was to make friends with the girl. All she wanted was to give her a second chance at a life that she couldn't give . . .

The thought stuck in her mind and Alice couldn't finish it. Wouldn't finish it. All she wanted. Tears began to roll down her cheeks.

All she wanted, she couldn't have.

All those old people in one place.

I hope Alice doesn't ask me to go again next time. The whole time I was there all I could think of was Granny D. And how she died. And how when she died that was when it all went wrong. I can't stand being around sick old people. Alice seemed to love it though. But then, she's not exactly normal.

For one thing, she's trying to help me. And that's not normal.

I mean, I broke into her stupid little café and ate her stupid bread and then she gave me a job. Who does that? Crazy people. That's who.

Maybe one of her secret burger ingredients is ground-up teenager and I'll be on next week's menu. The Becca Burger. She's just waiting for me to drop my guard.

I'll be ready for her, though, if she tries anything. She doesn't notice, but I watch her out of the corner of my eye. You get real good, real sneaky, at keeping your eye on people when you don't know where the next hit is coming from. And I'm fast. Faster than her, for sure.

She's got to be thirty at least. More. She's got wrinkles, around her brown eyes, but I reckon she was probably pretty cute when she was younger. Younger and thinner, probably. Not that she's fat. Comfortable. I've heard blokes use that word before to describe women. It's a horrible word. But I guess it kind of fits. She does run around this place all day, though, and then wants to chat all night. But that's not the same as being quick because you have to be. To survive. I'm fast.

And the singing. What's the go with that? Who sings to their food? Plants, maybe. But food? Crazy people. That's who.

Thing is, she doesn't seem crazy. Not proper crazy. I mean she has conversations with a photo on the wall. She doesn't think I know about that. Tries to hide it. But I see her. Every morning she talks to that old picture. And she likes garden gnomes. I guess that doesn't make her crazy, though. Weird, yes; but not crazy.

But the thing is, I've been wrong about people before.

'I'll change.' I believed him.

'It won't happen again.' I believed him.

Everyone lies. People just can't help it.

I won't stay in this shithole long. Just long enough to save up some money. And then I'll take off. Head north. It's not as if anyone here will be sorry to see me go. They give me funny looks, the women who come into the café. And I know what the men are thinking. Dirty old buggers are all the same. I hate serving them. Joey's always watching me. Alice thinks he's okay. More than okay, if she's being honest. Which she isn't. See, lies.

Not that any of it matters. Once I've got enough cash, I'll shoot through.

I've stuffed up a couple of times in the café, but Alice didn't get mad. She didn't hit me. She didn't even yell at me. And the fact that I haven't been turned into a burger, yet, is a good sign. I suppose. As long as I don't make her angry. Olds get angry really easily. I don't say much. I know when to shut up.

I dreamed about him last night. He just stood there. In the doorway. Hands on his hips, like that first night after Granny D died. Smiling. The way he always did, dripping with intent.

I woke up and pushed the chair Alice bought me up against the desk, up against the door. And I slept on the desk. Any little bump and I'd have been ready.

I'm saving money pretty quickly. That's the only reason I said yes to going today. It meant more cash. There's nothing else to do round here but work. No shops. No cinema. I suppose that means he won't think to look for me here. I mean, who even knows this place exists?

But he will be looking. You don't do what I did to him and get away with it. He'll be coming. It's only a matter of time. He'll want revenge and he'll keep searching for me till he finds me.

I will watch. I will work. I will stash away supplies.

And then, I'll run.

Eight

Kookaburra Creek, 2018

It was times like this that Hattie missed her sister most. Genevieve would have been able to talk her to a solution perhaps. At the very least she would have soothed Hattie's worries. And she needed that, as her anxiety was raging inside her. Genevieve was always good at talking Hattie down. Out of all the people in the world Hattie knew, Genevieve was the one person she could talk to about the café, who would understand just how she felt about the prospect of losing it. But she couldn't understand anymore. Not a word. And it was all Hattie's fault. This whole sorry mess was her fault. If only she hadn't caused the accident. If only she hadn't caused Genevieve so much pain. If only she'd taken better care of her, stopped her working so hard, maybe her mind wouldn't have gone downhill so badly, so early. If only she'd listened to the doctor.

Hattie remembered the conversation that day at the doctor's office. 'Miss Brookes, this latest assessment of Genevieve's condition would indicate her brain function is deteriorating more rapidly than we predicted. Not that we can accurately predict such things, especially in cases like this. It's all a bit unknown. But maybe it's time for you to give up your receptionist job and take over the café. Take some of the burden off her.'

'I've managed this long perfectly well,' Genevieve had insisted. 'I don't need you babysitting me.'

'That's not what the doctors are suggesting, Gen.'

'Of course it is, Hattie. Listen, I know exactly what's happening here. The absence seizures are getting worse and I know what that means. But if you take away my independence now, you might as well start digging my grave. Whatever time I have left, I'd rather spend it doing something I enjoy.'

'Stop being so stubborn.'

'Well, I did learn from the best.' She'd wrapped Hattie in a tight hug.

If only Hattie hadn't let her have her way, Genevieve might still be with her in mind as well as body.

Walking the green hills that surrounded Kookaburra Creek, Hattie could see laid out before her a patchwork of every blunder and fault of her life, the dawning light illuminating them so clearly: loving Buckley, trusting him, the accident, Genevieve's suffering, not forgiving Buckley when she had the chance, not realising the café was never really hers, that he'd never actually given it to her. Everything had started with Buckley Hargraves and now it seemed everything was going to end with him as well.

March, 1967

Closing night had seen the biggest ovation yet and a record number of seven encores. Harriett knew she couldn't go back to film after this. The stage was where she belonged; it was her place in the world. Until Buckley had brought her into the theatre, it was like she'd been sleepwalking through life. Now she was truly alive.

The air backstage was thick with smoke from the many bongs around the room. Jim Morrison's voice blasted throughout. Bottles of Dom Pérignon were being emptied as if they contained water. Stagehands were stealing kisses from extras and, in the darker shadows of the theatre, members of the main cast were celebrating the end of the show in more intimate ways.

But Harriett couldn't find Buckley anywhere. She headed to his dressing room and found his door slightly ajar. A quiet giggle floated on the air to Harriett's ears. She fought back the sense of dread rising inside her and stepped into the room. Buckley was perched on top of the chaise longue in the corner of the room. He turned his stretched-out body awkwardly and looked at Harriett.

'Hey, babe,' he said, grinning, his eyes glazed over, a tiny dribble of drool trickling from his chin. He was high. Again. Beneath his naked lower half, two legs that were definitely not his lay spread beneath a blanket. Two empty bottles of champagne lay discarded to the side.

'What do you think you're doing?' Harriett crossed the room in three long strides and pulled the blanket out from under him, sending him toppling to the floor. And there lay Delilah, a stupid grin splattered across her drunken face.

'Relax, Harry. This is just a bit of fun. You know, before I have to settle down.' His eyes were bloodshot and he couldn't focus on Harriett. 'Join us.' He drew another breath from the bong hanging from his right hand.

'I can't believe you'd do this.' She stepped back towards the door, picked up the vase sitting on the small table just inside the room and threw it at him.

Too stoned and drunk for his reflexes to engage, the crystal cylinder smashed into the side of his head.

'Uncalled for, Harry.' He touched his temple. His hand came away covered in blood. 'Uncalled for.' He fell to the ground and Delilah screamed.

Harriett turned and ran. She pushed through the throngs of cast and crew crowding the passageways backstage, searching for Genevieve. She eventually found her alone by the water cooler. Harriett grabbed her and dragged her out of the theatre.

'Why are we leaving the party? What's happened?'

Harriett pushed her into Buckley's Jag and started the engine. She took off down the street and drove and drove and drove.

'Hattie, can't we stop somewhere?' Genevieve yawned and stretched. 'We've been driving for hours.'

'Not far now. Close your eyes. I'll let you know when we're there.'

She knew they couldn't have been far now. At least she hoped they weren't. Fatigue enveloped her body, her mind. She wasn't sure she could drive much longer. She'd never heard of Kookaburra Creek before Buckley had bought her the house, but it was on the map. As long as she was following it correctly. She picked it up to double-check. They'd stay a few weeks, give him some time to think about what he'd done. Give her some time to decide what she wanted to do. Just a few weeks.

When she raised her eyes back to the endless black stretch before her, she saw a large, furry brown lump in the middle of the road. Was it a wombat? Harriett had never seen a wombat. Why wasn't it moving? Couldn't it see her hurtling towards it? It wasn't moving. Oh shit.

Harriett swerved to avoid the creature and lost control of the car.

The tyres screeched as she took the corner too fast and lost traction on the loose gravel shoulder. Genevieve screamed beside her as the tall gum trees sped towards them. They spun round and round, and the side of the Jaguar slammed into a tree.

'Are you okay?' Harriett reached across to her younger sister. 'Gen?'

Silence.

Harriett opened her eyes and saw Genevieve slumped forward on the dash, her face lying in a sea of shattered windscreen.

'Oh God, no.' She unbuckled her seatbelt and got out of the car. They weren't far off the road. Which way? She had no idea how close to town they were. Could she walk it? No. She couldn't leave Genevieve.

'Evening, ma'am. Need a hand?' A man with a thick, black beard peddled up beside her on a pushbike.

'My sister's hurt.'

He ran around to the side of car. When he saw Genevieve covered in blood he gagged.

'Oh hell.'

'Help me, please,' Harriett cried.

The man pulled off his jacket and held it to the gaping wound in Genevieve's head. 'Hold this here. Tight. I'll go get help.'

'Don't leave me,' Harriett pleaded.

'Ma'am, we need help. It isn't far. I won't be long.'

He turned and got back on his bike and sped off down the road.

*

The hospital was small and old, but at least it seemed clean. Harriett was worried about Genevieve. She wasn't sure what was more concerning: Genevieve's silence – she'd not even muttered a groan since the accident – or the blood covering her face and soaking her clothes. Then, of course, there was the number of doctors and nurses surrounding her little sister. The pain across Harriett's middle was not subsiding like she assumed it would, but she would not take her eyes off Genevieve. Not even when the mean matron asked her to move back. Now, an hour later, they prepared Genevieve for surgery.

'Miss Brookes? You're looking very pale.'

Where was that voice coming from? Why was everything so bright all of a sudden?

Harriett felt herself swaying. She had to focus. Focus on Genevieve.

'Miss Brookes?'

The room began to spin. She felt something wet and sticky between her legs. Then everything went black.

Harriett woke. Her head was propped up on a pillow and a white sheet covered her body.

'Welcome back, Miss Brookes.'

Harriett tried to sit up, but the doctor stopped her. 'You've suffered quite a trauma.'

'I just fainted. I'm fine.' A dull ache pulsed through her stomach and she placed a hand on her belly.

The doctor put his hand on her shoulder, gentle yet firm. 'You did more than faint. You suffered internal bleeding. I'm afraid you lost the baby.'

'What?'

'Did you know you were pregnant?'

Harriett shook her head.

'We couldn't stop the bleeding, unfortunately. We had to perform a hysterectomy,' he said in a matter-of-fact tone.

Harriett closed her eyes. His words made no sense. She squeezed her stomach tighter. Baby? Hysterectomy?

'How's my sister?'

'Did you hear me, Miss Brookes? We had to perf—'

'I heard you. How's my sister?'

'I'll take you to her once you've got your strength back. Is there anyone we should call?'

Harriett shook her head. Once the doctor left the room she began to sob. She wanted it to stop, but she couldn't hold back the floods of anger and sadness.

By the time they let her see Genevieve, Harriett had managed to pull herself together. What her sister needed now was Harriett's strength. What Harriett needed now was to focus on anything other than her loss.

When Harriett was wheeled in to see Genevieve her skin turned cold. Her baby sister lay there with two broken arms, a broken leg and her face covered in bandages seeped in blood. But Harriett would not allow herself to cry. Tears were no use to Genevieve.

She sat in her wheelchair at the end of Genevieve's bed and watched over her sister in silence.

2018

If only, if only, if only. Well, Hattie couldn't change a thing in the past, could she? No matter how much she wished she could.

Yes, it all began with Buckley Hargraves, but she'd be damned if he'd get the last say in how the remainder of her life would turn out. There must be something she could do. She walked through the quiet streets of town with a new purpose to her stride.

She'd been so young then. So naïve. Well, she certainly wasn't young anymore. She hastened her step. It wasn't just her life that was about to be ruined. She couldn't let this happen to Alice. Or Becca. The destruction of lives at the hands of Buckley Hargraves would stop today.

'I simply won't stand for this, Mr Buddle. This is thievery. Plain and simple.' She had rung the lawyer in Glensdale as soon as she got home.

'Calm down, Miss Brookes,' he replied harshly.

It wasn't surprising, Hattie supposed, seeing as she'd rung him at home and got him out of bed. But this was important, and he owed her a favour. So, really, an early-morning call was nothing to complain about.

'I need all the facts before I can advise you what to do. Why don't you make an appointment to see me next week?'

'How about now, Mr Buddle. I can give you the facts here and now and you can get to work as soon as you get to your office.'

'But Miss Brookes . . .'

'But nothing, Elliot. How is your lovely wife, by the way? Still blissfully ignorant about that trollop you visit whenever you go to Sydney on business?' Desperate times, thought Hattie, definitely warranted desperate measures.

'Tell me again what's happened.'

Hattie told him all she knew, leaving out the more salacious details of course, and all about the letter from Smythe and Smythe.

'It'll be a long shot. But if we can somehow prove intention, that Hargraves always meant you to have the property, maybe . . . Do you have any proof? Anything in writing? Anyone who can verify your story?'

Only two other people knew that Buckley had given her the property as an engagement present. One of them was dead, and the other hadn't spoken a word in nearly a decade.

The fact was, Buckley was gone. His children were as greedy as their mother, and there was nothing Genevieve could do to help. Besides, there was nothing in writing. Unless . . .

'Right then,' Hattie said with determination. 'You get to work on finding precedent or whatever you need and I'll get to work on finding proof.' She hung up the phone and ran into her bedroom, lifting the heavy lid of the old trunk. Genevieve had told her it wasn't healthy to hang on to the past. Obsessive, she'd called her. But maybe there was a reason Hattie hadn't been able to let go. Maybe this was the only chance to save the café. Surely somewhere in all the magazine and newspaper articles she'd collected over the years, there was something about Buckley and Harriett and the engagement and his generous gift. She just had to find it.

Nine

Kookaburra Creek, 2018

§aturdays hadn't been so busy in the café since, well, Alice couldn't remember when since, with an unexpected coach stopping by making things more hectic than usual. Thank God Becca was there. The girl was certainly earning her keep. Her Cajun chicken burgers had flown off the menu and Becca had had to whip up extra patties on the run after they'd sold out of the batch they'd already prepared for the day.

As the sun began to fall to the west, casting long shadows across the grass through the gum trees, Alice finally felt like they'd caught up with the day.

Becca took Joey a cup of coffee and then cleared table three. Alice thought she might just have seen a scowl cross the girl's face when Joey thanked her, but she couldn't be sure. He was the last customer left inside and Alice was quietly thankful he'd only popped in for a cuppa and not a meal.

Out on the deck only Freddy Harris was left, with his school books spread across the table.

'Studying again, Freddy?' she asked, taking him a chocolate milkshake. He always drank a chocolate milkshake when he was studying.

'It's too noisy at home. Mum's yelling at Fiona about wasting her life as a paralegal and forsaking the gifts God gave her.' He rolled his eyes.

'Ahh. Assignment due?' She looked at his schoolwork.

He nodded. 'Monday.'

Alice looked at him fondly. He was always leaving work to the last minute. 'Anything else I can get you?'

'One of those coconut lime cupcakes would be great.'

'Of course,' Alice said, and walked back to the counter.

'Table ten,' she said to Becca, handing her a plate with Freddy's cupcake in the middle. 'Thanks.'

Becca took the plate then hesitated before stepping out onto the deck.

'This isn't a library, you know.' Alice heard her say as she searched for a spot to put the plate down.

'Sorry,' Freddy apologised as he made room.

Alice couldn't be sure, but she thought she saw Becca blush.

'Alice, you with us?' Joey asked, placing his money on the counter in front of her.

'What? Yes. Of course.'

'I said can I take one to go?' He tapped the cupcake stand.

'I heard you.' She grabbed a small box from under the counter. She hadn't heard him at all. She was too busy watching Freddy do his homework, an idea forming in her mind.

'What kind of loser does their schoolwork in a café?' Becca grumbled as she came back into the dining room.

'Freddy's a great kid,' Alice said. 'He'd be in the same year as you.'

'I don't go to school.'

'Maybe we can fix that.'

'No bloody way.' Becca shook her head.

'School isn't that bad.'

'School sucks.'

'Maybe, if you just give it a chance . . .'

'I said no way.' Becca stormed out of the café.

Joey shook his head. 'Her temper hasn't got any better.'

'Thank you for stating the obvious, Joey.' She slammed his cupcake down on the bench in front of him.

After Joey left, Alice went out the back to find Becca on the jetty. She knelt down beside her.

'I didn't mean to upset you,' she said.

'You didn't.'

Alice raised an eyebrow.

'I just can't go back to school.'

'Maybe, if you just give it a try . . .'

'I said no.' Becca jumped up and ran back towards the café, taking the stairs to their apartment two at a time.

Alice sat and put her feet into the creek. This wasn't getting any easier.

She thought about Freddy, and a new plan started forming. She just had to convince Becca of it somehow.

No way I'm going back to school.

If Alice thinks for a second I'm going to put myself through that again, she's kidding herself.

They all knew what was going on, though they pretended they didn't. Teachers are useless. None of them helped. Too hard, I guess. The kids knew too and treated me like somehow they were going to catch it. I will never go back to that. Ever.

And seriously, what would be the point anyway? It's not as if I can do the stupid work.

It's like he said: 'A dumb cow like you isn't ever going to amount to anything.'

And he was right. The tests at school proved that. Learning is a waste of time.

Especially for someone like me. Besides, school would mean enrolment and enrolment would mean a paper trail. I'd be easier to find.

I knew what I did was wrong. I knew what it meant. If Alice ever finds out, she'd kick me out in a heartbeat. She can never know.

In the morning Alice sat alone in the living room and arranged the sheets of paper on the coffee table in front of her. She was nervous about her plan to convince Becca that finishing school was a good idea. The whole thing could backfire terribly.

Becca shuffled into the room, rubbing her eyes. 'What's this?' she asked, looking down at the paper.

'They're maths worksheets. Betty left them for you to try. She used to be a schoolteacher, you know.'

Becca sat down in front of the coffee table and inspected the worksheets. 'There's no point. I can't do them,' she said.

'Well, I was thinking you could get some tutoring, and Betty said she'd help. And Freddy. He's very good at English, you know. Between us I reckon we'll have it covered.'

'I'm not going back to school. You can't make me. I'm old enough to have left and I'm working. You can't make me.'

'I wasn't going to send you to school.'

'Then what's this about?'

'Betty's had a lot of success getting students through their exams through TAFE. There's one in Glensdale. I've just finished a marketing course there. They're pretty good.'

'Do you mean, like, homeschooling? That's for hippies.'

Alice shook her head. 'Not actual homeschooling. You'd enrol through TAFE, and when you're ready you'd do your exams.'

'Why would I want to do that?'

It hadn't even occurred to Alice that Becca might not actually want to get her HSC. When she was that age it was all Alice could think about. It was her ticket to freedom, a better life. Didn't Becca want that too?

'You don't have to,' she said. 'It's just an idea. One day you might want to move on and it might be handy if you've officially finished school.'

'Do you want me to leave?' Becca frowned.

'Of course not.' Alice shuffled off the lounge and sat on the floor beside her. 'I love having you work here. I'd have you here forever, if it were up to me.'

'Who's it up to?'

'Well, you, of course.'

Becca sat up straight and eyed Alice with suspicion.

'Here. Let me show you.' Alice grabbed a pencil and started showing Becca how to work out the first problem.

They went through the first page together. 'What are you, a maths genius?' Becca asked.

Alice hadn't been called a genius in a very long time. Her mind flashed back to that cool September day with Dean, when they'd sat under the grey gum by the dam.

'Well?'

'Not exactly,' said Alice. 'But I was pretty good at it at school.'

'So, you're a nerd?'

'I guess you could say that.'

Becca thought for a moment. 'You finished school and you were a nerd and you ended up here. Exactly where I am. So what's the point?' She stood up and went to her room.

Alice didn't know what to say. Granted, school hadn't worked out for her the way it was supposed to, but that was no reason not to try. Becca's situation was different. She had Alice in her corner for starters. It wouldn't end the same way for Becca. Alice wouldn't allow it.

She got up, went into the kitchen and started on breakfast. When she turned around she saw Becca back at the coffee table, head down, pencil in hand. She tiptoed closer.

'That's right.'

'What?' Becca looked up.

'That answer. It's correct.'

Alice could see a small smile touch Becca's lips, a look so familiar it tore at Alice's heart.

'Maybe we could give it a shot.' Becca shrugged. 'I mean, it might help pass the time until . . .'

'Until?'

But Becca didn't answer. Alice sat back down beside her and they went through the next sum. The unease she felt all morning would not subside, try as she might to ignore it. She'd hoped embarking on this new project with Becca might have distracted her, but all it did was bring back memories of sitting in her own living room with her mother going through homework, before everything changed and the world turned black. Alice had learned to lock away the memory of the day her mother was taken from her. It was kept deep down in a hidden part of her soul she rarely dared to open.

Ten

Lawson's Ridge, 2003

Alice wrote the day's date at the top of her English book and her stomach tightened. It had been doing that all day – tightening, turning into a knot every time she had to write the date.

She looked up at the big white clock above the whiteboard, the same clock her mum would have watched when she was Alice's age. The hands ticked over ever so slowly.

At exactly 2.48 p.m. Louise leaned forward and tapped Alice on the back, slipping her a scrap of paper. Alice unfolded it under her desk.

'What do you call a cow with no legs? Ground beef!'

Alice grinned. She could always count on Louise to remember what day it was. Count on her to tell some lame joke to try to make her laugh.

When the last bell of the day finally rang Alice stepped quickly and quietly through the corridors, avoiding eye contact with everyone.

Outside she could see Dean waiting for her beside the school gate. She really did wish she could walk with him, just for a bit, to take her mind off where she was headed. But he'd ask questions. He'd want to know details.

She doubled back past the maths rooms and came out of the main block near the canteen. She took a few steps beside the short wire fence that bordered the school before jumping over it and running off before he could spot her.

It wasn't long before she reached the cemetery and, as she made her way along the dirt path to her mother's grave, she fiddled with the white daisy in her hands. She'd taken it from the bouquet outside the general store as she'd run past. Mr Williams wouldn't notice. She came up to the grave and knelt down beside it and brushed the headstone clean of dirt and laid the flower at its base.

God didn't exist. She knew that without doubt. But she said the little prayer they'd learned in scripture at school anyway, the one about bread and trespassing. She never really understood it, but it seemed like what you were supposed to do under the circumstances. She was sure she'd mucked up the words, but it wasn't as if anyone was listening, so she figured it didn't really matter.

She sat down in the dirt.

She didn't cry. She never did. Not there. Not where her mum could see.

It was hard to believe it had been five years since her mum lost her battle with cancer. Five years since Bruce lost his battle with despair and let the alcohol consume him. Five long years of loneliness and pain for Alice, gone in the blink of an eye.

Every time Alice visited Sonia's grave haunting images flooded her mind. Her mum hooked up to what seemed like every machine in the hospital at Cutter's Pass; hair shaved, cheeks sallow, eyes staring blankly into the distance; her dad standing in the doorway of the room, eyes on the floor, unable to come in and hold his wife's hand or hug his daughter so desperate for him to come back to her, rescue her.

Every time Alice visited her mum's grave she waited for the images to pass, until she could remember the mum with long brown curls, happy chubby cheeks, and bright laughing eyes.

A cool breeze swirled the dirt around Alice's feet, and the sun, low in the sky, cast long shadows across the graves.

'I'd probably better get going. It's getting late.'

She stood and touched the top of the headstone. 'See you soon, Mum.'

When she arrived home, Alice quietly opened her front door. With any luck Bruce would have drunk himself unconscious and she could slip into bed unnoticed and wait for midnight so this day could be over and done with.

'Alice? Tadpole? Where are you? Where is she?'

Alice's shoulders dropped. They were going to do that dance again.

Bruce strode towards her, anger, adrenaline or some other force Alice didn't understand overriding the alcohol coursing through his veins. She could smell him well before he got to her.

'Sonia said she'd be home for dinner.' His eyes were wild and distant.

Alice breathed deeply. 'She's gone, Dad.'

'Gone?' He shook his head. 'Gone where?' He looked left and right, behind him, behind Alice.

'Dad.' Alice sighed. She just wanted to lie on her bed, turn her music on, let the day fade away. 'She's dead. Remember?' That was her mistake. She should have just turned away.

'She wouldn't die. She wouldn't do that to me.'

Alice could see his eyes full of rage as he stepped towards her. The same rage she'd seen in him that Christmas after her mum had passed away. The first of many alcohol-fuelled rages. She started to back away, finding herself pressed against the front door. He grabbed her shoulders, squeezing so hard Alice wanted to scream.

'Stop, Dad. Please,' she whispered.

'No. You stop.' He shoved her. The screen door gave way and Alice stumbled out onto the lawn. 'How dare you make up lies for your mother?'

'They're not lies,' Alice spat. 'She's dead. You should remember. You were there. Not for anything else. Not before. Not after. But you were there when she died and you left me.' She couldn't help herself.

Bruce stormed outside, fire in his eyes. He picked up Daisy, the last addition to Sonia's gnome family. The gnome Alice had searched for high and low for Sonia's birthday the year her life changed for good. She'd had to order it from a catalogue, and it took months to arrive, landing on her doorstep the Christmas of her twelfth birthday. The last Christmas with Sonia.

Bruce pelted Daisy at Alice. She turned and ran, heard the smash behind her as Daisy hit the pebbled path.

When she got to Faraway Forest, she slowed down and climbed onto her branch. She slumped forward and began to sob. In the fading light she closed her eyes and allowed all the anger and sadness and confusion she kept locked up every other day of the year to spill forth. Her shoulders shook, her neck dripped with salty tears and she pounded the trunk of the tree with closed fists.

'Pond? Is that you?' Dean's voice floated up from below.

'Go away.' Alice's voice cracked in reply.

'Like hell,' Dean said and he scaled the ironbark before Alice had a chance to escape.

'I said go away.' She looked into his eyes.

'And I said like hell.' He held her stare steadily.

'Go,' Alice said, a little less forcefully.

'Nope.' Dean shook his head, the edges of his eyes crinkling ever so slightly.

Alice fell forward and began to cry again, but Dean caught her in a strong embrace. And he didn't let go. She could hear his heart beating, her ear against his chest. She could feel the warmth of his arms around her. It was comforting, safe. This close to him, Alice could smell a slight hint of cloves and honey. Ever so slowly her sobs eased.

It was pitch-black when Alice finally pulled herself upright again. There was no moon in the night sky to offer illumination. She could no longer feel her left foot, but she could feel the crick in her neck. If Dean was suffering any discomfort, he wasn't letting on. He reached out, brushing the remaining tears from her cheeks. His touch was soft, his gaze staring deeper into her than anyone ever had.

'Th . . . thank you,' she stuttered. 'I . . . I have to go.'

She manoeuvred into position and climbed to the ground.

'Seriously?' Dean slid down behind her. He tried to catch up with her as she sped away, but his cramped legs gave way. 'Pond! Stop!'

She couldn't. If she stopped, then she would let him in. And she couldn't let him in. So she ran.

There were no lights on in the house when Alice got home and she exhaled in relief. Her dad was unconscious at last. She carefully swept up the shattered pieces of Daisy and put her in the bin, her thoughts drifting back to the branch, to Dean's arms wrapped tightly around her, to his eyes piercing right through to the heart of her.

There was no room in her plan for Dean McRae. She knew that. But she also knew that she hadn't felt much of anything for the last five years, and with that one embrace Dean had changed everything.

Alice pulled Gus the gnome out from behind the hose. Every anniversary Bruce smashed a gnome. Every anniversary Alice hid Gus from Bruce and later placed him back on his patch so Harry Brown wouldn't wonder where his target was early the next day.

Six gnomes now sat neatly on display.

Dean had changed everything and she hated him for it. A shiver tickled the back of her neck and she turned around and saw a tall, skinny shadow on the street corner. There he was, leaning against the lamp post, watching her.

Head down, she rushed inside just as he called her name.

For days Alice's thoughts had been a jumbled mess. Packing shelves at night in the store didn't help her focus. Neither did going for ridiculously long walks. Standing her dad's used beer cans into elaborate sculptures also didn't help, though it did pass an awful lot of time. Time she should have been using to study. At school her distraction was always worse and nothing she did seemed to alleviate the problem.

'Is this where you've been hiding?' Louise asked, finding Alice crouched down between the stacks of books lining the library wall.

'Oh, hi.' Alice stood and looked around, lowering the text on *Modern Economics for High School Studies* that she hadn't actually been reading.

'I've been looking for you everywhere. We have a party to plan, remember?'

'Sorry.' Alice looked out the dusty window to the handball games in the quadrangle. He wasn't there. So where was he? She looked behind Louise's shoulder.

'So? What do you think?'

'Sorry. What?'

'About a bonfire. For Brian's and my eighteenth. Hello? Earth to Alice.' Louise tapped Alice on the head.

'Sounds great.'

'The whole year's coming. Even Dean said he'd come.' She tucked her hair behind her ear.

The bell rang loudly and Alice picked up her bag. 'We'd better get to maths.'

Before walking out the door, Alice checked to see if the coast was clear.

'So, some of you did really well on Monday's test,' Ms Robertson said as she walked around the room. 'And some of you,' she placed Alice's answer sheet on her desk, 'not so much.'

Alice couldn't believe it. The mark just didn't compute. Perhaps she'd suddenly developed dyslexia and the numbers were backwards or upside down.

As Ms Robertson weaved through the little wooden desks that had been in the same position in the same room for who knew how many years, Alice's stare followed her. She would come back any second now, realising she'd given Alice the wrong paper. But she didn't come back. She sat down to go through the answers with the class, and Alice stared at her in disbelief.

*

Dragging her feet along the path through Faraway Forest, Alice patted the sturdy trunk of her tree before lifting herself on to her usual branch. She leaned back into the V and closed her eyes, trying to picture anything but those two tiny numbers. How on earth had that happened? She'd studied, right? She knew the work inside out. Never before had she got anything below eighty per cent for a maths test. Never. What had happened?

'Hey, stranger.' Dean's voice floated up from below.

Alice sat up. 'Ah . . . um,' was all she could manage and the reason for her failed maths test suddenly dawned on her. She wondered if she could scamper down the tree and past him before he'd realise she was gone.

'Can I come up?' Dean asked, one foot already on the rock below.

'I s'pose.'

'How have you been, Pond?' he asked as he sat beside her.

'Fine.'

'I haven't seen you much lately.' He shifted so he was looking directly at her.

She searched for a whole sentence with which to respond, but her mind was blank. She had to get out of there, but there was no way to leave.

'What's going on?' Dean asked, looking her in the eye. 'Why have you been avoiding me?'

'I haven't.'

'Really?'

'Okay, maybe a little.'

'So?'

'It's just . . .' All of Alice's excuses, both the genuine and made up, abandoned her as Dean brushed her hair behind her ear. 'I'm embarrassed. About the other night. And I don't want . . . I didn't want . . .'

'It's fine, Pond. You don't have to tell me anything you don't want to. But you do have to tell me this. Are you okay?' He took her hand in his.

'I will be.' Looking into his eyes, she knew that to be the truth.

He leaned in close, his lips nearly touching hers.

'Are you sure?'

He reached his hand up behind her head, his fingers entwined in her hair, and he pulled her to him. His mouth was soft and the sensation was strange and not at all like she'd imagined. It was a good strange. A tingle at the base of her spine prompted her to open her mouth wider and Dean's tongue searched for hers. It was unfamiliar and unexpected and wonderful. Her mind cleared of everything. Her whole body shivered.

As Dean's lips slowed and he moved away from her, Alice found herself not wanting to open her eyes, not wanting it to end. She pressed back into him, back into the safety of his embrace and allowed herself to simply be. There. With him. Warmth coursing through her every vein as he kissed her again. Deeper this time.

Alice pulled back, sucking in great gulps of air.

'Sorry.' She cast her eyes down.

'Oh no.' Dean cupped her face in his hand. 'Don't ever say sorry for that.'

Alice shifted on the branch.

'You're not going to run away again, are you, Pond?'

For the first time in Alice's life she felt perfectly still. Everything began and ended there, with him. She never knew a kiss could do that.

She leaned into his shoulder and he wrapped his arm around her. Dean held her hand, slowly moving his fingers over hers. They sat in silence, no need for words, their breathing one rhythmic movement. Dean traced his finger up Alice's arm, sending shivers down her spine.

'Do you think maybe we could stay here forever?' Alice whispered.

'That sounds perfect, but I should probably get you home. Mum's expecting me and she'll worry if I'm late.' Dean sighed and shifted his body. 'I went dirt-bike riding yesterday with Brian and she had a fit. And I didn't even tell her about the part when I crashed. She's such a bloody worrywart.'

It must be nice to have someone to worry about you, thought Alice.

'I can get home myself. You go.'

'No, Pond. That won't do. I'm going to make this last as long as I can.'

He waited for her at the bottom of the tree and as she lowered herself off the branch, he reached up and held her hips, guiding her down the last few feet. She turned into him and he kissed her again, more gently this time. Briefly. He put his arm around her and walked her home.

Outside her house, Alice stopped. Dean opened the gate and tried to step through, but she cut him off.

'Too much chivalry in one day,' she said, and forced a laugh.

'Sure?'

'Yeah. Dad had a late job last night. Burst toilet pipe – joys of being a plumber,' she lied. 'He'll be sleeping.' Not a lie. She couldn't let Dean in. She couldn't show him the truth, and risk scaring him off.

'No worries, Pond. Are you doing anything tomorrow arvo?'

'Hanging out with you after work?'

He leaned in and kissed her, holding her body tightly against his.

'See you tomorrow,' Dean said, letting Alice go. She nodded wordlessly.

Once he was well out of sight she opened the front door. The smell of stale beer assaulted her nose. No, she couldn't show him the truth. Not now, not ever.

Eleven

Kookaburra Creek, 2018

Fridays were wonderful, especially in summer when the café opened for dinner. Mondays were comforting with their routine, and, though she was loath to admit that it made her happy, they delivered Joey as her first customer of the week. Thursdays were fun as they meant Betty and her lawn bowls crew coming in for lunch and staying till close, giggling like teenagers all evening. But Sundays in spring, they were special. Alice never thought she'd love Sundays again, after an adolescence of drudgery working in the corner shop, subjected to Bertie's boxer shorts. But then she'd found herself at the Kookaburra Creek Café – and the first Sunday of spring was her absolute favourite. It meant all her friends descending on the café for brunch to raise funds for the Kookaburra Creek Rural Fire Service.

This morning she'd got Becca up extra early to help prepare the brunch, but hadn't warned her just how much work there'd be to get through. After all the chopping, dicing, slicing, shredding and spreading, fifteen platters of sandwiches, four bowls of salad and five trays of mini sausage rolls lay across the kitchen bench.

'Come and help me with the doors,' Alice said to Becca, who was wiping avocado from her chin.

'And we need to put these tables together.' Alice waved her hands around.

'Need a hand?' Joey asked, appearing in the doorway with a basket of knotted wholemeal rolls, long white baguettes, sweet croissants and parmesan sticks, which he placed on the service counter.

Becca jumped back, startled. Joey wasn't a tall man, but he had broad, strong shoulders and a widening middle-aged girth. His brown hair, speckled with grey, was closely clipped and his crooked nose somehow amplified his deep voice. Alice had hoped Becca was getting over her wariness of Joey. Apparently not.

She put her arms around Becca's tense shoulders. 'That would be lovely, Joey. Thank you.'

Within minutes there were two extraordinarily long tables running through the café and out onto the deck.

Betty arrived next and put some coins in a bucket on the counter, while Joey helped Becca bring the food to the tables. As the café gradually filled with noise and laughter, Becca stood against the back wall, hands clenched behind her back.

Sergeant Carson arrived and threw his jar of coins into the bucket before slapping everyone in the room on the back in greeting. Except Becca, whose back he couldn't reach, not that he'd have tried. All six of the Harris mob were there, including beautiful Fiona. Their red hair and bright blue eyes all lined up were quite the sight. Behind them stood Hattie, looking tentative.

'Come in,' Alice said, trying to catch Harriet's eye. What was going on with her?

Hattie, the consummate actress, brightened up immediately. She swanned into the café and greeted everyone.

It wasn't long before the café was full and happy voices filled the space. Claudine had brought an inconceivably large platter of cheese and crackers and dished up a hearty wedge or two on everyone's plate.

'Come on,' said Alice, reaching for Becca's hidden hands. 'There's a spot for you here.' She could feel the tightness in Becca's body as she guided her to the end of the table closest to the kitchen as everyone tucked in to the feast.

'. . . and you wouldn't believe what he said.' Joey reached the climax of his story.

'*And you call yourself Italian!*' shouted everyone from both tables. Fiona reached across and touched Joey's shoulder. Alice felt her cheeks redden and had to avert her eyes. Fiona Harris had been in and out of their lives, of Joey's life, as long as Alice could remember. Why seeing her there next to him today made her feel uneasy, Alice wasn't sure. Fiona touched Joey's shoulder again and Alice felt her heart beat a little faster.

She forced herself to focus on Hattie and Betty and their debate about the relative value of the arts in this modern world.

'But without art and music, the very soul of a culture is doomed,' Hattie countered.

'Perhaps. But without science, life itself is doomed and therefore there endeth the soul. So, you see, arts can only take a back seat to other learning.' Betty seemed to be enjoying herself.

'So, Becca, darling.' Mrs Harris leaned across the table, pushing her red curls behind her ear. 'How long do you think you'll be staying with our Alice?'

Becca shot Alice a quick look.

'She's proving herself very helpful with the café,' Alice said. 'So, I hope she stays on for a good while.'

'And where are you from, child?' Clive's voice boomed across the table, his hearing aids clearly on the wrong setting.

Becca stood up and started clearing the table. 'Sydney,' she mumbled, pushing her fringe over her eyes.

'Eh?' Clive shouted and Freddy whispered in his ear before getting up.

'I'll give you a hand,' Freddy said to Becca and winked at Alice.

She mouthed her thanks to him, relieved he'd picked up on Becca's discomfort.

'So, what else do you know about her?' Mrs Harris asked, watching her youngest boy disappear into the café with the strange girl.

'Now, Mrs Harris.' The reverend placed a gentle hand on his wife's arm, but she shrugged it off.

'I mean really, Hattie,' she continued.

'Oh, let the girl be,' Hattie said. 'I'm getting old and Alice needs a little help. Becca's doing a fine job.'

'Yes, well, taking in strays may be your thing, Harriett, but it's not for everyone.' Mrs Harris shot Hattie a look, but the old woman didn't flinch.

'And what is it the Bible preaches about being tolerant of those in need?' Betty came to Hattie's defence.

'Rightly so,' Reverend Harris muttered.

Hattie smiled. 'Betty, would you pass the tea, please?' she asked, flicking her green scarf over her shoulder and making sure it swiped Mrs Harris's cheek on the way past.

Yes, this was now Alice's Sunday norm and she'd grown to love it. She wasn't, however, loving the fact that Fiona Harris was leaning closer and closer to Joey the more the day wore on.

*

Clive, always one of the last to leave spring brunch, pulled one leg up and over his rusty bicycle and waved to Alice before peddling away. When Alice walked back into the café kitchen she found Becca and Freddy finishing the last of the washing up in silence.

'Thank you, Freddy sweetheart.' She hugged him.

'No worries, Alice.' He bent down to kiss her on the forehead. 'Gardens next week?'

'Absolutely.' She nodded. 'Be a gem and drop the takings off at the station, will you?'

Freddy saluted and turned to Becca. 'See ya round.'

Becca waved dismissively and Alice shrugged in apology to Freddy. He shrugged back before picking the bucket up off the counter and heading out the front door.

Alice put away the last of the dishes and handed Becca a bottle of water.

'Are you ready?' she asked.

'For what?' Becca took a step back. 'We're finished, aren't we?'

'A walk.'

'A walk? Are you kidding me?'

'Nope. My Sunday ritual. I always go for a walk after brunch.'

'Your ritual, maybe.' Becca folded her arms in front of her chest. 'Not mine.'

'It'll do you good.' Alice moved behind Becca and started pushing her towards the door.

'Oh, come on,' Becca groaned.

Alice, trailed by a reluctant Becca, followed the creek into town, a gentle stroll past pastures and green fields dotted with dairy cows. A brown and white Ayrshire lowed deeply as they passed and Alice waved.

'Hello, Patches,' she called out.

Becca paused a moment, but said nothing.

When they reached the white wooden bridge that crossed the creek at Dandelion Dell, Alice picked up a dandelion from a cluster by the water's edge. Holding it to her chest, she closed her eyes and threw it in the gently running stream. If Becca noticed, she chose not to say anything.

Across the bridge sat the town centre – two rows of old, wooden shopfronts lining High Street, the main strip that ran through the town. Moretti's Bread House, Curlz Hair Salon, the National Bank and the newsagent were all closed, given it was Sunday. Only the grocer was open, though the old pub, the Cow and Boot, would open in another hour or so, once Sam got back from his fishing. Each shop had a planter box of colourful flowers on its windowsill, dutifully cared for by Betty and Hattie and the town gardening club, and the street was lined with lemon-scented gums, tall and thin. In the middle of the grassed median strip that cut the road in half proudly stood the arch that proclaimed Kookaburra Creek as a Tidy Town winner five years running.

Behind the main drag were a mix of red-brick and weatherboard houses and the one school, right on the edge of town, where kindergarten to Year Twelve students were educated by seven dedicated teachers. They hadn't had their own school long in Kookaburra Creek, and any time they beat Glensdale at sport or spelling bees the whole town celebrated. A small but well-stocked library sat next to the town hall, and the public pool on the other side of town would reopen for the season in another month or so.

At the end of High Street was the cenotaph, the names of twenty Kookaburra Creek men lost in various wars engraved on the brass plaque.

'Just up here is the duck pond,' Alice said, breaking the silence. She pointed to the large park in the middle of town. 'I thought we could . . .' She held up the bag of stale bread she'd been carrying with her and handed it to Becca, who shrugged.

A green Holden ute driving through town slowed as it approached.

Becca froze. All the colour drained from her face.

'Becca?' Alice whispered.

Becca began to tremble and the car came to a stop a few metres away. Dropping the bag of bread, Becca turned on her heel and ran.

'Becca!' Alice shouted, stepping in the bread as she tried to follow, knowing it was unlikely she'd catch her.

'Becca! Wait!'

'I've looked everywhere, Joey. Where can she be?' Alice paced the café dining room. Becca had disappeared over an hour ago. Alice had called everyone she knew, which was virtually the whole town, and no one had seen her. Hattie had told her to go home and wait and, when she'd refused, Joey was tasked with dragging her back to the café.

'I know what it means to you having her here.' He held Alice's shoulders gently. 'You said she saw Carson's car and just took off?'

'She looked terrified.'

'And he's been out looking?'

She nodded. 'Oh, Joey. Where could she have gone?'

Joey squeezed her tightly. 'Well, if seeing a cop in a car is what scared her off, sending one to find her isn't going to work. I'll go.' He released Alice from his embrace and cradled her cheeks in his large, rough hands. 'I'll bring her back safe.' His warm brown eyes met hers. 'I promise.' His voice cracked slightly. 'I won't let you down.'

Alice took his hands in hers and squeezed them tightly. 'Hurry. Please.'

Joey took off, jumping from the deck.

'Come on, boy,' he called to Shadow, who'd been waiting dutifully outside.

Alice walked around the dining room pushing in chairs that were already snug against the table, moving salt and pepper shakers half a centimetre from where they sat, only to move them back again. She almost buckled under the weight of the memories of the past that had resurfaced. This was different, she repeated again and again under her breath.

Then why did it feel the same?

She went upstairs to the tiny office that sat off the living room and opened the cupboard. Her eyes drifted past the shelf of paperwork and dog-eared recipe books that she didn't use much these days – most of what she cooked she either knew by heart or made up as she went along – until her gaze stopped on the plastic tub pushed into the back corner.

Slowly she removed the lid and took out the small pink-striped box. Tammy's old jumper sat inside and she lifted it and pressed her face into its soft folds. If she breathed deeply enough, she could still catch the faint hint of Tammy's scent: vanilla and lavender. Under the jumper was Tammy's colouring book, a pressed dandelion glued to the front cover. Alice still couldn't bring herself to look inside, even now. She lay the book on the floor beside her, avoided looking at the photos that were tucked inside a yellow envelope, and put them to one side.

At the bottom of the tub was a sparkly rainbow headband. Alice picked it up and held it to her chest, memories of joy and laughter flooding her mind. Fear had stopped her opening the tub for years, fear that she would drown in emotion. But holding the headband, thinking of Tammy's sweet face, hearing her laughter again, she didn't want to let the memories go.

She opened the yellow envelope. Her daughter's eyes smiled back at her and Alice let the tears flow. It was eight years since she'd looked at her precious girl's face. Behind the sadness though, a hint of joy rippled as she looked into Tammy's eyes.

She touched each photo and a memory long pushed aside resurfaced with each new picture. Slipping the photos back inside, she held the envelope to her chest. She didn't return it to the tub, but left it on her bed before heading back downstairs.

She wandered into the kitchen and looked up to Sylvia. Chocolate fudge. She always said chocolate fudge when Alice was worried or upset. Pulling the mixing bowls from their shelf, she tied her orange apron around her waist.

Creaming butter, beating eggs, sifting flour. A dozen chocolate fudge. Two dozen chocolate fudge. Three dozen.

The sun set.

By the oven's dim light Alice mixed more batter. Five dozen chocolate fudge cupcakes.

When the kitchen bench was full, she cleared the serving counter out front. Six dozen cupcakes. Trays cooled on the tables in the dining room.

She ran out of eggs.

Chocolate frosting oozed from the piping bag. Squeeze, swirl, dollop. Squeeze, swirl, dollop.

The old brass bell on the café door jingled and Alice's head jerked up.

Joey stood behind Becca and gently guided her inside. It was only then, trying to get a proper look at her, that Alice realised there were no lights on in the place. She bumped into chairs as she hurried to get to the girl.

Becca didn't look up. Hands in her pockets, her left foot traced the tiny cracks in the floorboards. Alice placed her hands on the girl's shoulders and checked her over. No cuts or bruises – there was dirt on her clothes but no obvious sign of harm. She wrapped Becca in a tight embrace and looked at Joey.

'Thank you,' she mouthed. He nodded and slipped silently back out the door.

Becca sat on the floor in the middle of the rug holding the hot Milo Alice had made her, not taking a sip. Alice sat in her usual spot on the sofa, hands in her lap, waiting for Becca to break the silence that had shadowed them since her return.

Alice counted how long each in and out of her own breath took. One, two, three, four. One, two, three.

'I might go to bed,' Becca said without looking up.

Alice opened her mouth to speak, but stopped herself. Whatever had spooked Becca had done a thorough job and Alice knew she wouldn't get anything out of her tonight. A teenage girl with secrets was a creature she knew well.

When she heard Becca's door close, Alice headed outside onto the deck and stood watching the moonlight bounce off the ripples in the gently flowing creek.

'Alice?'

Joey's voice startled her and she turned round to see him standing on the edge of the deck. Shadow lay beside him, his head on his front paws.

'Thought I'd pop by and see how she is.'

'I don't know.' Alice sighed. 'She's in bed. Calm. At least.'

Joey nodded. 'And you?'

Alice's shoulders began to shake and Joey took three steps and enveloped her in a tight embrace.

'I know,' he said, as she sobbed into his shoulder. 'I know.'

'I just kept thinking, if I lost her . . .'

Joey nodded and held Alice's shoulders with outstretched arms.

'I know it's silly.' Alice sniffled. 'And I know it can never make up for what happened but, I don't know, maybe she's meant to be here. Maybe there's a reason.'

Joey's voice was doubtful. 'Maybe. I just don't want you getting hurt. Becca's got some serious stuff going on. You might not be able to save her.'

'But I can try.'

'Oh, Alice. Be careful. I couldn't bear to see you in that much pain ever again.'

'Don't you get it, Joey? Underneath it all, I'm always in that much pain. It never goes away.'

'I know. I lost her too, remember?' A single tear fell down his cheek.

They looked into each other's eyes, stuck in that moment, unable to move.

A tawny frogmouth landed on the deck railing, thrashing a tiny lizard in its beak.

Alice dropped her gaze. 'Thank you, Joey, for bringing her back. You always come through for me.'

Joey closed his eyes. A moment. He looked at Alice with a sadness that broke her heart all over again. 'Not always.'

He kissed Alice on the forehead before walking away into the night.

❧

I punched him.

And I kicked him and I hit him. But he wouldn't let go of me. I could see his face, grinning that awful grin at me. I couldn't get free. I spat and I scratched and I screamed.

He didn't shout back, didn't growl. He always growls.

His grip wasn't tight, sending searing pain through my arms, shoulders. He was gentle. He's never gentle.

I looked at his face and it slowly came into focus. Crooked nose. Dark eyes, kind. Stubble covering his chin.

Joey. Not him.

I screamed again. Then sobbed.

'No one will hurt you here,' he said to me, as if he knew why I'd run. 'Alice and I will protect you.'

I've heard those words before. 'No one will hurt you.' They mean nothing. People lie.

It always starts with the lie and then they hurt you. Bad.

'Let me take you back to Alice,' he said, releasing his hold just a little. Just enough to let me know he wasn't going to hurt me. Not enough to let me run.

He used to do that too. And that was when he'd strike. But Joey didn't strike.

He held me, I sobbed and he didn't strike. He didn't say anything else. Just held me and waited. This was his chance, and he didn't take it.

I don't know how long I cried and punched him in the shoulder. It felt like forever. But he didn't try to stop me. He just waited.

Where I was when he found me, I have no idea. Or how he found me, for that matter. But it took ages for us to walk back to the café. There was so much bush. We walked in silence.

I don't know what to say to Alice now. It's pretty obvious she was worried about me. I reckon she'd even been crying. I don't remember the last time anyone worried enough about me to cry. But what can I tell her? If I tell her the truth, I'm sure she won't want me around anymore. She's been good to me, sure. But that's because she doesn't know. If she did, she wouldn't want me here. Or the danger that follows me.

Who would?

But I can't tell her. I mean it isn't really the sort of thing you casually drop into conversation over Milo and a biscuit. I may not be an adult, but I know for sure there are certain things they just don't like to talk about. No one ever wants to talk about it.

Alice won't want to hear about it either.

I can hear her pacing in the living room right now. But she won't come in. I think she's scared to. Scared of what she might find out.

Twelve

Lawson's Ridge, 2003

For the first time in Alice's life, every waking moment wasn't dedicated to thinking about school, or her escape from Lawson's Ridge, or how to use school to escape Lawson's Ridge. For the first time since her mother's death, every dream wasn't filled with fractured images and silent screams.

She knew it couldn't be good for her to be distracted like this, losing focus for exams. But if Dean was the reason her mum's frozen smile and her dad's sad eyes no longer visited her dreams, then she wasn't about to complain.

Every afternoon they'd spend hours together – walking the dusty streets of Lawson's Ridge, climbing their ironbark, driving the endless gravel roads that led nowhere; talking about school, getting out of Lawson's Ridge, Dean's family, never hers, or saying nothing – just holding hands as they walked, or leaning against each other as they perched on their branch, or Alice resting her head on Dean's shoulder as they drove. Each day passed better than the last and Alice allowed herself just a spark of hope.

'I love it.' Louise hugged Alice. 'How on earth did you afford something so beautiful?'

Alice shrugged. The silver heart-shaped locket had three tiny flowers embossed on one side and 'Happy 18th' engraved on the other. Inside, on red velvet backing, Alice had placed a picture of the two of them taken when they were eleven. Big toothy smiles next to Pip's dam, before Alice's world changed.

'I've been saving up,' she said.

Someone turned up the music coming from Brian's ute.

'Let's see who else is here.' Louise grabbed Alice's arm and dragged her towards the gathering mass. 'Do you think Dean will show? It probably isn't his thing.'

Alice's cheeks burned and she was grateful for the cover of night. Not once in thirteen years had she kept anything from her best friend. Until now. She hadn't told her about the kiss, about spending every afternoon the past few weeks with him. Even at school she'd managed to keep her secret, keeping her distance from Dean under the deal that if they were going to spend the afternoons together she had to study at school. She didn't enjoy the lies, the sneaking about. But it was for Louise's own good. She'd be upset if Alice had a boyfriend and she didn't, so, really, she was protecting her feelings.

What garbage. The simple truth was she just didn't want to have to share these new feelings with anyone. Not even Louise.

The bonfire in the middle of the Jenkins' back paddock was tall and wide, encircled by utes with headlights on and teenagers arriving with cases of beer, carefully dodging the cowpats littered about. Alice and Louise joined the swelling crowd standing around the jumping flames.

'Hey, Pond.' Two arms grabbed Alice from behind and spun her around. Dean leaned down and kissed her on the lips.

'Happy birthday, Louise,' he said, not letting go of Alice.

'Thank you.' Louise frowned and Alice could see the confusion flicker across her eyes. 'I'd better go mingle.' She spun round and strode off.

'Is something wrong?' Dean asked, turning Alice into his embrace completely. 'You haven't told her about us, have you? I thought you two shared everything.'

'I wasn't sure how she'd feel about it.'

'Wouldn't she be happy for you?'

That was the thing. Alice wasn't sure. And she didn't know how to explain it to Dean. He hadn't known Louise very long; didn't know her history of always being the one in the spotlight.

'Or is it me?' Dean stepped back. 'Are you embarrassed to be with me?'

'No. God no.' Alice held his hands. 'I just wanted to keep you to myself for a while.'

'Really?'

'Really.' She hugged him tightly. 'I should go and check on her.'

Dean brushed Alice's fringe from her eyes. 'Okay, but don't be long.'

Alice found Louise away from the bonfire, leaning against the fence in the shadows of night.

'Lou?' Alice stepped closer and she thought perhaps she saw Louise wipe her cheeks. It was dark though, so she wasn't sure. 'I know I should have told you. I'm sorry. It's just happened and I wasn't sure . . .'

'All those times you told me you were studying, you were seeing him?'

'I know. I'm sorry. I didn't mean to lie to you.'

'But you did. I can't believe you'd do that to me. You cow.'

Louise had never called Alice names before.

'Lou, please . . .' A horrible thought occurred to her. 'Do you actually like Dean?'

'What?' Louise snapped, scratching her left hand. 'Don't be stupid. He's just another skinny idiot like the rest of them. I'm disappointed because you lied. We're supposed to be friends. Best friends. And best friends don't keep things from each other.'

'I'm sorry, Lou. Really.' Alice stepped closer and tried to take Louise's hands, but she put them in the back pockets of her jeans.

'This hurts.'

'I know. I'm really sorry. I'll never lie to you again. I promise. Please forgive me. Come back to the party.'

Louise stepped off the fence. 'Is it serious?'

Alice shrugged.

'Do you love him?'

Alice stared at her friend. She'd never been in love before. She wasn't sure she knew what it felt like. But surely this had to be close.

Alice looked down. 'Maybe. I think so.'

Louise stepped forward and hugged her tightly. 'Then I'm happy for you.' Her voice cracked.

Alice stepped out of the embrace. 'Really?'

'Of course.' Louise nodded, a beauty pageant smile plastered on her face. 'Let's get back to my party.'

'Hey, Pond.' Dean stepped towards her as she came out of the hall a couple of weeks later. 'How'd you go?' He leaned in to kiss her but she moved her head to the side so he would catch her cheek. Louise had only been two rows behind her in the exam and wouldn't be far behind now.

'Really good. I knew all the answers,' she lied. She didn't know them all, but she was fairly confident she knew enough. A couple of weeks of serious cramming had done the trick. She turned around to see Louise coming out into the sunshine.

'Well?'

'Pretty good.' Louise shrugged.

Alice embraced her. 'Can you believe we're done?'

'It's a miracle we survived.'

'Some of us have survived.' Brian came from behind and put his long arms around both girls' shoulders. 'Some of us still have one to go tomorrow.' He winked at Dean.

'And then we'll all be done.'

The four of them walked towards the gate and down the street. The boys ahead, the girls behind. There was no spring in Lawson's Ridge. Not a proper one. There was winter when the nights dropped as low as six degrees and a cold day was twenty-one. A week or two in September when temperatures didn't quite know what to do. And then summer. Hot, dusty forty degrees summer.

In the heat they walked to the Jenkins property, where Mrs Jenkins had homemade strawberry ice blocks waiting for them.

'So, tomorrow we're no longer high school students,' Dean said as they sat on the verandah that wrapped round Louise and Brian's home.

Louise sat next to him. 'And then?'

'And then we party at Pip's dam.' Brian said.

'Does the poor guy know we're coming?' Dean asked.

'Every Year Twelve goes there after exams.' Alice sat opposite him.

'It's tradition,' she and Louise said in unison.

'And brainiac here will be heading to Sydney.' Brian punched Alice lightly on the arm. 'While I stay put and take over this joint.' He spread his arms wide, the family's acres stretching as far as they could see.

'You're still coming with me, right?' Alice looked to Louise. First Sydney, then the world.

Louise shifted in her seat. 'Actually, Mum's lined me up with a job already. An old school friend of hers or something. Runs a nice clothes boutique in Sydney and said I can start whenever I like.'

'What? When are you going?'

'Christmas.' Louise looked to the ground.

Alice frowned. They were supposed to spend the summer together and go to Sydney at the same time. Why hadn't Louise said anything?

'That's only two months away!' said Dean.

'Well, at least we have a plan.' Louise shook her finger at Dean. 'Unlike some people.'

'Really, mate?' Brian threw Dean a can of coke. 'You still don't know what you're going to do?'

Dean looked up to Alice and she smiled back at him. 'Actually, someone convinced me I could do more with my life than go be some lackey in my dad's business, so I've applied to do PE Teaching at Sydney Uni. I might even have a shot at getting in.' He shrugged.

'Bloody great, mate.' Brian stood up and slapped Dean on the back.

'To all of us.' Louise raised her ice block in the air and the others raised theirs.

For the first time in Alice's life it felt as though the future was within her grasp.

Thirteen

Kookaburra Creek, 2018

Hattie stood in the shadows of the café, unable to go in. It had always been there in her life; her second life, at least. Tall and proud, watching over her and Genevieve, sheltering them, providing for them.

It may have had fresh make-up applied over the years, a nip here, a tuck there, but she knew its bones. She knew which floor-boards creaked, which bits of plaster had to be patched up every year because they never set right. She knew the sound the wind made blowing through the tiny gap in the dormer window of the second bedroom upstairs. She knew its very soul.

It had broken her heart the day she'd moved out. Not that she had much heart left to break. Putting Genevieve into full-time care had done most of that. The thought of being in their home without her had been just too much to bear. So she'd found herself the tiny house in town and left the café to sit there, forlorn and unloved for months. She'd known she had to sell it, but couldn't bring herself to do it.

Then Alice had appeared, as if by magic, and Hattie envisioned new life for her beloved old home.

How many lives did a building have, she wondered. Hattie herself had had two lives. One in light, one in shadow. Before she and Genevieve called this place home, how many incarnations had it seen? Would it have a life after this?

So much of Hattie's second life was contained within those walls. She remembered the first time she saw it. If only she'd known then. But she hadn't. She hadn't known anything.

June, 1967

They stood at the bottom of the steps of the two-storey weatherboard house. The paint was flaking, cobwebs hung from every corner and the windows were covered in a thick film of dirt and grime, preventing anyone from looking in. Probably just as well, thought Harriett.

'This is it?' Genevieve asked.

'This is it,' Harriett sighed. It wasn't quite the summer house in the country Buckley had described, but then not much about Buckley had turned out to be what she'd expected.

'And it's yours?'

Harriett nodded. 'Ours.'

They walked across the deck and opened the front door.

'It's big.' Genevieve looked around, hobbling on the walking stick the hospital had lent them. Three months of rehab had seen her walk again, with help. 'How long will we be here?'

'Just a few months. Till we're back on our feet.'

Genevieve laughed. 'So to speak.'

There was nothing inside, just a great big empty room, old white sheets covering the floor. So this is home, thought Harriett, fighting back tears. She had to stay strong. For Genevieve. She owed her that. Whatever it took to protect her baby sister, she'd do it. Their old life was gone now, shattered in an unthinking instant. And it was all her fault. They had to make a life here. A quiet, unnoticed life.

'There's a kitchen back here,' Genevieve called from behind a curtained doorway.

She turned and looked at Harriett with her skin so pale and soft, a smile so kind. The scars carved into her face were no longer red and angry, but they would never heal. Harriett had hoped they would. Genevieve was young and the young healed well. But the doctor had explained the damage was too great. She hadn't told Genevieve the disfigurement was permanent, though she suspected she already knew. There were no mirrors in the house, and there never would be.

'It just needs a thorough clean. The whole place does,' said Genevieve, limping into the centre of the room. 'And then we can turn it into a nice place for holidays.'

Harriett also hadn't told Genevieve about her baby, how she'd lost it, how she'd never be able to have children now. She didn't want to burden her. This was all her own fault and she didn't want to worry Genevieve unnecessarily.

This was not the life either one of them had imagined for themselves. Certainly not what Harriett had always dreamed of. There'd be no bright lights or applause or public accolades. But how could she ever go back to that now?

No. This was home. In time, when Genevieve was ready, Harriett would tell her.

July, 1968

Genevieve paced the kitchen floor. 'Do you think anyone will come?' She wrung the tea towel in her hands.

'Of course they will.' Harriett wasn't convinced, but she couldn't let Genevieve know she had doubts.

The menu was pretty basic and neither of them knew what they were doing. But it was worth a try. She'd do anything to make Genevieve happy again and this was what Genevieve had decided would make her happy. A café.

It had taken a while for her to come to that decision and even longer for Harriett to save enough money working for the accountant, but they'd finally managed to refurbish the house, buy all the equipment they needed and set up Genevieve's café.

'It'll just take us some time to build up, is all.' Until then Harriett would keep working for the accountant in Glensdale.

'You did deliver the flyers, right?'

They really had no idea what they were doing.

Genevieve stared ahead, silent, unmoving, her eyes vacant. Harriett moved into position in case she fell down. Not that she ever had. Yet. But the doctor could never guarantee that it wouldn't happen.

'Gen?'

No response. Harriett began counting, just as the doctor had instructed. Time the seizures, when they happened, how long they were. Over the past year they'd been getting worse. Not significantly so, but enough for the doctor to want her to take notes. Another constant reminder of the damage Harriett had inflicted upon her sister.

The old brass bell she'd found by the creek and hung above the door clanged loudly.

'You go,' Genevieve said, coming back to her. 'I can't face them.'

Harriett walked into the dining room, Genevieve's homage to white. White chairs, white tablecloths, white tables, frilly white doilies. Harriett would have loved some colour, but she wasn't going to take anything away from her sister. She owed her so much more than that.

'Morning, Harriett.' Clive stepped forward. His bike lay up against the side of the deck. It was fitting, Harriett supposed, that their first customer was the first person she'd met in Kookaburra Creek. With him was Betty, the headmistress of Glensdale School. Harriett wasn't sure if they were a couple, but it didn't seem likely. Betty didn't seem the type to be part of any couple.

'Morning,' Harriett greeted them. 'Take a seat.'

'It's very quiet,' Betty said, looking down her nose at her surroundings.

'Yes. Thank you for stating the obvious. You're our first patrons.'

'Well, we'd better behave ourselves, then.' Clive grinned.

'That would be nice.'

In the kitchen Genevieve prepared Clive's chicken sandwich and Betty's green salad. 'It's a start.'

Harriett squeezed her shoulder. The bell rang again. 'See? Told you people would come.'

She went back out to greet their next customer and stopped in the middle of the dining room, looking at the tall figure standing before her. Her legs felt weak. He hadn't changed a bit. There was Buckley standing before her, after all this time. She turned and went back into the kitchen.

'Harry, wait.' He followed her.

Genevieve spun round at hearing the familiar voice. 'Buckley.' She hobbled to him and threw herself into his arms.

He kissed the top of her head. 'Good to see you, squirt.' His face drained of colour when he stepped back and saw the scars down the side of her face. Harriett was thankful he at least had the sense not to say anything. 'My, you're all grown up now.' He faked a happy expression like the very good actor he was.

'That tends to happen when a year passes.' Harriett's voice was low.

'I'm sorry, Harry. I thought you needed time.'

'A few weeks, maybe. A month. It's been a year, Buckley Hargraves. A year and four months. What gives you the right to come waltzing in here like this?'

Genevieve went into the dining room, wrapping a scarf round her head before pushing through the shutters.

'What the hell happened to her?' He walked towards Harriett.

'It doesn't matter.'

'Of course it does.'

'It mattered a year ago. When we had the accident. Where were you then?' She ran out the back door and he followed.

'Why didn't you tell me?'

On the little white jetty Harriett spun around. 'Because I didn't think you were interested. Turns out I was right.'

'Were you hurt?'

She fought back the tears of what might have been, tears for their lost child, tears over her stolen future. 'No. Not like Gen.'

'I'm sorry, Harry. What I did was stupid. I know that. After you left, I fell into this hole of drugs and booze, but I'm better now. I got help. I'm working again. Doing pretty well. In film. Ironic, I know. There's this new movie and it's getting a lot of buzz.'

She'd read the article, cut it out, about how very successful he'd become. There was even talk of Hollywood. 'Congratulations. What's it got to do with me?'

'I want you back, Harry. I need you to forgive me and take me back.'

Harriett took half a step back. 'You're kidding.'

'No. I'm deadly serious.' He reached his arm around her body and pulled her in tight. She couldn't stop him kissing her. She didn't want to stop him.

For the first few moments of the kiss she'd been dreaming about for so long, it was as though her life was back where it belonged.

Buckley lifted his head. 'I want to marry you, have children, start a life together.'

She clutched her belly. The endless nights she'd cried herself to sleep, the lost hope, all welled up inside her. 'No.' She pushed him away.

'We're meant to be, Harry. You know that.'

'And where does Delilah fit into this lovely picture you've created?'

'I said I'm sorry. You have to forgive me.'

She heard the bell clang again. Another customer for Genevieve. 'I can't leave her.'

'She can come too.'

'You don't understand. So much has changed for us. I can't . . . she has these . . .' Harriett closed her eyes. 'She's happy here. She's finally got a smile on her face for the first time since the accident and I can't take that away from her.'

'Then we'll figure something out.'

'It's more complicated than that.'

'Please? If Gen's happy here, we can come back on weekends. Come back with me, Harry.'

'How? How can I ever trust you again?' All the anger she'd bottled up for so long came rushing out of her. 'You slept with another woman and it took you a bloody year to figure out you're sorry.'

'Can't we just let the past go? We could be so good together.'

Tears pricked at Harriett's eyes. Let the past go? Yes. That's what she needed to do. Let it go. But not the way he meant.

'Too much has happened, Buckley. Please, just go.'

'But Harry.'

'I'm sorry. This is how it has to be.' Her voice was low, strong. She would not let Buckley seduce her. 'Just go.'

He tried to grab her, but she pulled away.

'Is everything all right?' Clive appeared, pushing his bike as he came towards them. 'Harriett?'

'He was just leaving.' Harriett turned her back and stood looking at the creek, willing herself not to cry.

She heard Buckley walk back to his car and start the engine. She couldn't stop him. Her place was here with her sister. She'd ruined Genevieve's hope of a normal life, stolen any chance of a future. At least here the people of Kookaburra Creek had accepted her. They no longer stared at her ghastly scars and had been encouraging about starting up the café. To start over again somewhere else? No. Harriett would work every day for the rest of her life to make it up to Genevieve. Here, in their café together.

And that meant saying goodbye to Buckley Hargraves.

'What's the matter?' Clive asked.

Harriett didn't reply. Instead, she turned and walked back inside.

2018

Hattie gazed upon the café, all that so long ago now. If only she'd stopped Buckley driving off that day, how very different things might have been. But would they have been better? Genevieve still would have ended up in a home – maybe later, but still.

And, judging by the stories in the gossip magazines that Hattie so diligently cut out over the years, Buckley's eventual marriage to Delilah was less than ideal. If even half of what was written of Buckley's exploits with other women were true, had they ended up together, Hattie might still have led just as lonely a life.

Funny how time and distance play with perspective. She almost felt sorry for Delilah. Almost. But wounds so deep didn't ever truly heal.

Hattie drew up her shoulders. Buckley and Delilah had destroyed her first life. She'd be damned if she'd let them ruin her second. She wasn't just fighting for herself and Genevieve, either. She was fighting for Alice and Becca, and Tammy. All of Kookaburra Creek. And she still had some fight left in her yet.

Fourteen

Lawson's Ridge, 2003

A week after the final exam, Pip's dam was pulsing with laughing, splashing bodies. It seemed half the school were there as Alice and Dean walked hand in hand towards the crowd. Louise ran up to greet them.

'Hey, you.' She embraced Alice tightly before giving Dean a quick, awkward hug. 'Brian's picked out a spot for us over there with a blanket and esky.' She pointed to the tall gum. 'The water's really nice.' She ran towards the dam and jumped into the water.

'Shall we?' Dean winked, stripping down to his board shorts when they got to the picnic blanket.

Alice took off her clothes, revealing a sky-blue swimsuit with a small frill across the bust. She still felt guilty that she'd dipped into her savings to buy it.

'Wow,' said Dean as he looked her over, and Alice's guilt washed away.

Hands clasped tightly together, they ran towards the water.

It wasn't easy getting a turn on the rope, so Alice didn't even try. She was happy splashing in the dam, her arms wrapped round Dean's neck as they laughed at every funny face being pulled each time someone flung themselves into the cool water.

Louise, it seemed, was also quite content, with her arms first around Bobby Jones' neck, talking loudly, and then around Doug Trainor's. She splashed Mike Smith and made him chase her and then got bored with her game.

She swam over to Alice. 'Drink?' She pointed to their spot under the gum.

'Sure.'

Dean joined the rope queue.

As the afternoon drifted into early evening, Louise and Alice sat on the picnic blanket watching the boys try to outdo each other with tricks off the rope, some with courage heightened by beer intake, others fuelled by their natural teenage bravado. Triple somersaults were attempted, only to end in bellyflops.

'Look at those dorks.' Louise nodded towards the rope.

'There's no way you can do a backflip with a twist off the rope and end up diving in normally,' Brian shouted as Dean took hold of the rope.

'You reckon?'

'I know.'

'Only one way to find out.' Dean stepped back. He turned to Alice and winked before launching himself off the bank.

The almighty crack as the branch tore from the old gum set cockatoos screeching into the sky from trees all around the dam. Everyone turned, unable to believe what they saw as seemingly in slow motion Dean fell into the dam, tangled in the rope still attached to the three-metre-long branch. The branch that smacked into him with a sickening thud as he hit the water.

Alice and Louise stood and grabbed each other's hands, mouths open, eyes wide. Brian was the first to move, followed by Bobby. As they swam to reach Dean, everyone gathered on the edge of the dam. Except Alice. Louise pulled on her arm, but she couldn't move.

The gathered crowd blocked any chance of being able to see what was happening in the water. But Alice didn't want to see. She stared at the ground, counting her breaths as she tried to slow them.

'They've got him.' A shout rose up.

Six boys carried Dean slowly up the embankment, the crowd parting for them.

'Go get Pip,' Brian barked at the girl beside him and she took off, slipping in the dirt.

Alice's legs buckled beneath her and everything went silent. She couldn't hear the frantic instructions coming from Brian, though she could see his mouth moving. The mumbled concerns from those standing closest to the epicentre of Alice's imploding world didn't reach her ears, the skidding tyres of Pip's ute as he sped past her ten minutes later were strangely quiet. For what seemed an eternity, Alice heard nothing.

Until the sirens.

Slowly she stood and walked towards Dean's wet, still body. People moved out of her way to let her pass. The ambos were bent over him, a light moving across his eyes, a brace around his neck, a blanket covering his legs.

As they rolled him on to the gurney, Alice stepped closer.

'Pond?' Dean's eyes fluttered open but his voice sounded weak and strange.

Alice took Dean's hands in hers. 'You're okay. Thank God you're okay.' Relief flooded her body.

Dean smiled as he looked at her, but his eyes betrayed his fear, so desperate, so scared.

She leaned down and kissed his forehead.

'Told you I'm not smart enough.' He croaked, his fragile laugh becoming a hacking cough.

Alice stood still, watching the paramedics wheel Dean towards the ambulance.

Only when the ambulance doors shut did she break eye contact with him, immediately crashing to the dirt. Louise wrapped her in her arms and they both started to sob.

Hours later, Alice kept replaying the moment of the accident over in her head. The sickening crack. The hollow thud. Through the kitchen, down the hall and under the door, the phone cord snaked into Alice's bedroom. Under the covers she waited, willing with all her might for the phone to ring with any news at all. Louise had brought her home. She'd taken her shoes off, helped her change into the T-shirt she always kept under her pillow and got her into bed.

'It'll be okay,' she'd whispered over and over, before leaving her there. 'I'll wait at home. Mum's on shift tonight. She might ring with news.'

It was now dark outside. Alice wondered when that had happened. She could hear Bruce's loud snoring coming from the living room, oblivious as always. She wondered if she should call Dean's mum. She'd only met her the once, but she seemed nice enough.

Alice stopped. That sound. Whirring. A helicopter.

The only helicopter that ever flew over Lawson's Ridge was the emergency medical chopper. The one that took patients from Cutter's Pass to Sydney. Everything happened in Sydney.

She pulled her knees up tight, slipping them under the T-shirt. Dean's T-shirt. The one from the day they'd first swum together at the dam, which she'd never given back. Maybe if she closed her eyes tight enough and hugged his T-shirt close enough, maybe somehow he'd be okay.

Fifteen

Kookaburra Creek, 2018

The sick feeling Hattie was carrying around inside her was not going away. There was no way out of it. She'd had two sets of lawyers look over the paperwork and there was nothing she could do. Nothing. If only she'd thought to be so thorough all those years ago, or given it any thought at all, actually, this whole sorry mess could have been avoided. But she was so very young, so terribly angry. She'd taken Buckley at his word. How was she to have known?

In exasperation, she threw the letter and offending documents across the room.

'Curse you, Buckley Hargraves.' She cried. 'And curse your sodding spawn.'

Who did they think they were? The unbridled nerve. Whatever happened to moral decency? That's what she wanted to know. For fifty years they didn't even know that Kookaburra Creek existed and now they thought they could lay claim to their piece of it. *Her* piece of it. The nerve!

It wasn't theirs. Never was. Yet those wretched lawyers said otherwise. And they were going to fight for it. Although they did understand, of course, Hattie's sentimental attachment, and were very generously prepared for her to buy them out. At a price. They had to consider their own lost earnings and potential, naturally. Very generous her left foot. Hattie had read the stories, cut them out, how the Hargraves dynasty had fallen at the hands of Buckley's addictions – the fortune he and Delilah had amassed slowly frittered away on alcohol and drugs. Delilah may well have been long gone, but her greed lived on in her family.

What was she going to do? Hattie buried her head in her hands. There was nothing she could do. Absolutely nothing. She knew that. Tears dripped steadily down her cheeks.

Alice woke to the sounds of clanging pots and pans and the smell of strong coffee brewing. She padded downstairs and into the café and found Becca standing in the kitchen among a mess: open egg cartons, half melting nobs of butter, flour scattered everywhere and what appeared to be every pan and utensil Alice possessed strewn across the bench.

'I made breakfast,' Becca said, her smile an attempt to portray calm and confidence. She ushered Alice into the dining room and sat her down, then disappeared briefly, returning with a plate of pancakes that she set down in front of her.

'It looks delicious,' said Alice.

'I thought they'd be easy,' replied Becca, her eager expression faltering.

'They smell great.'

Becca shrugged and sat down opposite Alice. She took a bite of the overcooked batter and spat her mouthful out, but Alice finished her whole overly salted pile.

'I've been wondering,' Alice said, as she pushed her cutlery together. 'Do you want me to let your mum know where you are? Or that you're safe at least?' She tried to sound casual as she stood to clear the bench.

'She's long gone.'

Alice stared at Becca. 'Oh Becca. I'm so sorry.'

'Not dead gone.' Becca shrugged. 'I kind of wish she was. Runaway gone. She took off. Ages ago.'

Alice watched for the telltale sign of Becca's fringe being pushed to the left, but her hands stayed on the bench in front of her, her eyes looking directly at Alice. So she was telling the truth.

'Right, then,' Alice said, sensing she wasn't going to get any more out of her. 'What do you say to some therapy?'

'I'm not seeing a stupid bloody shrink!'

Alice laughed. 'Not that kind of therapy. *Retail* therapy.'

Becca stared at Alice.

'Shopping. You must be sick of wearing church hand-me-downs.'

'I s'pose.' Becca fiddled with the shirt that was just a tad too tight.

'There are some good shops in Glensdale.'

'Really?'

Alice nodded. 'Come on.'

Becca, it seemed, wasn't a born shopper. Not like Tammy. Tammy would try every outfit in the store on and want each one. Becca looked at the T-shirt Alice held up and shrugged. She shrugged at the shorts too. To get an idea of size, Alice had to hold the garments up to a fidgeting Becca and eyeball it.

Tammy used to pick out matching shoes for every outfit, and jewellery if Alice let her get away with it. Becca picked up one pair of black trainers and was done.

'Summer's not far away. They'll be hot,' Alice said, and held up a pair of sandals.

'They'll be fine.' Becca walked away.

The drive back to Kookaburra Creek was quiet. Alice knew she had no right to think it would be the same, shopping with Becca. No reason to suspect she'd feel the same joy. Yet she had expected it. Alice fought back the tears she could feel welling up inside her.

It wasn't wrong to see this as some sort of second chance, was it? There was a reason Becca came into her life. A reason the girl with eyes that carried echoes of Alice's past ended up in her café. There had to be. And maybe it wasn't even about Alice, or Tammy. Maybe it was just about Becca, about giving her a second chance. Or maybe it was about all of them. Alice would give anything in this world to have her life back. But that wasn't possible. Yet Becca was here, for whatever reason, and Alice wasn't about to waste this chance fate had given her.

She was afraid to speak. Her words would likely betray her foolish thoughts. As they passed tree after tree after tree on the long narrow road, Becca fell asleep beside her. And then Alice let the tears fall.

A single light was on in the café when they got back to Kookaburra Creek and Alice wondered if she'd forgotten to turn it off before they'd left. Becca jumped out of the car and ran up the external staircase as soon as Alice pulled the vehicle to a stop. Had she been feigning sleep? Oh no, Alice hoped she hadn't seen her crying.

'What are you doing?' she said to herself as she entered the café to turn off the light.

'Actually, petal, I was waiting for you.'

Alice dropped her shopping bag and spun round.

'Hattie! You scared me half to death.' Her initial fright dissolved into worry when she saw her old friend sitting in the shadows, scarf folded in front of her, no matching stripe clipped in her hair.

'Sorry.' Hattie started to stand, but sank back down again.

'What's wrong?' Alice moved quickly and sat beside her. 'Is it Genevieve?'

'No, no. She's fine.'

'Then what?'

Hattie took Alice's hands in hers. Her long, thin fingers were cold despite the warmth of the room. 'I do have to . . . There's something I need . . . Oh, Lord, this is harder than I imagined.'

'Hattie, you're scaring me. Are you sick?'

'Not at all.' She shook her head. 'Though that would be easier news to tell.'

'Harriett Brookes, whatever it is spit it out right this second.'

In all the time Alice had been in Kookaburra Creek, Hattie had never looked her age. Despite her wrinkles, she always somehow pulled off an air of someone much younger than she actually was. But there in the dim light Alice saw every moment of Hattie's seventy-odd years and then some – traces that only a painful history can etch into the lines of your face.

'It's the café.' She wrung her hands together.

'What about it?' Alice started to feel dizzy.

'Apparently, it technically isn't mine.'

'You mean it's Genevieve's?'

'No. It isn't ours at all.'

'I don't understand.'

'Neither did I.' Hattie laughed, sad, cynical. 'We were so terribly young, so innocent of the world. I misunderstood. I didn't know. I thought . . .'

'You're telling me neither you nor Genevieve own the place. So the bank does?' Alice's mind was racing to put the pieces of the puzzle together.

'My trip to Sydney was for a funeral. For Buckley Hargraves.'

'*The* Buckley Hargraves? The actor?'

'The one and only.' Hattie rubbed the fingers on her left hand.

'What's he got to do with all this?'

'Well, technically the café belongs to him. Belonged to him. His children technically now own it.'

'Stop saying technically, for God's sake, Hattie. Do they, or do they not own the café?'

Hattie looked down. 'They do.'

Alice shoved the chair back and started pacing the room. 'And I suppose now he's dead they want it back?' She threw her hands in the air.

'Yes.'

The quiet reply barely reached her ears.

'Shit, Hattie. How could you not tell me this tiny, insignificant, life-bloody-changing detail? All this time you never even owned the place?'

Fractured thoughts raced through her head. It was never Hattie's. Never hers. But they weren't really going to lose it, surely? It was more than painted chairs and thousands of cupcakes. More than gingham curtains and burgers and salads. The Kookaburra Creek Café wasn't just a café. It was home. And not just to her. It was home to everyone she knew. To Betty and her bowls crew, to Claudine and Mrs Harris, all of the Harris mob. To Joey. It was her home, Tammy's home. All those years ago it was the café that saved her from her broken life.

Every happy memory Alice had since leaving Lawson's Ridge was tied up with this café. Every memory of Tammy. No. She couldn't lose this place.

Alice shook her head decisively. 'Right, then. We'll fight them. The will. I assume this is about the will.'

'I've seen a solicitor. They'll win.'

'Then we'll get another solicitor. You can't just give up, Hattie.'

'I'm not giving up.'

'How did this happen?'

Hattie stared at her. 'I genuinely thought Gen and I owned it. I didn't realise we didn't.'

'How on earth could you not know? Contract. Payment. Exchange of title. Hello?'

'I was so young. So desperate. I didn't understand. I spoke to the solicitors again yesterday . . .'

'There must be a way. We can do better than Elliot Buddle. We can find a solicitor in Sydney. There must be a loophole.'

'Alice, he's contacted some colleagues. We don't have a legal leg to stand on.'

Alice paced the café floor. She had to think. Had to stop the tumbling mess inside her head and fix this. Save her café, her life, her memories. She'd lost so much already. And now with Becca here . . . No. She wouldn't lose again.

'We'll buy them out. Surely between us we can afford the land value. It couldn't be worth more than 200 grand. Three, tops. I've got forty put away. Can you get the rest?'

Hattie shook her head.

'A loan. Surely I'd be good for a loan now. For such a small amount.'

'Well, we don't know.'

'Don't know what?'

'What they'll want. If Buckley's kids are anything like their mother, it won't be that straightforward. They're sending someone over to evaluate the place.'

'What? When?'

'In the next week or so.'

That wasn't a long time to come up with any kind of money, any kind of plan.

Her legs buckled beneath her and she crumpled to the floor. Hattie lowered herself beside Alice and put her arms around her.

'We'll be okay, petal. We'll be okay.'

Alice shook her head. Here she was again, just like when she was eighteen, her life unravelling before her, beyond her control. She clutched her stomach and fought down the bile.

Sixteen

Lawson's Ridge, 2003

Three words. It was all Alice could do to remain upright after hearing those three words. Other words were being spoken, but they blended together into something quite incomprehensible and made no sense whatsoever. The mumbling and gasping of the crowd gathered outside the general store only made it worse.

One by one the group dissipated and Alice was left in the middle of the street, those three words echoing in her head.

She didn't want to move but she felt her shoulders turn. Then she saw her feet step, one in front of the other, and a force stronger than she could fight pressed down on her, pushing her to sit on the hot, concrete kerb.

'Are you okay?' a voice that sounded suspiciously like Louise's asked her.

'Uh-huh.' Alice nodded, not at all believing her own answer.

'Look at me,' said the voice and Alice raised her head. 'He'll be all right.' Louise's face came into focus. 'You need to believe that.'

Alice nodded.

The three words repeated in her head, pounding again and again and again. Spinal cord injury. Thud, thud, thud.

She didn't know what it meant. Not really. Only that it wasn't good. It was all the information Mrs Jenkins had. Spinal cord injury, St Vincent's, they'll keep Mrs Jenkins updated. Medical professional to medical professional. As soon as Alice saw her walking past the store she'd rushed out. And everyone else had seen her too, following her so they could also hear the latest. It was all anyone was talking about. The most exciting thing to happen in Lawson's Ridge in a long time.

'Come on, Alice,' Louise whispered, waving to her mum that she'd catch up later. 'Maybe it's not that bad.'

Alice looked up and saw the fear in Louise's eyes. Not that bad? The hospital were only taking calls from family members and even then, apparently, weren't giving much away. Alice knew enough of how hospitals worked to know it wasn't a good sign.

'Do you think Brian can drive me to Cutter's Pass?' she asked.

'Sure. Why?'

Alice stood. 'I need to go to the library.'

Once she was there, Alice pored over the only books she could find, hour after hour. Reading. Re-reading. Cross-checking. Louise and Brian had left her there after she'd insisted she could catch the bus home, and she'd entered the library determined not to leave without answers. Not that she was sure exactly what she was reading. Permanent loss of mobility in all limbs. Partial loss. Full recovery.

What did it all mean and which parts applied to Dean?

If she was understanding the information correctly, everything depended on how high or low the injury was, and that she didn't know the answer to. She knew he was in intensive care. She knew it wasn't good news. She knew she couldn't get the picture on page twenty-five of the third book she'd read out of her mind: the young boy in the wheelchair, on a ventilator, able to move only his head, after falling off his horse.

She stayed in the library until closing and took the last bus back to Lawson's Ridge.

A week was all she could wait. A week and no return of Mrs McRae and no further news from Mrs Jenkins.

Stuff hospital rules. She had to figure out a way to speak to Dean.

But what would she say?

Sitting on her bed, Alice wiped away nervous tears as her hand shook above the receiver. Could she pull this off? She'd rehearsed what she was going to say again and again. She wasn't sure they'd put her through, but she had to try. She'd gone too long without news.

Hopefully he'd take her call. Hopefully he'd be able to.

'Dean McRae, please.' She mustered as much confidence and maturity in her voice as she could. 'Intensive care.'

The switch put her through.

'It is rest time,' the nurse on the other end announced crisply. 'Are you family?'

'Yes,' Alice said. 'I'm his sister.'

'Don't be long.'

Alice waited.

'Hey, Pond.' Dean's weak voice struck Alice and she put her hand over her mouth to stop from gasping.

'How'd you know it was me?' she asked. 'I didn't even tell the nurse my name.'

'Who else'd be smart enough to say they were a sister I don't have?'

Alice laughed. 'Sorry. I wasn't sure they'd put me through otherwise.'

'It's really good to hear your voice,' Dean said.

The slight catch in his tone threatened to bring Alice's tears back to the surface. 'How are you?'

'Not bad for a bloke who humiliated himself in such a spectacular way in front of the whole town.' He laughed, then gasped with the effort.

Alice smiled and wiped away the salty drops on her cheeks. 'It was only the whole school, not the whole town.'

'Oh, that's all right then.'

'Everyone's worried about you.'

'I can imagine the rumours.'

'No, really.'

'Well, you can assure everyone that I'm going to be just fine.' Dean started coughing. 'Just fine,' he whispered when he stopped spluttering. 'It really is good to hear your voice.'

'You sound tired.'

'Humiliation can be exhausting.' His words were very soft.

She didn't want to push things, but she just had to know. 'What have the doctors said? L3? T1?'

'Pond, what have you been up to?'

'Just a little research.'

'I should have known. Maybe you should drop law and do medicine.'

'I'm not sure I'd be cut out for it.'

'You sound pretty convincing to me,' he said quietly.

'So?'

'Insistent, aren't you, Dr Pond? They don't really say much in front of me. Not the technical stuff anyway. T9, incomplete. That's what I've picked up so far.'

Alice wrote it down, recalling her research.

'T9'. Good. Lower limbs only.

'Incomplete'. Good. That meant hope.

'I pretend I'm asleep most of the time so I can listen in. They said my recovery so far is . . . encouraging. Yeah, that's the word they used. And they're happy my chest has cleared up. Bloody muddy dam water.' He faked a cough.

'And now you're a poet.' Alice giggled.

'I guess so. I'm going to be stuck here for a while no matter what, though.'

Alice could hear the strain in his voice.

'I'm sorry.' He sighed.

'What for?'

'Ruining our plans for summer.'

'Don't be silly. All you need to worry about is getting better. And then, when you're home, we can make new plans.'

'Sounds good. Oh shit. Nurse Ratched is giving me the evil eye. I'd better go.'

'Okay. I'll call again. Or maybe I'll write.'

'I'd like that. Here comes . . .'

'Dean?'

The phone went dead.

'Hey, Tadpole.' Bruce gave her a hug as she passed, blissfully unaware of his daughter's pain. 'Today's going to be a good day. I can feel it.' He looked expectantly at Alice.

She looked back at him blankly and left in silence.

Her shift dragged on, but at least she was occupied. Mostly. There was still plenty of time between rearranging stock on shelves and colour-coordinating the magazine rack for her mind to wander, and her thoughts kept turning to how she could help Dean. She'd been reading up on the power the mind had on recovery. Surely there was something she could do, even from so far away, to keep his spirits up.

'Take the rest of the afternoon off,' Mr Williams said, walking into the shop as Alice finished her third baked-bean pyramid. 'You've been doing so many extra hours lately, you'll run me out of business.'

'But . . .'

'No buts. Look at this place. If I leave you in here any longer today, you'll have the rice bags hanging from the ceiling and chocolates melted and formed into sculptures.'

Why hadn't she thought of that? She turned and caught a glimpse of Mrs Dobson's car speeding away. Ah, she thought, no date today. That explained things.

'Thank you.' She stopped by the counter to pick up her bag and looked at the postcards on display. Three tiers of faded pictures showing towns around Lawson's Ridge, towns people actually wanted to visit, and they'd been sitting there on the counter for years; as long as Alice could remember. Grandma Jenkins had bought one once, to send to relatives overseas, but Alice couldn't recall any other sale since she'd worked there. Ever.

Wiping the dust off the picture of sheep from Cutter's Pass, Alice pulled fifty cents out of her pocket.

'You can have that one, Alice. Take as many as you want.' Her boss waved his hand in front of the display.

Alice took a handful and slipped them in the pocket of her green cargo pants.

'Thanks.'

Sitting on her bed, with Dean's T-shirt pulled over her clothes, Alice twiddled a pen between her fingers. Over, under, over, under. She'd managed to write two words on the postcard before fear made her mind turn blank. What could she possibly say? In her head she imagined poetic words flowing forth, bringing hope and happiness. On paper, the lonely words 'Dear Dean' were hardly going to do the job. She would have to do better than that.

'So, I've been thinking about when I get to Sydney and all the things we can do together. What do you think about the City to Surf? We can do it while you're still in your chair and we can dress up and everything. A fun run to the beach. That's not something we could ever do here in Lawson's Ridge. What do you reckon? You game?'

It was funny how the days bled into one another. Alice had never thought of her life as anything even resembling exciting, or of Lawson's Ridge ever offering hope of excitement to come. But the monotony of her existence had made the days become even more blurred. She worked in the store. She came home. She picked up after her father. She sent off postcards. She worked in the store. She came home. And on it went.

The only event of any note in her narrow world was the end-of-year school formal. But it was hard to muster any genuine enthusiasm, or even any fake gusto for it.

'Come on, Alice.' Louise tried to get her to try on the green satin dress that Alice knew she simply couldn't afford. They'd been trudging round Cutter's Pass all afternoon in search of two perfect dresses. It was easier for Louise, who looked beautiful in everything she tried on and who had the budget to pick any dress she liked. Alice refused to put any of the dresses on.

'You can't go to the formal naked, you know.' Louise stepped out of the change room in a red gown.

'Wow.' Alice nodded her head. 'You look great. But I can't afford any of these.'

'You really need to find something to wear, Alice.'

'What's the point?'

'The point is you only finish high school once, so you may as well enjoy it. Do you think Dean would be happy seeing you mope around like this while Agony Annie is torturing him?'

'Agony Annie?'

'His new physio.'

'Excuse me?'

With a flourish Louise flopped onto the chair in the corner of the shop. 'I was talking to him. Yesterday.'

'Oh.'

'Brian made me ring.' Louise scratched her left hand. 'He pulled the helpless younger brother card. He only accepts I'm three minutes older when it suits him. He feels guilty about the accident. Reckons if he hadn't egged him on, then . . .' She shrugged. 'But, big bad Brian's too chicken to ring himself, so he made me do it. I gave the physio the nickname because it sounds bloody awful what she puts him through.'

Alice frowned. Dean had never told her anything about his physio sessions being hard, though she supposed they probably would be.

'Which do you like best?' Louise held up two stunning dresses.

*

At exactly 5.35 that evening the phone rang.

'That was quick, Pond.' Dean's voice floated to Alice's ears. 'Waiting for my call?'

'No. I'm far too busy to be waiting round for some guy to call,' she mocked. 'Just happened to be walking past when it rang.'

'Liar.' Dean chuckled.

'How's it going down there?' Alice really wished he'd tell her more. Whenever she asked him, he always dodged the question. 'How's the new centre?'

'Great.'

'Liar.'

'Nah. Actually, not too bad. This rehab joint is pretty good. Annie has upped the ante on my therapy. Strange woman seems immune to my obvious charms. She keeps wanting me to work harder. But one day I'll crack her defences and she'll give me a break.'

'Agony Annie?'

'You've been speaking with Louise.'

'Yes. Funny that, seeing as we're best friends and all. Why haven't you told me how hard it is?'

Dean sighed. 'I guess I just don't want to worry you with boring detail.'

'Being vague worries me more.'

'Sorry.'

'What about the doctors? You had your assessment today, right?'

'I can count on you to be paying attention.' Alice could hear the gentleness in his voice. 'They seem pretty happy. Though sometimes I switch off when they're banging on with their medical mumbo jumbo. The nurses and Annie are much better to talk to.'

'And?'

'They reckon it's likely I'm going to have a good recovery.'

'Really? You're not lying to me so I don't worry?'

'If I keep doing what Annie tells me to, I've got a good chance at walking independently again.'

Alice heard the slight catch in his voice and wondered if he wasn't telling her something. She hated speaking over the phone, unable to see him, read his body language. And once a week was nowhere near enough. Well, it wouldn't be long till she was down there and could see for herself how he was doing and if he was holding anything back.

'You will be fine, Dean. I know it.'

'Yep. Fine and fat.'

'Fat? What about all the physio you're doing?'

'All the physio in the world can't counteract the cakes and slices Mum keeps bringing in. She's found this amazing bakery and never visits without going there first. I think she feels a bit useless, you know? She can't fix me, so she'll feed me instead.'

Alice laughed.

'Every bloody day she forces cream puffs and cupcakes down my throat.'

'Sounds terrible.'

'You've no idea.'

'Well,' Alice chuckled, 'when you're up and about again and I'm down there, you can walk it off by showing me around Sydney.'

'I can't wait,' said Dean. 'Uh-oh. The nurse is here to check my butt for sores. Every three hours she comes in. I reckon she secretly has a thing for my arse and it's just an excuse. I might start charging her for a gander.'

Alice could hear someone talking in the background.

'I'd better go.'

'Okay.' Alice sighed. Their calls were never long enough. 'See you soon.'

'Oh, and Pond, keep those postcards coming. Please. Gives me something to smile about in between phone calls.'

Alice hung up.

She pulled out the next postcard from the pile beside her bed.

'So I've been thinking. When you're back on your feet – and you will get back on your feet – why restrict ourselves to activities just around Sydney? I mean, there's a whole wonderful world out there we can explore. I've always wanted to see the Great Barrier Reef. Dive with turtles. They are the coolest little creatures. Except they're not that small. But diving with them and swimming over the coral would be pretty amazing. What do you say? Are you game?'

Seventeen

Kookaburra Creek, 2018

In the early morning light, Alice moved around the café performing the usual tasks that she had to do before opening up for the day. Except that she wasn't really there. Her finger turned the coffee machine on, her arms lifted chairs down from their tables, her feet stepped across the floorboards avoiding table legs, but it was like she was on autopilot.

'Do you need a hand?' Hattie rested her hand on Alice's shoulder. She hadn't gone home last night, but instead slept in Alice's bed while Alice took the sofa. Not that either one of them got much sleep.

'I don't even know where to start.'

It was quarter to nine and she'd have to open soon. She wasn't ready for service. Wasn't ready to paint on her smile so no one would suspect anything was wrong.

'Why don't I take care of out here and you get started in there?'

Alice nodded.

In the kitchen she looked up to Sylvia.

'Don't fail me now, old girl.'

She leaned on the bench and waited, and Sylvia didn't let her down.

Alice grated the zest from a lemon and juiced it using her favourite hand juicer. She beat the butter and eggs and sugar. Surely a bank would give her a loan. She measured the flour. Without owning the building, though, all she had for equity was the business.

With a rocking action she used her biggest knife to finely chop the rosemary. Maybe she'd have to look for new premises to lease. She licked the back of the spoon. Sweet. Tangy. Earthy. An inspired combination.

It was worth a try, if nothing else. And if that failed, she'd come up with plan B, plan C, as many plans as it took.

'No harm in giving it a go.' Hattie nodded when Alice told her the plan. 'What have we got to lose?'

'Only the café,' Alice said, and laughed.

'We'll get through this together, petal.' Hattie embraced her.

'Oh, please. A woman your age, Hattie, should have more decorum in public,' Betty entered the café.

'And a woman your age should be so lucky as to have anyone who'd want to hug them back,' Hattie shot back with a wink.

Alice smiled. No, she couldn't lose this place.

Buoyed with a plan, Alice sailed through the rest of the morning and into the afternoon. She'd save this place, whatever it took.

The bell above the door clanged and Alice turned to see a young man in jeans and a red shirt standing there, looking uncertain. Tourists. A little early in the season, but you could always pick them.

'Miss Pond?'

'Yes.' Why would a tourist know her name?

'Sorry I'm late.'

'Late?'

'Sorry. You knew I was coming? I thought you knew I was coming. McKenzie. Stuart McKenzie from McKenzie Brokers. I'm here to value the property.'

Now? Already? Stuart McKenzie was not what she'd imagined – he was far too young and friendly to be in this line of work.

'If now's not a good time, I can come back later.'

She stared at him.

'Miss Pond?' He took a step closer.

'Sorry. Now's fine. What do you need?'

'Why don't we start with a tour?'

She moved him round the café into the kitchen, watching him scribble in his notepad. The tightness in her belly grew with each passing moment.

'Charming. This place is so darned charming. What's your annual turnover?'

'It's ahh . . . about . . .'

'Never mind.' He waved his hand. 'I'll need to see the books myself anyway. Whenever you're ready.'

Alice nodded.

'And how many employees?'

'Two. Myself and my assistant. Oh, and my partner.'

He narrowed his gaze. 'Just the three of you managing all this?' he flicked through the papers she'd handed him.

'Yes.'

Hang on. She snatched the papers back. 'The Hargraves don't own the business. They only own the property.'

'True.' The smiling assassin nodded. 'But it does help gain an overall picture of the potential for the place.'

'Well, you can't have my potential.' She folded her arms.

'Fair enough. May I see upstairs?'

They weren't entitled to her potential, but they were, unfortunately, perfectly entitled to her home. Alice almost retched.

'This way.'

Stuart McKenzie opened every cupboard, walked through every room, looked out every window, muttering 'charming' as he went. He peered into every aspect of her life and Alice had never felt so exposed.

'Thank you, Miss Pond. Can I trouble you for some afternoon tea?'

Surely he wasn't serious. But the smile on his face said he was.

She watched him from the kitchen as he made notes, his eyes constantly wandering around the room. Just looking at him made her feel sick. Having to serve him too, was almost more than she could bear. She brought him a lemon rosemary cupcake and Earl Grey tea.

'Mr McKenzie?'

'Stuart, please. Mr McKenzie is my dad.'

'How much will the valuation come in at?'

He shook his head. 'I really can't say just yet. I need to check out comparable sales which, given the unique nature of this property, might be difficult.'

My unique property, thought Alice.

'And until I speak with my clients, I can't really say anything.' He shrugged.

Yes, your clients. Your evil, hateful clients who are trying to destroy my life. Well, Mr McKenzie, I'll be ready for you and whatever price is named. In a few days' time when I'm done with the bank, I'll be ready.

'Of course,' she said, smiling. 'I understand.'

Never before had Alice been so happy to get rid of a customer in her life. She couldn't believe how much she was shaking when he left.

'Alice.' Becca burst into the café. 'Can you tell this psycho to stop following me?'

Freddy stepped in behind her, his hands up in surrender. 'I saw her leaving Betty's and thought we could walk together.'

'I was at Betty's studying. Why were you there? So you could stalk me?' She stepped towards him, her face full of anger. No, fear. Alice was beginning to recognise the difference.

'It's okay,' Alice said calmly. 'Freddy's here to do the garden.'

'What's that got to do with following me?'

'I'm really sorry,' Freddy said, lowering his arms. 'I was just trying to be friendly.'

'Freddy, why don't you go get started?' Alice suggested.

He nodded and backed out of the room.

'It was like he was waiting for me outside Betty's place,' said Becca.

Alice sighed. 'That's my fault, I'm afraid. I mentioned to him yesterday that you'd be there. I guess he decided to try and make friends.'

'I don't need friends.'

'Maybe not. But if you change your mind, he's actually one of the good guys.'

It took some fancy persuasive work to convince Becca that Freddy was in fact not a stalker, but eventually, after a snack and a debriefing of the day's tutoring session, she conceded enough to perch herself on the wooden picnic table outside, knees drawn in tight, watching Freddy move about the garden. As he mowed and weeded and edged, Becca looked on, occasionally passing comment but mostly scowling. Unperturbed, Freddy went about his work, his mischievous smile never wavering. And all the while Alice hovered by the windows, moving around the café to ensure she had a clear view.

'Don't tell me you're playing matchmaker again,' Joey said, interrupting Alice's spying.

She spun around and put her hands in her apron pocket.

'Nothing of the sort.' She threw her nose in the air as she brushed past him.

'It wouldn't be the first time,' Joey continued, as he followed her to the counter.

'And I learned my lesson.' Alice busied herself with the coffee machine, though she was pretty sure she wasn't fooling Joey at all. She was well aware – the entire town was well aware – of the disaster that ensued after she tried to set Carson up with Betty's niece who'd visited four summers previous. The fact the poor woman hadn't returned to Kookaburra Creek since, not even for a weekend, said it all really.

'Indeed.' Joey nodded.

'I just think it will do her good to have a friend. Someone her own age.'

'Uh-huh.' Joey was doing a poor job of trying not to laugh.

'Are you here for something, or to pass judgment?'

Joey threw his hands in the air. 'Coffee, Alice, simply a coffee.'

'Good. Go sit down then.'

'How is she?' he asked, nodding towards Becca.

'I think we've turned a corner, but it's hard to tell. She hasn't said anything, but whatever she's running from she's pretty darn scared of it.'

'Have you asked her?'

'I don't want to risk pushing her away.'

'Maybe that's what she needs, though. To know you'll listen.'

'Maybe.'

'I mean, between you and Hattie I'm surprised the poor thing has lasted this long without spilling state secrets.' He laughed.

'What are you suggesting?'

'Not a thing.' He bowed in surrender.

'You're impossible, Joseph Moretti.'

'Impossible . . . ly good looking?'

'Just impossible.' Alice threw her tea towel at him and smiled.

The doorbell clanged again and Fiona Harris walked in.

'Sorry I'm late.' Fiona grinned and kissed Joey on the cheek.

What? No. Alice's body felt unnaturally heavy. She'd watched Joey date before, on and off over the years. It was never anything serious. Nothing ever stuck. She'd seen Fiona waltz back into town plenty of times, have some fun with whatever bachelor within 100 kilometres showed an interest, and waltz right back out again. But something felt different this time. She wasn't sure what but, whatever it was, she didn't like it.

Becca came inside when Freddy left, went straight into the kitchen and started on the washing up. Maybe now was the time to ask her some questions? But Alice knew what it was like to have closely guarded secrets at that age. Becca would tell her when she was ready. If she ever was. Assuming they'd still all be there, of course.

Oh, Lord. In all the drama of the last forty-eight hours it hadn't occurred to her that losing the café wasn't just losing the café. It meant losing Becca. What would become of her if Alice had no job to offer? No roof over her head to provide?

'Are you deliberately trying to scald me?' Betty's voice broke sharply through Alice's thoughts. She was sitting with Claudine at the table beside Joey and Alice had just poured far too much coffee into her china cup.

'Sorry,' Alice muttered, trying to wipe up the spill.

'You are off with the fairies today, child. What's wrong with you?'

'Sorry, Betty. With Becca and the thought of losing —' She stopped herself, realising what she was about to say. Her cheeks burned. No one could know. Becca couldn't know.

'Losing what?' Betty stared over the rim of her thick glasses.

'Losing my mind, I think.' Alice tried to cover her mistake. 'Not with it at all today. Sorry.'

'I'll say. Leave your personal dramas at the door, Alice. This is a business you're running here.'

'Not for much longer,' Alice whispered under her breath as she walked away.

She went to take Joey and Fiona's order. Fate truly was a cruel master sometimes. They placed their order with Alice and went back to whatever hushed conversation they were so obviously engrossed in.

As she moved about the dining room seeing to the other customers, Alice kept an eye on Joey and Fiona, their heads close together the whole time.

'Which table?' Becca asked, coming into the dining room with two burgers.

'Would you mind?' Alice indicated table one, Joey's table.

'Oh.' She frowned. 'Sure.'

Maybe Alice couldn't do anything about Fiona Harris, but that didn't mean everything was lost. There was still the bank, and that meant hope. As dangerous as hope could be, she needed to hang on to it right now.

Eighteen

Lawson's Ridge, 2003

The music spilling out of the school hall was loud and fast. Alice stood back from the gate in the shadows of the gums, watching happy, loved-up couples and noisy groups skip, step and stumble their way inside. The boys looked mostly like they'd made an effort to shower at least and be presentable, some of them even looking almost handsome in the collared shirts and ties they'd rented or borrowed. The girls, dressed in dark satins, teetered on unfamiliar heels, their hair coiffed professionally and piled on top of their heads, soft ringlets framing their painted faces. Louise arrived, beautiful in a sapphire blue dress that had been the most expensive in the shop. Alice still preferred the red, but it wouldn't have mattered what Louise had worn, she would have been stunning.

She looked down at her own dress. A peach taffeta bridesmaid's gown her mother had once worn in the late eighties. She'd done her best to alter it – taking the bum-bow off, de-puffing the sleeves, shortening the length. She'd done a good job, compared to what it looked like originally. But compared to the parade of perfectly fitted frocks entering the hall, well, Alice's peach puff was a disaster.

She took a deep breath and stepped inside the large hall doors. Groups of girls started dancing in small circles and boys shuffled their feet left and right next to them in time with the music. Louise was the first to break the girl-circle, turning to dance with Bobby Jones. Then she turned again to move in sync with Doug Trainor.

The music changed and Louise went back to dancing with the girls. She didn't notice Alice pressed up against the wall, watching on.

Alice sighed. This wasn't right, being here without Dean. Slowly, quietly, she slipped back out into the warm November night and hurried down the path towards the protective darkness of Faraway Forest.

She could still hear the music from there, just, ever so softly carried on the light evening breeze. So many beautiful dresses. So many happy faces, and couples dancing together.

She slid her tattered ballet flats off and smiled at the relief her screaming toes felt immediately. Her mother's feet had been much daintier than hers. The earth between her toes was cool and in sweeping arcs she pushed away twigs, crushing the fallen eucalypt leaves into the ground, releasing their sweet, oily scent. Her legs started to move to the rhythm of the faint music and she closed her eyes and danced in the dirt.

'Those moves are wasted on an audience of trees.'

Alice spun round to see Dean wheeling towards her along the well-worn dirt path. A cry caught in her mouth. Even though she knew he was in a chair, to see him actually in it, to see the truth of it for the first time – she fought back tears.

'What are you doing here?' She ran to him. When she reached him she stopped suddenly, not knowing how to approach him.

'Come here.' He reached out and pulled her onto his lap.

Alice tried to stand up, but Dean held her firmly in place.

'I don't want to hurt you,' she whispered into his neck, the smell of cloves and honey tickling her nose.

'Then stay right here.' He reached up and cradled her cheek in his hand. 'God it's good to see you.' He kissed her firmly, gently. She could taste a lingering hint of coffee on his lips.

'So,' she said breathlessly. 'What *are* you doing here?'

'Not complaining, are you, Pond?'

'Not at all.' She rested her head on his.

'I convinced Mum that it was vital for my mental health and recovery that I come back for the formal.' He grinned.

'But you're not at the formal.'

'Neither are you.'

Alice punched him lightly in the shoulder. 'I'm glad you're here.'

'I'm glad I'm here, too. When I saw you weren't at the dance I had a hunch you might be here.'

Alice shook her head. 'I just couldn't face it.' She scrunched up the peach satin abomination in her hand.

'Hmm. I think this calls for something special. Hop up.'

Alice stood.

'On the back of the chair is a backpack. Grab it.'

She did as he said.

'Pull out the picnic blanket. You've already cleared a spot for us.' He laughed.

Alice lay the blanket down.

'In the bottom of the bag is a box. Careful, Pond. No, don't open it yet. Pop it on the blanket.'

She did.

'Now come here and help me out of this.'

Alice stared at him.

Dean beckoned her with his index finger. 'You can't do it from there.'

'I can't do it from anywhere.'

'Of course you can. I can almost do it by myself. Couple more months of physio and I won't need any help at all. But right now I do. Just a bit of support. Once you know the trick it's easy.'

Alice stepped towards Dean. He told her how to brace herself, how to shift her weight. As she lowered him towards the blanket, she could feel her grip loosen.

'I don't think . . . oh shit.' She dropped him the last few centimetres to the ground.

'Oh my God. I'm so sorry. Do I call an ambulance?' Alice saw Dean's shoulders shaking. 'Christ. You're having a fit or something. I'll go for help.'

She turned to run, but a hand on her ankle stopped her.

'I'm fine.'

She looked down. 'You're . . . you're laughing?'

'Gotta look at the funny side of it.' He pulled on Alice's leg and she crashed down beside him. 'Now we're even.'

Alice snorted. 'You're still as crazy as ever.'

'And you,' he brushed her fringe aside, 'are still just too cute for words.'

'I didn't hurt you?'

'Nope.' He shook his head and kissed her gently. 'Tough as, I am. Doctor says I'm lucky. If the branch had hit me any harder, well, I might not be getting out of that thing ever.'

Alice sighed. Surely if he could be bright and happy, so could she. She pushed all negative thoughts from her mind as he opened the cardboard box.

'These,' he said, placing a cupcake in Alice's hands, 'are the best I've ever eaten. You won't believe your tastebuds.'

'From your mum's favourite café?'

'The one and only. Go on.'

She took a bite and her eyes grew wider as she stared at Dean.

'Told you so.' He winked and started eating his own. 'Strawberry and white chocolate.' Dean shrugged. 'Who'd have thought?'

'Wow. These are good.'

'I know, right?' He sighed. 'We're moving back in with Dad.'

'Really?' She tilted her head to touch his shoulder and he squeezed her hand. 'So, you're getting out of rehab?'

'Just after Christmas. They're modifying Dad's house as we speak. I've still got a long way to go, but at least I won't be stuck in the rehab hospital every day.'

'That's fantastic. No more Nurse Ratched.'

'Nope. So, I guess there's an opening for a sponge-bath-giver-butt-gazer.' He winked. 'You know, when you come down.'

Alice hit him again. 'I was thinking more along the lines of you taking me to the Opera House and the Australian Museum. Far more civilised.'

'Yes, you can wheel me across the Harbour Bridge and cook me delicious meals from your dodgy student dorm.'

'You know I can't cook, right?'

'I know. It'll still be nice having you there, though. Someone who sees me, you know, without that thing.' He pointed to his chair.

'Is it that bad?'

'Sometimes. I try to ignore the looks, but it's hard.' With effort he turned himself to look at Alice. 'What's that in your hair?' he asked, reaching behind her head, undoing the peach ribbon she'd tied her ponytail back with.

'I thought it might help, you know, make the dress look better.' Her cheeks reddened.

'You are so beautiful without all this nonsense.' He leaned in and kissed her. Starting softly, sweetly, building till his ferocity forced her to brace herself with her elbows. From somewhere deep inside, a soft moan found its way into Alice's mouth and she let it escape when Dean's arm, wrapped around her waist, pulled her closer to him.

Alice felt the strangest tingling between her legs and she pushed forward. Such a peculiar feeling, so rapturous. He slipped his hand beneath her dress, tracing her thigh to her knickers. She moaned again.

Dean fell backward and gasped with pain as his head hit the ground.

'Oh, God. Did I hurt you? I'm sorry.' Alice sat up.

'No.' Dean shook his head. 'I am. This isn't exactly how I imagined our first time.'

'You've imagined it?'

Dean nodded. 'A hundred times.'

Alice could feel the heat rising over every inch of her skin. She traced a shaking finger across Dean's chest, undoing his buttons as she went. She had no idea what she was doing, no clue as to where her boldness was coming from. She just knew she needed him to keep wanting her like that.

Dean reached for the backpack on the ground behind him and propped himself up. 'Are you sure about this, Pond?'

She was nervous, certainly, but she'd never been surer of anything in her life before. 'Yes,' she nodded, 'as long as you . . .' her cheeks reddened.

'Come here,' he said, his voice low.

Alice knelt, her face close to his. He took her head in his hands and pulled her towards him, kissing her gently. His hands moved down her back to her hips and he lifted her on top of him, his arms stronger than she remembered. His hands moved quickly, slowly, gently, firmly over her body. Her undies fell to the dirt below and she unzipped his jeans. She could feel him growing beneath her and she gasped through his kiss. With Dean's hands cradling her hips, Alice let him push inside her. She gulped.

'Are you okay?'

She nodded. 'Is it . . . supposed to hurt? I mean just a little?'

'I think so. We can stop.'

'No.'

'Here.' He shifted his weight slightly. 'Is that better?'

As he rocked her backwards and forwards gently, the pain subsided and she felt every hair on her body stand on end.

'Yes.' She sighed and raised her eyes to the stars. 'Yes.'

Beneath the brightening sky they lay, half asleep. Alice's head rested on Dean's bare chest and the gentle up and down of his torso as he breathed made her smile.

'Morning, Pond,' he said, a slight croak to his voice.

'Morning.' She blushed as he kissed her cheek.

She wriggled to the side and looked into his eyes. He brushed the ringlet that always fell across her left eye behind her ear. She wished they could stay like that forever, under their red ironbark with strawberry and white chocolate cupcakes to sustain them.

'It seems I've kept you out all night.' Dean smiled. 'Will your dad be worried?'

Alice shook her head. He wouldn't have even noticed that she hadn't come home and it was far too early for him to be up yet. 'What about your mum? She'll be frantic.'

'She thinks I'm at Brian's.' He shrugged.

'So, you planned this?' Alice sat up.

'No. No way.'

She'd never seen him look so serious.

'I'm supposed to be at Brian's. Only reason Mum let me come – because I'd be in the care of Nurse Jenkins. I didn't plan this, I swear. Believe me, if I had there would have been roses and a horse and carriage. Even a bed perhaps.' He smiled.

'Don't be silly. It was perfect.' Alice looked into his eyes.

For a moment, they said nothing, just gazed at each other.

'Shit. Brian will be worried, though.' Dean pushed himself up on his elbows. 'Here, help me up.'

It was an awful lot harder getting Dean into the chair than it was getting him out, but they eventually managed with only a bruise or two each.

He sighed, taking Alice's hand before they left the clearing. 'I wish we could stay.'

'Me too. But it won't be long now and I'll be down there.'

'I know. That's what keeps me going. Knowing we'll be together. Thinking of all the things we'll do together.'

At the end of Jenkins Lane they stopped.

'Here.' Dean pulled a piece of paper out of his pocket. 'Dad got me a mobile phone. You can call me anytime without the nurses telling me to hang up, and I'll have it when I get out.'

'I don't want to say goodbye.' Alice fought back tears.

'Then don't.' Dean coughed heavily. 'It's only see you later.' He reached up and pulled her down till her face was touching his. Ever so softly he whispered something as he kissed her before wheeling himself towards the Jenkins house.

The shiver up her spine, the lingering smell of him, the memories of the night they'd just shared so vivid all mixed together with the echo of his fleeting words.

'I love you.'

*

Alice skipped back through Faraway Forest and blushed when she passed her tree. Their tree. Everything was set. She'd saved enough to get to Sydney, start the life she knew she was meant to be living. She would go to uni and be near Dean and eventually she'd save enough to get her dad the help he needed.

Oh, to be back in Dean's arms. Images of last night, perfect in her mind, awkward moments already erased.

She opened her front door and was greeted by silence. No snoring from the living room. No radio tuned to the racing channel. Had Bruce not drunk last night? Was he up? This early? Conscious? Was he looking for her? Alice allowed herself to hope. Would they have Christmas this year?

'Dad?' she called quietly. 'You here?' A little louder.

Room by room she checked. Empty. Hope turned to trepidation.

Kicking off her shoes as she entered her bedroom, she noticed her cupboard door was open. She dropped her bag and rushed to open the drawers. T-shirts and socks were strewn across the floor. Her chart had been ripped from inside the wardrobe.

'No,' she cried. 'No, no, no.'

She dug her way to the back of the cupboard. Searching. The feeling of bile rising in her stomach.

Nothing. She spun around and spotted the shoebox tossed into the corner of the room. She slumped to the floor and turned the box upside down. It was gone.

Every last cent of her savings. Every dollar she'd put into her escape fund.

All of it. Gone.

And in its place a note.

'Sorry, Tadpole. It's better this way.'

Alice leaned back against her bed, tears falling down her

cheeks. She reached up to her bedside table, but the photo of her mum was gone too.

The next morning Alice rang Dean. But he didn't answer. She tried a few times and when, by lunchtime, he still hadn't picked up, she began to worry. So she rang Louise. Maybe he was still at the Jenkins'.

'I can't believe you'd have the nerve to ring here.' Louise's voice was full of venom.

'What? Why?'

'Don't you have any idea how bad it was to keep Dean out all night? His lungs are still recovering from the accident. He's in hospital, you selfish cow. Pneumonia. All so you could have a bit of fun.'

'Louise. Stop. What are you talking about?' Alice's head was spinning.

'You're just lucky you didn't kill him. Thank God Mum was home when he finally rolled in yesterday. Once he's stable, they're flying him back to Sydney.'

'Lou, I had no idea. We didn't mean to stay out. I didn't mean to . . .'

'Well, it doesn't really matter, does it? The damage is done now. If you really loved him, you wouldn't have done this to him. I hope you're happy.' The line went dead.

Alice didn't know what to think. She should have known staying out wasn't good for him. She'd done enough research. But they hadn't meant to fall asleep. Oh God. What had she done?

Eventually Alice got hold of Dean. He was out of hospital, back at his dad's, and doing okay. He didn't blame her for what had happened and said he wouldn't change that night for anything in the world. But Alice did blame herself. She was silly and thoughtless. Every time he coughed when they spoke, guilt surged through her.

'It could have ended so differently.'

'But it didn't, Pond. I'm fine. Let it go.'

But she couldn't let it go. She'd almost killed him. Each phone call reminded her of that. Each day she tried to think of a way to make it up to him.

She desperately wanted to talk to him about her dad, but he'd only worry and she didn't want to be the cause of any more of his stress. She tried to speak to Louise, but she'd already left for Sydney and Mrs Jenkins wasn't giving out Louise's new phone number. At least not to her.

Alice was all alone.

Christmas came and went with no word from Bruce. He'd run away like that before, after they buried Sonia. He'd taken all of the money out of the cookie jar Sonia had kept for emergencies and disappeared for five weeks.

Alice hadn't told anyone, afraid they'd take her away and put her in a home. If anyone asked she'd told them he was too grief-stricken to see people. And they'd believed her. Not because her lies were all that convincing, but because it was easier for them that way. Two years later he disappeared again, for three weeks, and again she told no one.

This time was different, though. He'd never left a note before. Alice sat on the floor of the living room and sobbed. She'd sold the couch, and the dining table, but it still wouldn't be enough.

All she wanted was for Bruce to walk through their door and she would run into his arms and forgive him. She wanted to fall asleep to the sound of his snoring after she tucked the blanket under his chin. She wanted him to tell her that it was going to be a good day, and she'd believe him and would hold on to hope that things would get better.

All she ever wanted was for her dad to come back to her. But she knew this time he was gone for good.

His destruction of her life was now complete. He'd taken most of her childhood, obliterated her past, and now it seemed he'd ruined her future as well. It had taken her three years to save up that money. Three years. All her hope was pinned on that escape fund, and now that hope was gone.

She stared at the letter of acceptance from the university, her result, 99.2, and the letter from the accommodation college that had arrived the day before, saying she had to pay the deposit in just over two weeks. With tears streaming down her cheeks, she tore the letters from the pinboard above her desk and ripped them into tiny pieces. She could defer for a year, sure, but a year wouldn't be nearly enough to save that kind of money again.

The phone rang. She'd stopped answering it weeks ago. Dean was asking too many questions about when she was coming down, prying too deeply into every meaning behind every word, clearly sensing something was up. How could she tell him she wasn't coming? She'd caused him so much pain already. She needed time. Time to figure out what to say to him, to brace herself for his interrogation.

And if it wasn't Dean on the line it would probably be the estate agent chasing their money. Rent was two weeks overdue. In five years she hadn't missed a payment. They would know something was up. What would she say to them?

After six sharp trills the phone fell silent and Alice ran down the hall and pulled it out of the wall. She needed time to think her way out of this mess.

She trudged through town to work. Not that there was much point anymore. But she couldn't just not turn up. She'd never missed a shift, had never even called in sick. If she didn't show, Mr Williams was likely to turn up on her doorstep and start asking questions.

She had no will left to fight her situation and time had lost all meaning as she went through the motions of her facade – no goal, no plan, no hope. Just exhaustion.

Alice would keep going to work. She would smile through her shifts, sell Sally and Sue apples, ignore Bertie's boxers, and no one would suspect anything at all. And all the while she would wrack her brain to find a solution.

Alice's fatigue was starting to overwhelm her. Every day was a slog to try to get through. At the end of a long shift just after New Year's she took some vitamins off the shop shelf. She wasn't sure how long they'd been there, but figured they couldn't hurt. She also picked up a packet of pads. She must be due soon.

Wait. She counted. No. She was past due.

Before Mr Williams returned from the back room, she grabbed a pregnancy test and hid it in her handbag.

'See you tomorrow, Alice.' He waved to her as she rushed out the door.

The next morning Alice dragged her feet through the dusty streets of Lawson's Ridge. Her shift didn't start till the afternoon, but she couldn't sit at home with her tumbling thoughts. She had to keep moving. For all her careful planning, she'd come spectacularly unstuck. First her dad, now this.

What was that line she'd read in English? 'The best laid schemes o' mice an' men.'

She bypassed Faraway Forest, the scene of the crime, and when she got to the abandoned wool shed at the edge of town she sank to the ground and leaned against the rotting wooden wall. She let out the anger, fear and shock she'd been holding back all night. She cried. She shouted incomprehensible words into the wind. Her plans were in ruins now. Now she was just like every other stupid teenage girl that didn't get out of this deadbeat town. All alone and pregnant.

As her tears subsided she remembered something her mum once said not long after her diagnosis. 'Be the architect of your own future.' Well, she refused to become another cautionary tale. There was nothing she could do about it here. Or in Cutter's Pass. She'd have to go further than that for a solution.

But the thought of getting rid of it hurt just as much. Confusion clouded her brain. What was she going to do?

Later in the dark of night Alice sat on her bedroom floor, a tiny lamp shining a small bright circle on the postcard sitting on the table in front of her; the pen in her hand poised above the white space waiting for words to flow through her hands. But the pen wouldn't move. No ideas. No words.

As the clock ticked past ten, rain began to fall. Alice pushed the blank postcard aside and plugged the phone back into the wall. There was no point putting it off. Just like ripping off a Band-Aid. Do it fast. Get it over with. A small white lie. A necessary one.

She wondered if Dean would still be up. He had told her to ring anytime on his fancy new phone. He would understand.

With shaking hands she dialled his number.

'Pond?' Dean's warm voice answered.

'How did you know it was me?' Alice fought back tears.

'I always know when it's you.'

Alice could hear the smile in his voice.

'Where have you been? I've been ringing and ringing. I was beginning to think you were avoiding me.'

The tears started to drip from Alice's cheeks. 'I've been working a lot,' she managed to say.

'What's wrong?' Dean asked.

'I . . .' Alice couldn't find the words. 'I can't . . . I don't . . .'

'What? Talk to me, Pond.'

Alice steeled herself. 'I can't come to Sydney.'

'What? Why?'

How could she tell him the truth? Her drunk of a father had run off with her money and she hadn't been smart enough to prevent it. She was stranded and broke and embarrassed to admit she'd failed. She was pregnant with his child and she didn't know what she was going to do. If she told him, he would want her to keep it. And where did that leave her? What about her future? Until she could figure that out, until she knew without doubt what she wanted to do, she had to keep it from him. He didn't need the stress of all this. A white lie to protect him.

'I didn't get in.'

'What are you talking about? You would have easily got the marks.'

'I didn't.'

'You needed ninety-seven right? What did you get?'

Damn. Alice never was good at lying. 'No. I . . . um. That's not what I meant.'

'What did you mean then?'

Alice could hear the catch in his voice.

'I mean the college.' She knew she was scrambling.

'This isn't making any sense, Pond.'

'I know. I'm sorry. I don't have anywhere to live . . .'

'What about Louise? Live with her. Or live here with me.'

If only it were that simple, she thought.

'I can try again next year.'

'This is bullshit. If you're going to lie to me at least make it plausible.'

'I'm not lying.'

'Of course you are. I know you. Something's up.'

'Please, Dean. This is hard enough as it is.'

'Hard enough for you, is it? At least have the decency to tell me the truth. I didn't think you of all people would have trouble seeing me like this, have trouble dealing with this.'

'What? No. That's not it.' Her tears were falling heavily and she couldn't stop the breaking of her voice. She was doing this all wrong.

'I can cope with the looks of pity and disgust from others. The stares that turn quickly away when they realise you see them, the downcast glances from people who don't know how to look me in the eye. But not from you.'

No. He was taking this all wrong. 'You know me better than that, Dean. I would never . . .'

'I thought that night together was special. I thought we were special.'

'It was. We are.'

'Yeah right,' he growled. 'Pity sex with a cripple. The boys in rehab warned me about that.'

'What? What are you talking about?'

'That's why you've been avoiding me.' He went on. 'You can't handle me like this.' He spat the words from his mouth.

'What? No.'

Dean's voice became so low Alice had to strain to hear. 'Clearly I'm not the complete man you want.'

'Dean, stop. Please, if you'd just listen . . . you don't under-stand . . .'

'Fine. Explain it to me then.'

Alice searched for the right words. Her mind raced, her heart pounded.

'Now's your chance, Pond.'

'It's complicated, Dean,' she whispered.

'Yeah, right. Just like the boys in rehab said. They warned me, you know. They told me how quickly their girlfriends had run when they realised what they were in for. I was such a fool to think you were different. That you'd accept me like this.'

'Dean, no. That's not . . . this isn't easy to explain . . .'

'Well, let me make it real easy for you, Pond.'

The dial tone rang loudly in Alice's ears.

'Dean?'

She rang him back straightaway. No answer.

She waited five minutes then rang again.

There was still no answer.

In the morning light Alice could see the estate agent's car out front. She wasn't surprised, though she'd been hoping it wouldn't happen.

She was out of time.

She tiptoed out the back door and through the broken slats in the fence and bolted towards Faraway Forest.

But her once safe place offered little comfort, not least because of the painful, beautiful memories it evoked. Sleep had eluded her most nights, and now exhaustion weighed down every muscle.

Alice waited in her tree till the cover of darkness made it safe to sneak back home.

Pushed under the door was an envelope, the estate agent logo emblazoned across the top in warning red. She had a week to pay the rent. With no formal lease in place for years, there was no notice period. A week to pay, or she was out.

Alice gathered her things as quickly as she could. Not that she would take much. Not that she had much to take. Some clothes shoved in with her pillow, the small amount of money she'd put away over the last few weeks, some cans and packets of food.

Out the front she made sure Gus the gnome was in position. No one would know.

She opened the garage door as quietly as she could, hoping the neighbours wouldn't hear and poke their heads through twitching curtains. Once a month Alice took the beat-up Datsun for a short run. She would check it was still going, make sure it had half a tank just in case she needed it in an emergency. This situation, Alice determined, was most definitely an emergency. The car wasn't registered or insured, but she'd never taken it outside Lawson's Ridge before so she'd always figured it didn't matter. What she would say if she got pulled over outside the town limits, she had no idea. But there wasn't time to worry about that.

She had to leave. Right away.

Nineteen

Kookaburra Creek, 2018

Sitting in front of the bank manager on Thursday afternoon in her nicest blouse, Alice imagined what being called to the principal's office must feel like. She didn't know where to look or how to sit, and she couldn't stop fidgeting with her top button.

'Well, Alice, it looks like everything is in order here. We'd be happy to lend you $350 000 – our valuation of the property and the business. How does that sound?'

'That sounds wonderful. Thank you,' she said, ignoring the wobble in her voice. She forgot where she was for a moment and ran around the desk and hugged him. 'Thank you.' It was more than she'd hoped they'd give her. Take that, Hargraves.

'Anytime. Just let us know when you need it and we'll get it organised.'

Skipping through town, Alice hadn't felt so good in days. She was going to save her café. But she wouldn't tell anyone.

Not yet. She didn't want to jinx things. She'd wait until those rotten Hargraves lowlifes came back with their asking price and then she'd smile and say, 'Thank you very much, here's your money.'

And this whole horrible nightmare would finally be over.

Alice knew that spending a Sunday at the markets in Glensdale may not have been Becca's idea of fun, but she wasn't about to let that ruin her favourite day of the month. Not after everything else that had been happening. Not after her good news. There was always something special about walking around the markets, past the fresh fruit and vegetables, the clever crafts and handmade jewellery on a bright, clear Sunday – joy, excitement, anticipation, an intoxicating combination. And she wasn't going to miss out.

She'd tried to bribe some enthusiasm out of Becca with the promise of getting her something while they were there, but Becca's lack of interest in, well, everything really, left her no leverage. The mention of the local band that played on the mound at the north end of the oval did nothing to sway her, either.

'It's not really my kind of music,' Alice said, breaking the silence on the journey over to Glensdale. 'But the teenagers really seem to enjoy it.'

Becca shrugged.

'I sounded really old just then, didn't I?'

'Just a bit.' Becca allowed herself a small laugh.

'Oh well.' Alice shrugged. 'Can't help that. If we run into Freddy, maybe you won't have to hang around an old crone like me all day.'

Becca sat up straighter. 'Freddy will be there?'

Alice nodded. 'He usually is. Nobody misses the markets.' Not Joey, not even Fiona would be absent. Unfortunately.

'You know,' Becca turned her body slightly, 'you're not *that* old.'

'Gee, thanks.' Alice felt very much older than her thirty-something years right there and then.

As they pulled up to the showground car park, Alice searched for a free spot. There was one left, beside Carson. She turned the wheel and parked.

Becca started fidgeting and shifted her body closer to Alice, further away from Carson's green ute.

'Morning, ladies.' The sergeant smiled as he spilled out of his civilian vehicle, and Alice saw Becca's tense shoulders drop.

'Morning, Carson. Lovely day for it.'

Carson tipped his imaginary hat and joined the throng of people heading into the market.

'What's wrong?' Alice asked, winding up the window.

'Nothing,' said Becca, colour slowly coming back to her cheeks.

'Becca, if you ever want to talk, I'm here. Anything at all.'

'I'm fine.'

'Come on, then. This will be fun. I promise.' Alice coaxed her out of the car and headed straight for Claudine McCreedy's cheese stall.

When Claudine had approached four of the region's farmers about producing a local specialty many years back, they were sceptical at first. No one in the greater Glensdale area had even heard of Beaufort, let alone knew how to produce it. How on earth would they be able to sell it? But they underestimated Claudine, and the fact her father had been a cheesemaker back in France. She even travelled back to her ancestral home to learn the art properly and when she returned it wasn't long before the locals embraced the smooth, creamy cheese as their own.

It probably helped that Claudine's Beaufort made the most perfect fondue and, at the beginning of each winter, just after the first market in June, the Kookaburra Creek Café played host to boisterous evening fondue gatherings. Alice still hadn't figured out how to use the creamy deliciousness in a cupcake, but she was working on it.

'Sample?' Claudine asked Becca as they stopped at her stall. But Becca didn't hear her, her eyes searching the crowd.

'There's Hattie,' Becca said, and she wandered off in the old lady's direction. Hattie happened to be speaking with one Freddy Harris and Alice saw straight through the girl's ploy.

She put a round of cheese in her carry bag and checked out the vegetables at the next stall. The asparagus had a nice snap to it. Could she use that in a salad somehow? In her mind she went through possible flavour combinations and, as she lifted her head to see if there was any inspiration randomly floating through the air, she saw Joey's stall a little further down.

It wasn't that he needed to have a stall at the markets. Everyone in a 100-kilometre radius knew his bread was the best around. But he'd started his stall all those years ago when he was trying to build up his reputation and he just never stopped coming. Alice knew he loved catching up with all his customers outside of the shop like this. Selling loaves was really just an excuse. He hadn't missed a market in twenty years. Well, he had; but just one. And it didn't really count. Nothing really counted that summer.

As always, his customers were lined up deep. Then she noticed Fiona. Standing at the front of the line, batting her ridiculously long eyelashes, her stupidly long red curls falling over her freakishly slender shoulders just so, her impossibly adorable freckled nose sparkling in the sunlight.

'Anything we need to worry about, *ma chère*?' Claudine said as she sidled up to Alice.

'What?'

'Mrs Harris is beside herself thinking her smart beauty might throw her life away on the local baker. Her words.'

'And why, Claudine, would that worry us?'

'Doesn't worry me. But I thought it might worry you.'

'Oh, please. I have bigger things to worry about than Fiona Harris's love life.' She stepped away before Claudine could say another word. Truth was, she did have bigger things to worry about. Much bigger things. But that didn't stop her sneaking a peek back over her shoulder as she walked to the back of the market stalls.

'Alice, petal? Can we talk?'

Alice spun around to the soft voice behind her. 'Oh, Hattie. I have news.'

'So do I. Shall we sit?' Hattie indicated the vacant white wicker chairs under the slender gums.

Alice had wanted to keep it a surprise, but just seeing Hattie made her desperate to spill every detail.

'You first,' she insisted. Her news would trump Hattie's – Alice felt a swell of happiness at the thought of saving the best news till last.

Friends walked past laden with trinkets, laughing, smiling. Children pulled their mother's hands, desperate to get to the popcorn tent, while their mothers tried to walk in the opposite direction towards the potted succulents or vintage clothes. Dads milled about not far from the barbecue, deep in animated conversation about the Glensdale Goannas' latest loss and slow descent down the rugby league ladder, no doubt.

'How did you go at the bank?' Hattie found her voice.

'Well, that's what I wanted to talk to you about.'

'I figured.'

Alice's smile spread across her face. She couldn't wait a moment longer. 'They're going to give me a loan.'

'That's wonderful.'

'Then why aren't you smiling? This is good news. Great news. Hattie?'

'How much?'

'Sorry?'

'How much did they say they'd give you?'

Alice looked Hattie directly in the eyes. That was not the response she was expecting. 'Harriett Brookes, what aren't you telling me?'

'I've heard from the lawyers. The Hargraves have named their price.'

'Good. Let's buy them off and be done with it then.'

'They want five fifty.'

'Ha!' How Hattie could find humour in this was charming. 'Good one. You had me going there for a minute.'

Hattie held her gaze.

'You're joking, right?'

Hattie shook her head.

Suddenly Alice felt very cold. Very cold and very weak. 'That's nearly twice as much.'

'Typical Hargraves,' Hattie spat. 'Greedy and spiteful. They know on the open market they'll get nowhere near what they're asking. It's just a ploy to get at me.'

'How can they do that? Isn't that illegal or something?'

'They can ask anything they like.'

'Why? Why do they have it in for you so bad they're happy to ruin your life and mine? What happened?'

'So many things. So long ago. And who knows what spin their mother put on it all.'

'Don't you think you owe me an explanation? I'm going to lose everything in this. Aren't I entitled to at least know why?'

'Oh my sweet girl.' Hattie took Alice's hands. 'It was such a lot of silly foolishness, really. Plus a few cruel tricks from life.'

'I know about life's cruel tricks, Hattie.' Alice's voice cracked.

'I know you do.' She patted Alice's hands. 'Just as you know when you're young you don't always know what you're doing.'

Hattie was right. Alice knew all about youthful blunders. And Hattie had loved her and accepted her through hers. The why of Hattie's past really didn't matter in the end. Besides, it wouldn't change anything now.

'Oh, Hattie.' She reached out and embraced her old friend.

Tears streamed down the crevasses in Hattie's cheeks. 'We'll figure it out, Alice. Somehow we'll find a way to fix this. We're smart women and we've been in tougher scrapes than this. You know what they say: "The show isn't over till the fat lady sings." And I don't see any portly women around here about to burst into song.'

There might not have been any fat ladies singing but Alice could hear them warming up backstage. She never thought life could be so cruel as to make her start over from scratch yet again. But apparently she was wrong. Alice didn't know if she had the strength to go through that pain once more. But she knew she had to try.

Time for plan B. Whatever that was.

Twenty

Somewhere on the Newell Highway, 2004

With every white line that blurred past her windscreen, Alice could feel her eyes getting heavier. The clock on the dashboard hadn't worked in years, but she knew she'd been driving for hours and that dawn couldn't be far away. She took the next turn off the empty highway and found a clearing to stop at. If she could just get an hour's sleep she'd be able to keep driving. She climbed into the back seat and pulled her coat tightly around her body. Staring up at the stars through the window, she searched for the Southern Cross, just like her father had taught her when she was ten. They'd been camping for her birthday and Bruce and Sonia had lain with her in the grass, naming constellations. When Alice got older she realised that 'The Tea Cup' and 'The Gnome' weren't real constellations, but it didn't matter. That night under the stars was Alice's last happy memory of her family and she'd held onto it tight.

The Southern Cross was out tonight. And The Tea Cup. Now, where was The Gnome?

The heat of the early sun streamed onto her face. Alice sat up slowly and looked outside, her arms and neck aching. The clearing looked like it may have been a park once. Alice could see where the old swing set used to be, the dips where countless pairs of feet had worn down the earth. What was once probably a sandpit now overflowed with litter. A wooden seesaw, its every splintered inch covered in graffiti, was all that was left.

Where had the children gone? Alice walked around her car stretching her legs.

An old amenities block stood forlorn behind the car park and Alice hoped it still had running water. She just needed a quick wash before she kept going. Cold water on her face, the dirt beneath her fingernails flushed away.

Just keep driving. No direction. No plan. Just drive until she ran out of petrol and wherever she ended up, she'd get a job and figure out the next move. Whatever that might be. She put a hand on her tummy.

With three deep breaths she started the engine. As she drove, she counted. One, two, three, anything to stop herself from thinking about all that had happened. Three hundred, 301, anything to avoid thinking about what would happen next. Six hundred and twenty-six, 627, anything to stop thinking.

The further she travelled, the darker the sky became. Storm clouds built until they could no longer hold their own weight and they burst open with relief.

Sleeting rain made it impossible for Alice to see where she was going. She had no idea how long she'd been driving blind for. Twenty minutes? Two hours? How long had it been since she'd been able to see more than a few metres in front of the car? Was she even still on a road?

She cursed the window above her right shoulder that wouldn't quite wind up all the way, allowing rain to blow in and soak her shirt. She had to find somewhere to stop, somewhere to shelter, even just for a little while.

Up ahead, a little to the left, her headlights caught something and Alice slowed down. Perhaps it was just lightning. She rolled slowly closer and could see what was maybe a building. She turned the wheel and felt the ground, soft and slippery, give way under her tyres. She tried to speed up and her wheels spun. She tried again. Bogged.

No lights shone through the windows, no signs of life emanated from the wooden house at all. Perhaps it was empty.

She waited in the car. Twenty minutes? Two hours? No one came. No one went. No lights turned on.

Closing her eyes she took in a deep breath. She grabbed her things and bolted through the downpour and up the few steps to the house's front door.

She knocked quietly. No answer.

She knocked loudly. No answer.

Above her head a sign creaked as it swayed on metal chains in the wind. She couldn't read it, though, in the dark. Gently she leaned on the door. If it opened by itself, then she technically wasn't breaking in. It offered some resistance and she pushed it harder. She jumped back as a bell clanged loudly. She stopped, frozen, waiting for someone to come and shoo her away, but no one did.

She shoved the door again, her heart racing as the bell sang once more. Inside there were tables and chairs arranged in groups and a counter up the back. A café? A restaurant? Maybe there was food. She could eat and rest till morning, and get out before the owners came back to open up.

Alice woke in the morning stiff and sore. Apparently the floor of a pantry in a strange kitchen was not the most comfortable place to spend the night.

Standing up, Alice tried to stretch out. Her limbs ached, her back cramped. She rubbed it gently. The shelves of the pantry weren't particularly well stocked, but there were items there she could probably use: some tinned tuna, some crackers. She shoved them into her bag. A thick layer of dust covered every surface and Alice wondered how long it had been since anyone had been in there.

Not that it mattered. The safest thing for her to do would be to leave. Without delay.

'Can I help you?' A voice startled Alice and she spun around.

An old woman stood before her, dressed in finery Alice had never seen the likes of in Lawson's Ridge. Jewels dripping from every finger, and smothering her neck a silk scarf draped just so in purple – the same colour as the stripe in her grey hair. She wore heavy make-up that stuck in her wrinkles, and looked Alice up and down with shrewd grey eyes.

'Are you here about the job?' the lady asked, her voice thick with suspicion.

Alice wondered how long the woman had been standing there; if she'd seen Alice take the food.

'Ohh . . . yes.' How else she could explain her presence?

'Fantastic. Come and sit down and we'll have a chat. I'm Harriett Brookes.' The woman extended her hand.

Alice shook it briefly. She'd have to play along. If this woman rang the police, they'd send her to a home, or a shelter, or some other horrible place.

'As you can see the place has been a bit neglected lately. My sister owns it. Had a fall, you see, and, well, she's no longer able to run the place. I thought about selling, but it didn't seem right. I know so little about running a café, so I need to put in a manager. You do have experience managing a café, don't you?'

Alice nodded, too petrified to say anything.

'Very well, then. It will be full-time. The pay is terrible, but what can you expect from such an endeavour?' She shook her head. 'I always told Genevieve this place could be a comfortable nest egg, if she'd only realise its potential. Perhaps you can help with that?'

Alice nodded.

'You don't say much, do you, petal?'

Alice shook her head.

'I'll need you to cook something for me.'

'Cook?'

'Yes. Manager is quite a loose term, really. You'll be the cook, waitress, the, well, everything. Are you all right? You're terribly white.'

'I'm fine,' Alice swallowed the lump in her throat.

'Good. Now, I'll be perfectly honest with you. No one else has applied, not even a sniff, so as long as you can throw something basic together, we can start talking details.'

Alice stared at her.

'Take these.' The old lady handed her the shopping bags she was carrying. 'I'll get myself some more and I'll be back in an hour to see what you've come up with.' The woman turned and threw her scarf over her shoulder as she walked out. 'One hour,' she turned back. 'And I'll be back.' She looked Alice in the eye.

Alice collapsed with her hands on her knees. There was no way she was going to cook for the old lady, but she'd certainly take whatever was in the bags with her.

She rummaged around the kitchen for anything else she could take. As she backed away from the pantry, the picture above the oven caught her eye. It was a photo frame of an old lady wearing a lace bonnet. The eyes looked vaguely familiar, which was ridiculous, Alice knew, and the smile reminded her of someone too. She reached up and touched the old frame and it fell off the wall, smashing to the bench below. She immediately started to clear up the shattered glass, hiding the tiny sparkly pieces beneath an old newspaper in the bin.

As Alice re-hung the picture, a piece of paper fell down from behind the frame. A recipe for chocolate fudge cupcakes. Alice looked up to the woman now back in her place on the wall and could have sworn she saw the old duck wink at her.

Yep, she'd definitely lost her mind.

Reading through the ingredients, Alice checked the bags and the pantry. It was all there. She could try it, she supposed, even though she really ought to leave. But it did look pretty easy.

She looked back to the photo and tilted her head. She supposed, at an angle, with a slight squint, the funny old lady could have looked a bit like a Spinster Sister. Sally and Sue's long-lost cousin?

'You have lost the plot totally, Alice,' she said out loud, and reached for a bowl on the shelf beside her.

The voice inside her head tried to tell her again to leave, but as Alice measured out the ingredients it fell silent. She cracked the eggs, and the birds outside causing such a racket a moment earlier stopped their bickering. She whisked the batter and the whirr of the ancient fridge faded into nothing. All there was was the round beating of the whisk and the in and out of her breath. Nothing else. Cake batter. Breathing. Silence.

'Oh good. You're still here.' The old lady, true to her word, had returned exactly one hour later. She picked up a cupcake. 'These . . . are . . . divine. If the rest of your cooking is half as good, we'll be just fine.' She extended her hand. 'What's your name?'

'Alice Pond.' Damn. She should have given a false name.

'Well, Miss Pond, you are a little younger than I was envisaging.'

'I'm eighteen.'

'Still.' She frowned. 'Oh, why not?' A large smile spread across her face, deepening the fine wrinkles around her eyes. 'I'm too old to worry about such things. If you're game, I'm game.'

Alice had a job. Not one she was capable of doing, but it was better than nothing. After Hattie – that's what the old lady had asked to be called – had left, Alice had tried to drive off, far away from there. But the engine spluttered in protest and Alice was stuck.

Beads of sweat covered her forehead as she looked around the room. Everything was white: the chairs, the tables, the counter, the walls. Small and quaint. How busy could a place like this really get? If Alice could con the people of whatever town she was in for long enough, earn some money, keep a roof over her head, she might have time to figure out her next move.

She picked up a menu from the table and read over it, wondering what she'd be expected to make. Sandwiches. She could probably manage those without too much stress. Salads, how hard could they be? Burgers, hmm; a little more difficult. Lasagne. Her chest started to tighten.

Alice moved to the kitchen and in the pantry was an old cookbook. She flicked through it and started gathering ingredients. Eggs, flour, mince, vegetables. There wasn't a lot to choose from, but she needed to teach herself how to cook, and fast.

By the time the moon had made its way across the sky Alice was covered head to toe in flour and butter and scraps of things she really didn't want to think about, but she'd done it. Well, sort of.

Of the ten menu items, she'd managed to assemble three. She lined the plates up on the bench and picked up a fork. The sauce of the penne pasta with tomato and cheese was a little runny, but it tasted okay. In fact, it tasted good and Alice finished the whole bowl. The burger was a little bland and definitely overcooked. She'd have to fix that. Not that she knew how. Her mum would've known. She really wished she hadn't ignored Sonia every time she'd tried to wrestle Alice's attention away from books to teach her to cook. Not that it was the first time she'd wished that. Every day for the first year after Sonia's death, as Bruce drank away his grief, she'd wished she knew how to make anything other than a cheese sandwich.

The last of the three dishes was shepherd's pie. Alice brought the fork up to her lips, taking in the delicious smell.

'Argh.' She spat the mince and potato onto the bench. It was the most disgusting thing she'd ever tasted. Whatever she'd done wrong, she'd done very wrong and she threw the rest of the pie in the bin. She'd have to go over that recipe again and check the ingredients.

'It's a start,' she said, looking up at the picture above the bench. 'Not a particularly brilliant start, but a start. Isn't it . . . Jill, Petunia, Mabel . . . Sylvia?' Sylvia felt right.

She arranged her pillow and blanket and bag of clothes on the floor of the pantry into something resembling a soft place to sleep and lay her head down, intent on studying some more. But, within moments, her eyes closed and the menu for the Kookaburra Creek Café slipped to the floor.

Twenty-one

Kookaburra Creek, 2018

Hattie sat on the end of her bed and sighed. It appeared they were out of options and the Hargraves were going to win. Unless she could come up with a brilliant plan.

She stared at the *My Fair Lady* poster that hung on her wall and a long-forgotten memory rushed back. She'd taken Genevieve, fourteen at the time, to her first musical way back in 1964. Oh how she'd smiled that night. They'd stayed after the show and hung around backstage waiting to catch a glimpse of the cast. When Eliza Doolittle emerged, a bandage wound tightly around her ankle, Genevieve had gasped and rushed forward to hug her.

'What happened to your ankle?' she'd asked.

'Just a mild sprain. The show must go on.'

Though she was clearly in pain, Eliza still took the time to chat with Genevieve, and Hattie never forgot that kindness.

'The show must go on,' Hattie said out loud. Her whole life had been a show. Pity it wasn't a musical, singing her way to a happy ending. If only real life worked like that. Singing your way to . . .

'That's it!' she shouted, jumping up. She threw her scarf around her neck and raced outside into the street.

The café was quiet for a change, which was good because it made keeping an eye on Freddy and Becca a lot easier. Alice was able to loiter by the tables near the deck and hear snippets of their conversation. Granted, a busy café would have made her a little less obvious, but a busy café also meant she wouldn't have the time or space to really eavesdrop properly.

They were supposed to be studying English – the literary devices employed in *Catch-22*, if she wasn't mistaken. But there didn't seem to be a lot of discussion relevant to allusion or irony or anything resembling literature at all.

A busy café would have made Joey's presence less awkward. Especially seeing as he'd brought Fiona with him. Again. She knew there weren't any other places in Kookaburra Creek that served food as good as hers, but surely they could make the short drive to Glensdale.

She didn't quite know where to look or what to say. She was happy for him, really. If this meant he'd found joy. Only thing was, it didn't look like there was much joy today. Whatever they were discussing was serious and Fiona's face was a storm cloud of unhappiness.

Alice wanted to tell Joey about Hattie and Hargraves and the café. She was hopeful he might see a solution she hadn't thought of. But Fiona was always there beside him these days, and it didn't seem right reaching out to him like that in front of her.

'Alice, is something bothering you?' he asked as she handed him two espressos.

Yes, and I could really do with your help. 'No, I'm fine.' She smiled.

He took a sip of his coffee and spat it back into the tiny cup. 'Sorry, but are you sure?' He handed Alice the cup.

'Oh. Sorry. I'll redo it.'

'Ah, just the thespians I was looking for.' Hattie burst into the café, her perfectly blow-dried hair showing off a stripe the blue of a warm summer sky.

'Oh no,' said Joey, turning around.

'Nu-uh.' Alice shook her head. Didn't Hattie have enough to worry about? Surely she could let this year's play slip. Just this once.

'Stuff 'n' nonsense.' Hattie grinned.

'Costumes.' Alice raised her left hand in offering.

'Props.' Joey put his right hand in the air.

Fiona came closer, all freckles and wide smile.

'Not this year, petals.'

Alice looked to Joey hoping he was quick enough to think of a way out for both of them.

Apparently he wasn't.

'This year we're doing things a little differently. I've been think-ing about our little situation, Alice.'

'What situation?' Joey frowned.

Hattie blurted out the truth before Alice had a chance to protest. 'The café is in jeopardy.'

'What?' He turned to Alice. 'Why didn't you tell me?'

'You've been busy.' Guilt rose in her. He had a right to know – so many of his own memories lived within these walls. 'I didn't know how.' She cast her eyes down.

'How? What's happened?'

'Those details we can fill you in on later. I have had an ingenious idea and have come up with the perfect plan. We'll start a Keep the Café Fund and, instead of doing a play, we're going to do a musical.' She threw her blue, floral scarf over her shoulder. 'If we're going to pull off this fundraising, this year will need to be our best ever show. I've managed to get that snivelling reporter Sinclair from Glensdale to cover it to increase our sales. And you'll never guess what we're doing.'

'I'm afraid to ask,' Joey murmured.

'Well? Guess.'

Neither answered.

'Okay, I'll tell you. *Anything Goes.*' Hattie clapped her hands.

'What's that got to do with us?' Joey asked.

'Too long have the two of you hidden away in backstage obscurity. But not this year. If we've got any chance of pulling this off, then I need some actual stars on stage. I simply cannot let Mrs Harris take the lead again. Not if we want people to come. No offence, Fiona. Or you, Frederick.' She turned as Freddy and Becca entered the café. 'But your mother's voice is not the instrument she believes it to be. We're all witness to that in church.'

'What's going on?' Becca whispered.

'Smile and back away.' Freddy took her hand and tried to pull her back outside.

'No way.' She grinned.

'I'll get to you two later.' Hattie waved in their direction, the sun streaming through the windows flickering off the gems covering her fingers.

'We really should go.' Freddy touched Becca's shoulder and she shrugged his hand away.

'Right now I need to secure my leads,' said Hattie. She smiled at Joey, Alice and Fiona.

'But I can't sing,' Alice protested.

'Codswallop. You're not in the same class as Betty, granted, but I have heard you enough times, especially in that kitchen of yours, and your voice is pleasant enough. And let's be honest, Betty is quite a few decades past being able to pull off Reno.'

'Reno?'

'Reno Sweeney. Surely you know the show. You're my Reno and you,' she looked at Joey, 'you are my Billy Crocker.'

Joey opened his mouth but nothing came out.

'I've heard you singing, too, in the wee hours of the morning as I pass the bakery. Gene Kelly you're certainly not, but you're not too bad. And you've got that rough around the edges charm we need.'

'Thanks.' Joey frowned.

'And the audience can just imagine you are taller than you really are.'

'Thanks again.'

'But Hattie,' Alice found her voice finally, 'I can't act.'

'Codswallop. Everyone can act. And you'll have me there to guide you.'

'But . . .'

Hattie raised her bejewelled hand. 'Time to let yourselves be guided into glory.'

'Hattie —' Joey tried to interject.

'Unless either of you has a better idea on how to raise the funds, then this is the best we've got.' She shot them both a look.

They said nothing.

'And I think you, Fiona, would make a lovely Hope Harcourt.'

'Oh, I love that musical. Thank you.'

'I'm sorry, Hattie.' Alice's voice was weak. 'But won't Mrs Harris be upset if she's not the lead?'

'Of course she will be.' Hattie tapped her foot. 'But this is for the future of the café, so she'll just have to, what do you young ones say, take one for the team and take a minor role. Something that won't stretch her acting ability too much.'

'You said everyone can act.' Alice was looking for any way out of this.

'Yes. But I didn't say everyone can act well. Sorry, young Harris offspring.'

Fiona didn't look the least perturbed that her mother was on the receiving end of Hattie's barbs. She was probably too busy imagining herself beside Joey singing romantic numbers.

'Mind you, I did think about asking Mrs Harris to play Evangeline Harcourt, you know, to keep the peace, but given the seriousness of the situation and the need to draw a significantly more sizable crowd than we've ever had before, I think,' she thrust her chest out proudly and took a deep bow, 'it's time.'

'Really?' Alice couldn't believe it. In all her time in Kookaburra Creek, Hattie had only ever directed the amateur productions, her days on stage 'in the past where they belong'. Every year someone tried to get her to take on a role. Every year she said no.

'How else do you think I got Sinclair to agree to cover the event? Even he could see the value in the headline "Australian Acting Royalty Harriett Brookes On Stage Again".'

'Please can we go?' Freddy whispered in Becca's ear.

'Are you kidding?' Becca's smile could not possibly have been any bigger. 'This is just getting good. Don't s'pose you've got any popcorn?'

Alice didn't know about popcorn, but she could have done with a shovel and some very soft ground right about then. What was Hattie thinking? And to spring it on her like this.

'Miss Hattie, I think . . .' Joey tried again to find his voice, but Hattie wasn't about to be paused.

'Sweeping changes.' Hattie twirled towards the door, parting Freddy and Becca with a determined smile. She waved her silk scarf in the air. 'All for a good cause.'

'What was that?' Becca snorted, unable to hold her laughter in.

'That was Hurricane Hattie,' Freddy snorted. 'Been dormant a while, but boy when she blows in she does it in style.'

Joey lowered himself into a chair and stared at Alice. 'So you've got some stuff to tell me, it seems.'

But Alice stood frozen. How could Hattie not have run this by her first? Not only would everyone in town now know their dirty business; not only would everyone now know how much trouble they were in; but now Becca knew too. And Hattie's idea to put Alice and Joey front and centre of this ridiculous plan was just plain . . . well, ridiculous.

Twenty-two

Kookaburra Creek, 2004

Alice hid her bedding in the back of the pantry and started cooking before seven. If she was going to make the day anything other than an utter disaster, she had to get some more practice in. She knew if she just kept the menu simple, a burger, a sandwich, the cupcakes, she might just be able to pull it off. Maybe.

At 11.30 the old brass bell rang announcing Alice's first customer. She peered over the shutters that divided the kitchen and dining room. An old man, his beard grey and un-brushed, held out a chair for an old woman. The woman was incredibly short, but she held herself with such confidence you'd be forgiven for thinking she was six foot tall. She took her seat slowly, casting her eyes around the room. A third person, considerably younger than the first two, sat with them.

'There's not much on offer.' The short woman's sharp voice carried through the near-empty room right to Alice's ears.

'*Non, non*, Betty.' The young woman's French accent was strong. 'Be nice.'

The old man grumbled. 'It'd want to be a damn sight better than that muck of a joint you took us to last week, Claudine.'

'Hattie has assured me it will be up to standard and I'll have no qualms telling her if it isn't.' Betty turned to Claudine. 'But I will give the girl a chance at least.'

Alice's knees started to buckle and she held on to the wall in order to stay upright. She looked to the back door, but her legs wouldn't move.

'If anyone takes our order,' said Betty, raising her voice.

'Well, what have we got to lose, hey?' she whispered, looking up to Sylvia staring down at her from the wall. 'Either way we're screwed, right?'

She stepped into the dining room.

'Ah, there you are.' Betty smiled, but Alice could tell it was forced.

'Good morning. I'm Alice. What can I get you today?' Alice could feel the three sets of eyes boring into her.

'Claudine will have the salad and Clive and I will try the burger. Not much else we can have really, is there?'

'I'll also have a coffee. *Merci*.' Claudine's smile was genuine.

Alice nodded. 'Won't be long.'

'I should hope not,' Betty stated, loudly enough for Alice to hear.

Alice hurried back into the kitchen. The salad was easy enough and actually looked quite pretty in the bowl. Alice had burned the first two beef patties, though, and had to throw them in the bin. The next two she managed to cook properly, but one of them fell apart and she 'glued' it back together with a little melted cheese and hid it under the tomato and lettuce that topped off the burger. She served that plate to Clive.

She waited for the echo of chairs being pushed back and angry footsteps heading to the door, but no such sound came. There was the clink of glasses and the clang of cutlery. The echo of the near-empty room ensured Alice could hear every detail of the meal she was too frightened to watch.

'Hattie's very brave to take a chance on a stranger like this. With her sister's legacy.' Alice could hear Claudine's accent clearly.

'Hattie's a sentimental old fool.' Betty, apparently, didn't like to hide her feelings. 'But this food isn't half bad.'

'What?' shouted Clive. 'Speak up, woman. You're not in church.'

Alice smiled and looked up to Sylvia, who winked, and she knew what to do next.

After clearing the table, relieved they'd eaten everything on their plates, she brought out cupcakes and placed one in front of each of them.

'We didn't order these.' Betty frowned.

'On the house.' Alice smiled. 'A thank you for being my first customers. You can take them to go, if you like.'

'Not necessary.' Betty picked up her cupcake and took a bite.

'Oh, *mon dieu*. What's in these?' Claudine asked. 'They're heaven on a plate.'

Alice smiled and left them the bill, retreating back to the kitchen.

'What did she say?' Clive shouted.

'Do turn your hearing aid up, old man,' said Betty with a sigh.

Alone in the café, Alice sat on the floor, and she stayed there for the rest of the afternoon, hoping with all her heart the brass bell wouldn't clang again.

'So.' Hattie's sharp trill made Alice turn around. The old woman was standing in front of the pantry. She must have come in the back door. Her short, grey bob was freshly blown under, a pink stripe running down the right side. Her pink and peach scarf sat open around her neck. Her face wore an expression Alice found hard to read.

'When, my dear girl, were you going to tell me that you're not just my manager, but also my tenant?'

Alice stood slowly, cursing that she hadn't hidden her stuff well enough. Her eyes darted round the room, looking for the quickest way out, if she could only get past the pantry door.

'Well?' Hattie pushed Alice's bedding forward with her foot.

Alice sighed. 'I'm sorry. I didn't mean . . . I'll pack up and I'll go.'

'Not so fast, young lady. It seems we have a situation here.'

'Please don't call the cops.' That's what people did in situations like this, right? Call the cops.

'Codswallop,' Hattie waved her hand. 'I take it you have nowhere else to go?'

'No.'

'I ran into Betty this afternoon. She enjoyed your cupcakes very much. Said she might bring a group by next week.'

Alice stood still, her heart beating fast. Afraid to speak. Afraid to move.

'You don't bring trouble with you, do you?'

'No,' Alice shook her head quickly.

'And you're definitely eighteen?'

'Yes.'

Hattie raised an eyebrow.

'Last month.'

'Then it would appear we find ourselves in the position of needing one another, Miss Pond. I require someone to get this place back up and running, and Betty can be a cantankerous old cow at times, but when she gives a compliment she means it. So, you're doing something right here. And you need . . . well, probably a whole lot more than I can give you, but let's start with this job.'

'Really?' Alice's voice was thick with tears.

'As long as you promise trouble isn't on your heels.'

'It's not.' Growing inside her belly, perhaps, but not chasing at her heels. And she still had time to figure out what she was going to do about that.

'And you simply can't keep sleeping on the pantry floor. Good God, child. What are you thinking? You'll stay with me. On a trial basis. A month or two and then we can reassess things.'

Unable to stop them, Alice let her tears fall. 'Thank you.'

'None of that nonsense. This is a business deal, pure and simple. And you've got work to do.'

Alice thought perhaps she saw the hint of a smile cross Hattie's finely lined face before she left the kitchen, but she couldn't be sure.

She wasn't sure where to start, but she knew she had to face the onerous task of teaching herself how to make a decent lasagne.

'Smells good.'

Alice turned round in the fading light to see a figure of a man standing in the evening shadows. She reached for the knife lying on the bench beside her.

'Sorry.' The man stepped forward and turned on the light. 'Miss Hattie said you might need some help. I'm Joey. Joey Moretti.' He reached out his hand.

Alice looked at his hand, held there in the air waiting for her. Joey. Joseph? Hattie had mentioned a Joseph. She took his hand and shook it. 'Nice to meet you. I'm Alice.'

'Yeah. I know who you are. The whole town knows who you are.'

Alice felt her cheeks redden.

'It's a very small town. And Betty has a very big mouth.'

'Oh God.' Alice frowned.

'No. It's a good thing. Well, at least this time it is. She's been pretty complimentary about your cupcakes. And let me tell you, if you've made her happy then you're doing something right.'

'I hope so. I don't want to let Hattie down.'

'Then you'd better let me have a look at that.' A crooked smile stretched across his face and he nodded to the slightly burnt lasagne Alice had put on the bench to cool.

'Oh. Okay. But I've never done anything like it before.'

Joey raised a forkful to his mouth, taking in the aroma before tasting. 'Not bad. Apart from taking it out five minutes too late. I'd try adding a pinch of cinnamon, though.'

'Cinnamon?'

Joey nodded. 'My Nonna's secret ingredient.'

Alice smiled. 'Okay. But if it turns out horrible, I'll be blaming you.'

'Blame away.' He bowed, lowering his head.

'Thank you, Joseph.'

'Joey, Alice. Call me Joey. Give the cinnamon a try and, if it isn't a huge success, I'll bring round one of my finest loaves to make up for it.'

'Sorry?' Alice took a step back.

'Bread. I'm the baker. Moretti's Bread House.'

Yes. That was it. Hattie had said something about *Joseph who made bread*. She was surprised, though, that this was him. So much younger than she expected. He wasn't as young as her, but young enough. Mid-twenties, she supposed, as she took in his open face, crinkles at the edges of his dark eyes, his solid frame.

'Oh. Yes.' She nodded.

'Come on, Alice. Let's clean this up and I'll walk you back to Miss Hattie's.'

'You'll what?'

'She told me, and I quote, "Check how Miss Pond is going and then bring the child home."' He flicked an imaginary scarf over his shoulders.

Alice laughed as Joey started cleaning up the bowls.

Twenty-three

Kookaburra Creek, 2018

'Harriett Brookes, I think you've gone and descended into complete madness at last.' Betty shook her head.

'It's a wild idea, *oui*, but maybe . . .' Claudine shrugged.

'Well, we have to try something.' Hattie pulled herself up to her full height. 'And in the absence of any other suggestions, then we have no choice.'

Alice had called this little meeting, assembling the key people she knew could help. They sat around the table in the centre of the café.

'Trust me,' she said. 'The thought of taking centre stage fills me with more dread than you can imagine. But if it means we keep the café, then I'll do whatever it takes.'

'Me too.' Joey nodded, despite the fear in his eyes.

'You'll never raise enough money,' Clive grumbled into his beard. He wasn't exactly invited to the meeting, but he and Betty and Claudine came as a job lot.

'That's why we're here.' Alice would not be perturbed. 'We don't need to raise the whole amount. Just the shortfall after the loan.'

'We should be able to charge more per ticket, seeing as it's Hattie's *retour triomphant*,' Claudine offered.

'Well, I'd certainly pay a premium to see her make a fool of herself,' Betty said, laughing.

'We see you do it every day and don't have to pay a cent.' Hattie smiled.

'Now ladies.' Alice knew they hadn't tipped over into dangerous territory, yet, but she wasn't about to take a chance.

'The church could put on a barbecue or something,' Freddy piped up. He and Becca had been on the bench spying on proceedings.

Joey nodded. 'Claudine and I could talk to all the foodie joints in town. Get things donated.'

'Now we're talking. Hattie, do you still have memorabilia from the olden . . . from your time in film or on stage? I know you had a photograph signed by Chips Rafferty,' suggested Alice, as the ideas bounced around inside her head.

'Of course. I have quite a few trinkets that could be of interest to collectors.'

'I like where you're going with this, girl. I've always fancied I'd be a hit with an auctioneer's gavel,' said Carson, slamming his fist on the table.

'I suppose,' Betty drew out her words slowly, 'I could persuade the council to waive their fee for hiring the hall. They do owe me a favour.'

'This might actually work,' Alice said hopefully.

'Claudine. Write this down.' Betty started dictating lists and schedules and instructions and Claudine took notes dutifully.

Alice glanced at Joey and his smile, though not completely convincing – she suspected he was having even more trouble than her
with the thought of acting in front of an audience – reassured her
enough to allow hope to creep into her heart.

The very first rehearsal of the new-look Kookaburra Creek
Amateur Dramatic Society's production of *Anything Goes* was not
at all going to plan. Whether Hattie hadn't factored in how much
turmoil changing everyone's usual role would cause, or she simply hadn't cared, Alice wasn't sure. She was sure, though, that the
poor lady was probably regretting her decision right about now.

Clive kept shouting over the clang and bang of props being
made, or possibly destroyed, backstage, wondering where he
needed to stand and why he had to be on stage anyway, because
usually he was behind the scenes, and why was Hattie insisting
he could do this acting malarkey when even a blind man could
see he couldn't?

'That staircase will need to be repainted. And that prop looks
terrible. We cannot let Hattie and Alice down.' Reverend Harris
barked orders at the backstage crew, the power of being named
stage manager apparently going to his usually mild-mannered
head. Or perhaps it was simply because he actually *was* in charge
of something for the first time in a long time. He may well have
been the reverend, but everyone knew it was really Mrs Harris that
ran his church.

And she was busy right now, loudly lamenting that she was no
longer allowed to be the star and what had she done to deserve
such harsh treatment.

Betty sat in the corner of the hall on one of the old school
chairs, crocheting a blanket in hues of purple and teal, chuckling

discreetly to herself and looking up every now and then to shake her head.

Out of habit Alice looked at Joey, whose shoulders were being squeezed by Fiona's elegant hand. He was not coping at all with his new role in the company, and everyone could see it. But he wasn't about to let anyone down.

Between crashes and clashes she could hear Becca and Freddy chatting just offstage.

'There's no way they're going to pull this off,' Becca whispered.

Alice angled herself slightly so she could hear them better.

'You don't know Hattie,' Freddy said grinning.

'Are you watching what I'm watching? I'd bet anything the whole show's a disaster.'

'What are the stakes?'

'What?' Becca asked.

'The stakes. Of the bet.'

'Name it. There's no way you'll win,' said Becca with a broad smile.

'Okay. If the show's a success, I get to take you out on a date.'

Becca's cheeks went red. Alice fought the immediate temptation to step in. She wanted to see where this went.

'Whatever.' Becca shrugged. 'It's never going to happen.'

'And if you win? Not that you will.'

'When I win you do my shifts in the café for a week.'

'That's it? I'd do that without a bet.'

Becca rubbed her ear. 'And, you have to teach me how to ride your Harley.'

Freddy seemed unmoved.

'And I get to have it for a week.'

Alice watched the colour drain from Freddy's face. He reached out and gingerly shook Becca's hand.

Tap, tap, tap.

The fractured sounds of the disgruntled company did not subside.

Thud, thud, thud.

Hattie pounded her walking stick into the wooden floor with such force that everyone stopped and looked in her direction.

The walking stick was a prop, not needed for mobility. Hattie was surprisingly spritely for her age. But every now and then she pulled out her father's antique for dramatic effect. Council meetings were definitely a favourite occasion, and any meeting with anyone from Glensdale.

The gold-tipped mahogany stick looked quite striking teamed with Hattie's deep red scarf, which had slipped from her shoulder and down her arm so it flourished whenever she moved. Alice was convinced it was no accident that Hattie let her scarf, normally so secure around her shoulders, drape like that.

'This simply isn't good enough. Do none of you understand the gravity of what's at stake?'

'Yes, Miss Hattie, but . . .'

'Uh-uh, Joseph.' Hattie tapped the stick. 'No interruptions. I will make this a success.'

Joey looked at Alice helplessly, but she had no answer. They all understood exactly what was at stake and they were doing their best. She just wasn't sure their best was enough. They weren't actors, clearly, and this kind of pressure wasn't going to help. If she could get out of this ridiculous show she would. But no other brilliant ideas had fallen into her lap and, with the Hargraves only giving them another four weeks to come up with the money, there was nothing else she could do.

'Hattie, everyone is really trying.' She glared at her old friend, hoping she would see she was overstepping the line.

'I know, I know.' Hattie nodded. 'I understand I've placed most of you in positions well beyond your comfort zone, but back when I trod the boards we were constantly pushing to do things we didn't think we could and the results were always spectacular. Trust me, petals. We can do this. For the café, for our friends, for our town.'

There were a few murmurs of agreement.

'I see potential in each of you and, if you follow me, I'll lead you to theatrical greatness.'

'I'd settle for not embarrassing myself,' Clive muttered.

'What was that?' Hattie stepped forward, leaning on the walking stick.

'Nothing.'

'I thought not. Right, then. Let's sort this debacle out and make some magic.' She spun around, making sure her scarf floated behind her.

'Clive, I need you to imagine you are back commanding your regiment.' Clive looked instantly taller.

'Claudine . . .'

Joey stepped up beside Alice. 'Do you think we can do it?' he asked.

'The fundraising? I hope so. The performance is another matter. I think if we don't give it our best, though, Hattie will use that stick for something other than emphasis.'

Joey nodded. 'You know, we could always squeeze some extra rehearsals in.'

Alice tilted her head slightly.

'I'm only thinking of our physical safety.' He nodded towards Hattie waving the walking stick in front of Sergeant Carson, who wasn't standing quite where he was supposed to be.

Alice liked it when Joey's crooked mouth turned up like that. 'We should probably concentrate on what our director wants us to do for now.'

'For now.' He winked and Fiona called him over.

He was a good man. The best. He deserved better than her. He deserved absolutely everything. Maybe Fiona could give him that.

'I said from the top, Alice. Are you paying attention?'

Alice refocused. 'Sorry, Hattie.'

Joey wagged his finger at Alice behind Hattie's back in mock chastisement and Alice struggled to supress the laughter she could feel rising in her throat. But then he focused his attention back onto Fiona as they began to run lines, and Alice sighed.

Twenty-four

Kookaburra Creek, 2004

By the end of two months' running the cafe, Alice was serving around twenty people a day. Hattie took care of getting in supplies and popped in every lunchtime to make sure things were running smoothly. Alice had finally mastered the tuna burger and was slowly coming to terms with the spinach pie. But what gave her the most pleasure, what surprised her most, was how she felt whenever she got the patty tins out. Every morning the brass bell would clang as Alice entered the café and she would go straight to the kitchen and look up at Sylvia. Sylvia would tell Alice what flavour cupcake to bake and she'd get going. Before long she would enter The Silence. For those few blissful minutes each day as she mixed her cupcakes, Alice was carefree. No stress about how well or not she was doing in the café. No worry that Hattie would discover her secret. No pressure to decide what to do before it was too late to make a decision.

At the end of each day her feet were swollen to the point of not even resembling feet anymore. Hattie would often run her a much-needed bath. The guestroom at Hattie's was small but comfortable, and every night Alice thanked the stars for Hattie's kindness.

'Today was busy,' Hattie said as they walked along the creek path on their way home.

'Yeah. Felt good, though.' Out of the fifteen lunches she'd served, she'd only burned two.

'You're doing a fine job, I have to say.' Hattie linked her arm with Alice's as they approached the white wooden bridge that led back into town. 'But how are you feeling?'

'Why?'

'I've noticed.'

'Noticed what?'

'How tired you get. And I heard you throwing up this morning. Again.'

'Must have been the leftover fish pie.' Panic filled Alice. Hattie knew.

Hattie stopped and took Alice's hands. 'Are you seriously trying to tell me you don't know what's going on?'

Alice shook her head. What would Hattie do? Throw her out?

'Is there any chance, petal, that you might be . . . well, that you might be pregnant?'

'What? No.' Alice shook her head. 'No. I'm not . . . I . . .' She looked into Hattie's grey eyes and found warmth. 'Yes.' She looked down. 'I am.'

She burst into tears.

Later that night Alice sat on the end of her bed, her thoughts messy and incoherent. Hattie hadn't said anything, just hugged her

tightly a while and then gave her some space. Alice had been waiting all evening for the woman to come back and tell her to pack
her things.

'May I come in?' Hattie pushed the door open, carrying a cup
of tea. 'I thought you could do with this.'

Why did people think tea cured everything? A broken heart?
Have some tea. Failed your exams? Have some tea. Fall off a ladder? Have some tea. You're eighteen, alone and pregnant? Have
some tea. Alice shook her head.

'There's no delicate way to ask this, but do you, well, do you
know who the father is?'

Alice nodded. It was a fair enough question, she supposed.
Hattie knew nothing of Alice's life before Kookaburra Creek.

'Do you think you should tell him?'

'No.' She shook her head. 'I'm not even sure I'm going to . . .'
Alice couldn't say the words out loud and in that moment she
knew what her decision was.

'Actually, I am. Do you want me to leave? Taking me on is one
thing. Taking on a baby isn't what you bargained for.'

Now that she knew she was keeping the baby, Hattie's answer
meant so much more.

'Not what I bargained for? I'd hazard a guess it isn't what
you bargained for, either.' Hattie looked down at Alice and
smiled. 'I've suspected for some time this might be the case. If
I was going to throw you out, I'd have done so already. You
can stay here till the baby's born and then we'll figure out what
happens next.'

Alice smiled and threw her arms around Hattie's neck.
'Thank you.'

*

Alice was grateful Hattie hadn't pressed the issue of the baby's father at any point in the last month. Grateful the woman was giving her space to think. That's all Alice had done for four weeks straight. She thought about the tiny life growing inside her, making her fatter and fatter. About how that tiny little thing would change everything.

She thought about Dean.

Alice sat by the creek under the little white bridge that crossed its width, watching the autumn leaves float on tiny ripples. It had been a long day in the café and she was exhausted. Her growing belly itched and she scratched it lightly. She wasn't sure she'd ever get used to the idea she was having a baby – four and a half months along and she still struggled with the concept. The news was out now. Everyone knew. So she needed to get used to it and quick.

'Hey, Alice. How's it going?' Joey strolled up beside her.

'Hey, Joey. Evening walk?'

He sat down next to her. 'Yep. You?'

'Just taking some time out.'

'Oh.' He got up to leave. 'Should I go?'

'No.' Alice smiled. 'The change in company will be nice.'

Joey sat back down. 'Hard day at the office?'

'Let's just say, as long as you're not planning on quoting Bible verses to me about my sins,' she rubbed her belly, 'then you'll be the best company I've had all day.'

'Mrs Harris giving you grief?'

Alice sighed. 'I get it. I'm an affront to her religious sensibilities. But if I upset her so much, can't she just not come in to the café?'

'What? And deprive herself the chance to prove her moral superiority? You've a lot to learn about the characters in this town.' He laughed and so did Alice.

'I guess so.'

'Don't let that meddling old biddy get to you. We've all been subject to her moral outrage at some point. Consider it a rite of passage.'

'Okay, I will. How long is this rite going to last?'

'Hmm.' He scratched his chin. 'Probably until the next time someone makes a moral blunder.'

'Don't suppose I can convince you to rob a bank or something? Take the heat off me?'

'Sorry, Alice. While I like to think of myself as someone who'd do just about anything for a mate, I draw the line at getting on Mrs Harris's bad side.'

Alice smiled. 'Well, then maybe you can help me with something else?'

'Anything.'

'I've heard whispers in the café that Hattie is on some sort of drive for the dramatic society?'

'Do you mean the recruitment drive?'

'Yes. That's it.'

Joey jumped up and held out his hands. 'Run, Alice.' A crooked smile spread across his face.

Alice took his hands and let him pull her up.

'Save yourself and your unborn child while you still can.'

'Surely it isn't that bad.'

'You haven't met Hurricane Hattie yet. If she's looking for new blood, no one is safe. I'll have to get in first and put my name down for props.'

'Really? There's not a hidden Hugh Jackman in there somewhere?' She poked him in the chest. 'A shorter, Italian Hugh Jackman?'

Joey dropped to one knee and sang something really loud and

really fast in Italian. It was hard to tell, with him making such a joke of it, but his voice wasn't actually that bad.

'Fine! You're off the hook. What about me?'

'Well, I've told you to run and you refuse to. So now you're on your own.'

'So, you won't rob a bank for me, and you won't save me from Hattie. What kind of a friend are you, then?'

'The type that will walk you home?' His eyes danced, his crooked smile quivered. He put his hand on his hip, inviting Alice to link her arm with his.

Together they crossed the bridge and headed into town.

'I'm glad you're not going to run,' Joey said as they walked up High Street. 'You make a pretty mean cupcake.'

'Well, seeing as this is where I ran to, I'm not sure where else I'd go.' Alice's cheeks burned as she realised what she'd said.

'What were you running from?' Joey kept his eyes forward, his voice soft and calm, and Alice felt a sudden urge to open up to him.

'My life. My dad . . . well, he was a drunk.' She'd never said those words before. 'He took off a little while back. Mum died when I was twelve. And there aren't a lot of options for a pregnant teenager where I'm from.'

'So you got the hell out of Dodge?'

'Something like that.'

'Well,' Joey stopped and turned to face her, 'in the interests of ensuring you don't have to run again, and my own selfish cup-cake addiction, I'll see if I can run interference for you with Hattie and her recruitment drive. At least for this performance season, anyway.'

Alice laughed. 'See. I knew there was a chivalrous soul in there somewhere. Now, about that bank heist . . .'

'Will you bring me cupcakes when I'm locked up in the slammer?'

'Of course.'

Joey put his arm around her shoulder and they continued up the road. 'Then you might just have a deal.'

Twenty-five

Balmain, 2004

After three hours on the road Alice drove into Sydney. This wasn't how she'd always imagined her first trip to the city would be, but little about her life right now was as she'd imagined. She still wasn't convinced it was a good idea, but Hattie hadn't exactly given her a choice.

'Morning, petal.' She'd given Alice a hug. 'Should be a slow day today.'

Alice had nodded. The Glensdale Winter Show meant most of her regulars wouldn't be in.

'I believe I can handle things here. If you had something else to attend to.' Hattie let the words linger a moment. 'It's a lovely day for a long drive, don't you think?'

'Hattie, no. I can't go to Sydney.'

'Why not? If you leave by lunch, you'll make it before rush

hour. It's time.' Hattie had handed her an envelope of money. 'For petrol. If you decide to go, that is.'

Alice pulled into the narrow street and manoeuvred her car into a park a few doors down from his address. She waited, trying to summon the courage to step out of the car.

The door to Dean's house opened.

She lifted the lock on the driver's door and pulled the handle just as Dean wheeled out of his house. His hair was long, tucked behind his ears. His cheeks were plump, his eyes hard. Her heart started racing. There it was, right in front of her. Her future.

But she couldn't get out of the car. She couldn't move.

Dean's eyes softened, ever so slightly, as a girl stepped out on the landing beside him, pushing the chair. Louise? What was she doing there?

Alice watched in shock as Louise bent down and kissed Dean. Not on his cheek, but on his lips. A long and slow kiss.

Together they moved down the path, Louise's hand gently resting on Dean's shoulder. Alice couldn't believe what she saw. Eventually they vanished from sight, disappearing into the long afternoon shadows.

Alice opened the door just in time to vomit into the street. She wiped her mouth and stared ahead, tears soaking her cheeks. How could he do this to her? With Louise? How could he not know she'd find her way back to him?

Alice's head was a mess of confusion. She knew she should drive after him. Demand an explanation. But who was she to make demands? She was six months pregnant with his baby and she'd never told him. She was in no position to make a claim. But, a little voice inside suggested, if she told him surely he'd come back to her. Or would he be furious? He was with someone else now, after all. He had moved on so quickly. Maybe he never really loved her in the first place. Maybe he would reject both Alice and his baby.

She sat, one hand on the steering wheel, one across her stomach, her eyes looking ahead but not seeing.

'You okay, love?' An old man tapped on her window and Alice turned to look at him. 'Do you need help?' he shouted.

Alice blinked. She nodded and started the engine. And then she pulled away from the curb. She pressed down on the accelerator and drove.

The traffic on the main roads was thick and she surrendered to the pulse of the cars around her, following whichever vehicle was in front of her. The blue hatchback turned left, so she turned left. The red sedan merged right, so she merged right. The roads straightened and the traffic thinned. Street lights flashed by her windscreen less frequently.

In the distance a low rolling rumble. Alice pushed her foot deeper onto the accelerator, following the sound of thunder.

Twenty-six

Kookaburra Creek, 2018

'Joey? I'm surprised to see you here,' Alice said as Joey entered the café at lunchtime. No Fiona. She smiled, but Joey didn't smile back.

'What's wrong?' Her heart start beating faster, and not in a good way.

'It's Hattie. She's had a fall.'

Alice dropped the coffee cups she was holding and they smashed as they hit the floor.

'She's been taken to Glensdale. I'll help out here with Becca. You go.'

Alice looked at Becca, who'd just taken an order from Betty and her crew.

'We'll be fine,' said Becca.

Alice made for the door, but Joey grabbed her wrist. 'She's a fighter – try not to worry.'

She nodded and ran out, the bell to the Kookaburra Creek Café ringing loudly as she left.

When she got to the hospital reception desk she asked the nurse where Hattie was and let out an audible sigh when the young woman told her Hattie was in room 203. If she had been seriously hurt they would've flown her to Sydney.

Even before she saw the number on the door, she knew she'd reached Hattie's room. The doctor was cowering outside the door, pale-faced and hands shaking. A smile spread across her face as she approached.

'Are you sure you want to go in there?' the doctor asked.

Alice glanced at his name tag. 'Don't worry, Dr Kumar. She's a softie underneath,' she said, still grinning, but Dr Kumar didn't look the least bit convinced. Alice leaned in and whispered, 'Peanut brittle is her weakness.'

'Right, then.'

'How's she doing?'

'For a woman her age, well, she's lucky she didn't do more damage. I'd say, given how bossy she's being, she's in more pain than she's letting on.'

'Maybe.' Alice smiled. 'Though bossy is her natural state.'

'What about rude? Is she normally rude?'

Alice frowned. 'No.'

'I've tried to give her something stronger for the pain, but she's insisting she doesn't need it. Maybe you can talk to her.'

'I'll try.'

Dr Kumar nodded and headed off in the direction of the Pink Lady gift shop at the entrance, which sold newspapers, crossword books, stuffed toys and delicious homemade peanut brittle.

'I hope you're not doing this just for attention,' Alice said loudly, entering the room. She stopped suddenly when she saw Hattie lying in bed.

Her face was devoid of any colour at all and Alice had to blink several times to convince herself that what she was looking at was, in fact, real. There was a tube in Hattie's nose and her left shoulder, exposed by the less than adequate hospital gown, showed blood and extensive bruising.

'Stop staring, Alice Pond, and come closer so I don't have to shout.' Though she was clearly trying to muster her usual force, Hattie was in a weakened state, and it shocked Alice.

'That's better,' Hattie said when Alice reached her bedside. 'Grab that pen and paper,' she grimaced, pointing to the small table next to the bed. 'I need you to take care of some things for the show.'

'Forget the show.'

'I'll do no such thing. This is far too important to let a silly little thing like a fall get in the way.'

Alice stepped closer, ignoring Hattie's glare.

'What are you doing, child?'

Alice smiled. 'I'm checking on my friend.'

'Nonsense. I'm perfectly fine.'

Taking Hattie's hand gently, Alice could see her fight back tears. 'So,' she said, 'I guess you'll be needing that walking stick for something other than scaring the rest of us now.'

Hattie chuckled softly.

'What have the doctors said?' Alice wasn't sure Hattie would tell her the truth.

'They said I'm a silly old cow who shouldn't be trying to hang a new lampshade from the ceiling on my own.'

'Hattie, you didn't!'

'Of course I did. When have I ever needed any help with anything?'

'But Hattie . . .'

'Don't "but Hattie" me. All this fuss and nonsense. I fell. They're
patching me up. No permanent damage. Except perhaps to my pride.'

'No permanent damage?'

Hattie shook her head. 'Arm's bruised, but that will recover.
The leg will take a bit longer to heal,' she rubbed her left leg softly.
'Takes more than a fall to keep this old girl down.'

Alice smiled. Despite Hattie's best efforts, Alice could see through
her bravado plain as day. It was in her eyes: Hattie was scared. And
it wasn't just the fall. Genevieve had only been in her fifties when she
fell all those years ago and she'd never recovered properly. Before she
was sixty she was in Kookaburra Cottage. By sixty-five, her mind
was almost completely gone. Hattie was about to turn seventy-six –
surely thoughts of her younger sister were foremost in her mind.

'What can I do for you, Hattie?' Alice knew the best way to
help would be to keep Hattie focused on the practical tasks.

'Well,' Hattie began. 'We must forge ahead. No time to waste.
The show must go on.'

By the time Alice got back to the café, Becca had closed up and the
lights were off. On the little wooden jetty sat a familiar figure and
his dog; a sight that offered Alice some relief.

'You still here?' she asked as she sat beside Joey.

Shadow pushed his snout under her arm, but she ignored the
old dog.

'Wait,' Joey commanded, and Shadow limped to the end of
the jetty and sat.

'How is she?' Joey asked, his brow furrowed.

'Bossing the staff around.' Alice smiled.

'That's a good sign.'

'She's pretty beat up, but looks like she'll be all right.' Alice's voice began to crack. 'You know how tough she —'

Joey put his arm around Alice's shoulder as she broke off. He held her tightly to him, stroking the back of her head.

'Just the thought of anything happening to her.' Alice looked up into his eyes.

'I know.' He squeezed her. 'I know. But a fall isn't going to stop that woman.'

Alice lay her head on his shoulder. Her one constant rock, through all these years. She breathed in his smell of bread and sweat, felt the comfort of his embrace.

'Are *you* okay?'

Alice nodded.

'I'd better go,' he said, gently releasing his hold. 'Early start.' He helped Alice to her feet.

'Thank you,' she whispered, placing her hand on his chest.

Joey stepped back. 'I'll check in with her tomorrow.'

'Sure.' Alice nodded and he started to leave. 'Joey?'

He stopped and turned.

'I don't like to ask, but I think maybe I need your help.'

'I don't think you've ever come straight out and asked for my help before. Must be serious.'

'Not serious. But important.'

'Anything.'

'It's to do with the show.'

'Oh. In that case, almost anything.' He flashed his crooked smile.

'Hattie swears she'll be fine for the performance, but we've only got two weeks left. We have to keep up the rehearsals, and I don't know if I can do it on my own.'

Joey stepped forward. 'You don't have to do it on your own, Alice. You don't have to do anything on your own. You have the whole town behind you.'

Alice nodded.

'And you have me. Whatever it takes. Whatever you need. You've always got me.'

'Thank you.'

Problem was, that wasn't quite true. She didn't have him. Sure, he'd help with the show and probably anything else she asked. But Alice had seen with her own eyes how close he and Fiona had become.

She watched him walk along the edge of the creek, his broad silhouette melting into the night with each long stride.

All these years he'd been there for her, through joy and pain. All those chances they'd had that she was too scared to take. Too wounded to take. And now with the plight of the café, Hattie's fall, Becca depending on her, and all their history weighing on her, her life was thrust sharply into perspective.

Alice finally understood just how much she wanted to be with Joey, and it was too late.

Twenty-seven

Kookaburra Creek, 2004

Alice doubled over in pain, clutching her belly.

'Alice, what's the matter?'

'Oh . . . my . . . argh.' The pain passed and she stood upright again to see Hattie smiling. 'What?' she managed to ask between deep breaths.

Hattie pointed to the puddle of water Alice was standing in.

'It's time.' Hattie's grin widened.

'Time? What? No, it's not. I've still got . . . but.'

'My dear girl. Babies have a habit of coming when they're good and ready, not when it suits us. It would appear this little one is good and ready.'

'Now?'

'Yes. Let's get you over to Glensdale, shall we?'

'But I'm not . . . but . . .'

*

Alice screamed. It was like someone was cutting her open from inside.

'Breathe.' A voice floated to her from somewhere across the room.

'I am breathing! What do you think I'm doing?'

The pain, if it could even be called that, surely there was a stronger word. Yes. Torture. The abject torture subsided and Alice threw her head back on the pillow.

'Sorry,' she said through sobs, looking at the poor midwife she'd yelled at.

'Think nothing of it,' said the midwife. 'We've seen and heard it all before.'

'How much longer?' Alice sighed.

'We're well on our way now. In fact, I think I'll go grab the doctor.'

'I can't do this.' Alice turned to Hattie, who hadn't let go of her hand since she was admitted, no matter how hard Alice squeezed it.

'Yes, you can. You've done a sterling job so far and we're almost there.'

'I can't.' Alice's tears welled up again.

'You can. We'll all be here to help you.'

Alice looked into Hattie's grey eyes. Thank God she had Hattie.

'I think it's probably time we pushed,' the doctor said, entering the room.

'We?' Alice found the particular pronoun used amusing.

'We.' Hattie squeezed her hand.

'One more push,' Alice heard someone say, but she couldn't. No more. She'd had enough. It was three in the morning and the darn baby could stay right where it was. She didn't care. In fact, she couldn't care less if the earth opened up and swallowed her whole right then and there. She wished it would. Then it would all be over.

'Miss Pond?'

Alice closed her eyes, hoping they would all disappear.

'Alice. One more push and your beautiful baby will be here.'

No. Not today, Alice decided. She forced her mind out of the hospital and let it float back to her ironbark. She just wanted to sit in its branches and rest. Maybe come back tomorrow and finish this off. Maybe.

Hattie squeezed Alice's hand. 'Come on now, petal. Last one.'

Alice felt a surge she couldn't ignore and opened her eyes. She looked at Hattie and she bore down. She pushed harder than she ever knew was possible.

Then she heard it: cries coming from the end of the bed.

'Congratulations, Alice. It's a girl.'

It felt like forever before they put her baby in her arms and yet when they did it was far too soon. She wasn't ready for this. For this tiny little life. How could something so small cause so much pain? And what was she supposed to do with it now?

She held her baby in her arms, looking down at the strange creature.

'Oh, she's adorable,' Hattie cooed. 'Do you have a name picked out? I hear Harriett is becoming popular again.'

That was the one part of this whole mess Alice was certain about. She'd known from the day she found out she was pregnant what she'd call her baby if it was a girl. The name her mum had always loved. She'd wanted to give the name to Alice but Bruce didn't like it and had said no.

'You'll always be my Tammy Tadpole,' Sonia would say as she kissed her goodnight.

Alice ran her finger gently over the baby's forehead.

'Tammy Sonia Pond,' she said.

'Beautiful.' Hattie sighed. 'Welcome to the world, Tammy.'

Alice walked back to her room from the bathroom with the help of the midwife.

'Thank you,' she murmured as the midwife left the room.

Alice stood in the doorway watching as Hattie sang quietly, rocking Tammy in her arms, a sense of dread rising in her as she looked on. What did she know about raising a child? What if Tammy got sick and Alice didn't know what to do? What if she stuck a pencil up her nose? What if Alice couldn't get her to sleep at night? How did you teach a child to walk? What if she couldn't cope on her own? She'd never missed her mother so much in all her life. What if Hattie decided to kick them out? Where would she go? What would she do? Oh, Lord. What if she was a terrible mum? She knew nothing about kids. What if she turned out just like her dad?

Alice felt a sudden urge to run – to sneak out of the hospital and get as far away from Glensdale and Kookaburra Creek as she could and just keep running. Hattie would look after Tammy and do a much better job than she possibly could, she was sure. She started to retreat from the doorway.

Hattie turned around. 'You're back.' She stepped forward and put Tammy into Alice's arms. 'Are you all right?'

Alice looked down at Tammy, her arms shaking. The little girl looked around with wide eyes, as though she were searching for something just beyond her comprehension. Then she looked at Alice directly with eyes that seemed to see into her heart, which Alice knew was ludicrous. She'd read cover to cover the baby book

Betty had not-so-subtly left on the café counter for her. And she knew it was impossible. But here was Tammy, looking at her, staring at her, asking her to be her mum.

Tears fell down Alice's face. 'I'm fine.' She held Tammy tight to her chest.

It had been a good first week back at work; busy, but not stressful, thankfully. Betty had brought her lawn bowls crew by again, and each of the old women had cooed over Tammy, giving Alice hope that her baby girl would be accepted here. Joey brought fresh bread round every morning and Hattie helped her clean up each night.

With her back against the tall, white post at the end of the jetty behind the café, Alice sang quietly while Tammy slept beside her. As she sang the lullaby her mum used to sing to her, she looked down at the piece of paper in her hands. The folds in the paper were ingrained with dirt and worn through in the corners. How many times these past few months had she taken it out and stared at Dean's phone number? But he'd made his choice and it wasn't her.

The lyrics of 'Hushabye Mountain' floated on the soft night breeze as she looked at her sweet girl, wondering what would be in store for her. Was it fair to bring her up without a father? Would Dean even accept his baby if she told him?

'You have a beautiful voice.'

Hattie's interruption made Alice jump and she looked up.

The old woman lowered herself beside Alice with a groan. 'It's not my place to say anything, but do you think, perhaps, you should try again?' She cast her eyes down to the paper still in Alice's hand.

'The song?' Alice tried to hide the note.

'Please, my girl. I'm old, not stupid.'

Alice sighed. 'He made his choice.'

'But without some rather vital information.' She shook her head. 'I'm not here to judge, but you've been holding on to that piece of paper for a rather long time. Ever since we met, in fact. So perhaps you need to tell him for your own sake.'

Alice stared at her with wide eyes. 'You saw?'

'Don't look so surprised. These old peepers don't miss much. You were hanging on to that like your life depended on it when I found you in my pantry. You looked so scared that morning.'

'I was.'

'You know, I was going to sell this place off before you arrived. But, when I saw you raiding the shelves like that, I came up with a better plan.'

'There was no job?'

Hattie smiled.

'How did you know it would work out?'

'I didn't.' She shrugged. 'I actually thought you'd run off that morning. But what a good hunch it turned out to be. Now, clearly Tammy's father isn't quite out of your mind, so do you think maybe you should try to talk to him again?'

Alice let her tears fall. 'Oh, Hattie.'

The old woman put her arm around Alice's shoulder. 'Maybe he'll understand. If you give him a chance.'

'He's already moved on. What's the point now?'

'She's the point.' Hattie nodded to Tammy. 'But so are you. Maybe if you tell him and the boy's fool enough not to see the light, then you can move on and get rid of that dirty scrap of paper, if nothing else.'

Tammy woke and gave a contented gurgle. Alice picked her up.

Would Dean understand that Alice had had his child without telling him? Tammy wriggled in her arms. Perhaps he could forgive her for that. Tammy's tiny nose twitched. Perhaps.

'I'll leave you to it.' Hattie stood up, squeezing Alice's shoulder before she left.

In the dark of night while Tammy slept, Alice pulled out the last blank postcard from Lawson's Ridge.

'Dear Dean,' she began. 'This news will no doubt come as a shock to you, but I can't keep it from you any longer.'

With each word written a shooting pain coursed through Alice's chest.

I know you're with Louise now and I hope you're happy. I really do. You deserve it.' Alice pulled a piece of paper out of her notebook and continued. 'But you also deserve to know that you are a dad. We have a beautiful little girl. Her name is Tammy. She has your smile. And your eyes.

'I'm sorry I didn't tell you. I don't expect anything from you. That wouldn't be fair. I just thought you deserved to know. My address is here if you want to be part of Tammy's life. All you have to do is write back. But only if you want to. I will understand if you decide not to respond. I really am sorry. Alice.'

Alice signed the letter, leaving Hattie's address and phone number at the bottom of the page. She wiped the tears from her eyes and sealed the envelope. She'd send it in the morning and then she'd wait.

Twenty-eight

Kookaburra Creek, 2018

'Joseph Moretti, what are you doing here? We're about to close,' Alice said as she put the last of the chairs on top of the tables.

'Thought it might be good to rehearse that rotten "The Top" number. Now that Hattie's out of hospital, no one is safe. Maybe we can get in a bit of practice without the threat of a certain cane tapping at our heels. What do you say?'

Alice was starting to have nightmares about that infernal walking stick of Hattie's. Alice ran the first two weeks of rehearsals, but this third week with Hattie back in charge had been intense. And Alice and Joey still hadn't managed a clean run-through of that particular number.

'I don't suppose it will do us any harm,' she said at last.

Joey chuckled. 'We couldn't really get worse.'

'Speak for yourself.' Alice did a twirl and almost fell over.

'Ahem. Just let me finish this up,' she moved the mop and bucket into position, 'and we can get started.'

'Let me help.' Joey reached out and took the mop, brushing Alice's fingers. A bolt of energy shot through her and she quickly stepped away. Alice had no right to feel this way about Joey. He was with Fiona now. She busied herself with the last of the washed cutlery.

Joey put the music in the stereo and Alice stood in the middle of the deck, trying to remember the intricate steps. And the words. And how the two went together.

'Shall we start from the top?' He stepped up and took her hands. 'No pun intended.'

'Good a place as any.' Alice shrugged.

They began quite well. Better than they ever had, in fact. But half-way through Joey lost his timing and stepped right instead of left. They crashed into each other, and went down, crashing onto the deck.

'That didn't quite go according to plan,' Joey said. He reached out a hand to help Alice up. Her legs were splayed, and her back-side was stinging.

'That's going to bruise,' Alice said with a laugh as he lifted her to standing.

'I'm so sorry,' said Joey, not letting go of her hand.

'It was my fault as much as yours,' she smiled, 'but we are definitely not *the top*.'

Joey raised a hand to her cheek, brushing aside her hair. 'How are you doing really? With all this café business?'

Alice sighed. 'If I lose this place, I don't know what I'll do.' Her shoulders slumped, she looked at the deck.

'We'll figure it out,' Joey said, lifting her chin with his hand. 'You'll be okay.' He stared into her eyes.

He leaned in close, his lips almost touching hers. How easy it would be to stay in his arms.

'Joey?'

'Yes?' He breathed heavily.

The weight of their past hung between them.

'Alice?' He cradled her cheek in his hand.

'There's something I need to say,' she whispered.

'What's that?'

'I'm sorry.'

'For what?' He frowned.

For everything I've ever put you through. So many words she wanted to say yet none of them seemed adequate. He was in a good place now. She had to let him go.

'Alice?' His eyes bore into her, waiting, searching.

Alice shook her head and closed her eyes. She stepped back. 'I'm sorry.'

Joey's hand fell from her cheek. He took half a step forward, then moved back. 'I'm sorry too.' He turned and strode across the grass clearing.

Alice let out a long sigh, her shoulders dropping, and she leaned against the wooden railing surrounding the deck.

'Don't you like him?' Becca asked softly, coming out of the café.

'Yes,' Alice nodded, 'I like him a lot. He's one of the best men I've ever known. *The* best.'

'So,' Becca jumped up and sat on the railing, 'what's the problem?'

'Fiona Harris, for a start.'

'And?'

'Isn't that enough?'

'Nope.' Becca shook her head.

'And a whole lot of history, I guess.' Becca was too young to understand.

'You know there's nothing in it, right?'

'In what?'

'This thing with Fiona.'

'What?' Alice frowned.

'I know what you're thinking. While you've been stuffing about trying to decide how you feel, Fiona's swooped in and stolen your man.'

'He's not my man.'

'But you wish he was.'

Becca was sharper than she gave her credit for on matters of love, not that Alice was going to admit that. 'Now you're just making things up,' she said.

'I don't think so. And I see the way he looks at you.'

'I think Cupid's arrow must have struck you right in the eye, Miss Giggling-in-the-corner-all-night-with-Freddy-Harris. Don't think I didn't see you.'

A mischievous expression crossed Becca's face. She jumped down from the railing and threaded her arm through Alice's, leading her down the deck stairs to the creek. Alice loved these walks they took together at the end of the day. They reminded her of the strolls she used to take with Hattie when she first arrived in Kookaburra Creek. Funny how life moved in circles like that – her turn now to offer comfort and shelter to a scared lonely girl.

'Don't try to make this about me,' Becca said. 'This is about you two old folks sorting your stuff out, and stop pretending you're not into each other.'

Alice opened her mouth, but no words came out.

'Personally I don't think he's all that special, but he's totally into you. And he's fine, I suppose, as far as old men go. And, let's face it, it's not like this town is drowning in hot bachelors.'

Alice had to hand it to her. Becca certainly did have a unique way of looking at things.

As the sun began to set, Alice and Becca wound their way through town. They stopped by the white bench in Dandelion Dell. Sitting down, Alice pulled two cupcakes out of her bag and Becca handed Alice the thermos of tea.

'Ladies,' came a voice from behind them. They turned around and saw Sergeant Carson waving to them from his green ute.

Alice waved back. 'Looking forward to rehearsal tomorrow?' she called.

'Absolutely.' He saluted and drove on.

Becca let out an audible sigh.

'He's one of the good ones, you know. No finer country cop than Bob Carson. A good mate, too,' Alice said.

'It's not him.' Becca shrugged. 'It's his car.'

'His car?'

'It's the same.'

'The same as what?'

Alice waited for her to continue.

'Same as his. My mum's boyfriend.'

'Did he hurt you?'

Becca stared into the distance.

'It's okay, Becca. You can tell me.'

'He . . . he hit me.' Becca shrugged. 'A lot. Once Gran died there was no one to protect me.'

Alice reached out and squeezed Becca's hand and the girl didn't pull away.

'And . . .' Becca looked up with desperate blue eyes, scared blue eyes. A look so familiar to Alice a wave of grief hit her.

'You're safe here, Becca. You can tell me anything.'

'But you'll think I'm . . .'

'I'll think you're a brave young woman who's carried this burden alone long enough.'

'And he . . . he touched . . . he made me . . .' Tears broke through Becca's defences. 'The first time was in his green ute.'

'Oh, sweetheart.' Alice took her in her arms and Becca sobbed into her shoulder. 'It's okay,' she whispered. Her own problems faded into insignificance. 'He won't find you here.'

'And if he does?' Becca wept.

'He won't. But if he does, we'll protect you. All of us. You're family, Becca, and in Kookaburra Creek nothing means more.'

Through sniffles Becca nodded. They sat there till dusk turned to night, then Alice suggested they head back.

I'm running.

As fast as I can, but it isn't enough. I'm screaming, but nobody hears. He's behind me. He's in front of me. He's on top of me. He's yelling. I'm screaming. He's sniggering.

He slaps my face and strokes my breast. He punches my stomach.

I run.

He catches me.

I scream. He smacks his lips together. I run.

It's dark. I can hear him breathing, all around me. I can smell his cheap cologne. A bright light. A pain in my head.

He stands below my window, outside the café, looking up. I hide behind the curtain, but he sees me.

I scream.

'It's okay.'

A voice.

'You're safe,' I hear again. It's Alice's voice.

'It was just a dream.'

I open my eyes. She's holding me.

'Shh. It's just a dream. You're okay.'

Alice wipes the hair from my brow. I'm dripping with sweat.

'He's here,' I spit at her.

'No one's here,' she says.

'He was here.'

She holds me tight. 'It's just you and me.'

'He found me.' I'm sobbing.

'Shh. It's all right. He won't find you here.'

She rubs my back.

'Out the window. Look,' I shout.

She stands to look, but I can't let her go. Together we walk to the window.

'There's no one there.'

I feel dizzy. My legs give way.

Alice helps me back to bed. She lays beside me, stroking my hair. My breathing slows.

She stays. One hour turns into two, but she doesn't leave my side.

Twenty-nine

Kookaburra Creek, 2005

In the kitchen of the Kookaburra Creek Café Alice scrubbed the pots and pans she'd put off washing the day before and cleaned out the pantry. She wrote a list of ingredients and supplies she needed. The sugar was running very low, and she'd need to top up her herbs and spices soon. She threw out the empty rice sacks and wiped down the shelves. She moved the spare flour canister to behind the larger main container, checking that the zip-lock bag of money was still safely hidden inside.

After all the cleaning was done Alice drank a cold glass of water and looked round the kitchen. It wasn't easy running the café now that she'd built a bit of a reputation. And with Tammy underfoot and into everything, it wasn't getting easier. Not that she was complaining. She'd never complain. She knew how lucky she was.

The roster Betty had come up with was certainly helping. These rare moments without Tammy were a godsend when it came to getting work done. She couldn't believe how willing everyone was to chip in and look after Tammy for her. Joey took her Monday afternoons, Claudine and Hattie alternated Wednesdays, even Clive took a turn every now and then for an hour or so when Betty had an errand to run on her rostered Sunday afternoons.

What could she prepare for tomorrow? Mondays always brought Mrs Harris's church group and that meant burgers, salads and cupcakes. The bus that ran from Glensdale to Sydney had had a timetable change and would be stopping for morning tea too, so that meant even more cupcakes. There wouldn't be enough time in the morning to bake them all.

She looked to Sylvia.

Rocky road cupcakes.

Alice mixed the marshmallows, shredded coconut and cashew nuts into the chocolate-cake batter as she hummed quietly. She soaked the raspberries in sugar so the coulis would be ready to add to the chocolate frosting. At least she'd be half a step ahead in the morning instead of three steps behind like she normally was.

With aching feet at the end of the day, Alice made her way to Hattie's and went into the guest room. She quickly changed, put on a load of washing before going to pick up her girl. All along the wall of the hallway were photos of Tammy. Hattie loved her as if she were her own granddaughter.

She touched the last photo on the landing. The one with Tammy sitting in the dandelions by the creek. It was her favourite picture – Tammy dressed in her pretty white dress, the dimple in her left cheek deep with joy, her eyes so blue it looked as if they'd been painted in. It wasn't always easy, seeing so much of Dean in her, but she managed to push aside foolish thoughts most of the time. Except when he visited her dreams. Thankfully that was happening less and less.

Alice walked into her room and looked at the mail on her small desk. All bills from various suppliers – the usual suspects. She thumbed through them again. It was silly, she knew, to think maybe she'd missed something, that a letter might have got caught behind another, or had slipped to the floor unnoticed and would somehow reveal itself now. Yet, she still held foolish hope. Even after all this time.

She sat on her bed. Deep down she knew it, even if she didn't want to admit it. He wasn't going to respond. Dean had made his choice.

Alice put the letters down.

October, 2006

Somehow Alice had made a life for herself and Tammy in Kookaburra Creek. Of all the places to end up. She'd never imagined her life like this, but the years passed by and here she was, running a successful café with Tammy having just turned two.

'Good morning.' Hattie greeted her with a cup of tea in bed and a thick envelope.

'What's this?' Alice's eyes widened.

'Look inside.'

Alice peeled the flap open frantically, her hands shaking more violently as she read the opening words on the paper inside.

'I don't . . . you can't . . . I don't understand.' She stared at Hattie, her bottom lip quivering.

'Now, petal, don't go getting emotional over nothing. This is strictly a business deal. I can't afford to have you running off to greener pastures when some big-city headhunter comes calling for your cupcakes, and I can't afford to pay you any more than I already do. So this is the perfect solution, wouldn't you agree?'

'You're giving me the café?'

'Not giving. Leasing. At a much reduced rate, granted, but if you read the paperwork you'll see there are quite strict terms and conditions. Profit margins have to be met and the like. And you're free to decorate as you see fit, change the menu, run the place as you like. But any ideas about changing it into a massage parlour or such, and I'll have none of it. Now, keep reading.'

Alice read the whole thing over three times.

'And you're giving me the apartment, too?'

'All part of the lease deal.'

'It's too much.'

'Codswallop. You need your own space. Not much fun living with an old codger like me. It makes sense for you to live in the apartment above the café. That way, you can bake all night and quite literally fall straight into bed. Well, you have to make it up the stairs first. A pain when it rains, but you'll mana—'

'Oh, Hattie.' Alice embraced the old woman. She had her very own business. 'Thank you so much.'

'Stop that nonsense, or I'll change my mind.' Hattie chuckled and hugged her tightly.

August, 2007

It was funny how life sometimes made decisions for you. Alice often stood in the dining room of the café, still not quite believing it was hers. She kept expecting to wake up and find it all a dream. But it was real. She now had a secure future for her daughter, for herself. Which was so much more than she'd hoped for in recent years.

Betty had convinced her to go to TAFE in Glensdale and do a business course and she was loving it – learning all about the ins and outs of proper bookkeeping and tax practices. Maybe one day she'd even do the marketing course they ran. Not that the Kookaburra Creek Café needed marketing. It was successful enough without it. But it sounded like it might be fun.

'Mummy bake.' Tammy tugged on Alice's apron strings, staring up at her with big blue eyes. Sometimes she looked so much like Dean.

'Sure, sweetie.'

In the kitchen Alice got the ingredients and utensils ready.

'I want to scoop.' Tammy held out her hand, stopping Alice from measuring the sugar.

'Okay. This is how we do a Tammy scoop.' She showed her how to level off the cup measure.

Tammy licked her fingers and smiled. 'Del-i-soso.'

'Del-i-soso?'

Tammy nodded and they baked a dozen chocolate fudge cupcakes.

While Tammy sat under the bench colouring with her crayons, Alice tidied up.

The doorbell to the café jangled and Alice sighed, wondering who it could possibly be.

'Jo-jo, Jo-jo,' Tammy squealed and jumped up, running into the dining room.

'He's not due back for a few days, sweetie.' Alice followed Tammy out.

'How's my favourite girl?' Joey asked as he picked Tammy up and spun her round. 'My, you've got big.'

'Jo-jo.' Tammy threw her arms around him, kissing him on the cheek three times.

'Something smells delicioso. Have you been cooking?'

'Del-i-soso.' Tammy nodded. 'What's that?' She pointed to a basket at Joey's feet.

'Thought we might go for a picnic dinner,' he said with a smile.
'If Mum says yes.'

Tammy clapped.

'Welcome back,' said Alice.

'Good to be home.' He winked at her.

'Picnic.' Tammy clapped her hands again and Joey looked to
Alice.

'Of course,' she said.

Before they reached the bridge that lead into town, Joey set Tammy
down from his shoulders. Dandelion Dell: a small patch of long,
green grass covered in tall dandelions, nestled against the creek
edge. Tammy took off her shoes and sat in the middle of the patch,
talking to the delicate white seed heads, a crooked grin spread
across her face. Joey sat down beside her and joined in.

Alice leaned against the bridge, wondering how often they did
this on their Mondays together; making up dandelion stories. It
was Tammy's favourite place in all Kookaburra Creek.

Tammy rose to collect some twigs to balance into a pile in the
grass. In her imagination that pile might become a princess castle,
or perhaps a fairy house.

Joey stepped up beside Alice.

'So, what's new in town?'

'Please, you know the answer to that.'

Joey laughed and poured them each a glass of sparkling water.

'How was Italy?' Alice asked.

'A bit hard this time. Nonno isn't doing too well.'

'I'm sorry.' Alice reached out and squeezed his hand.

Joey shrugged. 'He's eighty-two. Had a pretty good life.'

'And your nonna?'

'She's the strongest woman I know.' He looked Alice in the eye. 'One of the strongest, anyway. Mum's fussing over her, and she's shooing Mum away. In the end I felt a bit like I was in the way.'

'Do you ever think you'll move back?'

'I was supposed to.'

'When?'

'Not long after Mum and Dad went back. They'd moved us out here when I was only six and Dad set up the bakery. It was their new life. When I was twelve he put me in the kitchen and that was supposed to be our future. Baking together for the rest of our lives.'

'But then your grandfather got sick?'

Joey nodded. 'Then Nonno got sick. About six months before you got here Mum and Dad went home to help out a bit. They were supposed to come back. But it was obvious Nonno wasn't going to get better and they decided to stay over there.'

'And you stayed here.'

He sighed. 'About a year later Dad told me to sell up and head over.'

'Why didn't you?'

'Well, by then I'd figured out there was stuff here worth sticking round for.'

He looked deep into Alice's eyes and her cheeks burned.

Joey looked away. 'This is the only home I've ever really known. I don't remember much of Italy.'

'Of course.' Alice smiled. 'Well, I'm glad you're back. That sorry excuse for bread from the Glensdale bakery will not be missed now you've returned, I can assure you.'

'Yeah, you lot only want me for my bread.'

Alice nodded. 'And your picnics.'

'That'd be right.'

'The truth is sometimes hard to hear, my friend.' She shrugged. 'It is good to have you back, though.'

'I got you something,' he said, pulling out a small parcel from the bag Alice only now noticed he was carrying. He handed her the gift. 'I thought maybe, if you wanted to, if you don't like them, it's okay. Anyway . . .' He shrugged.

Alice suppressed a smile and undid the red ribbon. Inside were two Leaning Towers of Pisa. One for salt, one for pepper.

'They're so cute. Thank you.' She leaned over and hugged him. 'That's really sweet of you.' She looked into his eyes and couldn't turn away.

'If you don't want to use them, I'll understand. I just thought with all the colour you've been putting into the place, maybe they'd fit in.'

'They're gorgeous. I'll use them, for sure.'

For the first time since she'd met Joey, the silence between them felt awkward. Their little picnic didn't feel quite so innocent anymore.

'Jo-jo, come back. Playtime.' Tammy came up and tugged his arm.

'I got you something, too.' Joey handed her a small gift.

Tammy tore open the wrapping paper. Inside was an elastic rainbow headband stitched with metallic thread that caught the sunlight. Joey helped her put it in her hair and she ran back to her dandelions.

'You are so good with her. How do you do it?' Alice touched his shoulder.

'It's easy. She's easy.' He sighed. 'I always figured I'd be a dad someday.'

'Jo-jo, come,' Tammy called.

'Never keep a princess waiting.' He smiled and Alice had to turn away, her cheeks burning with colour.

With three dandelions in her hand, Tammy ran to Alice, followed by Joey, who only needed a few long strides to keep up.

'Mummy make a wish.' She handed Alice the longest stem. 'Jo-jo make a wish. Me make a wish.'

All three faced the creek and blew on their dandelions together, tiny white seeds floating on the wind across the water.

'I wished for a rainbow unicorn.' Tammy smiled. 'Jo-jo? What you wish for?'

'If I tell you it won't come true.' He glanced at Alice and she couldn't hold his gaze.

'But . . .' Tammy's happy face clouded over.

'Oh, no. That's only for grown-ups.' Joey knelt down beside her. 'Kids are allowed to tell their wishes.'

Tammy accepted Joey's explanation and went back to her dandelions as Alice and Joey started setting up the picnic.

'Mummy, Mummy, Mummy, can we keep him?' Tammy called.

Beside her sat a frightened little puppy. It was looking at Tammy, who was holding a piece of her bread out for him.

Alice stepped lightly towards them and the dog inched backwards. 'He might already belong to someone, sweetie.'

The black-and-white patched puppy looked clean, but Alice wasn't sure she liked it being so close to her little girl.

'Please, Mummy.' Tammy clasped her hands in front of her chest.

Alice looked around, but there was no one else nearby. The dog wasn't wearing a collar, either. 'I don't know, sweetie.'

The dog put its head on its front paws and crawled forward on its belly.

'I'll call the vet in Glensdale later and ask if anyone's reported a missing pup. He seems pretty tame,' said Joey. He poured some water into a bowl from the picnic basket and placed it on the ground in front of the dog. It drank eagerly.

'I suppose we can look after it till then.' Alice nodded.

The puppy didn't leave Tammy's side for the rest of the afternoon. When she stood, it did. When she rolled in the grass, it did.

'What should we call him, Mummy?' Tammy skipped over as Alice and Joey packed up the picnic.

'He's not ours to name,' Alice smiled.

'But we have to call him something, Mummy.'

'She's right.' Joey knelt down and patted the dog. 'For now, why don't we call him Shadow?'

Despite the late-summer sun slipping towards the horizon, the searing heat had lost none of its bite. Tammy skipped around Alice and Joey as they walked back to the café, Shadow ducking in and out between her legs, licking her hand every chance he could. To give Tammy and her new friend more room for their circle, Alice and Joey closed the gap between them and Alice felt Joey's hand brush hers. She was surprised at the tingle she felt at the base of her spine, the red rising in her cheeks.

'La la la-la la la,' Tammy sang as she skipped with flapping arms. 'Smurf the whole day long.'

As they reached the steps of the café, Tammy threw herself into Joey's arms.

'I love you, Jo-jo,' she said, kissing his cheek three times.

'And I love you. Though if you don't stop growing, I won't be able to pick you up much longer.' Tammy patted Joey on the cheek and bounced up the stairs, Shadow following close behind.

'Thank you for today,' Joey said, his voice just above a whisper. 'I always hate leaving my family, but spending time with you guys helps.'

'Well, we're always happy to have you home,' Alice smiled.

Joey took her hand and held it to his lips.

'Bath, Mummy, bath.' Tammy jumped back down to the grass and Joey dropped Alice's hand.

'I'd better get her in.'

'I'll let you know what the vet says.' Joey nodded. 'Night, princess.' He bent down and kissed Tammy. He stepped forward, then back again. 'Night, bella.' He kissed Alice quickly on the cheek.

Three renditions of 'Hushabye Mountain' were needed to settle Tammy for the night. She'd cried when Alice said Shadow had to sleep outside, but had settled down once Alice agreed that Tammy could make Shadow a bed on one of the deckchairs using her favourite blanket.

Alice kissed her daughter on the forehead, her nose and her chin and said goodnight.

'Night, night, Mummy.'

'Love you to the moon.'

'And back.'

Alice leaned against the doorframe and watched Tammy until the rise and fall of her chest fell into its usual rhythm.

In her own bed Alice lay against her pillows and thought about her dandelion wish. She'd asked for some clarity with Joey, but this was no closer to coming true after the day they'd just spent together. She couldn't deny she liked him. But she didn't know how she felt about being with another person again. She'd locked the memory of Dean away in the hidden part of her heart she didn't dare open, but he was still there. And what would it mean to allow someone in again? Look at what had happened with Dean, with her mum and dad. It only led to pain.

Her eyes felt heavy. At least there was no pain with Tammy. Tiredness, yes. Frustration, certainly. But no pain. With Joey, there was confusion. A past not yet resolved. A future that couldn't quite begin. Her tumbling thoughts started to give her a headache. She closed her eyes and dandelion seeds caught on a summer breeze danced through her mind.

Thirty

Kookaburra Creek, 2018

The cast of the Kookaburra Creek Amateur Dramatic Society sat on the deck of the café as Freddy and Becca brought out coffees and plates of bacon and eggs.

It was hours before the opening night of the show, and Hattie had decided they all needed a hearty breakfast in preparation. Alice couldn't eat, though. She wrapped her hands around her teacup, but it never made it to her lips. She was too nervous about the show. She was too worried about Becca. She watched her closely. As long as she was near Freddy she seemed relaxed, but as soon as he left her side she started playing with her fringe and her eyes would dart round the room.

The nightmares were getting worse. Alice stayed with her all night, but it didn't seem to help. She was exhausted. How was she was going to get through tonight's performance? Maybe she could steal a nap this afternoon, if Freddy could stick round. She'd only have to ask.

'Good idea, Fiona,' Betty said, cutting across the chatter. 'What do you say, Alice? We all come back here and toast our amazing success after the show?'

'Sure,' Alice answered.

'That settles it, then.' Fiona put her hand on Joey's arm. 'A post-performance party at the café. Now I think I might head home. Big night tonight.' She rose, pushing down on Joey's shoulders. 'Walk me home?'

Oh shoot me now, thought Alice.

'Girl has a point.' Clive got up and stepped off the deck, mounting his bicycle. And everyone except Freddy followed.

'See you all tonight.' Alice waved, her cheeks feeling decidedly warmer than they should have as she watched the group walk away, Joey walking beside Fiona.

'Carson?' She grabbed the sergeant's arm before he left.

'What's up, Alice?'

'Actually, I don't know. I wonder . . .' She thought about how to raise the issue without actually raising it. 'Do you think . . .'

'Out with it, love.' He smiled.

'Can you just keep your eye out for any green utes. Other than your own.' She laughed, hoping it would cover her nerves.

'I can. Why?'

'It's probably nothing.' She shook her head.

'In my experience, Alice, when someone says it's nothing, it's usually something.'

Alice shrugged.

'Okay,' Carson sighed. 'I'll be on the lookout. But the second your nothing becomes a something, you tell me.'

'Thank you. And I was wondering if I could have the number of your cousin, Andrew?'

'Andrew? The locksmith?'

Alice nodded.

'Do we need to have a proper chat?' he asked in a serious tone, squaring his shoulders and looking down at Alice. He could be really intimidating when he wanted to be.

She shook her head. 'I'm sure it's nothing.'

Carson scribbled the number down and handed it to her before giving her a look that made her feel like she was a teenager who'd been caught drinking. She should have known she couldn't fool Carson. He had good instincts. But the truth would have sounded ridiculous.

'Thank you,' said Alice, and she walked Carson down the stairs of the deck.

Magic was not something Alice believed in. But she did believe that sometimes in life things happened without any explanation. That sometimes things were connected in inexplicable ways.

She knew it was purely coincidence that a frightened girl happened to turn up in her café, yet that girl had Dean McRae's eyes. She knew that Sylvia was just an old photo, yet that old photo had spoken to her so many times over the years, and always knew exactly what to tell her. She knew that Becca's dreams were just dreams, yet she couldn't shake the feeling that there was more to it than that. One thing she was absolutely certain of was that she wasn't willing to take any chances.

She turned and watched Freddy and Becca set up the dining room for lunch. It would be a slow day. Everyone was going to be getting ready for the show. Even those just coming to watch had hair appointments and manicures in Glensdale organised. And everyone knew the café was closing early. Maybe she could have a rest. Just a little one.

'Alice, petal, walk me home.' Hattie came up beside her.

So much for her rest.

They walked slowly along the creek till they got to the bridge.

'I need to pause a moment.' Hattie lowered herself down onto the bench.

Alice sat next to her.

'Becca and young Freddy are getting on well.'

'It's good for her to have someone her own age to talk to. I'm sure she thinks I'm a hundred years old sometimes.'

'Remind you of someone?' Hattie asked.

'I never once thought that of you,' Alice replied. 'I wasn't game enough to.'

'Rightly so.' Hattie nodded, a hint of a smile showing at the corners of her mouth, the edges of her faded grey eyes crinkling. 'You've come a long way since those days. A long way.'

Alice sat in silence. Most of the time she felt she hadn't come any way at all in the time she'd been at Kookaburra Creek. She'd never meant to stay here. It had sort of just happened. Yet now she so desperately didn't want to leave.

'Thanks to you,' Alice said. 'If it weren't for you, who knows what might have become of me.' She shrugged her shoulders.

'True.' Hattie nodded. 'So really, you'd be a fool not to take my advice.'

Alice smiled. 'And what advice would that be?'

'To sort this malarkey out with Joey once and for all.'

'Hattie, please.'

'I'm not finished. Didn't anyone ever tell you it's dangerous to interrupt a woman my age? I could drop dead mid-sentence. Now, I don't know what this thing is with Fiona Harris and, frankly, I don't care. But they are spending an awful lot of time together and it's making me nervous. Regardless of what happens with the café, which we are going to save, by the way, the question you really need to be asking yourself is, do you want to lose Joey on top of everything else?'

'It's too late,' said Alice.

'Codswallop. You lost love once, and Lord knows I understand how that hurts. But you have a second chance. We don't all get that. You want to think twice before you go throwing it away.'

No words came out of Alice's mouth.

'Good. No more nonsense. I'll manage the rest of the way on my own. Now make me proud tonight.'

She let Alice's hands go, pushing the purple stripe in her hair behind her ear as she stood up. She bent down with a flourish of her right arm and when she came back up again she held a dandelion seed head in her hand. Without another word she handed it to Alice and turned on her heel and sashayed away, as best she could, given she was relying on the walking stick, leaving Alice alone with her thoughts.

Backstage the atmosphere was buzzing. Hattie looked radiant, her hair set in a perfectly turned-under bob with a lemon-yellow hairpiece clipped into the left side. She moved from person to person, reassuring them they were in fact ready and she had no doubt they'd do her proud. Whether Hattie actually believed that or not, Alice couldn't tell. But she was convincing and that was all that mattered really. When she got to Alice they exchanged a smile and squeezed each other's hands.

From her vantage point behind the stage curtain Alice watched Betty escort Mr Sinclair to his chair, front and centre. As the skinny reporter took his seat, his face pinched in a look that suggested he wasn't expecting much from the night, Betty caught Alice's eye and gave her a thumbs up. Alice had never seen Betty do that before. She didn't recognise the man sitting on the other side of Betty, but then there were a lot of people in the audience she didn't recognise. It seemed the drawcard of the legendary Harriett Brookes' return had worked and the hall was packed.

'All right, petals.' Hattie gathered the cast. 'Mr Sinclair has an uninterrupted view, so let's give it all we've got.'

'We've put in the work,' Joey chimed in. 'We're ready. Let's make everyone proud.'

He put his hands into the middle of the circle of Kookaburra Creek Amateur Dramatic Society misfits and everyone followed. 'Let's do this!'

A cheer went up, just as the overture started and the main lights in the hall dimmed.

Alice's hands began to shake.

'You'll be great,' Joey whispered in her ear as they took their places.

The curtain fell for interval. Apart from Mrs Harris missing a cue because she was too busy poking her head through the gap in the backstage partition to see the audience reaction, everything had gone smoothly. Well, that and the fact the stairs didn't turn all the way round like they were supposed to, but no one seemed to notice that. At least that's what Joey told everyone as they changed costumes.

'It's going great,' Becca told Alice. She and Freddy had made their way backstage during the break.

'Can you hear us up the back?'

'Clear as day,' said Freddy, taking his now customary position behind Becca's left shoulder.

'And Mr Sinclair?'

'Seems to be enjoying himself,' Becca said. 'Though it's a bit hard to tell his happy-smug from his unhappy-smug face.' She shrugged.

Alice could hear Carson on stage starting up the auction. He was working the crowd beautifully and the first few bids were being shouted out with joyous abandon.

The cast changed costumes and the stage crew readied the set for the next act.

As the auction drew to a close, Hattie gathered the cast and tapped her walking stick. 'Not bad. Not bad at all.'

Everyone stopped where they were and held their breath.

'An admirable job so far but, remember, the closing number is the most important. That's what people will remember. Joey, a little more projection.'

'Yes, ma'am.'

'Mrs Harris, a little less. Alice, make sure you breathe properly, or you won't be able to reach that high note.'

Alice nodded.

'Don't let me down.' She tapped her stick again and Freddy and Becca took one arm each and helped Hattie back on stage.

'You heard the lady.' Alice clapped her hands, jolting the frozen cast back into action. The sooner they got back on, the sooner they could finish.

The music started, the curtain rose, the final act began.

It was the final number, and the cast belted out the last of Cole Porter's delicious lines.

Resounding applause went up from the audience as the curtain closed. When it opened again Alice looked out to a standing ovation. Mr Sinclair was on his feet beside Betty, who, if Alice wasn't mistaken, actually looked quite proud.

Shouts of 'Bravo!' and 'Encore!' filled the hall.

Hattie motioned with her hand that they should perform another number and Alice looked to Joey, panic across her face. They'd all been hoping simply to not embarrass themselves and be booed off stage. No one had thought about having to do an encore.

The clapping and cheering continued and Joey made a trumpet gesture with his hands.

Alice shrugged and nodded. The cast took their positions.

Hattie began with the opening lines to 'Blow, Gabriel Blow', and soon the rest of the company followed, their proud voices ringing out through the hall.

The chorus received a mighty cheer, though not as big a reception as Clive when he took his individual bow – slowly down, slowly up, holding his back in a ploy, Alice suspected, to milk his applause. Mrs Harris soaked up the adoration, blowing kisses into the audience when she curtsied. Six times.

Joey, Fiona and Alice took their bow together, stepping forward with Joey between the two women, their hands clasped in the air.

But the biggest applause of all was for Miss Harriett Brookes. Audience members threw flowers on to the stage as Hattie bowed and, if Alice wasn't mistaken, there might have been a tear or two slide down the star's cheek.

The entire cast and crew were squashed together on the deck of the Kookaburra Creek Café for the afterparty, patting each other on the backs, gulping down wine and beer and champagne.

An exhausted Hattie had been given a seat next to the door and was surrounded by Betty and her bowls gang. Freddy and Becca were on drinks duty, ensuring no one's glass was empty for long. Funny how people who needed topping up were always near each other and Freddy and Becca had to attend them at the same time. Mr Sinclair may have had a smile on his face, though he seemed a little put off by the close press of the crowd.

And everyone, it seemed, wanted to make a speech. Thanking Hattie, thanking Alice, asking Joey if he was going to abandon them for Broadway, thanking whoever happened to be standing next to them, praising the crew, praising the cast, thanking their grandmother who first made them listen to Cole Porter, thanking Cole Porter . . .

Eventually Hattie rose and all eyes turned to her, all voices stilled.

'I'm terribly proud of each and every one of you,' she said with considerable effort, ignoring the tear at the corner of her eye. 'I'll be expecting even more from you next year.'

Everyone cheered.

'Mr Sinclair?' She invited his critique.

'Best local production I've ever seen,' he muttered.

Everyone cheered.

'And,' Hattie continued. 'I'm pleased to say that, while we don't have the final tally yet, of course, it looks like the proceeds of the night, ticket sales, food takings, the wonderful auction, might be enough to save the café.'

A cork flew out into the night, a wet plonk suggesting it had landed in the creek in the distant dark.

Everyone cheered as Joey started pouring the champagne into upheld glasses.

They'd done it. They'd actually pulled it off.

From across the deck Alice caught Joey's gaze. All she wanted right there in that moment was to run into his arms, celebrate there. But Fiona stood right beside him, cheering with the rest of the crowd.

Alice forced herself to hide behind a smile as friends and strangers alike patted her on the back.

Thirty-one

Kookaburra Creek, 2009

It hadn't been easy to convince the newsagent in Glensdale to get *The Courier* sent over from Cutter's Pass when she'd first arrived, but three batches of free cupcakes and the promise of more had sealed the deal.

Alice knew it was silly, after all this time, to still want news from Lawson's Ridge. She'd stopped thinking of it as home long ago, but part of her, a part she didn't like to admit existed, had to know if her dad ever went back for her. She scoured every article, every classified, for any mention of Bruce Pond, any clue that he'd returned to his daughter. But his name was never there.

Today's paper was no different. Nothing in the articles on drought in the first few pages, nothing in the sport pages – though it seemed the footy team were doing well this year – no advertisements for Pond's Plumbing and Pipes.

She read the birth announcements. No names she knew. She scanned the obituaries. Bertie had passed away. A wave of sadness washed over her as she remembered his Sunday visits to the shop in his boxer shorts and dressing gown. What a lonely death that would have been.

And then she spat hot tea across the table.

A name. Not the name she'd searched nearly six years for, but one that sent a shiver down her spine nevertheless.

Mr and Mrs Jenkins were apparently thrilled that this coming Saturday their only daughter Louise was to marry Dean McRae.

Alice paced the kitchen. She couldn't quite understand it, but there it was in black and white.

How foolish she'd been, hoping all this time he would change his mind and decide to be part of Tammy's life.

So this was his final choice. His declaration to the world. But it made no sense to her.

Alice pulled out her bowls and measuring cups and started on a vanilla batter. She cracked the first egg and pieces of shell fell into the bowl. Dammit. She threw out the batter.

Closure. That's what she needed. She grabbed another bowl and started measuring again. Perhaps if she saw it for herself, then she could believe it.

She had everything here in Kookaburra Creek to move on with: Tammy, the café, friends. Even an orphaned dog that had somehow become hers. Yet, she knew she was holding back. Maybe a chance to say goodbye was just what she needed.

She looked up at Sylvia. 'I'll keep my distance. I won't speak to him. I'll just watch.'

Sylvia stared back at her.

'Really. It's only so I can close that book once and for all.'

*

The familiar sight of Pip's sprawling farm came into view as Alice passed the flood sign just out of Lawson's Ridge that was only ever needed once.

Alice slowed the car as she pulled into town. She turned into her old street. Number two's picket fence was still there, its yellow paint looking fresh. Mr Jones always was so houseproud. Number four looked pretty much the same, apart from a new letterbox. The lamppost on the corner, Dean's lamppost, was gone, however. By the looks of the metal stump that stuck out of the pavement, it was mostly likely knocked over and never replaced. She pulled up next to number ten and stopped. There was no lawn, only brown weeds. Instead of cheap white curtains, the windows were covered in taped-up newspaper. A 'for lease' sign, splattered with dirt, hung from one corner off a wooden post in the centre of the front yard where Gus used to stand so proudly.

Getting out of the car, Alice tiptoed up to the living room window. The newspaper was yellowed and faded, but she could still make out the stories printed on it. Drought, tractor sales, footy wins and losses. All dated four weeks after she'd fled. Had the place really remained empty all this time?

She returned to the car and continued driving, past the corner store, towards the cemetery.

Kneeling beside her mother's grave, she placed daisies against the headstone.

'Hi, Mum. Sorry it's been so long.' Tears fell down her cheeks into the dirt below. She traced Sonia's name with her fingers. What else could she say? She'd abandoned her mum, left her there alone in the dust for all these years. 'I'm so sorry,' she sobbed. It was her only regret leaving Lawson's Ridge.

'I have a baby girl.' She sniffled. 'Well, she's not a baby anymore. Tammy Sonia Pond. She's nearly five. You'd love her . . .'

After tidying the gravesite, pulling out brown weeds, sweeping away years of neglect and dirt, Alice stood and slowly walked away.

She unwrapped the sandwich she'd packed and took in the view. Climbing her old ironbark hadn't been as easy as she'd remembered, but she'd made it up there. The path below was overgrown and the whole area looked less green than it had when she was younger. And it was smaller. It was definitely smaller.

Leaning back against the trunk, memories flooded her mind and she tried, pointlessly, to push them aside. All the kisses they'd shared. That night. How safe she felt with him, how he'd made her laugh. Pointless, wasted memories. He was marrying Louise. She had to accept that, for her own sake and for Tammy's. She climbed down from the tree and started to walk, a new plan forming in her mind as she headed into town. The boarded-up windows of abandoned shops that lined the main street had multiplied since Alice left.

'What are you doing here?'

Alice turned round to see a familiar figure behind her. 'Louise? Hello.' She was face to face with the friend she'd once shared her entire life with.

Louise's long blonde hair was piled on top of her head in large soft rollers and Alice realised they were standing outside the hairdresser.

Louise took a step forward. 'What are you doing here?'

'I . . . I heard. I wanted to wish you both well.'

'Seriously? You expect me to believe that? Do you know how much you hurt him when you left? You shattered him. You can't come back now and change that.'

'That's not . . .'

'I won't let you hurt him again. The best thing you can do for him is leave. Right now.'

'I'm not here to hurt anyone.'

'No. I won't let you. He's marrying me. And we're going to have a good life together.' She shook her head. 'It took him so long to get over you, Alice. Properly over you. I won't let you ruin the peace he's finally found.'

Alice could see Louise's hands shaking – the old telltale sign that always gave away how uncertain she was behind her confident bravado.

'I'm not here to cause trouble.'

'Then don't.' Louise's eyes were wide now, pleading. 'Please, just go. If you ever cared for him at all, let him have his peace.' She turned and went back into the hairdresser.

Alice didn't know what to think, what to feel. Why was she there? Really? What did she hope to achieve? She doubled over, but quickly pulled herself upright and walked away.

The little wooden church shone brightly in the late afternoon sun, its whitewashed walls as clean as they had been when Alice was growing up.

From behind a large gum she could see the guests arriving without any chance of being seen. She'd hidden there often as a child when she didn't want to go to Sunday School. The initials she'd carved when she was twelve, a dark scar on the pale bark, A.P., inside a crooked love heart. She'd always planned on coming back to add the letters of her true love, the one she'd marry one day in the church across the field, when she found him.

With her finger she traced D.M. beneath her initials and then erased the ghost letters with a sweep of her palm.

Sally and Sue arrived dressed in the brightest purple dresses Alice had ever seen, their lime green fascinators holding up their grey hair. They looked towards the old gum, but Alice was sure they didn't see her. They smiled and entered the church.

Mr Jones wore the same brown suit he'd trotted out for Sonia's funeral and every wedding and funeral ever since. Mrs Jones teetered on heels that were clearly new and an uncomfortable contrast to the wellies she normally wore. Mr Williams helped Donna Dobson out of his car and they walked arm in arm into the church. Alice wondered when they'd gone public with what the public knew all along. Pip hobbled in with a cane, a new addition, and Alice wondered how he was managing his great property so encumbered as he clearly was now. How had he aged so much in the few years Alice had been gone?

'Pond? Is that you?'

Alice spun around, a familiar shiver shooting up her neck. Dean stood before her in a neat black suit, an electric blue tie loosened around his neck. His hair was shorter than she remembered and flecked perhaps with grey. So young. His chest was thicker, his belly too. In his left hand he held a walking stick. His blue eyes stared at her with the same bright intensity that haunted her dreams.

'No chair?' Her voice cracked and tears filled her eyes at the sight of him.

'Been back on my feet for a long while now.'

Alice's thoughts tumbled over themselves. Here he was in front of her. Healthy. Handsome. She wanted so desperately to embrace him.

'What are you doing here?' Dean stared at her. 'Not that I'm complaining.' He smiled, his left dimple deepening. 'I'm just surprised.'

Alice sighed and shook her head.

'I'm sorry. I shouldn't be here.'

'No. It's okay. It's good to see you.'

He stepped a little closer, reached out and touched Alice's cheek. She turned her head so he couldn't see her tears.

With his free hand he turned her face back towards him and wiped her tears away. Alice took his hand, held it tightly and inhaled.

'You're getting married.' She forced a smile.

'Yes.'

'Louise, huh?'

He shifted his weight. 'She's been amazing . . .'

'You don't need to explain. Congratulations.'

'Pond.' Dean leaned in so close Alice could feel his breath on her face. 'There's so much . . .'

'None of it matters now.'

'Pond.'

A white limousine pulled up to the church gate. Out stepped two girls Alice didn't recognise, dressed in the electric blue halter-neck dresses she and Louise had always planned on having for their weddings. They helped the bride out of the car. Louise's simple, elegant gown looked perfect. She glanced around, but Alice and Dean were well hidden.

Alice closed her eyes and pictured Dean's two lives. The one with her and Tammy, the time lost, a past missed, always playing catch up. The one with Louise, the hope she represented, the future. His future.

The past didn't matter now.

'Go, now. Marry Louise, Dean. It's meant to be.'

'I never stopped loving you,' he said, so matter-of-fact it hurt her more than if he'd been filled with emotion.

Alice cast her eyes down. 'But now you love Louise.'

'We have a good life together.'

All of a sudden Alice felt incredibly foolish. Foolish for being there and thinking it would change things, for holding out hope all this time, for believing he ever loved her enough. She could actually feel it, the shattering of her heart into tiny pieces as a past of hopeless choices slowly crushed her. And she knew she had to get out of there as fast as she could.

'Go. They're waiting,' she whispered.

She raised her head and looked into his eyes, mustering more conviction than she thought possible, as those tiny pieces of her heart imploded one by one.

'Goodbye, Alice.'

He squeezed her shoulder. With slow, deliberate strides he walked back to the church. At the side door he stopped, shoulders slumped, and ever so slightly he turned.

Alice waited.

Dean pulled himself up straight and opened the heavy wooden door.

Alice gulped in great breaths of air and turned her back on the church. She lifted her chin, squared her shoulders and walked across the field.

'Goodbye,' she said out loud, a single tear escaping down her cheek.

Thirty-two

Kookaburra Creek, 2010

'Not too fast, sweetie.' Alice put her hand on Tammy's as she stirred the batter with a wooden spoon. 'That's better. Just a little slower.'

With her spare hand Tammy took a handful of grated carrot and threw it into the bowl, accidently dropping some onto the floor under the bench where Shadow just happened to be lying in wait.

That dog really loved cupcake time, and no wonder. Alice always had to prepare double the special ingredient – blueberries, coconut, carrot – because somehow Tammy managed to spill a little, every time. The poor kid had learned the hard way though that, despite Shadow's pleading eyes, she couldn't drop chocolate on the floor. A few days at the vet last month had brought that message home. Neither Tammy nor Shadow coped well being separated for the first time since becoming best friends. Tammy was now very careful when it came to chocolate and her dog.

Alice slid the trays of carrot and ginger cupcakes into the oven and Tammy and Shadow ran outside to play by the creek.

It was their favourite game. Tammy would throw a stick into the water, Shadow would launch himself in to fetch it, Tammy would call him back out and Shadow would bound back up the bank, shaking water all over a protesting, giggling Tammy. Then she'd throw the stick back into the creek again.

Alice smiled. It had been six months since her visit to Lawson's Ridge and the 'closure' she'd searched for turned out not to be what she'd expected. She thought perhaps there would be an overwhelming sense of joy; an epiphany, like the weight of the universe had been lifted off her shoulders. She thought the world would take on a colour the vibrancy of which she'd never seen.

But it wasn't like that at all.

It was more a subtle acceptance that came over her. A letting go of what could never be and being content with what was. She had Tammy, her café, her friends. It was enough. More than enough. And somewhere in there lay happiness.

As she arranged the painted chairs around the café, Joey entered as he did every morning. Something about him was different, though. Was it his hair? His shirt? She gave him his espresso and cupcake and he lingered.

'I was wondering, Alice,' he turned his coffee cup round and round, 'if you'd be interested in maybe going on, well, on a date with me?'

Alice felt her cheeks redden and wasn't quite sure where to look. There really was no reason to say no. Not a rational one. Not anymore. But she didn't know if she was ready; if she'd ever be ready.

'No pressure.' He smiled. 'Just two friends hanging out.'

Just two friends hanging out. 'I . . . um . . . yes. I'd like that.'
And with those words Alice realised just how much she would.

'Friday at seven? I'll come get you.'

'What about Tammy?'

'Hattie's already said she'd look after her.'

'Oh, has she just?' Alice raised an eyebrow. 'Confident I'd say
yes, huh?'

Joey grinned and bowed as he left the café.

What did single mums wear on dates? Alice had no idea. Nothing
in her cupboard seemed right. Not that she knew where he was
taking her. It was hot out, so maybe a summer dress. She picked
one out at random and checked herself in the mirror. This one
would have to do.

'Mummy looks pretty.' Tammy stood in the doorway patting
Shadow's head. 'Can we come too?'

'We have our own fun planned for tonight,' said Hattie, coming up behind her. She wrapped the little girl in a tight hug. 'He's
here, Alice. You'd better go.'

'This isn't what I imagined when you said date.' Alice looked
around the kitchen of Moretti's Bread House. Granted she didn't
have a lot of experience with dates – any experience, for that
matter – but weren't there supposed to be roses and candlelit
dinners? Not flour and butter and stainless steel benchtops. Joey
tied an apron around Alice's waist, his fingers brushing against
the small of her back. 'I thought this might be more fun,' he said,
as though he could read her thoughts.

*

'Don't be afraid to throw it down hard,' Joey said, showing Alice how to stretch the dough. 'That's better.'

'This is kind of fun.'

'I thought you'd like it.' He flicked some flour at her.

She flicked some flour back. 'How do you know when you've kneaded it enough?'

'That pretty much comes down to experience. You kind of get a feel for it.'

'Ah, see, I knew there was a catch. You're not going to tell me because you don't want me to get as good as you.'

'Sorry to tell you this, Alice,' he shrugged, 'but, when it comes to bread, you will never be as good as me.' He took some dough and threw it at her, the sticky mix landing in her hair.

'Is that so, Joseph Moretti? I accept the challenge.' She threw a big lump of dough, smacking him right between the eyes and he stumbled back and fell to the ground.

'I'm so sorry.' She took the three steps to get to him, trying not to giggle.

'No worries. But when I retell this story it'll be a rolling pin that knocked me down and not a lump of dough.'

Alice reached out her hand to help and the laughter she'd been holding back burst forth.

'Oh, that's charming.'

'S—sorry.' She doubled over, unable to stop.

Taking her offered hand, Joey pulled her down to the floor beside him, rubbing flour into her hair.

'That's nice. Make me look like an old woman with white hair.' She smiled.

'You look beautiful.' He touched her cheek. 'You are beautiful.' His hand reached behind her head and he pulled her closer to him. 'And amazing,' he whispered. His lips were so close. She tilted her head. With a gentle touch he parted her lips. Softly, slowly, he drew her lips into his. Softly, slowly he released them.

Alice felt a tingle at the bottom of her spine and leaned into him.

His kiss slowed and he cupped her chin in his hand, breathing deeply.

'We'd better get these rolls in the oven, before I take advantage of you.'

'You think you have the advantage?'

'Oh, I know I don't.' He kissed her again.

Joey's hand slipped further down her back. Lower, lower. He squeezed her bottom, lifting her into his embrace.

Alice's skin burned with desire as she pressed herself against him. Pleasure filled her. Joy. Then in rushed fear.

'I'm sorry.'

'Don't be.'

'It's just . . .'

'What is it, Alice?' Joey stroked her hand.

'This is all . . . the only guy I've ever kissed is Tammy's father. And, well, that didn't quite turn out the fairytale.'

'What happened?'

'Long story short? Dean didn't have room in his life for Tammy.'

'His loss.'

'Well . . .' Alice told him the whole story. Most of it, anyway.

'I'm so sorry, Alice.' He hugged her tightly. 'I can't promise you a fairytale, but I can promise you this. You and Tammy mean the world to me. However fast or slow you want to take it, that's okay. I'm in.'

Alice leaned against him. 'You might just be one of the good ones, Joseph Moretti.'

'Might be?' He kissed Alice deeply and she felt her desire rise again.

She broke the kiss. 'I think you're right.'

'About?' Joey panted.

'Getting these rolls in the oven.'

'Of course.' He nodded, pulling himself up slowly to standing. 'No point doing the hard work and not reaping the doughy rewards.'

Alice smiled, reassured by his response.

She really didn't want to stop kissing him. Yet she knew she couldn't let things go any further. Not yet. Not so fast. This, whatever it was with Joey, had to be right. Pure. If only they could stay there on the floor in each other's arms and just be.

He helped her to her feet and they put their rolls in the oven. They cleaned up the bench, sticking to small talk and idle gossip as they waited for the timer to ding.

The first batch of rolls came out perfectly cooked, but the fruit loaf they were making for dessert was a disaster. It might have had something to do with the fact that neither one of them could concentrate on baking when they were concentrating so hard on not falling into each other's arms again. Alice was determined to do this right. Take it slow. Build something worth hanging on to.

'I know they're not traditional,' said Joey as he reached below the bench, 'but I hope you like them.' He handed her a bouquet of rolls shaped like roses, tied with a red gingham ribbon.

'How did you do that? They're wonderful.' She put the bread bouquet up to her face. 'And they smell divine.'

'Ordinary roses just wouldn't do. Can I walk you home?'

Alice held out her hand and together they walked through the quiet streets, moonlight guiding their way.

Thirty-three

Kookaburra Creek, 2018

Alice had never seen Becca take so long to get ready. While she never would have admitted it herself, the girl was obviously excited. And nervous. Freddy had won the bet fair and square and Becca had been moaning for days about not being able to back out of their date. Alice knew Freddy would have let Becca call it off, but she suspected Becca didn't actually want to.

Becca came into the living room, a new red blouse sitting over jeans, her hair pulled back in a neat ponytail that allowed the world to see her bright blue eyes for once.

'I look stupid, don't I?' she grumbled, pulling at her shirt.

'You look fantastic.' Alice smiled, a sense of pride welling up inside her. 'Too late to change now anyway,' she said as Freddy appeared at their door.

'Have fun,' Alice said as she ushered Becca outside.

*

Alice looked at the clock. It had just gone nine – far too early to expect Becca home just yet. She opened the yellow envelope she'd been keeping by her bed. She'd been looking at the photos every night lately. Reliving happy memories. Sad ones, too. She pulled out her favourite shot of Tammy and Shadow playing by the creek. They both looked so happy, so carefree.

She stared at it a while and smiled.

Beside her bed there was a picture of Becca, taken in secret as she sat on the jetty. Alice took the two photos and put them side by side into a frame.

'Alice, petal? You in?' Hattie's voice called from the top of the external staircase.

'It's cold out here, girl. Let a couple of old fuddy-duddies in before we catch our death,' Betty barked.

It was a balmy twenty-four outside tonight.

Alice met them at the door. 'Evening, ladies. To what do I owe this pleasure?' She let them in.

'Hattie here had some notion that we should march these papers over to you right away.' Betty handed Alice a wad of papers from the bank. 'But you and I both know she's simply sticking her nose in where it isn't needed. I told her the young love-birds wouldn't be back yet. Why she had to drag me into this, I do not know.'

'We need a witness to sign the documents.' Hattie shook her head. 'Even you know that, Betty.'

'I'll tell you what I know, Harriett Brookes.'

'Cuppa, anyone?' Alice held back her laughter as best she could.

'Thought you'd never ask.' Hattie sauntered over to the sofa and Betty followed.

That was weird.

It was nice. But it was weird. And I was a mess.

I thought dates were supposed to be all romantic and stuff. Stumbling on the chair leg as your date pulls it out for you? That's not romantic. Neither is realising you have toilet paper on your shoe when you get back from the loo, or spilling your dessert down your front. Definitely not romantic. But he did pretend not to notice. That is kind of sweet, I suppose.

Then there was the kiss on the cheek in front of the café under the moonlight. That was pretty romantic.

But finding out Alice was watching the whole bloody thing from the window above and enduring her hundred questions when I got inside?

Mortifyingly not romantic.

But I guess it was still a good night, all things considered.

I can't seem to get to sleep, though. And it's not just because of the date, or the kiss, though I can't stop thinking about that. Freddy told me the rest of Alice's story over dinner. He was only little when it happened, but it's kind of a part of town history, a horrible part, and people don't forget that sort of thing. Even if they don't talk about it.

I mean, holy cow. No wonder the woman hasn't let Joey in.

This is a lot more complicated than I first thought. Fiona Harris is nothing. Even I can see that, though it seems Alice can't. But this new revelation, well, I get it now, why she and Joey are the way they are with each other.

So, now I have the big picture, what do I do with it? I can't change the past. I know that. And wishing things to change doesn't work.

But maybe there's another way I can help Alice somehow.

Freddy and I talked about it a bit and I think together we can come up with something. As long as you know someone cares, you have hope. At least that's what Freddy said and I reckon he's right.

There's something in his eyes, you know. When he looks at me he's simply . . . looking at me.

He's the closest thing to a real friend I've ever had.

Thirty-four

Kookaburra Creek, 2018

Alice woke coughing, her head pounding, her mouth dry. She coughed again. Why was it so hard to breathe? Her eyes started to sting. Then she recognised it. The acrid taste in her mouth. The bitter odour in her nostrils. Familiar terror gripped her and she jolted upright.

'Becca?' she screamed, running into Becca's bedroom. Empty. 'Where are you?' Her voice hoarse.

Thick black smoke filled the living room. She blinked, unable to see. 'Becca!'

She could hear whooshing and cracking below her, and the sounds of things crashing.

She had to get outside and downstairs. She pulled the neck of her nightie over her mouth. It didn't help much, but it was better than nothing. She fell to the floor and crawled on hands and knees, feeling with her fingers as she made her way along the hall, past the living room and kitchen. The floorboards radiated heat. Floorboards. The door was to her right. No, left. Stop. Think.

She coughed. Left.

Her knees slid along the floor, not carrying her fast enough. Just ahead was the door. She reached up. She fumbled for the handle. Using all her weight to push forward, she shoved it open. She tumbled out into the early morning light, smoke streaming behind her. She slipped down the stairs, wet with morning dew, and landed hard on the deck. She stood up. Where was Becca? Maybe she had gone for help. No, her bike was leaning against the ancient gum.

A scream cut through the silence and Alice spun round.

Black smoke and orange flames danced in the windows of the café in a menacing waltz.

The windows exploded.

Alice wrapped her arms around her head as shards of glass shredded her skin and blood dripped onto her nightie.

No, no, no. This wasn't happening.

'Becca!' Tears ran thick down her ash-coated cheeks.

Behind her a car skidded to a halt. Joey raced out, his mobile up to his ear. 'You'd better get here quick, Carson,' he shouted, dropping the loaves of bread he was carrying.

'Are you hurt?' He gripped Alice's shoulders. 'Where's Becca?' He shook her. She stared back into the building.

Part of the top floor caved in, crashing into the café.

'She's inside?'

Alice nodded.

'Bloody hell.' He raced back to his ute and put on his protective Rural Fire Service jacket.

'I'll get her out. I promise.' He kissed Alice on the top of her head.

'Stop,' she shouted, but the word had no sound.

Shadow jumped from the tray of the ute and stopped beside Alice. She watched Joey leap through the space where the window was just moments ago and fell to her knees. Shadow lay his head in her lap.

Gulping sobs escaped from deep within her chest.

'Did he go in?' Carson shouted as he pulled up. He yanked on the handbrake and jumped out without turning off the engine.

'Alice, are you okay? There's blood everywhere.'

She couldn't answer.

'Can you hear me?'

She nodded.

'Did Joey go inside?'

She nodded.

'Idiot!' He shook his head.

Sirens sounded and the RFS truck screeched to a stop. The volunteers jumped out.

'Sam, you get the hose. Reverend Harris, you ring Glensdale for backup.' Carson continued barking orders as the men sprayed water onto the café.

Alice stared ahead. She was back there, back to that black day when her life stopped once before.

No. She shook her head. Not Becca. Not Joey. She rose slowly. Not this time.

A spare jacket hung inside the RFS truck. She pulled it on over her bloodstained nightie and tightened the buckles. She put one foot in front of the other towards the café.

'No way, Alice.' Carson grabbed her arm.

She turned and glared at him. 'That's my family.' She didn't recognise her own voice.

'I said, no way.' He tightened his grip.

Shadow barked and through the rain of water falling from the café roof Becca stumbled out, coughing. She made it down from the deck and fell to the ground.

Alice ran towards her and hugged her tightly. 'Are you okay? Where's Joey?'

'He was right behind me. I was trapped,' she rasped. 'He freed me. He pushed me out the door.'

Alice looked up, but Joey didn't emerge.

Becca began to cry and Alice cradled her against her chest.

Carson ran towards the building and Alice and Becca gripped each other tighter, staring into the flames, searching for Joey's silhouette to appear.

Every second felt like hours.

Carson disappeared behind a wall of black smoke. Every inch of Alice's being wanted to run after him, to help find Joey. But the sobbing, crumpled girl in her arms wouldn't let her go.

Through the smoke Carson backed out of the café, his shoulders slumped as he dragged Joey along the deck. Carson fell down the steps, pulling Joey with him to get clear of the fire.

'He's not breathing,' he shouted.

The reverend and Sam ran to Joey's still body. Alice watched on helplessly as they tried to revive him.

Thirty-five

Kookaburra Creek, 2010

Alice was pulled from a heavy sleep by Shadow's incessant barking. What was his problem?

'Quiet, Shadow,' she called, but as consciousness dawned an acrid smell filled her nose. She forced herself out of bed and went to the window. In the distance she could see an amber glow.

There was a moment before it hit her. Bushfire. Not far to the north. She ran into Tammy's room, forcing her little girl into the first clothes she could get her hands on.

'I don't want to get dressed,' Tammy whined.

'We don't have time.' Alice rushed her downstairs, Shadow leading the way.

Standing in the middle of the café she didn't know what to do. She'd seen bushfires on the news before, and she'd read about them. But they were always so far away, so they never seemed real. In Lawson's Ridge there was never enough bush to catch alight.

Joey. She'd ring him. He'd know what to do. As she picked up the phone the bell above the café door rang.

'Good morning. How are my two favourite girls?'

Alice spun round. There was an urgency in Joey's voice, concern in his eye, not matched by his happy words.

'Is it close?' Alice stepped towards him.

'Close enough and moving fast.' He leaned close to her ear so Tammy wouldn't hear. 'Best get you out of here.'

He turned to Tammy. 'How about a little adventure?'

Tammy frowned. 'I'm not a baby. Something's wrong.'

'You always were too smart for me.' Joey patted her head. 'There's a small fire and we just need to head to school to make sure everyone's safe.'

'I don't want to go to school.'

'That's where everyone is going to be. It won't be for long.' Alice forced a smile. She turned to Joey. 'What do I do?'

'You've got one minute. Grab a few things and we'll head. I'll start the car.' He turned and walked out.

Alice shoved the spare flour jar with her hidden stash of cash in it into a plastic tub. She looked around. What else was there? Did she have time to run upstairs? She could hear Joey outside calling her name. She decided against it, and headed out, locking the café door behind her. 'Where's Tammy?' she asked.

Joey looked around and started calling her name.

Alice ran to the back of the café and found Tammy standing in front of Shadow's water bowl.

'I was getting him some water. Shadow?' she called for her dog. 'Where is he, Mummy?'

'Shadow! Here, boy.'

Joey appeared beside Alice. 'He's probably got a head start on us. Dogs are pretty smart and Shadow's smarter than most of them.'

Tammy put her hands on her hips. 'He wouldn't go without me.'

The wind picked up and smoke moved in, wrapping itself around the café.

'He's probably just making sure it's safe for you. Let's get in the car and get going.' He took Tammy's hand, but she wouldn't move. 'We have to go. Now.' He picked her up and carried her to the car.

'The school will be safe. It's the other side of the creek and they're expecting the wind to shift west soon, and that'll blow it the other way.'

Alice looked back to the café as Joey started the engine.

'It'll be okay. The boys know what they're doing.' He tapped the RFS logo on his bright orange shirt. 'Let's go, hey?'

Tammy wound down her window and called for Shadow, each call of his name sounding more desperate than the last. Alice looked to Joey, who frowned. That didn't alleviate her rising panic.

By the time they arrived, the school hall on the edge of town was packed, yet eerily quiet. People huddled in small groups, speaking softly. Even Mrs Harris was hushed as she directed her church ladies to hand out drinks.

Tammy stopped as they entered the room. 'Shadow's not here.'

Alice got down on one knee. 'Joey's right, you know? Dogs are smart. Smarter than humans. They know what to do in situations like this. He's probably found himself a nice place, the safest place to be in all Kookaburra Creek.'

'Then why didn't we go with him?'

Alice had no answer to that.

'I need you to be a brave girl for Mummy. Do you think you can do that?'

Tammy frowned, but nodded.

'Good girl. We'll find Shadow when this is all over.'

Clive and Betty sat on old wooden chairs inside the entrance to the hall marking off names as people arrived. Alice looked around but couldn't see Hattie.

'Ouch, Mummy.' Tammy pulled her arm away and Alice realised how tightly she was squeezing her hand.

'Sorry, sweetie. Stay with Mummy, okay?'

Sergeant Carson stood on the stage and tapped the microphone.

'We have two crews already out and Glensdale are sending over what they can. Moretti, your crew can take the North Road. Sam, you boys head to the lower pass. Rev, you'll be first relief so get some rest now. Mrs Harris, you'll have twenty hungry, thirsty lads coming back in around six.'

Mrs Harris nodded. Carson continued to mobilise the volunteers and Alice looked round the room.

'Have you seen Hattie?' she asked Betty.

Betty checked her list. 'She hasn't come in yet.'

'Sit here,' Alice said to Tammy, directing her to the spare chair next to Clive and Betty's table. 'Remember, be a brave girl. Wait here for Mummy.'

'Stubborn old mule probably thinks she's impervious. I'll check with the reverend.' Betty shook her head. 'She may have been in the church garden picking flowers.'

'Is anyone else not accounted for?' Joey asked.

'The Smiths haven't come in yet.' Clive checked the list. 'But they were going away this week, I'm pretty sure. And we're still waiting on Peter Albert.'

Betty strode back towards them. 'The reverend hasn't seen her.'

'Mummy,' Tammy said, tugging on Alice's shirt. 'Can we go and find Shadow now?'

'In a minute.' She brushed Tammy's hand aside. Peter Albert came into the hall coughing. 'Have you seen Hattie?' Alice asked him. He shook his head.

'Mummy?'

'Sweetie, Mummy just has to do something important. I need you to be very brave and stay right here till I come back. Then we'll go look for Shadow.' Her eyes searched the room. Maybe she'd just missed Hattie in the confusion. 'Can you do that?'

Tammy nodded. 'Be brave.'

Alice looked to the back of the hall and took a few steps forward, tapping the first person she came to on the shoulder.

'Have you seen Hattie?'

No. She pushed past him to the next person.

'Hattie?' Her mouth was dry.

No.

She pushed between clusters of quietly murmuring people, asking each group the same question. With each 'no' her heart beat louder in her ears.

Where could she have got to?

Oh, God. If something happened to Hattie . . .

She reached the back of the hall and turned round, pushing once more back through the crowd.

'You've already asked, Alice.'

Spinning round.

'Sorry, Alice. Still no.'

To the left.

A slight shake of the head.

'Alice?' Joey tapped her on the shoulder and she turned round.

'What's all the fuss about?' Hattie adjusted the violet scarf around her neck, standing in front of Alice, not a worry in the world.

Alice let out a cry and threw her arms around the old woman. 'Oh, thank God. Where were you?'

'I'm not as fast as I used to be, is all.'

'I'd better get my crew organised.' Joey rubbed Alice's arm. 'You go see if Mrs Harris needs some help. I'm sure she'd even find something for Tammy to do.'

Alice nodded. She looked over to the desk Betty and Clive had been manning. With everyone accounted for they'd made themselves useful elsewhere. The chair where she'd left Tammy was empty.

Alice's heart dropped.

She pushed her way through the crowd looking for her girl.

'Tammy?' she shouted.

She looked under trestle tables. She looked in the bathrooms. She checked the whole hall and Tammy was nowhere to be found.

Oh, God, where was she? Panic coursed through every fibre of her being.

Alice ran up to Joey, who was briefing his crew. 'I can't find Tammy.' She grabbed his shirt.

'She probably just found a quiet place to colour.' He rubbed her shoulders.

They did another sweep of the hall together.

'She's not with you?' Mrs Harris asked and Joey shot her a look. 'No. I haven't seen her.'

Alice's breathing quickened.

One of the young school kids pointed to the hall doors.

Joey grabbed him by the shoulders. 'Did you see Tammy?'

The shy boy nodded and pointed again to the doors. Joey stood up, face to face with Alice.

'Shadow,' they said together and ran towards the hall entrance.

'You stay here.' Joey grabbed Alice's shoulders. 'In case she comes back.'

'No. I can't.'

'Stay,' Joey said with such force Alice took a step back.

'He's right, petal.' Hattie came up behind Alice and placed her arm around her waist. 'If she is out there, best to leave it to the professionals.'

Alice threw Hattie's arm off. 'No,' she growled. 'If my baby's out there, then I'm going to look for her.'

'Alice, I really think . . .'

Her glare stopped Joey mid-sentence.

'Get her some gear, Kirk.'

'What?' Alice stepped back.

'If you're going out there, you're not doing it unprotected.' Joey wrapped an RFS jacket round her and buckled her in. 'You stay right beside me.'

Joey and Kirk led the way, while Alice and Sam followed through town to the outskirts where the eucalypts stood thick.

Heavy steps. Fast steps. Familiar landmarks were shrouded in grey as they headed towards Dandelion Dell. The smoke was black and thick and the midday sky dark.

Alice caught a movement to her right.

'Over there.' She took off.

A branch exploded next to her and she fell.

She tried to stand, but couldn't. Searing pain shot up her leg.

'Over there,' she screamed. 'She's over there.'

Kirk ran past her and Joey bent down to help her up. 'Can you walk?'

'No.'

Kirk ran back, coughing heavily. 'There's no one there.'

'But I saw her.' Alice gulped.

'Smoke can do things to your vision.'

Joey's calm voice irritated her.

'I saw her.'

'Let's keep moving. I don't like the look of that wall of flames.' He pointed just off in the distance.

Alice tried to step forward, but fell to the ground.

'Sam, you'll have to take her back. She can't be out like this.'

'No!' Alice screamed.

'Alice.' Joey grabbed her shoulders, hard. 'It's too dangerous. You can't walk. You can't be out here.'

'Don't do this, Joey.'

'I'll bring her back. I promise.'

He kissed her forehead.

'Get her out of here,' he barked at Sam.

Sam heaved Alice onto his shoulder and started trudging back in the opposite direction.

'Tammy!' Alice continued to shout, as they headed back towards the hall.

Sam dropped Alice on the steps to the hall and Hattie came running out with water for them both.

The men in their RFS jumpsuits were climbing into trucks, Carson making sure each knew their job, Clive grumbling as he tried to move through the press of people, delivering water on Mrs Harris's order. Inside the hall Betty wrangled the schoolkids and their siblings – the toddlers thought it was all a great adventure, but the older kids were hushed, sensing the gravity of a situation they didn't quite understand.

Alice sat on the steps, watching for any movement in the distant smoke. Then an orange blur appeared from the haze, floating down the street.

She turned to Hattie. 'Help me.' The old woman put her

arms round Alice's waist and they shuffled towards the figures approaching.

She saw Tammy resting in Joey's arms, her head nestled into his chest, the threads of her headband sparkling. Behind him Kirk followed, carrying Shadow.

'Tammy!' Her little girl was safe. As she got closer, she could see a bunch of dandelions clutched in her girl's tiny fist. 'Sweetie?'

As soon as they were clear of the smoke, Joey fell to the ground. Kirk placed the whimpering pup on the ground and tore off his RFS jacket and laid it on the road. Joey placed Tammy on the jacket and put his hand on her chest.

'One, two . . .' Joey counted.

'Breathe.' Kirk put his hands over Tammy's face.

'What are they doing?' Alice cried.

'Maybe we should wait here.' Hattie's voice was soft.

'No.' Alice broke free of Hattie's hold and launched herself towards her girl, falling to the ground, crawling the rest of the way.

Joey and Kirk continued their disjointed movements, speaking words to each other she couldn't hear.

Reverend Harris appeared beside Alice, holding her hand gently, as Doctor Knight raced up and came to a sliding halt beside Tammy. Kirk fell back, shaking his head. Doctor Knight put his face close to Tammy's.

They continued, pushing and breathing and pushing and breathing.

Again and again and again. Then they stopped.

Joey slumped back on his heels and Doctor Knight touched Tammy's forehead and closed his eyes.

'No!' Alice screamed. 'Keep trying!'

Joey lifted Tammy into her arms.

'No,' she whispered.

'I'm sorry. I was too late. She was already . . . the smoke was so thick.'

'No.' Alice's tears fell on Tammy's perfect serene face. 'Wake up, sweetie. Wake up. Please.' She brushed Tammy's ash-covered cheeks, smearing her beautiful girl grey.

'I'm so sorry.' Joey's voice sounded far away.

'No.' Alice shook her head. 'Wake up, Tammy. Wake up!' she screamed, shaking Tammy's tiny body. The dandelions fell on to the road. 'No, no, no, no.'

Alice rocked back and forth, holding Tammy tightly to her chest. She tried to breathe in the vanilla scent of her hair, but the bitter stench of smoke filled her nose.

And time ended.

Thirty-six

Kookaburra Creek, 2010

By the water, the residents of Kookaburra Creek gathered, dressed in all the colours of the rainbow, a dandelion each in their hands. Reverend Harris spoke quiet words of loss and hope that Alice couldn't hear.

She stood, supported by Hattie and Carson. If they let her go, Alice was sure she would sink through the ground. She closed her eyes, but opened them again, the image of Tammy's lifeless body persistent, haunting her behind her eyelids. The phantom smell of smoke, smoke that stole her little girl, always mocking her when the image returned.

Whispers of 'such a sweetheart', 'saving her Shadow, bless her', 'best friends till the end', floated on the air as one by one people stepped forward and tossed a dandelion seed head into the creek. Some silently, some with prayer.

Hattie led Alice to the water's edge and handed her a stem.

Alice knew she should've been grateful to Hattie for this small gesture and for organising the whole day, but there simply was no gratitude in her heart. There was nothing but pain. She turned and limped through the crowd, which parted as she stepped through. Except for Joey, who stood in her way at the back of the group. Shadow lay at his feet, the dog's dark eyes looking up at her.

'Alice?' Joey didn't try to hide his tears. 'I'm sorry I didn't get to her in time. I . . .'

Alice looked up, shook her head and stepped round him, dropping the stem at his feet.

The bell above the café door echoed through the empty dining room. It had remained closed this past week, and the room felt stale, cold. Alice couldn't bear to be in there so she went back outside and dragged herself up the stairs to the apartment. She tore off the dress Hattie had forced her to wear to the funeral. She slipped into her pyjamas and laid herself on Tammy's bed. The sweet vanilla scent of her hair lingered on the pillow and Alice buried her face deep into it, searching for any sort of comfort.

Hattie knocked on Tammy's bedroom door before opening it. 'I thought I might stay over. Just in case you need anything.' She waited for a response. 'The couch will be fine,' she continued. 'I've slept on worse in my time.'

Alice rolled over, her back to Hattie.

'Right, then. Let me know if you need anything.' She pulled the door to, not quite closing it.

Alice could hear Hattie's soft, rhythmic snoring coming from the living room. She sat up in bed, her knees held tightly to her chest, watching the clock. It had taken Hattie one hour and twenty-seven minutes to finally fall asleep.

In the distance Alice could hear thunder rumbling. Closer and closer.

Tap, tap, tap. Loud drops on the tin roof.

A flash.

A rumble.

Then the rain came down, but it was too late. For Sam, who'd lost his shed. For the RFS, who'd lost two trucks fighting the blaze. For Betty's young nephew, now lying in hospital with first-degree burns to thirty per cent of his body after he tried to save the trucks.

Too late for Tammy.

As the sky lit up with jagged flashes, Alice stood. She slipped on her dressing gown and opened Tammy's elephant money box and took out some coins. Tiptoeing past Hattie she stepped out into the wet night.

Outside the post office stood an old phone booth. Alice fumbled in her drenched dressing gown pocket for Tammy's coins.

Rain fell on her shoulder through the holes in the booth ceiling. She dialled the number, not knowing if he would answer.

'Hello?' His deep, familiar tones caused Alice to gasp. 'Hello?'

'Dean?' her voice rasped.

'Pond? Is that you?'

Alice sobbed into the handset.

'Pond? What's happened? Where are you?'

All she could do was cry. No words were adequate to tell him his daughter was dead.

'Christ, Pond. You're scaring me. What's going on?'

'I'm sorry,' she cried. 'She's dead.'

'What? Who? Talk to me, Pond.'

'I'm so, so sorry.' She held the receiver to her heaving chest in a futile attempt to muffle her sobs.

'Just tell me where you are and I'll come get you.' Alice could hear his distant words.

She raised the receiver and paused.

'I'm so sorry.'

'Pond!' she heard him shout before she hung up.

Sliding down the glass wall, Alice sank into a pool of water and dirt. She dropped the piece of paper she'd kept all this time and watched it soak into the mud. She closed her eyes, letting herself slip into the vast, empty Nothing where she now belonged.

Thirty-seven

Glensdale Hospital, 2018

Standing outside the ICU, Alice took deep breaths and closed her eyes before entering. She wouldn't ever get used to the sight. The room was dark, with only a lamp in the corner and the blinking lights from various machines offering illumination. Bandages covered Joey's eyes and dressings covered his left arm and shoulder and upper torso. The burns would heal in time, the doctors had said with confidence. There was no way to avoid scarring, but it could have been much worse. His sight would eventually get better, too.

They were not so confident about his heart, though. The strain of the rescue, the smoke, the burns – it was all too much and Joey had suffered a heart attack. Everything else would heal. As long as his heart could recover.

Alice stepped closer and adjusted the oxygen tube that had come loose from his nose. His heart monitor beeped quietly and

Alice looked at the numbers. She'd learned very quickly what the data meant, had bugged the nurses until she knew almost as much as them.

With the specialist passing through Glensdale tomorrow they'd decided not to send him to Sydney. Being around people who loved him was more important, they said. Alice wasn't sure she found that comforting. When the specialist came she'd make sure she was there to get to the truth of it.

Watching the rise and fall of Joey's chest, Alice held his right hand gently.

'Hey, Joey,' she whispered, letting him know she was there. 'It's me.'

Maybe tomorrow everything would be better. Maybe tomorrow he'd wake up and speak. Maybe tomorrow she would see him smile again and her world would be put back together. Never in her life had she longed to hear him tell her that her bread would never be as good as his. She settled into the chair next to him and continued to watch him closely.

A light cough roused Alice from sleep. Hattie had joined her. She sat up and rubbed her shoulders, cursing the hospital chair for its hard discomfort.

'Hey,' she said.

'Any change?'

Alice shook her head. Hattie squeezed her hands and kissed her on the forehead.

'What time is it?'

'Just gone seven. I don't know how you convinced the nurses to let you stay, but you've been here all night. Becca's asking for you.'

'How is she?'

'Physically, she'll be fine.' Hattie shrugged. 'She's worried. Go. I'll stay with him.'

'No. You shouldn't be . . .'

'Don't you dare say I'm too old to be sitting watch. I've known Joey since he was knee-high to a grasshopper and I'll bloody well stay if I want.'

'Thank you. How do you do it, Hattie?'

'Do what?'

'Find the strength?'

Hattie's smile was tinged with sorrow. 'Women like us have a habit of finding strength when we think we have none. We'll get through this. We always do.'

Alice nodded and stepped lightly down the corridor. Despite Hattie's reassurance, she didn't know where she'd find the strength to go on. There was nothing left. The café. The apartment. It had all gone up in flames.

She squared her shoulders and entered Becca's room.

Becca was sitting in the hospital bed against a pile of pillows, scratching at the IV drip in her hand.

'Why do I need this?' she complained. 'I'm fine.'

'They're just making sure your fluids stay up. It won't be for long.' Alice pulled the sheets up to cover Becca's legs.

'Stop it. I'm fine.' Becca smiled.

'You gave me such a scare.' Alice sighed.

'I know. I'm sorry.' She fiddled with the tube coming out of her hand. 'I was just trying to put it out. I didn't mean for Joey to get hurt.'

'Shh. It's all right. What matters is that you're okay.'

Tears started to fall down Becca's cheeks. 'I'm so sorry. It's all my fault.'

'What are you talking about? The investigation said it was an electrical fault. It's an old building. It was no one's fault.'

'Not the fire. Joey. If Joey doesn't make it, it will be all my fault.'

'Don't you think that for a second. Joey has never run from danger before and never turned his back on those he cares about.' Alice threw her arms around the sobbing girl. 'Stop that. You are not to blame.'

'Of course I am. I'm a bad person and I do bad things. Even when I don't mean to.'

'You've had some bad luck in your life, sure, but that doesn't make you a bad person.'

Becca started sobbing. 'You don't know the whole story.' She sat herself up straighter. 'When I ran away, I stole a great big wad of cash from my mum's boyfriend.' The confessional words came quickly now. 'I nicked the money he owed his dealer so I could escape, and he'll be coming after me for it. And you'll be in danger. Karma. That's what this is. Bad people like me deserve bad things.'

'Stop that right now. You did not deserve anything that monster did to you.'

'Except . . .' Becca wiped her tears and spoke so softly Alice had to lean in. 'Except, I knew when I took that money his dealer would go after him and I wanted him to. I wanted him to get caught and . . . and be killed. Good people don't think like that.'

'Oh, Becca.' Alice squeezed her tightly.

'It's karma.' Becca began to cry again. 'I wanted *him* dead and now I've killed Joey.'

'Joey isn't dead. And your rotten excuse for a guardian deserves everything he gets.'

'But if Joey . . .'

'Shh.' Alice rocked her back and forth, stroking her hair. 'It will all be okay.'

She held Becca until the tears subsided and the poor girl fell into an exhausted sleep. It *would* be okay. She needed to believe that. It had to be.

When night fell again, Hattie insisted Alice go back to her place and get some sleep. She didn't have to worry about leaving Becca or Joey alone. Betty had a certain pull with the hospital staff. None of them were game enough to tell her she couldn't have her roster, which saw someone with Joey and Becca twenty-four-seven. Alice obeyed Hattie but she only got as far as the hospital car park. She stood there and closed her eyes, gulping in the cool night air. Truth be told, she didn't want to go back to Hattie's and spend the night alone. She was afraid to close her eyes and see the fire, see Becca weak and struggling for breath, Joey lying in the dirt, unmoving. She was afraid to see the ghost of Tammy's sweet, ash-covered face that had begun haunting her again.

'Alice?'

She turned to see Fiona standing by the lamppost.

'How are they?'

'Becca's going to be fine. Joey's still touch and go. Visiting hours are over, but in the morning . . . Haven't you been in?'

'No. This is a time for family. I just wanted to ask how they were. You know this town, sorting rumour from truth isn't always easy.'

Alice nodded.

'Dad's constantly praying.'

'He's a good man,' Alice said. She started to wobble.

'Alice?'

'I'm just tired.' But Alice looked down and realised her hands were shaking so hard, her car keys were jiggling loudly.

'Maybe I should drive you home.'

'I think that would be good.' Alice felt her knees were about to buckle beneath her.

Fiona helped her into Hattie's house and took her to her old room. Hattie hadn't changed a thing since Alice had moved out a decade ago. The quilt was still the same on the bed. The dresser still displayed the same photo in the small, brass frame – the one taken of Tammy and Joey in Dandelion Dell.

'I'll go make you a cuppa, hey?' Fiona said as Alice sat on the bed.

'Thank you.' Shadow nuzzled his snout under Alice's arm as she leaned against the pillows.

The very same pillows she'd found comfort in when she first arrived in Kookaburra Creek. How far she'd come since then. Yet here she was right back where she started – alone, homeless, afraid.

She picked up the photo of Tammy and Joey. She hugged it tightly and began to weep.

Everything was gone. Every memory, every hope. She knew this crippling pain – when life ended and all that remained was a black void. How could the shattered pieces of what was left of her possibly recover this time round?

Thirty-eight

Kookaburra Creek, 2010

Alice could hear them downstairs. Talking, moving, laughing. Living.

For days now, she wasn't sure how many, they'd come. Perhaps it was weeks. She couldn't tell. She didn't care. Talking and moving and laughing. Living. She knew who they were, their voices familiar – quiet and hushed at first, though no longer, speaking now in cruel, loud tones so that she could hear.

Every day, though she wasn't sure how many, Joey and Hattie came. Sometimes Betty. Sometimes Clive or Claudine. Sometimes Harris or Carson. Always Joey. Always Hattie.

When she lay on the floor, ear pressed down, she heard the snippets clearly.

'She'll come down when she's ready.'

'Should we take her something to eat?'

'Surely this isn't healthy, *c'est pas*?'

They knocked on her door, but she wouldn't answer. Hattie would come in, though, uninvited, unwanted. She forced Alice to eat. Every few days, she wasn't sure how many exactly, Hattie made her bathe and sat behind her and brushed her hair.

And every day, Alice listened to the snippets.

'This isn't right.'

'It'll take some time.'

'How much time?'

Alice's legs ached. Every step was torture. Five painful steps from Tammy's bed to the sofa. Eight agonising steps from sofa to bathroom. One step from sofa to rug. Tammy's favourite rug, soft, warm.

'I'm worried.'

'She's been through a lot.'

'*Mon Dieu*, this is too much.'

They continued to come. Talking, moving, laughing. Living.

The sun continued to rise and set. The birds continued to sing.

'I think we should call someone.'

'Is she any better?'

'This has gone too far.'

'Shh,' Alice whispered, rocking back and forth on the rug, squeezing Tammy's rainbow headband in her hand.

Alice woke. How long had she slept? Three hours? Three weeks? Sometimes when she slept, she'd drift off into a world where colours were still bright, where laughter still promised joy, only to wake and be reminded that the world was now lost.

Sometimes she dozed. In and out, never quite managing to leave the grey and cold behind. Sometimes she didn't sleep at all.

A noise. A sharp, beeping sound that wouldn't stop. Was it in her head? Or maybe it was coming from below. *Beep, beep, beep.*

She looked at the door. Ten steps. She shuffled.

Stairs. Fifteen steps.

The café bell jangled happily, cruelly.

Twelve steps to the kitchen, to the beeping.

Alice stopped and stared.

On the bench in the middle of the kitchen were glass bowls, spatulas, beaters, canisters of flour and sugar, eggs, packets of butter, patty cases, cupcake tins. All laid out neatly around an alarm clock with a note attached.

'It's time.' Joey's handwriting read. 'She'd want you to.'

Alice looked to Sylvia.

Chocolate fudge. Tammy's favourite.

With shaking hands Alice measured the butter and placed it in a bowl. How much sugar? She hesitated. Then she pictured Tammy holding the cup measures in her hand. One and a half Tammy scoops. She smoothed the top of the brown sugar with the flat palette knife, just like Tammy used to do, and she let her tears fall. She reached for the flour, her hands remembering each step, one by one.

She plopped the batter into the waiting patty cases and spilt some on the floor. No tiny hands running tiny fingers round the bowl, a cheeky chocolate-rimmed grin declaring innocence. And she mixed another batch.

As she pulled the trays out of the oven, the rich chocolate aroma hit her in a rush of hot air. She placed the cupcakes on the cooling rack and sighed.

'Del-i-soso,' she said, and the tears began to flow again. She sunk to the ground and rested her head on her arms, eventually falling asleep.

'Alice?' A deep voice stirred her and she woke, lying on the floor, oven mitts her makeshift pillow.

'Joey?' She stood, six dozen chocolate fudge cupcakes on the bench in front of her.

'I've come to open up.'

'Oh.'

Alice started to arrange the cupcakes on trays and plates and Joey stepped forward to help her, Shadow limping beside him.

'Out!' she shouted at the dog. Shadow bowed his head and went out onto the deck.

'He only wants to . . .' Joey started.

'Don't,' she said.

'I'm sorry, Alice. I did everything I . . .'

'Don't. Please don't.' She refused to look at him even though she could feel his stare boring into her.

'Shall I start on the salads?' he said quietly.

'Thank you, but I think I can manage today.'

'Right.' Joey stood there as Alice continued around him, unable to look at him, knowing if she did she would see her girl in his arms, limp, not breathing.

'Right. I guess I'll be off then.'

Alice watched him leave the café and stride along the creek until he was out of sight, Shadow following slowly behind. Alice collapsed to her knees, sucking in great gulps of air.

She stood back up and with trembling hands she set the tables, one by one.

'It's so good to have you back on deck, petal,' said Hattie as she entered the café. 'Feels right, this place, with you in it.' She embraced Alice in a tight hug. 'We've been long enough without you. Where's Joey?'

'Gone.'

'You know he's been running this place on his own?'

'I thought it was you.'

Hattie shook her head. 'He worked every night in the bakery till Betty and Mrs Harris came in the morning to take over while he came in here. Every day.'

'Really?'

'Of course. Why are you surprised?'

Alice wished she hadn't been so dismissive of him earlier. She wished she could thank him. Above all else, though, she wished she could face him.

'What can I do to help?' Hattie put on a gingham apron, the exact same pink as the stripe in her hair.

Carson was the first customer of the day, coming in to get his turkey sandwich and cupcake.

'Good to have you back, love.' He hugged her tightly before sitting down.

Alice felt her chest tighten and forced herself to smile. A small part of her was glad the day was moving so slowly, allowing her an easy re-entry. The rest of her wished she were busy, busy, busy so she didn't have to think.

'*Mais oui*!' Claudine ran through the door with tiny steps and kissed Alice on both cheeks. 'So good to see you.'

'Thank you, Claudine. Coffee?'

She knew Hattie was watching every move so she forced herself to appear perfectly normal, perfectly capable. It was exhausting.

By the end of the day the ache in Alice's legs had disappeared, replaced with a throbbing. But the throbbing wasn't so bad. Physical pain was far preferable to the dull emotional ache that possessed her constantly.

Alice tried not to think of the weeks she'd missed. She tried not to think at all, letting years of routine and habit take control of her every move. And that did feel good, to surrender to a more primeval force. To simply do, not think, not remember.

'What are we going to do with these?' Hattie asked, pointing at the five dozen left-over cupcakes.

Alice shrugged.

'There's a fundraiser tomorrow. They're raising money for a new truck for the RFS. I could take them along?'

'I can take them.'

'That would be nice. Everyone will be pleased to see you again.'

At the thought of seeing all those people, Alice's heart began to race.

Hattie held her in her arms. 'You'll be fine.'

Alice wasn't convinced, but she'd taken the first uneasy steps back into her life, what was left of it anyway; and, despite her certainty that she would, she hadn't actually imploded. Perhaps she could take a few more tentative steps.

Thirty-nine

Glensdale Hospital, 2018

Becca refused to leave her hospital room.

'I'm not leaving till Joey does. We came in together, we leave together.'

Freddy looked to Alice, not knowing whether to put Becca's bag down.

'I understand.' Alice took Becca's shoulders and sat her down on the edge of the bed. 'But the best thing you can do for Joey right now is show him you're recovering. And the best way to do that is to come home.' Alice needed her to come home, too. She needed something to keep her going.

'Why hasn't he woken up yet?'

'He's not young like you, petal. His body needs a bit more time,' Hattie said.

'It's all my fault.' Becca started to cry.

'No, it's not.' Alice rubbed her back.

Hattie stepped closer. 'It was an accident. Pure and simple. I know no one believes in accidents anymore these days, but they happen and sometimes they're bad and no one's to blame. I'll hear no more of this nonsense. What we should be spending our energy on is figuring out how we're going to help Joey,' Hattie said.

Alice looked up.

'You heard me.' Hattie tapped her stick. 'The doctors are doing their bit. Joey has someone with him all the time. Now, we need to start being practical.'

'I have an idea,' Alice said quietly.

'Out with it, then.' Hattie clicked her fingers.

'The bakery. We can keep it open for him so he has something to come back to when he's well again.'

'I like it,' Hattie said.

'He did the same for me.'

'Can I see him before we go?' Becca asked timidly.

Alice nodded and steered her down the hallway to Joey's room.

∽

That image is burned into my brain.

Joey lying there like that. Perfectly still, as if he weren't really there, bandages everywhere. All because of me.

Why would he do such a stupid thing as risk his life for me?

I can still feel his arms lifting me up from the kitchen floor, shielding me with his body. Like a dream. I wasn't awake. But I wasn't asleep. I was there. I remember it. But it was like I was looking on from a distance.

Alice's plan to help Joey is a good one. I heard her crying last night. She's putting on this brave face that everybody's buying. But not me. I know she's scared for him. I am too.

The plan will help keep her busy, though. And me too. I never understood that concept before, staying busy in the bad times. But I do now. Anything will be better than sitting beside his bed waiting for him to wake up.

I can't believe Alice still wants me around, after everything that's happened, after everything she knows. I thought for sure she'd want nothing to do with me once she found out I was a thief. But I was wrong.

I'm looking forward to tomorrow. Not the getting up early bit, but the rest of it. And I can't wait to tell Joey all about it. When he wakes up.

If he . . .

No.

When he wakes up.

With no café to run it seemed only natural to try to keep the bakery going. A debt long owing that Alice was finally able to repay. If she had any say in the matter, Joey would have a business to return to when he got better. Whenever that might be.

Alice showed Becca how to knead the dough exactly the way Joey had taught her, throwing it in ropes onto the bench. Becca yawned constantly. Four in the morning did not altogether agree with her, but she never once complained. And she was slowly getting her head around the art of baking Moretti's traditional bread.

Unfamiliar with the industrial ovens in Joey's bakery, Alice burned the first dozen rolls, and she had little hope of being able to produce the range of breads and pastries Joey did, but she was managing the basics. And three weeks into the project, they weren't doing too badly overall.

Covered in flour, Becca opened the doors at nine. Hattie arrived, bringing much needed coffee for them, and by ten Claudine and Sam came to take over serving. Apparently, Betty had made another roster.

That evening Alice meandered through town and came to the white bench. Tammy's white bench. She sat and watched the moonlight dance across the tiny ripples on the creek's surface.

Alice picked one of the stems that hugged the bench's leg and stepped towards the water. Her life had been so very different the last time she'd made a wish this way – the picnic when Tammy was three and Shadow turned up and Alice had wished for clarity regarding her feelings for Joey. Well, she had that clarity now, even though it had taken years to get it.

Closing her eyes, she took a deep breath and blew the tiny seeds onto the evening breeze, wishing with all her might for Joey to get better.

She made a second wish, too. She didn't know if that was allowed, but she figured it couldn't hurt.

'Well, my sweet Tammy, the fight's not over yet.' She let out a deep sigh. 'But I will keep on fighting for our home.'

'Alice? Are you okay?'

She looked up to see Becca standing before her. 'Of course.'

'Seriously? I know you're keeping something from me.' Becca sat beside her.

Yes, she had been keeping this from Becca. Until she could find a solution. The poor girl was carrying enough guilt as it was.

'Is it Joey?' Becca's voice dripped with fear.

'No. There's no change.'

'Then what? You're frightening me. Tell me right now what's going on.'

Alice couldn't believe how very much Becca sounded like Hattie just then.

'It's the café. The bank. Now that . . . now that there is no café, no business, they won't loan me the money. I have no equity. Not even enough for the land value.'

A single tear fell down Becca's cheek. 'What do we do now?'

'Well, I'm still working on that. We need to come up with a plan C. We'll get the gang together again and we'll come up with something.'

'If anyone can do it, you can.' Becca slipped her hand into Alice's and squeezed it tightly.

Yes, Alice could begin again. She hadn't lost everything. She still had Becca and Joey.

Somehow she'd find a way.

Forty

Kookaburra Creek, 2018

Hattie stepped quietly into Genevieve's room so she didn't startle her. In front of the window her sister sat, the sun on her back, warming her on this cold morning.

'Hi there, sweetie.' Hattie sat beside her. 'How are you?'

Genevieve stared ahead.

'Would you like me to do your hair?' Hattie got back up and fetched the brush from the dresser. The mirror was completely covered, as it always was, by a green scarf, and the familiar pang of guilt rushed through her.

'It's over.' She brushed Genevieve's soft, thin bob – fifty strokes on each side, making sure her grey strands fell over the extensive scars down her left cheek. The nursing staff never quite got it right, no matter how often she showed them.

'I haven't told Alice yet. How can I?' What a confounded mess.

She returned the brush to its place and sat back down. 'I wish you were here, Gen.' She pulled the lilac afghan up over Genevieve's legs. 'Are you warm enough? Let's take a walk.'

She wheeled Genevieve out of her tiny room, through the living area and into the garden.

Spending time with her sister always calmed Hattie, and by the time she got back home she was feeling marginally better. She kicked off her shoes and sunk into her old, floral sofa. She still didn't know how to break the news to Alice, but she was in a better place to deal with it. She'd been keeping it from her for a week now and she just had to find the courage. She opened the letter from Smythe and Smythe and reread the words that changed everything.

'Dear Miss Brookes, We are writing to inform you that an offer has been made on the property at 1 Mini Creek Lane, despite the substantial damaged sustained in the recent fire, and the Hargraves family have accepted it. The new owner, who wishes to remain anonymous at this time, will be taking possession in fourteen days . . .'

Buckley Hargraves had done it. From the grave he'd managed to throw one more spanner in the works. But she'd be damned if she'd let him ruin Alice's life. She'd find out who the new owner was and come to some sort of arrangement. Hattie could be very persuasive when she wanted to be.

Forty-one

Kookaburra Creek, 2011

For the first time since the fire, Alice entered Tammy's room and saw it as it actually was. A mess of clothes and toys strewn across the floor, the bed a crumpled mess of linen. Alice had lived in the room since Tammy's funeral and she could now smell the evidence of that.

It was time, she knew, to tidy up. To give Tammy's room the love and care it was owed.

She started with her own mess, picking up her clothes and throwing them in the washing basket. Then she picked up Tammy's toys, left as they lay the day fire tore their lives apart. With each stuffed bear, each half-clad doll, Alice could see Tammy's crooked grin. The one she always wore when playing with her favourite things.

The empty tub under Tammy's bed was just the right size to fit everything in. The suitcase in the cupboard, the one ready for emergencies, would fit all of Tammy's clothes. Alice took in a deep breath and got to work.

With the room clear, she sat on the bed. Beside her was Tammy's favourite colouring-in book, her box of pencils, and her rainbow headband. Alice looked around the room, her life dismantled. She picked up Tammy's favourite jumper, infused with the lavender fabric softener Claudine had given her, and held it to her face. She cried into its soft folds. In a small rainbow-striped box she put those last few things, steeling herself to put one foot in front of the other.

Those next few days routine and mundanity kept Alice going. Baking, cooking, running the café – an insincere half-smile painted on her face, a carefully crafted mask hiding the truth.

'She's doing so well.'

'Such a brave girl.'

If only they knew. Alice was hanging on so tightly to her daily chores she was afraid she'd simply disintegrate if she stopped. And at some point in the repetitive haze, getting out of bed each morning had become just a little less onerous.

'She's moving on so well, bless.'

Alice hated that expression. Moving on. To her it carried connotations of leaving something, someone, behind. Abandoning the past. But Alice didn't want to abandon anything. She hadn't moved on at all. She had simply kept going, carrying the past inside her deeper every day, but never forgetting.

'You there?' Joey called, arriving with two loaves of bread.

'Hi,' Alice said in a clipped tone, as she came into the dining room. 'Thank you.' How long would it be, she wondered, before she could look at him and not see Tammy? Another month? A year, perhaps? Ever?

'I hear business is picking back up.' Joey rocked back and forth on the spot.

'The regulars are all back.' She busied herself with the cutlery, polishing what she'd already polished only half an hour before.

'Do you . . . do you think you'll maybe, ah, come to the markets next week?'

Alice wanted to utter the words, give him the smile that would ease his pain, make things right.

'I . . . I don't know, Joey.'

'Alice . . .'

'Please don't.' She forced herself to look him in the eye. 'I can't. We can't.' She fought back tears, looking at him, seeing Tammy's lifeless body in his arms. 'We just can't.'

He grabbed her hands. 'I can't lose you too, Alice.'

She could see the tears in his eyes.

'I won't.' He stepped closer.

She shook her head. 'I'm already lost.'

She moved to the other side of the café and started setting the tables.

Hattie burst in. 'Ah! I'm glad you're both here. I've had the most amazing idea. Sorry. Am I interrupting something?'

'No,' said Alice. She looked Joey in the eye. 'We're done.'

Joey turned away and placed some menus on the tables. Alice saw him wipe his cheeks, despite his efforts to hide doing so.

'Good, then. The fundraiser for the RFS got us nowhere, so I've been wracking my brain to come up with a better idea. I want to hold a picnic. Charge for the privilege of attending and really get this thing going. Sunday is the first day of spring so what better time? Can I count on you to bake for me?'

Alice knew that it wasn't so much a request as it was an assumption.

'I think it's supposed to rain on Sunday.' Alice frowned.

'Bother. What about having it here, then?'

'I suppose . . .'

'Splendid.' Hattie kissed her on both cheeks. 'I'll rally the troops. Joey, you spread the word. Expect us at eleven on the dot.' She spun on her heel, flicking Joey in the eye with her purple scarf as she did.

'Hurricane Hattie strikes again.' Joey looked to Alice, hope in his eyes. When she didn't respond he straightened his shirt and cleared his throat. 'Right, then. I'm off.'

'Joey. I'm sorry. I wish . . .' She had no words.

'It's okay, Alice.' He reached out and brushed her cheek. 'I understand.' His voice cracked and he rushed out the door.

'I'm so sorry,' she whispered into the empty room.

Days drifted, weeks waned, months meandered and somehow Alice found a way to move from one season to the next. She wasn't sure when, but at some point her new half-life without Tammy became her normal, though the pain never went away.

She would often catch herself talking to her little girl when baking, or going into her room to check on her at night, only to remember she was no longer there.

During the day she kept the constant ache at bay with work and would bake late into the night when sleep was plagued with ashen images.

She thought about leaving Kookaburra Creek, but it was Tammy's home, and when she was still and quiet she could feel her baby with her.

In the twilight of a mild December night, Alice and Joey walked beside the creek. Things would never be the same between them.

That she knew. But they had found a way to move through their lives, together yet separate, two shadows that never quite overlapped.

'What is this surprise you want to show me?' Alice glanced sideways at him.

'Well, if I tell you, it won't be a surprise.'

They turned in the direction of Dandelion Dell and Alice hesitated. She hadn't been back. Not once.

'It's all right,' Joey whispered in her ear.

When she saw Tammy's dandelion patch, renewed with life as Mother Nature was so expert at doing, she couldn't believe her eyes.

'What's that?' She stared at the shiny white bench sitting in the sea of fluffy white seed heads.

'I . . . we, wanted to do something, you know, to remember her, to mark tomorrow.'

Alice put her hand on her chest. She'd been trying to ignore that the anniversary of the fire was here. 'I can't believe this.'

'The whole town chipped in. She was special to all of us.'

'You guys are amazing. This place is amazing. You did this for her?' She shook her head.

'And for you.' He took her hand and held it to his chest. 'You're special to us too.'

'Joey.' Alice shook her head.

'I know it's going to take time, Alice. And that's okay.' He kissed the palm of her hand. 'I'll leave you to it.' He bent down, plucked a stem and handed it to her, before stepping off into the shadows.

Alice sat on the new bench, there in Tammy's special place. There where life had so instantly and brutally changed.

She could hear Tammy's laugh, loud and infectious. She thought perhaps she might cry, but instead she smiled.

With Joey's delicate gift in her hand, she stood and stepped to the edge of the creek. 'Sorry I'm late, sweetie,' she said. She bent down and laid it on the water, watching it float past her feet.

Forty-two

Kookaburra Creek, 2018

Arm in arm Alice and Becca walked along the creek, Shadow padding along slowly beside them. They hadn't been back home since the fire. At first, Hattie hadn't let them. She'd organised someone to gather some clothes for them and insisted they live with her till something more permanent could be arranged. Secretly, Alice was relieved. She wasn't sure she could cope with seeing the aftermath. And then there seemed no point now it was no longer hers. That was just rubbing salt into the wound.

There was nothing else to do but cry when Hattie told her. But she'd reminded herself she still had Becca, and even though Joey hadn't woken up yet he hadn't got any worse. And in the strange mess that was her life right now, they were both things to be grateful for. She would find another home for her café. She would find another home for her and Becca.

'So plan C's out the window,' said Becca. 'What do we do now?'

'Well, there are twenty-three more letters in the alphabet, so we keep thinking.'

'Does anyone know who the owner is yet?'

Alice shook her head. 'No. Which is really unusual. In a place like this news like that normally spreads pretty quickly. And I can't believe they haven't shown themselves by now.'

The talk around town was all conjecture, though that didn't stop it gaining momentum and, if any of it was to be believed, either Hattie was making up the whole story about Buckley Hargraves for publicity and actually still owned the café, or a celebrity chef had bought the place to turn it into a posh country retreat. And they were two of the less ridiculous rumours.

'A mystery.' Becca tried to hide a smile.

'What do you know?'

'Nothing.'

As they rounded the bend that led to the café, Alice noticed cars and utes parked out front. Standing around in a large group of KingGee blue and khaki were a dozen or so men including Reverend Harris and Clive, and there was someone in the middle of the group barking instructions.

'Hey, there.' Freddy ran towards them. 'Glad you two happened by.' He winked at Becca. 'Phase two is about to start.'

'Phase two?' Alice asked.

'Yep. Operation Café Recovery.' He turned around and spread his arms. 'Bringing the café back to life. The new owner's here and the engineer's been by and given the go-ahead to get started.'

'What? The new owner? How is this a good thing? Why are you all smiling?'

'Because they all know something you don't.' Betty stepped out from the middle of the circle.

'What's that?'

'I'm the new owner.'

Alice stared at her. 'I don't understand.'

'There's nothing to understand. We had a problem. I stepped in.'

'How? They wanted so much.'

'Oh, I'm rich. Filthy rich, actually. Stocks and bonds and whatnot.' She waved her hand in the air. 'My lawyer, Jim,' she pointed to a man with a phone pressed to his ear, 'released some extra funds and I bought the place.'

Alice recognised him from opening night of the play. He was in the audience.

'So you bought the café?'

'Yes. I wasn't going to let anything or anyone take away our town café. I made an offer. They accepted.'

'And everyone knew?'

'Just about.' Freddy grinned. He stepped aside as Hattie joined the group. 'Everyone except you two.' He laughed.

Hattie took Alice's hand. 'Thank you for the call, Becca.'

'You knew?' Alice looked at the girl smiling smugly beside Freddy.

Becca shrugged.

'There's no point doing something like this if you can't have a bit of fun with it, now is there?' Betty smiled. 'Harriett Brookes isn't the only one in town with a flair for the dramatic.'

'So Betty owns the café?' Alice needed to make sure she was fully grasping the situation.

'Oh, good. You've finally caught up. But if you're going to continue running the place, you'll need to be a bit more on the ball. I only own it on paper. You two are still in charge. We can work out the details later. Maybe we can come up with some sort of purchase plan, Alice. I hear the market has had a sudden and dramatic downturn.' Betty winked. 'But right now, we've got a lot of work to do. Hattie, do close your mouth. Gaping is not becoming in a woman your age.' She spun round leaving Alice and Hattie staring after her.

Fiona and Mrs Harris and ladies from the church group had arrived armed with sandwiches and kegs of water and set up a trestle table.

Alice heard a series of clicks and turned to see Mr Sinclair in the shadows taking photos and jotting things down in his notebook.

He walked towards Alice. 'I heard about the community rallying to rebuild. Thought it might make a good story. If you don't mind?' Sinclair lowered his camera.

'That's fine. I guess.' She fought back tears as she looked at her friends, who'd banded together to rebuild the café. They were all in on it – coming up with this plan, keeping it a secret. They did this for her, and for Hattie. She wiped the tears from her cheeks, staring at her family, her home.

'I know, petal. I know.' Hattie squeezed her.

Reverend Harris came up to them and embraced them both. 'I hope you know just how much you mean to us all.' He adjusted his collar and stepped back to Clive and the other men surrounding them who were eager to get started.

'What can we do to help?' Hattie and Alice asked together and rolled up their shirtsleeves.

Betty walked past and whispered in Alice's ear. 'I wasn't about to let you go. Either of you.'

Hattie brushed Genevieve's hair gently. 'Well, I never thought Betty would be the one to save the day, but she bloomin' well has. I do wish she had let us in on her plan. Would have saved us a lot of heartache. But I guess in the end, as long we get to keep the café, it doesn't matter.'

She finished with Genevieve's hair and fixed the cardigan across her shoulders. She was always cold.

'Alice is going to buy it off her. Once it's back up and running and things have settled.' She leaned over and whispered in her sister's ear: 'Our home will be in good hands long after we're both gone.' She wiped a tear from the corner of her eye and squeezed Genevieve's hand.

If she hadn't known it was impossible, she'd have sworn Genevieve squeezed back.

Hattie climbed the steps of her small home and sat on the end of her bed. Alice and Becca wouldn't be back for a while yet and she enjoyed the quiet. She loved having them there, of course, but it did get noisy sometimes. She wasn't as young as she used to be and she'd lived alone a long time now.

Still, at least they were safe, and now they had a future. The café was saved; her home, her legacy, was intact. Now all they had to do was see Joey safely out of hospital and Kookaburra Creek would be back to normal. Everyone's tomorrow could begin.

Even hers. Not that she had many tomorrows left at her age. But, however many tomorrows she did have, she'd be damned if she was going to waste them. If nothing else, the fire had taught her that. She looked at the trunk at the end of the bed.

She opened the wooden box and pulled out all the old newspaper and magazine articles, the photos, every last relic of Buckley Hargraves, and took them outside to her small yard, dumping them unceremoniously in the metal garbage bin.

'Goodbye,' she said softly, as she lit a match and threw it onto the pile. The yellowed paper went up quickly; the photos curled at the edges and slowly melted. As she stared at the dancing flames, she smiled. 'Goodbye.'

'Hattie, what are you doing?' Alice ran towards her.

'Nothing. It's just a little going-away party,' she said, taking great pleasure in the confusion that crossed Alice's face. 'It's time we all looked to the future.' She dusted off her hands. 'Now, I think we need to have a party. A proper one. My birthday's coming up and we'll need to reopen the café. Besides, I think the whole town could do with a pick-me-up.'

Alice stared back at her. 'How can you think of throwing a party when Joey's still in hospital?'

'Even more reason. That boy needs something to look forward to. People who are unconscious can hear. They've done studies, you know? There's no way he'd be game enough to miss my birthday party. Might just give him the impetus to come back to us. It's all part of my cunning plan.'

Alice closed her mouth.

'There's a good girl. You'll get that organised for me, won't you?' She patted Alice on the shoulder and turned her back on the small bonfire, striding into the cottage, feeling lighter than she had in years.

Forty-three

Kookaburra Creek, 2018

As the sun began to set Alice and Becca entered the hospital. Fiona came out of Joey's room and walked towards them. 'Hi.'

'How is he?' Alice asked. She knew Betty had Fiona rostered on for the afternoons, but she didn't normally stay this late.

Fiona reached out and took Alice's hands. She smiled, relief in her eyes.

Alice and Becca ran to Joey's room.

Just inside the doorway Alice stopped. Becca ran past her to Joey, who was propped upright in the bed. The bandages had been removed from his eyes and he smiled when he saw them.

'Hi.' Alice fought back tears.

'Hey,' he said.

Becca launched into telling him how she'd made a plaited loaf that morning.

'It was a bit wobbly.' She shrugged. 'But Mrs What's-her-name with the fluffy poodle didn't seem to mind.'

Joey laughed and stopped himself, clearly pained with the effort. The right side of his face was covered in dressings that restricted his movement.

'Alice here's been turning out wholemeal rolls like she's been doing it forever.'

'Yeah, but they're not as good as mine, right?' He winked at Becca.

Alice stepped into the room.

'You're awake,' she said.

'They took me off sedation last night apparently. I came round an hour or so ago.'

'You're awake.'

Becca looked at her phone, which hadn't actually made a sound, and stood up. 'It's Hattie. We've got a party to plan. Oh, and did you know Betty's the new owner of the café? Alice can tell you all about it.' She leaned over and kissed Joey on the cheek before skipping out of the room.

'You know, you're her hero now,' Alice said.

'If I'd known that was all it took to win her over . . .'

'Joseph Moretti, you stupid old fool.' The tears she'd been holding tightly back burst forth. 'Don't you ever risk your life like that again.' She hit his uninjured shoulder. Hard.

'I couldn't let her . . . not again . . .'

'Don't.'

'Alice, please . . .'

'Don't,' she sobbed, falling into his pillow, and as he wrapped his good arm around her he allowed himself to cry too.

They stayed like that, without words, until evening turned to night, and Alice knew there was nowhere else in the world she'd rather be.

'You know,' Joey eased Alice back up, 'they're probably going to come past and kick you out soon.'

'I'd like to see them try.'

Joey smiled. 'I'm glad you're here.' He sighed and reached out to brush Alice's fringe to the side, the stiffness in his muscles making him grimace with pain.

'I'm glad *you're* here.' She smiled, taking his hand in hers. 'I saw Fiona on the way in. She's been visiting every day.'

'She's a good friend.'

If the last few weeks had taught Alice anything, it was to fight for what you wanted.

'Is that all she is?'

'What do you mean?'

'The two of you have been pretty tight ever since she came back to town. I figured you were, you know . . .'

'No. I don't know.' He looked mildly amused.

'You mean you're not?'

Joey's smile grew. He was definitely amused.

'Alice Pond, I'm thinking maybe I'm not the fool here. Fiona is a friend. That's all. She came back all conflicted about her career and Mrs Harris was giving her grief. A lot of grief. She just needed a friend to lean on. Someone with perspective who'd be honest with her.'

'At the markets, Claudine said . . .'

'Alice, you know better than to listen to idle gossip.'

'So you're not . . .'

He shook his head.

'You and Fiona aren't . . .'

He shook his head.

'I'm rather happy to hear that.'

'I'm rather happy to be heard.' He squeezed her hand.

*

Six long weeks after the fire, Joey was allowed home and his first day out of hospital was celebrated with a gathering at the Cow and Boot. Alice was in a particularly good mood at the pub and not just because Joey was back. The café rebuild was nearly all done, except for a few finishing touches. And she and Becca were moving back in. She'd have to find a way to thank everyone for what they had done to get it ready so quickly, but how did you thank a group of people for giving you your home back?

Words would never be enough. She'd have to think of something else. But not tonight. Tonight was about Joey.

Freddy circulated the third round of drinks, smiling at Becca as he handed her a lemonade. She took the glass with a grunt and a frown.

'What's up with them?' Hattie whispered in Alice's ear.

'Oh, she's cranky he didn't stop by the bakery for lunch yesterday.' Alice laughed.

'I didn't stop by. She's not cranky with me,' Hattie said.

'Yes, but she isn't in love with you.'

Mr Sinclair burst through the pub doors.

'Howdy, good folk of Kookaburra Creek,' he said, his feeble voice doing its best to cut through the noise. 'Look what went national yesterday.' He held up the article he'd written about the café's rescue.

COURAGEOUS CREEK COMMUNITY in thick black letters stood proudly above a photo of the building crew at work restoring the burnt-out café, with Alice and Becca in the background watching on. The pub hushed.

'*The Herald* have been doing a series on small towns, you know, the whole tree-change phenomenon, and they thought this would fit. *The Age* are running it, too. I'm . . . we're famous.'

A cheer went up from the crowded room. Kookaburra Creek

had only once before made it into the news. Fifty years ago when a once-famous actress crashed the car she'd 'borrowed' from a once-famous actor, on the edge of town.

'Give the man a drink,' Reverend Harris called out, and Mrs Harris shot her husband a look.

Eventually, the excitement settled and guests broke off into small groups of animated but quiet conversations. Mrs Harris chatted with Betty about the imminent bowls trip to Wollongong and how keen the crew were to flog the team from Kiama, who they were yet to beat at a meet. Hattie was filling Joey in on the grandeur that her birthday-party-slash-café-reopening was turning into. At the back Clive was chewing Mr Sinclair's ear off about doing a series of stories on local Vietnam Vets, perhaps. Becca and Freddy circled the group in opposite directions, clearing and refilling glasses. Becca doing her best to maintain her scowl, Freddy, grinning, seeing straight through the ruse.

The pub doors opened slowly and Alice turned to see who was coming to join the celebration of Joey's return. One look at the man who entered and it was clear from the hard set of his face that he wasn't there as a friend. Her heart started to race. Through the large bistro windows she saw a green ute parked crookedly out front. Carson never parked crookedly.

She turned to Becca, who was rolling her eyes again at Clive's exaggerated story. But then Becca caught sight of the man and all colour drained from her face.

Alice looked back to the stranger, who was searching the dining room off to the side, then back to Becca, and she stood up.

Freddy, it seemed, had also been watching and, while he wouldn't have known exactly what was happening, he could tell it wasn't good. He put a hand on Becca's back and guided her behind the bar before stepping into the middle of the room.

'Can I help you, mate?' he said loudly enough that everyone stopped and watched. He knew his town well. 'You look a bit lost.' He gave a false smile that Alice was both proud of and somewhat unnerved by.

'I'm looking for Bianca,' said the man.

'No one here by that name. Sorry.'

Alice noticed that Hattie had positioned herself to block any view of behind the bar. The rest of the gang shuffled around it too, ready for whatever was coming next.

'Don't mess with me, kid,' the man warned, pulling himself to his full height, which was considerable. 'I know she's here.' He pulled the article out of his back pocket. 'Drove all night to find my precious girl,' he sneered, stepping closer to Freddy, who didn't move.

'You!' The man pointed to Alice and moved towards her. 'You're in the photo with her. Skinny little bitch stole my money and I want it back.'

Joey rose and stood between the man and Alice, his thick arms folded across his chest. Alice could only imagine how menacing he must have looked, covered in half-healed scars.

The man stopped, assessing his situation.

'She's nothing but a thief and a liar,' he said. 'I'm just trying to track down what's owed me. She's nothing but trouble. If she's here, you'll want to get rid of her.'

Alice could see he was getting more and more agitated. She stepped out from behind Joey.

'Show me,' she said, reaching out for the article, hoping her shaking hand wasn't too obvious. 'Ah, yes. The fire was well over a month ago now, though.' She paused. 'I remember her. But her name wasn't Bianca. It was . . . Simone.' She pretended to look more closely at the picture. 'That's right. She was looking for work.'

'Where is she?' he asked, clearly battling to remain calm, but smart enough to know he needed to keep himself in check.

'I'm really sorry, but she moved on. I couldn't offer her work, obviously, so she kept going. Never saw her again after that day.' Alice handed back the clipping.

'Where the hell did she go?'

Alice shrugged.

'Simone?' Freddy asked.

Alice nodded.

'I'm sure she said something about heading up past Brisbane. Loads of resorts up that way with lots of work on offer.'

'Brisbane?'

'I think that's what she said, mate.'

Becca's tormentor stood his ground. 'Brisbane? How the hell do I get to Brisbane from here?'

'I'll help you get on the right road,' Sergeant Carson, dressed in civvies, offered. Alice had noticed him leaning casually against the bar, watching everything, the tight vein in his neck the only indication that his cop instinct was on alert.

'It's pretty straightforward.' He smiled, steering the man back out of the pub.

Alice let out the breath she hadn't realised she'd been holding. Freddy jumped over the bar to a shaking, crying Becca.

They stayed crouched on the floor, the pub abuzz with speculation and gossip, until Carson returned, which felt like hours.

'He's gone,' he announced, making his way behind the bar.

'Are you sure?' Alice asked.

He nodded. 'Followed him to the highway and stayed there a while to make sure he didn't double back. Made sure I told him I saw Simone,' he finger-quoted, 'get on a bus headed north. Old

Reggie's on patrol a hundred clicks up and I asked him to let me know when he sees the green ute go by.'

'Thank you.' Alice sighed, helping Becca to her feet. She'd stopped crying, but was still pale.

'Is it about time we had that chat?' Carson whispered in Alice's ear, though she suspected he'd probably already pieced together something pretty close to the truth.

'Not right now.' She hugged Becca tighter.

Sergeant Carson nodded in understanding.

'Surely you're not still planning on moving back into the café tonight?' Hattie said, handing a drink to Alice. 'Not after this.'

Alice shrugged. 'I don't know. Becca might feel more comfortable in her own surroundings.' She looked to her charge, who gave a slight nod in response.

'I'll stay with them, Miss Hattie,' Joey declared.

'You're hardly in any shape . . .'

'I'll stay, too,' Freddy announced and Alice saw the corners of Becca's mouth turn up ever so slightly.

'And I'd like to see what's been done to the place.' Claudine clapped her hands.

'It's my investment.' Betty stepped forward. 'Don't think you're doing this without me.'

'Or me,' Clive mumbled. 'Someone needs to keep you lot in line.'

'Oh, Lord.' Hattie threw her arms in the air. 'I'll stay, too, shall I?'

'Slumber party!' said Freddy, and Alice felt Becca's shoulders jiggle.

On their way out, Carson handed Alice a piece of paper with his mobile number on it, which of course she already knew, and underneath was written 'any time'. She nodded at him in appreciation.

A new brass bell clanged as Alice opened the door to the Kookaburra Creek Café. Claudine clapped. Hattie cheered.

'Doesn't look too bad,' Clive mumbled as he stepped through onto the new whitewashed floorboards.

Where the old blue counter once stood, a wood-panelled bench now sat. Each plank of recycled timber was stained in a different colour – pale lime, soft blue, light lemon, bleached rose. Country chic had been the brief and, as Alice looked around at the eclectic mix of distressed-white second-hand tables and chairs, she was thrilled with the result.

On the new counter sat a glass cupcake stand, five tiers tall. Alice reached out and touched it.

'A new beginning,' Betty said. The old stand Alice had used since she'd arrived in Kookaburra Creek hadn't survived the fire. 'But I expect to be able to choose the first flavour that adorns those lovely tiers.'

Alice thought Betty could just about choose anything she liked at this point.

The windows were now dressed with wooden shutters that matched the bench. A chalkboard on the back wall was ready for the daily specials to be written across its black surface and Alice couldn't wait to write them up.

'*Très chic*,' said Claudine, running her hands along the communal table that ran the length of the French doors. In soft grey calligraphy across the stripped-back tabletop was written: 'Come gather at our table: family, food, friends.'

'The lights will be fitted tomorrow,' Betty said, with pride in her voice.

'A couple of dry runs in the kitchen and we'll be good to go.' Alice beamed.

Joey stepped up beside her and placed his hand on the small of her back. 'It's fantastic.'

She looked up into his eyes. 'It's all because of you lot.' She turned to face her friends and tears started to well.

'All right. Enough of this. Let's see upstairs.' Hattie coughed.

With the new build, the café had been redesigned with the staircase inside. No longer would Alice have to worry about getting to and from work in the rain.

The flat was painted white, with a big red rug in the centre of the living room. A new couch, grey and soft, nestled against a wall, and a television sat in the corner. The kitchen was now open plan, making it look twice as big as it actually was. But it was the hallway that took Alice's breath away.

'We know what you lost, so we all went through our things. We hope it's okay.' Betty squeezed her shoulders and Alice stood, mouth open. She couldn't stop the tears now pouring freely down her cheeks.

One entire wall of the hall was covered in a collage of photos and painted sketches, some small, some enlarged, of Tammy and Alice, Joey and Tammy, Hattie and Tammy, Claudine and Betty and Clive and Tammy; of Alice, pregnant, standing behind the café counter; of the whole group at Sunday brunch. All in elegant black frames.

'Thank you,' Alice whispered. She turned and on the opposite wall was a photo of Becca and Alice taken, it appeared, when neither one was aware they were being watched, sitting on the jetty, their toes in the creek.

'You can fill that wall up as you go,' said Hattie, squeezing her into a hug.

'Right, then.' Clive's grumble was pitched higher than usual. 'Where are we all going to sleep?' And everyone looked to someone else for an answer.

Beneath a midnight velvet sky Alice sat on the deck looking up at the stars. The lights in the café behind her were off, the torches on the new deck long extinguished. She counted the white twinkling dots above, lost her place, and started again.

'Couldn't sleep?' Joey asked, startling her. 'Sorry.'

'Hi. You neither, huh?'

Joey shook his head. 'That motley crew strewn about your living room make for very noisy bedfellows.'

'Especially Clive,' they said together.

As if on cue, they heard a shout. 'To the trenches!' Clive's voice cut through the night and Alice and Joey started laughing.

'Sorry this wasn't quite the homecoming we had planned for you.'

'Oh? This wasn't part of some careful ruse to get me to stay over?'

'Not quite.'

Joey sat beside her. 'How you holding up?'

Alice thought about lying. Thought about telling Joey she was perfectly fine. But she'd never lied to him before. Kept things from him, yes. But never outright lied. And she wasn't about to start. Not now they'd been given a second chance.

'What if he comes back?' She looked into his eyes.

'Then we'll be ready.' He leaned in. 'I'd be more worried about her taking off.'

'It's on my mind.'

'Regardless, it might be wise to start using that new lock on your door. Just to be safe.'

'Will it keep you lot out, too?' Alice nodded towards the upstairs door.

'Hardly.' He laughed.

'Freddy's harmless enough, I suppose. And Claudine,' Alice said, grinning.

'Yeah, it's that Miss Hattie you have to watch.' Joey leaned in even closer, his warm breath tickling her cheek.

Curled up on a blanket in the corner of the deck, Shadow barked in his sleep and Alice jumped. 'Does he always dream?'

'Most nights.' Joey smiled. 'It'll be okay.' He steadied Alice's shaking shoulders. 'I reckon you and Becca have had your fair share of drama. You're overdue for a break.'

'I hope so.'

'I know so.' He pulled her into his embrace.

'When you hold me like this I almost believe anything is possible.'

'I'd better not let you go, then.' Joey tilted his head and Alice could almost taste his lips.

'I have something for you.' He reached into his pocket and pulled out a small white box wrapped in yellow gingham. 'I've wanted to give it to you so often, but it was never the right time. Recent events have made me realise there's no such thing. The only right time is now.'

Alice opened the gift and pulled out a long silver chain. Dangling at its end was a small clear disc and sprinkled inside were dandelion seeds.

'It's beautiful. Are they real?'

Joey shifted his weight. 'Yes. They're from . . . I picked it up . . . when you dropped it . . . I had it preserved in resin.'

Tears fell down Alice's cheeks as she realised it was the dandelion she'd dropped at his feet all those years ago. 'From Tammy's funeral?' She looked into his eyes.

He nodded.

Alice couldn't speak. She handed Joey the necklace and turned so he could put it on her. As his fingers brushed the back of her neck a shiver ran down her spine.

'I don't know what to say.' She turned back to him, the distance between them so small now. 'Thank you.'

He smiled and brushed the hair from her forehead.

'Does this mean you've forgiven me?'

'Forgiven you? What on earth for?'

Joey cast his eyes down. 'For not saving Tammy,' he whispered.

'Oh, Joey.' She pressed her hand into his chest. 'You think . . . God, no. I never blamed you for that.'

'But all that time you kept me at a distance, I thought it was because you couldn't forgive me.'

Alice's heart broke for the pain she'd caused him all these years. 'My sweet, sweet, Joey. I never blamed you. It was just, for the longest time every time I looked at you I saw her smiling face and it was just too hard to bear. God, I'm so sorry you thought . . . Oh, Joey. It's you who needs to forgive me.'

'So that's what's kept us apart all this time? That I remind you of Tammy. Not that you couldn't forgive me?'

Alice shook her head. 'Over time that got easier. But there was just so much history. So much between us that was unresolved.'

'We can't change history, Alice. Our own or anyone else's. All I need to know is how you feel about me, now.'

She touched Joey's cheek. 'All this time, through the darkness and the light, it's been you. You, Joseph Moretti, are the reason I'm breathing. In more ways than one. I didn't realise it at first, and then once I did it seemed all too late. You've loved me all this time and I just never knew how to love you back. Not the way you deserve.'

'Just by being you.'

'It's taken me a while to understand that.'

'And now?

She slipped her hand behind his head. 'And now . . .' She leaned in and pressed her lips into his.

There were no birds singing in the trees, no breeze rustling the leaves overhead. There was just Joey; his arms wrapped round her and his soft lips moving in time with hers.

I told Freddy everything.

He sat with me once everyone sorted out their place. Hattie to go in to Alice's room, Clive on the sofa, Betty on the blow-up. Claudine said she was fine on the rug, but I reckon she might regret it in the morning, and Joey said the armchair was more comfortable for his burns than lying down. I think he was lying. But it's an okay lie, I guess.

Freddy sat on my chair at my desk and said he'd stay watch there all night, which might sound creepy but it was really nice. So, I figured he had the right to know what he might be getting himself in for and the whole bloody story came pouring out of me.

He just sat there and listened. If he was shocked, he didn't let on. If he was upset, he didn't show it. He just listened.

When I finished spilling my guts, he came over to me and wiped the tears from my cheeks. He didn't freak out. Didn't say anything. He tucked me into bed and sat back on the chair.

He's asleep now. He snores. Just a little. It's kinda cute.

Every time I close my eyes I see his face, so I've given up on sleep tonight.

I know now that no matter where I go, he can find me. I know that I can run, whenever I want, wherever I want. But no matter where I go, he'll still find me.

So, I guess I might as well stay here. I know they will always have my back.

I know now what family is.

Forty-four

Kookaburra Creek, 2018

Alice lay in the grass, her arms stretched above her head. The breeze was light, the sun warm. The smell of fallen eucalypt leaves crushed into the dirt so familiar, so distant.

She smiled as his face came closer, his breath on her cheek. She could taste the coffee on his lips, smell the scent of cloves and honey on his neck, as he kissed her gently, briefly.

He rose, the edges of his face fading into mist.

'Too smart,' he whispered, tapping her on the head. 'Not smart enough.' He touched his chest and looked at her with eyes so sad she began to cry.

'Goodbye,' she whispered.

The sound of pots and pans crashing woke Alice and she realised she was on the deck, with her head on Joey's shoulder. The two of them must have fallen asleep there at some point in the early hours of the morning.

She rubbed her eyes. Her cheeks were wet. The taste of coffee lingered on her lips, the smell of cloves and honey in her nose. She abruptly sat up, pushing the dream from her mind.

She stretched and shook Joey's arm.

'What? Who?' He jumped up.

'It's okay. We fell asleep. I'm guessing the others are in the kitchen.'

Hand in hand, they stepped through the open sliding doors into the café dining room.

'Morning,' said Freddy, startling them as he pushed his way through the shutters into the dining room.

Joey clutched his chest. 'Jesus. You do remember I'm recovering from a heart attack, right?'

'Sorry, petal.' Hattie sashayed into the room, carrying a plate of fried eggs. 'The two of you just looked far too cosy for us to wake you.' She winked and patted his cheek. 'Becca's cooking breakfast. For all of us.' She placed the eggs on the long table in the middle of the room.

Clive and Betty came in, raising their coffee mugs in salute.

'*Bonjour, mes amours*,' Claudine smiled, carrying a large platter of pancakes.

Alice fell into Joey's good shoulder and burst out laughing.

Scrambled eggs, bacon, banana smoothies – the food just kept on coming out of the kitchen. Becca had even thrown together a fruit salad and muesli, in consideration of Joey's recovering heart.

Joey ignored the salad. Instead he piled some waffles onto his plate and began to eat them.

'Well, well, well.' Carson appeared at the front of the deck. 'What's going on here?' He crossed the deck in one stride and sat beside Alice.

'Breakfast,' Alice said, frowning slightly. What was he doing here so early? Had something gone wrong?

'Just thought I'd pop by and see how the sleepover went,' he said with a broad smile.

'Smashingly well, my dear.' Hattie handed him a plate of eggs and bacon. 'Could you smell it from your car?' She grinned and Carson winked. Apparently he'd also spent the night there. Nothing got past Hattie.

He leaned into Alice. 'Pulled over in Queensland,' he whispered in her ear. 'Seems someone tipped them off up north that they might want to check out his vehicle. Turns out that someone was right. He's been arrested. Possession.'

She sighed and her shoulders dropped. 'Thank you.'

While the crew started cleaning up Alice found Becca sitting on the jetty, her bare feet in the creek, and she joined her.

'What's the matter?' she asked.

Becca shrugged. 'I'm worried he'll come back.'

Alice put her arm round her and was pleased Becca didn't back away. 'I suppose that's a possibility. Unlikely, but I guess you never know. All I can promise you is that we will always be here for you. We'll always protect you.'

'I know.' Becca nodded.

'And if you ever want to find your mum or real dad, I'll help with that. But this is your home. Forever more.'

Becca smiled. 'I know. They made their choices, Alice, and I reckon it's about time I started making my own.'

She hugged Alice tightly and Alice hugged her back.

Forty-five

Kookaburra Creek, 2018

Alice swept the deck of the café and wiped down the tables. The dry run had gone well and they would be ready to reopen in a few days. In the week since she and Becca had moved back in, they'd checked off their list of finishing touches – a touch of paint here, a wobbly table leg fixed there – and there was nothing left to do but make sure the café was sparkling clean. And that was a job Alice insisted she do herself.

She'd sent Becca to Glensdale with Freddy to buy serviettes and cupcake cases, and Joey had a big day in the bakery ahead of him. Truth be told, she was grateful for some peace and quiet after the last few days.

Inside, Alice pulled the chairs down from the tables, the mopped floor now dry. She hummed softly as she set up the dining room.

The new replica doorbell of the Kookaburra Creek Café rang loudly and Alice turned around.

Through the café door stepped a woman. Her blonde hair was shorter, her face was gaunt and her posture was just ever so slightly less straight than it used to be. But, despite the distance of time, Alice recognised her old friend immediately.

'Alice,' the woman said.

'Louise.'

'I wasn't sure you'd still be here.' Louise held up an envelope – the envelope Alice had sent Dean all those years ago with news he had a daughter. 'But I had to try. Someone in town said I'd find you here.'

'It's been a while.' No other words came to Alice's mind.

'Do you mind if we go somewhere to talk?'

In silence Alice and Louise walked along the creek until they got to Tammy's bench. They sat, staring into the water.

'It's Dean,' Louise started. 'He's gone. He'd spent so much time over the years taking more and more risks. Skydiving, scuba diving, rally car racing. But in the end it was pneumonia. His lungs never did recover properly from the dam.' Louise's voice was thick with tears.

'When?' asked Alice, trying to keep a neutral expression.

'Seven days ago.'

The night of the slumber party. The night of that dream. Alice bowed her head.

'I found these. In his drawer.' She handed Alice a bundle of postcards tied with a peach ribbon. 'I had no idea how much you loved him.'

Alice gulped.

'I just had to come and find you. Tell you I'm so sorry.'

'Sorry?'

'I was trying to protect him. You have to understand that.'

'What?'

Louise handed Alice the envelope she'd been carrying. 'I never . . . I thought you didn't really care. I thought . . .' She shook her head. 'I never showed it to him.'

Alice struggled to take in what Louise was saying. He never got the letter. He never knew. All those years she spent thinking he didn't want to know his daughter. All those tears she cried over his rejection of her, and he never even knew. He died not knowing Tammy existed.

Alice turned to Louise. 'But you read it? You knew what was inside?'

Halting sobs escaped Louise's throat. 'I did love him, you know. Right from the very start. That day at the lookout. He treated me, like, well, like he did genuinely care. About me. No other guy had ever treated me like that. I tried to stop the way I felt. For you. But when you took off, I was so angry at you. That you could do that to him. I was just trying to be his friend.'

Alice couldn't even speak. She tried to process what Louise was saying.

'Why didn't you tell him, Alice, as soon as you found out?'

'I didn't know how.' Alice's head hurt. 'Would it have made any difference?'

'I don't know. All I know is he was crushed. When you left. He looked for you. For so long. Then he gave up. Then he let me in. He was just starting to get over you when that letter came.' She looked at the envelope in Alice's lap. 'I had to protect him.'

'Did he love you?' Alice's voice was soft.

'I believe he did. In a way. We had a good life together.'

'Kids?'

'No. We tried. The chances were always slim though after the accident.'

Alice shook her head. So much wasted pain.

'I don't expect you to forgive me, Alice. Or even understand why I did what I did. But I wanted you to know about Dean. Closure, I guess.'

Alice closed her eyes for a second. Closure.

'Mostly, I wanted Tammy to know her father never abandoned her. Not by choice. It was me. It was all me. And I'm sorry.'

Too many emotions ran through Alice's mind and filled her soul.

'If you'll let me, I'd like to apologise to her. Tell her what her dad was like.'

'Ease your guilt?'

'Maybe.'

'You can't.'

'I understand. Your decision.' Louise nodded.

'No. I mean, you can't – no one can. Tammy died. Eight years ago.'

'Oh, Alice.' Louise threw her arms around her.

Alice stiffened under the embrace, then she softened. Louise wasn't the only one at fault – it was such a tangled mess of secrets and lies and mistakes.

They sat there watching the sun fade behind the trees.

'Are you driving back to Sydney tonight?' Alice broke the silence.

'Yes. I should get going. Here's my number. Just in case . . . I don't know.'

'Drive safe.'

'I am sorry, Alice.'

'So am I.'

Alice watched Louise walk over the bridge and in to town, waiting for hate to fill her. But all she felt was regret and pity. So much was lost already. Hate seemed so pointless now.

*

By the time Alice got back to the café, the night was cloaked in darkness. Two lights shone down from the windows in the apartment and all was quiet. There was no need to hurry. She'd go up in a minute.

With her feet dangling in the creek beneath the jetty, Alice fingered through the bundle of postcards. Every unanswered note she'd ever sent Dean after the dam accident, every word she'd written him, tied neatly with the ribbon she'd wrapped her ponytail in the night of the school dance. She'd always thought she'd lost it on the way home that night.

This wasn't how she'd thought it would end. She'd often imagined that they would run into each other, in Sydney probably, on some crowded street, quite by accident. They'd stop and get coffee, catch up. There was a time once, in her imaginings, that they'd go to dinner and end up back at his place, in each other's arms. Sometimes she'd tell him all about Tammy. Sometimes she wouldn't. Sometimes in her daydreams they'd simply meet on that crowded street in Sydney and smile and go their separate ways.

But it wasn't to be. Now all that was left were memories.

Footsteps sounded behind her and she turned to see Joey and Shadow walking towards her.

'Quiet day?' Joey lowered himself beside her, and Shadow put his head in Alice's lap. 'What's that?' Joey looked at the bundle of postcards beside Alice.

'I had a visitor. Dean's passed away.'

Joey stared at her with wide eyes.

'He never knew about Tammy.'

'Oh, Alice.' He wrapped his thick arms around her. He traced his fingers through her hair as she told him about Louise's visit.

⁓

So, this is what I've learned in my seventeen years.

The older the ties that bind us, the harder they are to break. And sometimes they don't break at all. I suppose that's not really an issue for me seeing as I don't have any old ties. But I don't know if old ties are a good or bad thing. Sometimes, it seems they can get in the way of new ties. New ties have the potential to become old ties and can maybe be just as strong, if we only let them. Maybe this is something I'll have the chance to find out now.

The older you are, the slower you are at getting your life together. But you do eventually get there. I suppose it can't be easy sorting through that much baggage, so I figure I'm going to sort through mine now. Leave it behind so I'm not, like, forty and ancient before I pull it together and almost miss pulling it together because I'm so old.

Kookaburra Creek isn't that bad a place to be stuck in. I mean, if you have to be stuck somewhere, it might as well be in a place where people actually give a damn, right?

Forty-six

Kookaburra Creek, 2018

Alice was woken by a swift pillow to the head.

'We can't be late today,' Becca sang.

It was the morning of the great birthday-party-slash-café-reopening.

'I'm coming,' Alice muttered from beneath the covers. 'And ouch.'

Before they headed downstairs Becca stopped Alice. 'I got you something.' She handed Alice a small box wrapped in green ribbon. 'I know it's not exactly what you're missing, but maybe . . .' She shrugged. 'Well, new beginnings and all.'

Alice opened the gift.

'Oh, Becca.' She pulled the girl into a tight hug. 'I can't believe you remembered.'

She looked at the salt and pepper shakers – a tiny gnome boy in blue overalls and a gnome girl in a spotted red dress. 'Sonia and Bruce.' She sighed.

'Who?' Becca pulled a face.

'My parents.' Alice shrugged. 'The gnome-collecting started with them. Dad gave mum her first one and then she just kept on collecting them.'

'Right. Well, as I said, not quite the same, but . . . oh don't you go getting all soppy on me!' Becca started to walk away when she saw tears well up in Alice's eyes.

'Sorry, no. Shall we?' They headed down to the café.

Standing in the middle of the dining room, Alice smiled and placed the salt and pepper shakers Becca had just given her on the very centre table of the café. They would eventually build up their collection again. In time. Betty had already declared she'd definitely bring something back from Portugal when she went next month. Wouldn't come home without a pair, in fact.

Alice knew the birthday-party-slash-café-reopening was never going to be a quiet affair but, even in her wildest imaginings, she could never have foreseen just how grand Hattie's plans would get. The plans had kept Alice so busy for the better part of a week, she'd hardly had time to stop. Placing orders, arranging deliveries, tweaking menus, organising extra staff, pre-baking. Alice was exhausted before the day even began.

Freddy arrived on cue and saluted Alice. 'Where do you want me, boss?'

'Back here,' Becca answered from the kitchen. 'I've got your apron ready.'

Alice arranged into tiers the cupcakes she'd stayed up till midnight baking: key lime pie, chocolate chilli and the ever popular chocolate fudge.

'The cavalry is here.' Hattie entered the café with a flourish, with Carson in his civvies close behind.

'Ready for duty, love.' He saluted.

'Put me to use,' Hattie demanded. 'No point standing around gathering dust.'

Alice gave Hattie a pen and pad and ran through the table numbers. It was her fault, after all, that the day was going to be so darn big. Her and her flyers and her insistence that the *Herald* most certainly would be interested in a follow-up story about the café's rebuild.

She wanted to cancel the whole thing once she knew the *Herald* was coming, but Becca wouldn't let her. She would stay in the kitchen, make sure she wasn't in any photos, and Hattie had convinced the paper to give her final approval, so Becca felt it would be safe. Besides, it would prove to *him* she wasn't there, if photos without her in them were published in the papers. And if that wasn't enough, well, she had all of them to watch out for her.

'Where do you want these?' Joey entered, carrying a large basket of breads and rolls and pastries in one hand, saluting with the other.

'Thank God,' Alice sighed. 'Back there, Joey. Freddy's waiting for you.'

'Breathe.' Joey smiled, putting his basket down and taking Alice's hands.

'I'm sorry this week's been crazy,' she said.

'Breathe, Alice.'

She did as she was told.

'Assuming we get through today, we'll have plenty of time just for us.' He kissed her softly, gently and took his bread into the kitchen.

Big wheels crunched the gravel road outside and Alice shook her head as the first of many buses arrived.

What had Hattie got her into?

'Showtime.' Hattie sashayed into position.

The borrowed tables on the grass below the deck were just enough to cater to the extra customers and Alice made a mental note to thank the reverend for their loan. Mental notes seemed to be the order of the day for Alice. Reimburse Claudine for the flowers on every table. Buy Mrs Harris a gift for stepping in and clearing tables when asked, give Becca a pay rise. If only she had a few moments free to make the notes on actual paper.

Flashes of light from cameras and phones came in fits and starts, one person's photo prompting others to follow, then nothing for a while, before another storm of light. Photos in front of the new sign that hung on chains on the front porch, photos in front of the cupcakes on display, group selfies, selfies with Alice.

Carrying out what felt like her thousandth beetroot burger, Alice noticed Joey, who was serving tables on the deck. Mental note, *buy Joey a massive thank-you present for today.*

Enjoying every moment of her party, Hattie mingled through the crowd as only Hattie could, making everyone feel like their being there was the reason she was so happy. The red stripe in her hair was the exact shade of the roses sprinkled over the chiffon scarf around her neck and she was glowing with the attention.

In the corner of the café sat the real reason for Hattie's joy. Genevieve had a blanket across her knees, and Betty was fussing about, making sure she was comfortable. Alice thought that perhaps the smallest light of recognition flickered in Genevieve's eyes every time Hattie wafted past her.

With the sun low in the sky, soft voices floated through the evening air. The long table on the deck was covered in glasses, some half full, some empty, some toppled over spilling sticky liquid onto the white tablecloths. The crowds had finally left and only those closest to Alice and Hattie remained. The reverend was chatting quietly with Betty at one end of the table. Fiona was sitting with her mother at the other, enduring Mrs Harris's loud laments about her daughter leaving town to sit the bar, the abject gloating barely disguised. Fiona smiled at Alice and she smiled back. Hattie was trying to convince Sergeant Carson to pursue acting properly because looks like his shouldn't go to waste, even at his age. While Carson blushed, Clive snored quietly next to him, chin on his chest.

Becca's head was resting on Freddy's shoulder and Alice could see from the rise and fall of her chest she wasn't far off sleep. Freddy smiled down at her, playing with the stray hair that fell across her forehead. Mental note, *take those two to Sydney for a weekend.*

Alice kissed Joey and squeezed his shoulder as she got up and took the empty bottles of wine into the kitchen.

From beneath the bench she pulled out the charcoaled remains of Sylvia. The firefighters had found her wedged between the steel bench and splashback after the fire, the metal having protected her somewhat from the flames. Only Sylvia's eyes remained un-scorched, though, and Alice had placed her on a piece of cardboard in the hope of hanging her on the wall again. But the paper was so badly damaged, to touch it was to crumble its brittle edges.

'We did it,' Alice said, smiling at her old friend. 'The chocolate chilli Joey suggested was a hit and I've got orders for the chocolate fudge that will keep me busy till next Christmas.'

On the wall where Sylvia once hung was now a photo of Tammy and Joey walking beside Kookaburra Creek, hand in hand.

Carefully Alice picked up the cardboard backing Sylvia rested on, opened the back door and carried her to the creek.

'Thank you.' She knelt down and placed Sylvia in the gently flowing water at her feet. 'For everything.'

'Did she ever talk back?' Hattie's voice made Alice jump and swivel around.

'How long have you been standing there?'

'Long enough,' she said with a grin.

'Everyone's starting to head off.' Becca joined them by the water's edge.

Hattie smiled. 'Time to go home.'

The three women linked arms and took the few steps back to the café together.

Alice smiled. Home. Kookaburra Creek, her café, Hattie, Joey, Becca. Funny how 'home' could sneak up on you like that, a place where you never meant to stay, with people you never meant to love.

Kookaburra Creek Café Cupcake Recipes

Sylvia's Chocolate Fudge Cupcakes

Makes 24

1¾ cups caster sugar
180g butter
200g dark chocolate
2 cups self-raising flour
½ cup cocoa

½ teaspoon vanilla paste
3 eggs
²⁄₃ cup water
24 × 1cm squares of dark
    chocolate

Preheat oven to 180°C. Line cupcake tins with cupcake cases.

Place 200g chocolate, sugar and butter into a heat-proof bowl. Heat in microwave in 20-second bursts, stirring between, until chocolate is melted.

Place remaining ingredients into bowl of an electric mixer. Beat on low and gradually add melted chocolate mixture. Increase speed to medium and beat until combined.

Spoon into prepared cupcake tin. Push a square of dark chocolate into the centre of each cupcake.

Bake till cooked – when top of cupcake is lightly pressed and cake springs back (approx. 15 mins).

Cool.

Top with chocolate frosting, piped in a swirl.

Chocolate Frosting

125g butter, soft
2½ cups icing sugar
½ cup cocoa

4 tablespoons milk
½ teaspoon vanilla paste

Place all ingredients into the bowl of an electric mixer. Beat until combined, fluffy and lighter in colour.

Strawberry and White Chocolate Cupcakes

Makes 20

1 punnet of strawberries

180g butter, soft

1 teaspoon vanilla paste

1 cup caster sugar

3 eggs

2 cups self-raising flour

¾ cup milk

½ cup grated white chocolate

1 tablespoon cornflour

20 × 1 cm squares of white chocolate

Preheat oven to 180°C. Line cupcake tin with cupcake cases.

Cut strawberries up into chunks and lay on a piece of paper towel to remove excess moisture.

Beat butter, sugar and vanilla until light and fluffy. Beat in eggs one at a time. Fold in flour, milk and grated white chocolate. Place strawberries in a bowl and stir together with cornflour. Fold into cake batter.

Spoon into prepared cupcake tins. Push a square of white chocolate into the centre of each cupcake.

Bake till cooked – when top of cupcake is lightly pressed and cake springs back (approx. 15 mins).

Cool.

Top with cream cheese and berry frosting.

Strawberry Coulis

4–5 strawberries   ¼ cup caster sugar

Make strawberry coulis by cutting up strawberries and placing them in a cup or jar with caster sugar and set aside to macerate. Once strawberries and sugar have become liquid, blitz with hand blender.

Cream Cheese and Berry Frosting

30g butter, soft   strawberry coulis
250g cream cheese   ¼ cup grated white chocolate
500g icing sugar

Beat butter, cream cheese and icing sugar until fluffy. Drizzle strawberry coulis down the sides of a piping bag, then fill piping bag with cream cheese. Pipe onto cupcakes in a swirl. Sprinkle white chocolate over top.

Lemon and Rosemary Cupcakes

Makes 18

1 cup caster sugar
180g butter, soft
3 eggs
2½ cups self-raising flour
¾ cup milk

zest and juice of 1 lemon
1 tablespoon finely chopped
 rosemary
¼ cup lemon curd or lemon
 butter

Preheat oven to 180°C. Line cupcake tin with cupcake cases.

Beat butter and sugar till fluffy and light in colour. Beat in eggs one at a time. Fold in flour and milk. Add rosemary, lemon zest and juice and mix well.

Spoon into prepared cupcake tins and bake till cooked – when top of cupcake is lightly pressed and cake springs back (approx. 18 mins).

Cool.

Using an apple corer, take out the middle of each cupcake (approx. 1½ cm deep) and fill with lemon curd/butter.

Top cupcakes with piped lemon Italian meringue.

Lemon Italian Meringue

3 egg whites   ¼ cup water
1 cup of caster sugar   2 teaspoons lemon zest

Beat egg whites until soft peaks form.

In the meantime make sugar syrup – place sugar and water into a saucepan and cook over medium heat until sugar dissolves. Stir often. Once sugar is dissolved, bring to boil without stirring. Boil for approx. 2 mins, or until soft ball state is reached (when a teaspoon of syrup is dropped into chilled water you can form it into a soft ball between your thumb and finger).

With beater running, add sugar syrup to egg whites in a slow stream. Add lemon zest. Continue beating till meringue is cooled. This does take some time.

Fill piping bag with meringue and pipe onto cupcakes.

Choc-Hazelnut and Frangelico Cupcakes

Makes 20

180g butter, soft

1 teaspoon vanilla paste

½ cup brown sugar

½ cup caster sugar

2 cups self-raising flour

3 eggs

1 cup water

½ cup cocoa powder

½ cup hazelnut meal

4 tablespoons Frangelico

20 Ferrero Rocher chocolates

Preheat oven to 180°C. Line cupcake tin with cupcake cases.

Place butter, vanilla, sugars, flour, eggs and water into bowl of an electric mixer. Beat until light and fluffy. Divide batter evenly into two bowls. Into one bowl add cocoa and mix well. Into other bowl add hazelnut meal and Frangelico and mix well.

Fill each cupcake case with half chocolate batter and half hazelnut batter. Bake till cooked – when top of cupcake is lightly pressed and cake springs back (approx. 18 mins).

Cool.

Top with whipped ganache and a Ferrero Rocher chocolate.

Whipped Dark Chocolate Ganache

400g dark chocolate, broken
  into pieces

½ cup cream

3 tablespoons Frangelico

Place chocolate and cream into a microwave-safe bowl. Heat in 20-second bursts, stirring between, until chocolate begins to melt. Remove from microwave and stir the chocolate and cream until all chocolate is melted and combined with the cream. Stir in Frangelico. Leave to cool. Once thickened, but not set, place into bowl of electric beater and beat until lighter in colour and holding its shape.

Pipe onto cupcakes and top with Ferrero Rocher.

Lime and Coconut Cupcakes

Makes 18

180g butter, soft
½ cup brown sugar
½ cup caster sugar
1 teaspoon vanilla paste
3 eggs
2 cups flour

¾ cup milk
zest and juice of 4 limes
2 cups of toasted shredded
  coconut
¼ cup lime curd

Preheat oven to 180°C. Line cupcake tin with cupcake cases.

To toast coconut, line a baking tray with grease-proof paper and spread coconut out evenly. Place in oven until coconut begins to turn brown. Remove and place in bowl to cool.

Beat butter, sugars and vanilla paste until light and fluffy. Beat in eggs one at a time. Fold in flour, milk, zest and juice. Fold in 1½ cups of toasted coconut. Reserve ½ cup of coconut.

Spoon into prepared cupcake tins and bake till cooked – when top of cupcake is lightly pressed and cake springs back (approx. 18 mins).

Cool.

Using an apple corer, take out the middle of each cupcake (approx. 1½ cm deep) and fill with lime curd.

Top with lime cream cheese frosting and remaining toasted coconut.

Lime Cream Cheese Frosting

30g butter, soft   500g icing sugar
250g cream cheese   zest and juice of 1 lime

Beat all ingredients until light and fluffy. Pipe onto cupcakes and sprinkle toasted coconut on top.

Acknowledgments

Thank you to the 'Knitting Circle' – Claudia, Eva and Hilary – who read some very early, very awful, work and didn't abandon me. Friendships like our Knitting Circle are rare and beautiful, and if I've managed to portray the power of female friendships well it's because of you. I miss you every day.

Kelly Baker. Your random act of kindness so long ago meant more to me than you'll ever know, and there you were again, recently, giving me my first writing break, which has made all the difference.

Thank you to my first professional editor, Nicola O'Shea, for helping me find the true heart of Kookaburra Creek.

Shell, El, Max, Georgie and Benison – my writing 'tribe'. Finding you girls two years ago when this fraught writing journey nearly drowned me was the life-raft I needed. Thank you.

To the team at Penguin – the art department for my stunning cover; the publicity team for getting my baby out there; my editor Elena for polishing my baby till it shined; and my publisher Kimberley for seeing what I see in the people of Kookaburra Creek, and loving them enough to take me on – thank you, all.

Thank you Sonia Lidbury for sharing your medical knowledge in regards to Dean's story. The wonderful staff at FFPS enthusiastically put their bodies on the line to taste-test all of Alice's cupcake flavours. Your waistlines might not be thanking you, but I certainly am.

Special thanks to Mishell Currie and Jen Johnson for reading draft, after draft, (after draft), giving me valuable feedback, and being my constant cheerleaders.

Léonie Kelsall, my brilliant critique partner, thank you for your insights and for riding every high and low with me.

To my unofficially adopted mentor, Dianne Blacklock, thank you for being a wonderful teacher, for picking me up when I was down, and for helping me find a way to keep going when I didn't think I could.

To my mum, Irene, thank you for keeping me grounded throughout this experience and for being one of the strongest women I know.

For her brutally honest feedback, and for believing in my stories from the beginning, thank you to my sister, Karen. We don't always see eye to eye (ever?), but these last few years, with both my writing and personal journeys, you have been my single greatest source of support and for that I am more grateful than you know.

My long-suffering husband, Chris – without you none of this would be possible. Thank you for giving me the time and space to chase this crazy dream. Now that it's published you can finally read it and see what I've been doing all this time.

And to my daughter, Emily – you show such courage and maturity in the face of the challenges life has dealt you. And for that, in every way, in every day, you are my every inspiration.